A
Dinah Harris
MYSTERY

# Deadly
## DISCLOSURES

# Julie Cave

First printing: March 2010

ISBN: 978-0-89051-584-6
Library of Congress Number: 2010920641

All characters appearing in this novel are fictitious. Any resemblance to real persons, living or dead, is purely coincidental.

**Printed in the United States of America**

Please visit our website for other great titles:
www.masterbooks.net

For information regarding author interviews,
please contact the publicity department at (870) 438-5288

Master
Books®
A Division of New Leaf Publishing Group

# *Acknowledgments*

I wish to thank Steve Ham for his invaluable assistance in providing feedback, criticism, ideas, and solutions during the development of this book. I could not have completed the book successfully without his knowledge and creativity. He has made a huge impact on our family and for this we thank him from the bottom of our hearts. We miss him and his family very much.

Thanks also to Ken Ham who edited many parts of the book to ensure that the arguments presented therein were flawless. He took time out of his busy schedule to ensure the book is right and his attention to detail is much appreciated.

Thanks to Tim Dudley for taking a chance with me.

Thanks to my parents for instilling a love of books in me.

Thanks to my husband, Terry, who has always supported my passion to write and believed in my ability, offered advice and ideas, and gave me time and space to do it. I love you.

Glory be to God, forever and ever.

# Contents

Chapter 1 ...............................................................................6

Chapter 2 .............................................................................18

Chapter 3 .............................................................................30

Chapter 4 .............................................................................42

Chapter 5 .............................................................................54

Chapter 6 .............................................................................68

Chapter 7 .............................................................................82

Chapter 8 .............................................................................98

Chapter 9 ...........................................................................112

Chapter 10 .........................................................................126

Chapter 11 .........................................................................138

Chapter 12 .........................................................................154

Chapter 13 .........................................................................166

Chapter 14 .........................................................................178

Chapter 15 .........................................................................194

Chapter 16 .........................................................................206

Chapter 17 .........................................................................218

Chapter 18 .........................................................................232

Chapter 19 .........................................................................250

Chapter 20 .........................................................................268

Chapter 21 .........................................................................278

Excerpt from *The Shadowed Mind* ....................................284

About the author ...............................................................286

Thomas Whitfield climbed out of the Lincoln Towncar and stood in the snappy, early morning fall air, breathing deeply. The temperature had fallen a few more degrees overnight, signaling that winter was truly on its way.

Thomas glanced up and down the wide street. There was nobody around at this early hour, and he took a moment to drink in the sights of his beloved city. The graceful willows, their branches arching over the street, were turning gold and red and, in the gentle yellow morning light, threw off highlights like burnished copper. This street was like many others in the center of DC — wide and tree-lined, with magnificent government buildings standing one after the other. That was another thing that Thomas found so delicious about this city — so much of it hinted at the enormous wealth and prosperity of the country, and yet only a few streets behind these world-famous landmarks, the seedier side of American poverty flourished. It was a city of contradictions, Thomas thought.

His gaze fell finally to the building right in front of him — the main complex of the Smithsonian Institution. Enormous stone pillars flanked the entryway into a marble lobby, and behind that were laid out the evidence of mankind's brilliance. Everything about the institution was testament to the scientific and anthropological advances of man over the pages of history — the inventions, the discoveries, the deductions, the sheer radiance of a human being's intelligence at its finest.

Thomas Whitfield had always been immensely proud of this place, and everything it showcased. He had boasted about it, defended it, nourished it, and protected it, the way a proud father would his prodigious child.

He was the secretary of the Smithsonian, after all, and he felt a strange kind of paternal relationship with the buildings and their contents.

He stood for a moment longer, a slender whippet of a man dressed immaculately, with highly polished shoes gleaming, thinning dark hair cut short, and a gray cashmere scarf to ward off the cold. Then he purposefully strode down the path and into the main building, scarf fluttering behind him.

To the malevolent eyes watching him through high-powered binoculars down the street in a non-descript Chevy, he presented a painfully easy target.

Thomas settled in his large office with the door shut, turned on the computer, and shut his eyes briefly as he contemplated what he would do next. The course of events he had planned for this day would change everything, and the impact would be felt right up to the president himself. *Courage, Thomas*, he told himself silently. *What you are about to do is the right thing to do.*

He began to type, slowly and decisively, feeling within himself a great sense of conviction and purpose. He was so lost in concentration that he was startled by the door suddenly swinging open.

"What are . . . ?" he exclaimed, almost jumping off his seat. Then he recognized his visitor and he glanced at his watch.

"What are you doing here?" Thomas asked. "It's a little early for you, isn't it?"

"I wanted to be sure I caught you," his visitor replied, moving closer to the desk. "Without any interruptions."

"I see. What can I do for you then?" Thomas asked, trying to hide his irritation. He hadn't wanted to be interrupted during this most important task.

"What are you working on?" the unannounced guest asked, ignoring him and moving around the side of the desk and trying to look at Thomas's computer screen.

"Oh, it's nothing," Thomas answered with a falsely airy tone. "It's just a family project. Nothing to do with work. Is there something I can help you with?"

Thomas was suddenly aware that his visitor was standing close by him. He felt uncomfortable, and tried to roll his chair away to maintain some space.

"You see," his visitor said in a quiet voice, "there are people out there who don't agree with you. They think the project you are working on could be very dangerous. In fact, I believe they have already tried to warn you about continuing with this project."

Thomas now felt distinctly uncomfortable and a little afraid. He decided to assert his authority. "Listen here," he said, in a voice that betrayed his anxiety. "What I am working on is none of your business. The subject is certainly not up for discussion with somebody like you. I suggest you leave my office immediately."

The visitor managed to fuse sorrow and menace into his words as he said, "I'm afraid I can't do that. You will have to come with me."

Thomas retorted, "I'm not going anywhere with you. In fact, I. . . ." He broke off abruptly as he saw the small handgun in the visitor's hand, pointing directly at him. There was no sorrow or pity on his face — only menace.

"Do I need to force you to come with me?" the visitor wondered, his tone like flint.

Thomas leapt to his feet, his eyes darting about wildly. He needed to get out of here, to try to get away from this situation that had so rapidly gotten out of hand. A hand shot out and grabbed Thomas by the collar with surprising strength. Thomas was shocked as he strained to get away from the man, who was intently staring at the computer screen.

"You traitor!" Thomas spat. "I should've known you were nothing more than a trained monkey!"

The visitor chuckled heartily. "That's ironic, Thomas."

The visitor, much younger and stronger than Thomas, began to drag him out of the room. Thomas was determined not to go down without a fight, and drove his heel backward into the visitor's shin. There was a yelp of pain, but the unrelenting grip did not lessen around Thomas's arm. Instead, a thick arm curled around Thomas's throat and squeezed, applying pressure to the carotid artery. It took only a few seconds for Thomas to fall limply into the arms of his abductor as the blood supply to his brain was cut off.

That was the last anyone saw of the secretary of the Smithsonian Institute.

\* \* \* \*

Dinah Harris woke with a scream dying in her throat, the sheets twisted hopelessly around her legs. Her nightgown was damp with panicked sweat, her heart galloping like a runaway horse. She stared, blinking, at the pale dawn light streaming through the window, while the shadowy vestiges of her nightmare slithered from her memory.

As she lay in bed, joining the waking world from sleep, the familiar blanket of depression settled over her, dark and heavy as the Atlantic winter. The dread she felt at facing another day was almost palpable in the small bedroom. Dinah glanced across at her alarm clock, where the flashing numbers showed 6 a.m.

She threw aside the sheets and stumbled into the tiny bathroom, where she purposefully avoided looking at herself in the mirror. She was only in her mid-thirties and had once been relatively attractive. Certainly not beautiful, but with what her first boyfriend had once told her — a pleasant face and athletic body. Now her eyes were always underscored by dark bags, her skin pale and paper-thin, and the weight fell off her in slow degrees without ceasing. She dressed in her trademark dark pants suit, pulled her black hair from her face in a severe ponytail, and washed her face.

She made strong coffee and sat in the kitchen as she drank the bitter liquid. The dining alcove was still stacked with moving cartons, filled with books and music that she couldn't face opening. The gray light of morning lent no color to the apartment, which suited Dinah just fine. Her world didn't contain color anymore.

Though traffic often seemed at a standstill in the mornings, Dinah always arrived early to the J. Edgar Hoover building. She turned directly to the teaching wing, avoiding the eye contact and morning greetings of many she knew in the building. She knew what they whispered about during after-work drinks and at the water cooler. Her fall from grace would go down as one of the most spectacular in FBI history.

So she kept up the ice-cool veneer until she arrived at her desk, checking her e-mails and teaching schedule for the week.

She didn't look up as an imposing shadow fell across her desk.

"Special Agent Harris, how are you?" boomed the voice of her former colleague, David Ferguson. He was a big man, six-four and two hundred pounds, with a loud, booming voice and a penchant for pork rinds. He stood above her, his hand resting easily on the holstered gun at his hip; the twin of a gun Dinah no longer wore but kept underneath her pillow.

"Ferguson," she replied. "Fine, how are you?"

"Feel like a coffee?" he asked.

"Don't you have a killer to catch?" Dinah asked, dryly.

He waved his hand dismissively. "Oh, they can wait. Come on."

He took her to a tiny Italian café a block away from the FBI headquarters. While they ordered, Dinah wondered at his ulterior motive for bringing her here. *It certainly isn't for my sparkling wit and charm,* she thought. Rumor had it that the freshman criminology classes were afraid of her.

"So I'm just wondering if I could get your opinion on something," Ferguson began, tentatively testing the water.

She scowled at him. "You know I don't get involved in cases."

He held up his hands in mock surrender. "Okay, calm down, Harris. I just want your opinion. I know you've given up your real talents to teach some snotty freshmen."

His comment stung her, but she narrowed her eyes at him and pretended she hadn't even noticed. "So get on with it already."

"I don't remember you always being this prickly," complained Ferguson, draining his macchiato. "Anyway. What would you say if I told you the secretary of the Smithsonian Institution had gone missing?"

"Missing?" Dinah raised her eyebrows and slurped her latte. "In what context?"

"As in, turned up for work at six this morning and disappeared off the face of the earth shortly thereafter."

"How do you know he turned up for work at six?" Dinah asked.

"Security cameras have him arriving in the lobby and heading for his office. After that, who knows?"

"So he's an adult, maybe he took a trip to get away from work stress or his wife has been giving him grief or his kid is in trouble." Dinah frowned. "Why are we even involved at this early stage?"

Ferguson paused. "It's due mostly to his rather prestigious position. It wouldn't do for the secretary of the Smithsonian to simply disappear. Congress is rather anxious."

Dinah knew of political influence that ran high in this city but didn't press the issue. "Is there evidence of homicide?"

"Not really, although I haven't been to his office yet." Ferguson made it sound like a confession, and he looked at her sheepishly.

Dinah stared at him. "What do you really want, Ferguson?"

He gathered up his courage. "I need you to work this case with me, Harris."

Dinah opened her mouth to respond indignantly, but Ferguson held up his hand and continued with a rush. "You know I'm not good with sensitive cases. I. . . ."

"Or complex ones," interjected Dinah, bad-temperedly.

"I'm operating on a hunch that this is a bad case, that it involves people in the White House." Ferguson must have needed her very badly to allow her comment to go unheeded.

"Well, I'm sorry, but I have a heavy teaching workload," she said. "So I'll have to limit my involvement to opinions only."

Ferguson didn't say anything but looked even guiltier.

"What have you done?" Dinah demanded.

"I may have cleared your schedule so you could work with me." Ferguson examined his fingernails with great concentration.

Dinah waited for a beat. "I see. You've spoken to my superiors?"

He nodded. "They've agreed to lend you to me for as long as the case takes."

Dinah stood abruptly. "Thanks for the coffee." She walked angrily from the café.

Ferguson stared at her as she walked off, then slapped down some crumpled notes and heaved his bulk out of the chair. "Where are you going?" Ferguson asked, struggling to keep up with her.

She wheeled around and glared directly at him. "Who do you think you are? Do you think I'm lesser than you so you can sneak around behind my back?"

"Dinah, we really need you back in the field. You were — *are* — brilliant." Ferguson spoke softly, hoping to calm her down.

"My field days are behind me, with very good reason," snapped Dinah. *I can't see a dead body anymore. I can't feel desire to catch the person who did it. I just want to lie down beside the body and feel the same endless peace of sleep.*

"Please, I'm begging you. I need you back," Ferguson said. Then it hit her. Dinah realized that this situation was very serious. Ferguson was the last person on the planet to beg anybody.

"I don't really have a choice, do I?" she said dully. She knew that this case could break her.

Ferguson didn't reply, and his answer was in his silence.

❋ ❋ ❋ ❋

The Smithsonian Institution was bustling with tourists and school kids as if nothing had gone wrong. Dinah and David strode into the main lobby, trying unsuccessfully to look casual. When they flashed their badges discreetly, they were allowed into the inner sanctum, where Thomas Whitfield's personal assistant was fielding phone calls.

The secretary was young and pretty, with thick, dark hair waving gracefully to her shoulders, startlingly blue eyes, and a creamy olive complexion. Her only downfall was the thick eye makeup, applied to make her eyes stand out but which had the effect of making her look like a scared raccoon. "I'm afraid Mr. Whitfield simply cannot be interrupted at present," she snapped into the phone. "I'll have him call you back if you'd leave a message."

She glanced up and saw the two agents standing at her desk. She gave them a wave to acknowledge their presence, repeated the details of the caller, scribbled furiously, and then hung up.

"Good morning," she said, jumping to her feet. "If you caught the end of that conversation, you'll know that Mr. Whitfield is in an extremely important meeting and. . . ."

"Save it," interrupted Dinah, showing the secretary her badge. The young woman blushed. "We're here to investigate the disappearance of Mr. Whitfield. What is your name?"

The secretary sat down hard, looking relieved. "I'm Lara Southall. I'm so worried about Mr. Whitfield."

Ferguson flashed his partner a frown and took charge. "I'm Special Agent David Ferguson and this is Special Agent Dinah Harris. You'll have to excuse her; she's been out of the field for some time and has forgotten how to relate to people."

Dinah opened her mouth to reply with outrage, but Ferguson continued, "Can you tell us about this morning?"

Lara Southall regarded Dinah with a mixture of amusement and fear, which Dinah filed away for future reference. "I got to work at eight o'clock as usual," she replied. "Mr. Whitfield always arrives before me. I usually turn on my computer, get settled, and then get us both a coffee. When I opened his office door to give him the coffee, the room was empty." As the girl spoke, she tapped perfectly manicured fingernails together absently. Dinah hated manicured fingernails: they reminded her of her distinctly unattractive, chewed-to-the-quick fingertips.

"Mr. Whitfield was due to give a presentation at eleven o'clock," Lara continued. "So I didn't really start worrying until about ten-thirty. He hates to be late, and he had to come back to get his presentation and make it uptown in less than half an hour. At eleven, I started to make some calls."

"Has he ever been absent from the office before?" Ferguson asked.

"Sure, he often has meetings or goes out into the museum to talk to visitors. The thing is, I always know what he's doing. That's part of my job. He never goes anywhere during the day without letting me know."

"So you started making calls at eleven. Who did you call?" Dinah asked impatiently.

Lara ticked off her fingers as she remembered. "I called his cell phone, and I called the other museums. I thought maybe he'd just forgotten to tell me he had a meeting. Nobody had seen him and his cell just rang out. So I called his home. His wife told me he'd left for work at about five-thirty and she hadn't seen him since. Then I called some of the senior executives. I thought they might've had an emergency. But nobody had seen him."

"Did the people you called — his wife, the executives — seem concerned about his whereabouts?" Ferguson asked.

"Yes, they did. It's so unusual for Mr. Whitfield to act this way that everyone I spoke to was concerned. I think his wife is actually here somewhere at the moment."

"So then you called the police?" Dinah said.

"No, one of the directors came over to look at the security tapes. She specifically told me not to call anyone until she'd viewed the footage. I thought that Mr. Whitfield might've had an accident on the way to work. Mrs. Whitfield was calling the hospitals when Ms. Biscelli — the director — came back from security."

"What did the tapes show?" Dinah asked.

"They showed him arriving at six-thirty or so. That's all I know."

"Did any of the tapes show him leaving?"

"Not as far as I know."

"Right. So what then?"

"I called the police."

Ferguson nodded. "What did they tell you?"

"Basically they won't do anything until he's been missing 24 hours." Lara stopped clicking her nails together and started twisting her hair with one finger. "So I told Ms. Biscelli, and she wasn't happy with that. I think she must've pulled some strings, because here you are."

Dinah and Ferguson both raised their eyebrows at her in confusion.

"The FBI," explained Lara. "You guys wouldn't normally get involved, would you?" She may have been a very pretty secretary, but Lara Southall was an intelligent girl. She'd asked the very question Dinah had been mulling over all morning.

"We're going to look in his office," Ferguson said, ignoring the question. He handed her his card. "Please call me if you think of anything else that might be helpful."

She nodded and picked up the ringing phone. "No," she said, sounding very weary. "Mr. Whitfield is in a meeting at the moment and can't be disturbed."

\*\*\*\*

Ferguson opened the door to the office while Dinah waited to get the log-on details for Thomas Whitfield's computer. Dinah stood in the doorway, looking into the impressive room, and felt the thrill of the chase wash over her like a wave. It had been a long time since she had felt anything.

The office was furnished with heavy cedar furniture that consisted of a large desk, a leather-bound chair, a couch, and two armchairs grouped around a glass-topped coffee table and one entire wall of built-in bookcases. The floor was covered with thick burgundy carpet, and the drapes at the picture window were also burgundy. The walls contained portraits of several great scientists and inventors — Dinah recognized Charles Darwin, Thomas Edison, and the Wright Brothers — as well as photos of the secretary with the president, the queen of England, and other dignitaries. The room itself was clean and uncluttered, likely symbolic of the man himself, Dinah thought.

Ferguson was moving around the room, muttering to himself, as was his habit. Dinah had forgotten how intensely annoying she found this habit. She preferred silence so that she could concentrate.

Having received the log-on details from Lara, Dinah strode to the desk and pulled on her latex gloves. The top of the desk was shiny and would be a great medium to obtain fingerprints. She was careful not to allow herself to touch the desktop while she turned on the laptop.

"By the way, Harris," Ferguson said from the wall of bookcases, "I forgot to mention that if something has happened to Mr. Whitfield, the media scrutiny is likely to be intense."

Dinah scowled at the screen of the laptop. She hated the media, and it was a long-term grudge she held from the last case she'd been involved in. "You can handle it," she said. "I want nothing to do with those vultures."

Ferguson glanced over at her. "Of course I'll handle it. But I can't guarantee that they'll leave you alone."

Dinah tapped her foot against the leg of the desk impatiently as the laptop struggled to come to life. "Sticks and stones, Ferguson," she said tightly. "Words can never hurt me."

She could see that Ferguson didn't buy the lie, but he'd decided to let it go. He at least knew not to push too far.

"This whole office is giving me a weird vibe," he said after a moment. "It's too . . . organized."

Dinah logged onto the laptop. "I'm listening."

"Look at the desk," Ferguson mused. "No files or paperwork. Not even a pen or a Post-It note. No diary."

"Maybe he's just really neat," Dinah said, opening Outlook on the laptop.

Ferguson went back to his muttering as he continued drifting around the room. Dinah frowned as she clicked through the folders in Outlook. Then she opened the other programs on the computer and looked through the folders there.

"That's odd," she commented at last. Ferguson looked up and came over to her.

She clicked through the inbox, sent items, and calendar of the e-mail program. There were no entries in any of them. "They're completely clean," she said. "The calendar is the strangest. You'd think the secretary of the Smithsonian Institution would have at least a couple of meetings a week."

"Maybe he uses a paper diary," suggested Ferguson.

"Certainly a possibility," agreed Dinah. "But couple the empty calendar with the fact that he's neither received nor sent an e-mail from this computer and something isn't right."

Ferguson opened the desk drawers and started looking through them.

"Also," added Dinah, "there is not one single saved document in any other program — no letters, articles, presentations, anything. The entire computer is as if it's never been used."

Ferguson sat back on his heels. "You think someone has wiped his computer?"

"Well, the sixty-four-thousand-dollar question is: did Thomas Whitfield wipe his own computer before disappearing or did someone else wipe his computer before abducting him?" Dinah began to shut down the programs. "After all, there is no evidence to suggest that he has been abducted. There's no sign of a struggle in here or blood stains, is there?"

Ferguson shook his head. "No, there isn't. But there is something off about this office. Nobody, least of all a man in his position, can get through a working day without sending an e-mail or doing paperwork of some kind." He gestured at the desk drawers. "There's absolutely nothing in them."

"I agree," Dinah said. She closed the laptop and picked it up. "I'm going to have the lab look at the hard drive. What else?"

"I'll call in crime scene to lift some fingerprints and check for blood." Ferguson paused, thinking. "I'd like to talk to Ms. Biscelli, and I'd like to talk to his wife."

Dinah nodded. "If Mr. Whitfield has been abducted, what do you suppose is the motive?"

Ferguson considered. "I don't know. Money? Fame? Half the time I think these loonies go around killing people just so they can get their name in the news."

Dinah stared at him. "Do you think Thomas Whitfield is dead?"

He shrugged. "Right now, Harris, I know nine-tenths of absolutely nothing. Let's talk to Ms. Biscelli. Maybe she'll know what happened and we can solve this case before dinner time and I'll get a decent night's sleep."

Flippancy, Dinah remembered, was just Ferguson's way of dealing with the intensity of this job and the horror they'd witnessed over the years.

Lara Southall called Ms. Biscelli on her phone and showed the two FBI agents to a small boardroom. She also gave them a copy of the last 12 months of Thomas Whitfield's schedule and appointments, as Dinah had asked her.

"Just for the record," Ferguson said, before Lara left them. "What is Ms. Biscelli's position, exactly?"

"She's the Director of Communications and Public Affairs," Lara said, and shut the door.

"I guess that's why she's so worried about Thomas Whitfield," murmured Dinah. "It can't be very good for the institution's public image for the secretary to vanish into thin air."

"I just don't know how you got to be so cynical, Harris," sighed Ferguson. "What with all the loving, caring, generous human beings we deal with on a daily basis." Dinah managed to smile. Even Ferguson knew that was a small victory.

The door burst open and a very small woman walked briskly into the room. She was five-feet all told, with short, curly dark hair and a rather masculine jaw.

"I am Catherine Biscelli," she announced, extending her right hand to the two agents to shake. Ferguson introduced himself and Dinah and they sat down again.

"We'll have coffee," decided Catherine Biscelli, and she buzzed Lara. The two agents glanced at each other. This was clearly a woman used to giving commands and having them obeyed. She wouldn't have been out of place in a marine corps, Dinah thought. *Sir, yes sir!*

"I'm in charge of public affairs," explained Ms. Biscelli. "You can understand that I'm concerned for Thomas."

Dinah noted the familiarity with which the small woman referred to Thomas Whitfield. "Are you concerned for him personally, Ms. Biscelli, or concerned for the institution?"

Catherine Biscelli narrowed her eyes. "Both, of course. I must say that it would be most out of character for Thomas to simply disappear. I'm dreadfully worried that something has happened to him."

"You worked closely with Mr. Whitfield?" Ferguson asked.

"Yes. I managed all of his public appearances and speeches, as well as managing the institution's press releases and exhibition launches." She paused, thinking. "He was a very polished, precise person. Do you know what I mean? He was always early, never missed an appointment or meeting, re-wrote every speech until it was perfect. He was very structured, he would never just disappear."

The coffee came in and Ms. Biscelli busied herself with cream and sugar.

"So you believe that he's been abducted?" asked Dinah.

Ms. Biscelli flinched. "I haven't had time to think about it, but I suppose I do. I certainly don't believe he's disappeared of his own volition."

"Let's keep both options open for a moment," suggested Ferguson. "Have you noticed any differences in Thomas's behavior recently?"

Catherine Biscelli looked blank.

Ferguson continued, "Has he been edgy, upset, anxious, losing sleep or weight, sad?"

*Sounds like he's describing me,* Dinah thought with a start.

Ms. Biscelli pursed her lips thoughtfully. "I don't remember anything specific. He was always very professional in his interactions with staff and visitors. I think that if there was something bothering him, he would never let it affect his work."

*She has a serious case of hero worship,* Dinah scribbled on her notebook and edged it to within Ferguson's line of vision.

"Did you notice any tension or arguments between Thomas and other staff or visitors?" Ferguson asked, and then wrote in reply to Dinah, *Does that mean she's covering something up?*

"Oh no," breathed Ms. Biscelli, as if the idea repulsed her. "Everyone here respects and idolizes Thomas. Nobody would want to start an argument with him. There is nothing to argue about."

"Were you aware of any trouble in Thomas's personal life?"

"No, I really wasn't. I've only met his wife briefly at social events, and she seems very nice, although obviously upset right at the moment."

"So as far as you know, Thomas Whitfield was an organized, dependable saint with whom nobody dared argue?" Dinah asked, her voice as caustic as vinegar.

Ferguson flashed a warning look at her.

Predictably, Ms. Biscelli's hackles rose. "Special Agent, I am trying to help by answering your questions as best I can. I worked with Thomas and I sent him a Christmas card every year and that was the extent of our relationship. If he was having problems, he certainly did not confide in me." She glared at Dinah, who simply stared back without blinking. They reminded Ferguson of two feral cats, poised in the moment of stillness before attack.

"Have you notified the board of regents?" asked Ferguson, trying to negotiate a ceasefire. "And will you notify the media?"

"I'm about to do that," Catherine Biscelli said. "I won't issue anything to the media until the board advises me to do so." Her demeanor was noticeably frosty.

"Do you know what Thomas's presentation to the Congress this morning was going to be about?"

She shook her head, dark curls bouncing. "No, I don't."

"Wouldn't you, as Director of Public Affairs, at least see an outline of what Thomas was going to say? I would think that even the secretary would be required to have his speeches vetted."

Catherine Biscelli flushed and Ferguson knew he'd hit a sore point. "That is generally the case," she admitted. "But I trusted Thomas's judgment implicitly. He chose not to tell me what was in today's presentation and I respected that."

"But that's not normally the procedure."

"No. Anything released into the public domain must be signed off by me." Catherine Biscelli would have been a hard taskmaster, Dinah thought.

"And generally speaking, why is that?" Ferguson pressed.

She looked a little non-plussed. "Well, to ensure that the information aligns with our mission statement and our culture; to make sure there is nothing offensive in it; to make sure there are no personal agendas. *Generally* speaking."

"But you are absolutely certain that Thomas's presentation to Congress this morning would not have contained any of those things?"

"Yes. I am. He is the secretary of the Smithsonian. If he can't be trusted, nobody can." Catherine Biscelli turned her hard obsidian gaze on Ferguson. He decided he'd harassed her enough.

"Thank you, Ms. Biscelli. Here is my card. If you think of anything, please call me." Ferguson stood and saw the small woman out.

"She's lying," said Dinah. She was scribbling furiously in her notebook.

"I agree," said Ferguson. "But I don't want her to know that we know that. Do you think she has any idea?"

Dinah shrugged. She didn't care, but then, she didn't care about much these days.

\*\*\*\*

Eloise Whitfield was waiting for news of her husband in the institution's cafeteria.

The two agents hurried over to the staff cafeteria where Mrs. Whitfield, a blond, fine-boned woman who looked like a scared bird, hunched over a half-eaten sandwich.

"Thanks for meeting us," Ferguson said as they sat down. "I'm sorry for the situation we're in."

She nodded, a short, sharp gesture. "He's in trouble," she said. "Thomas is in trouble. I can feel it."

"You think he hasn't done this of his own accord?" Ferguson asked.

"No, absolutely not. That just isn't Thomas's style. He's been taken." Her words were jittery and spilled over each other, like someone who had consumed too much coffee in a short space of time. Her thin fingers clenched an empty coffee cup so hard her knuckles were white.

"By whom?"

"I don't know. I don't know. I just know he's in trouble."

"Do you know who would want to take him? And why?"

Her brow furrowed. "I can't think of who they might be . . . all I know is that he had upset some people in recent times. He was so mild-mannered usually; I can't remember him ever getting into a fight. Just recently, though, I overhead him arguing on the phone."

"And you don't know who he was arguing with?"

"I have no idea. He wouldn't tell me. He just said he was having a difference of opinion with someone at work." Her hand moved to smooth her hair, then scratch her arm, and then tap the table. "I came here to ask who that someone was. Nobody would tell me."

"So you were told that Thomas gets along with everybody and there had been no tension or conflict recently?" Dinah caught Ferguson's gaze and rolled her eyes.

"Yes. All I know is that he was arguing with *somebody* and now maybe that somebody has gotten mad and tried to hurt Thomas." She looked up at them. The fear she was feeling roiled across her features like waves across the face of the ocean. "Please. You must find him."

"We're trying, ma'am," said Ferguson, gently. "Did he happen to tell you what his presentation to Congress was going to be this morning?"

"No, we've always kept work and home life separate. I probably wouldn't understand it even if he did tell me."

She glanced around, seemingly checking to see if there was anyone within hearing distance. "Listen," she said, leaning forward. "I picked the phone up one night, during one of Thomas's arguments. I wanted to see what they were about. I shouldn't have done it, but I was curious." She glanced around nervously again. "I heard Thomas being threatened."

Ferguson glanced at Dinah. "What exactly did you hear?"

She shivered involuntarily. "The voice told him to stop what he was doing, or they'd come for him."

"Was the voice male or female?"

"Male."

"Do you know what he was referring to with respect to Thomas's activities?"

"No."

"Was Thomas involved in anything . . . out of the ordinary or unusual?"

"Not that I could see. Our lives were normal. He went to work and came home. On weekends we'd visit friends, have brunch in Georgetown, or . . . or. . . ." Her eyes welled with tears and she looked dismayed.

"We'll stop, Mrs. Whitfield, if this is too hard for you," suggested Ferguson.

"No," Mrs. Whitfield said fiercely. "I'll tell you whatever you need to know. Whatever will help to bring Thomas back home."

"Have you noticed Thomas acting differently in recent times?" Ferguson asked.

Mrs. Whitfield was quiet, thinking. "In ways only a wife would notice, now that I think about it. I caught him very recently looking at me in the way he does when he has something important to tell me. He used to put his head to one side and look very thoughtful, like he was trying to gauge my mood. And " — Mrs. Whitfield blushed — "he did start to take a bit more notice of me."

The two agents were silent, digesting this new information.

Mrs. Whitfield drew a deep breath and took the opportunity to say, "I heard some idiots in Thomas's office say that he might have gone missing of his own free will. I'm telling you now, he would never do that. And now that you know about the threat, you know something bad has happened to him."

Ferguson scratched his head and closed his notebook. "Thanks for your time, Mrs. Whitfield. This can't have been easy for you. Where can we reach you if we need to?"

Mrs. Whitfield recited her phone numbers dutifully and stood. "Please find him. Please trust me when I tell you that something terrible has happened to him." She shook their hands again briefly and was gone.

Ferguson felt a little bewildered. "Well, I guess we're a little closer to the truth," he said. "If the threat she overheard on the phone is true."

"Who on earth would Thomas Whitfield be associating with that would be capable of making a threat like that, let alone carrying it out?" wondered Dinah.

"Maybe the highly respected Thomas Whitfield was a drug mule," suggested Ferguson with a smirk.

Dinah groaned. "Why are you such an idiot?"

\* \* \* \*

Thomas Whitfield had lost track of time and space.

The secretary of the Smithsonian — he who had once hosted presidents and entertained queens — lay in the trunk of a car, hands and feet tightly bound and eyes blindfolded with a rag that smelt of motor oil. Whenever the car would turn a corner tightly, he would roll helplessly and smack his head on the exposed wheel brace. As a result, he also had a pounding headache. There was little oxygen in the confined space, and this caused panic to rise like bitter bile, threatening to choke him.

The only thing he could do was pray desperately. Every so often, he would intersperse his prayers with thoughts of his wife of 34 years, who would surely understand. It was the only way he could stop from giving into the panic altogether and screaming like a caged baboon.

Then the car stopped.

Thomas tensed as dread flowed through his entire body. Soon it would be over, one way or the other.

He heard fumbling with the trunk lock, and then the light that filtered through his blindfold suddenly brightened. Rough hands grabbed him, hoisted him out of the car, and stood him shakily on his feet. The binds around his ankles were loosened, and a voice commanded, "Walk."

Thomas had no idea in what direction his abductor would have him walk, and in any case wasn't sure he could, and so simply put one foot in front of another. He swayed, disoriented by the fuzzy vision and his headache.

A hand clapped his back between the shoulder blades and propelled him forward. He stumbled several times as he negotiated a sidewalk he couldn't see.

Finally, he was shoved into a chair, and the blindfold was ripped from his eyes. He squinted, trying to adjust to the sudden light. Thomas was sitting on an old schoolroom chair inside what looked like an abandoned industrial building. The floor was filthy concrete and the walls bare cinderblock.

In front of him stood his visitor who had abducted him from the museum. Thomas could barely stand to look at him, so he looked at his surroundings, trying to establish any escape route. The windows were tiny and at least nine feet high, and there were no doors apparent.

"What are you doing, Thomas?" his abductor asked softly.

"I can't stand to look at you," said Thomas.

His abductor chuckled. "You'd be surprised how many times I hear that."

"No, I don't think I would," said Thomas truthfully.

The smile left his abductor's face. "Let's get down to business then, shall we? You must know why you're here, Thomas."

"I guess you didn't want me to make that presentation to Congress."

"That's certainly true, but there's more to it than that. I must insist that you stop taking this course of action." The abductor suddenly grinned. There was no apparent joke.

"What do you mean? Do we not live in a democratic society with free speech?" Thomas was angry. "Do I need to remind you of our constitution?"

The abductor barked a harsh laugh. "You'll forgive me if I ignore your questions, enlightened though they are. The truth of the matter is that you don't have a choice. I don't care what you do in the privacy of your own house. We will not allow you to brainwash untold thousands of people with this nonsense you've come up with."

"Who is 'we' exactly?" Thomas demanded.

"You don't need to know. Now, I will have your answer. If you resist us, you will pay dearly. Do you really want to make a widow of your wife?"

Thomas shivered, knowing that he was certainly in the valley of the shadow of death. For a brief moment, he searched his heart. Then he faced his abductor resolutely. "I absolutely will not," he said clearly. "I answer to a Higher Authority than you or the ones who sent you. Do with me as you wish." His face and conscience clear, he bowed his head and waited.

"Higher Authority!" snarled the abductor, who was clearly upset with the direction the conversation was headed. "Thomas, I want you to think about everything we have done for you. I want you to think about why we put you in the position of secretary. Think about what we wanted you to achieve. This is your last chance. Do you understand?"

Thomas looked directly into the eyes of the abductor. "I understand."

The abductor removed his Armani jacket. "Perhaps the next half an hour will influence you to change your mind."

Thomas continued to pray.

\* \* \* \*

The two agents parted ways at the cafeteria. Darkness was swiftly descending over the museum, and both Ferguson and Dinah felt that during the coming days there would be precious little time for rest.

By the time Dinah arrived at her small apartment, the initial excitement at being involved in a case again had worn off. There had been a time when her instincts for catching the worst types of killers had been keen and sharp. She had been, as Ferguson said, one of the very best. Yet it had all changed in the blink of an eye.

She turned on the television for company and was relieved to find two bottles of good New Zealand semillon in the refrigerator. The first mouthful glided down her throat coolly and seductively, and she felt the ever-present anxiety begin to subside.

She thought fleetingly about dinner, and settled for toast and yogurt, staring unseeing at the animated television screen and trying not to let the self-pity strangle her.

This existence was what she hated so intensely. It wasn't anything remotely resembling a life. She felt she was only surviving and nothing more. The worst part of the existence was the time she had alone, where she could think and her brain would betray her with memories and recriminations.

The television caught her attention. Catherine Biscelli, director of the Office of Public Affairs for the Smithsonian Institution, had organized a press conference. The diminutive woman stood behind a blond wood lectern and shook her dark curls.

"The Smithsonian Institution has received news today that the secretary, Mr. Thomas Whitfield, did not appear at work today and his current whereabouts are unknown. The police have been advised and are conducting an investigation. At this point, while there are those who certainly fear for his safety, there is no evidence of foul play. The

Smithsonian Institution will continue to open as normal and all visitors are welcome. Thank you."

The press had a barrage of questions, but Catherine Biscelli held up a hand and walked from the room without acknowledging any of the reporters.

Dinah recounted the events of the day and what was to come. Today Thomas Whitfield had disappeared. In three days the media coverage would be at fever pitch. Then the pressure to solve the case would build inexorably, until something gave.

Her cell phone rang from her handbag and as she stood, somewhat shakily, she observed that she had downed almost two glasses of wine already.

"Hello?"

"Hey, Harris, it's me," Ferguson said. "You free to talk?"

Dinah bit back a cynical laugh. *No, I am hosting a dinner party for my dozens of friends. Call you later, darling.*

"Yeah, what's up?"

"The crime scene preliminary findings have come in," Ferguson said. "No bloodstains, recent or otherwise, found in the office. They combed the office for torn fingernails, hairs, you know the drill. Nothing."

"Nothing at all?" Dinah frowned.

"Nope. So really we still don't know whether Thomas Whitfield has gone to ground of his own volition or been taken against his will." Ferguson paused. "Although, I gotta say, if someone did want to take him, it wouldn't have been hard. He weighed about 120 pounds, dripping wet."

Dinah massaged her temples. "It would be interesting to see what can be recovered from his laptop. The only other evidence we have that an abduction has occurred is the fact that everyone thinks he's Mr. Wonderful and that he would never just disappear like that."

"Maybe it's a former life catching up with him," suggested Ferguson. "He might be pure as snow now, but perhaps he's got a few skeletons in his closet. Do we know anything about his past?"

"Not really. We'd have to ask his wife," said Dinah absently. She was thinking about the past catching up with her.

"I love a good skeleton," Ferguson said cheerfully. "There's nothing more satisfying than getting that skeleton right out in the open."

"That's because you don't have any skeletons," snapped Dinah, more angrily than she'd intended.

There was silence on the other end of the phone. "Harris, I didn't mean . . ." he began tentatively.

"I know," she said, trying to keep the savagery she felt out of her voice. She took a long swallow of wine, hoping it would dampen the thunderstorm of anger breaking inside her.

There was another silence, and then Ferguson said, "Are you drinking?"

Dinah closed her eyes briefly. "Do you have a point?" she demanded.

"I just . . . no, I guess I don't have a point," Ferguson admitted. "I'm just concerned about you."

"I'm fine. There is no need to waste your energy being concerned about me." Dinah topped her glass. *Is that the third or fourth glass?*

"I know, but. . . ."

"Was there anything else you wanted to discuss?" Dinah interrupted.

Ferguson sighed. "No. See you tomorrow."

Dinah hung up, feeling brittle and exposed. Although she trusted Ferguson implicitly, if he thought she had a drinking problem, he would feel compelled to report her. Then she would lose everything that had ever held any meaning for her.

She lay in bed, hoping to find release within the numbness she craved. As she slipped into the heavy, silent world between wakefulness and sleep, she imagined that a small, chubby hand caressed her cheek and whispered, *"Mommy."*

There was a strange, comforting light in the distance, and Dinah was trying to get to it. She was in pitch darkness, struggling against what seemed to be a wind tunnel, an invisible hand holding her back from the light. No matter how hard she tried, she couldn't seem to get any closer. She threw her body into it, straining her arms and legs to try and propel herself forward. Her sense of desperation grew. The light was the answer, the meaning of life. She *had* to get there!

*You can't do it on your own.*

Then the light began to ring, a slow, insistent buzz, and Dinah rose through the layers of sleep like a diver coming up for air. Dinah half sat up, blinking, and saw that the room was still dark and that her cell phone was ringing on her night table.

"Hello?" she answered, squinting at her alarm clock. It was just after two in the morning.

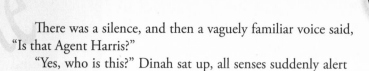

There was a silence, and then a vaguely familiar voice said, "Is that Agent Harris?"

"Yes, who is this?" Dinah sat up, all senses suddenly alert and sharp.

"It's Lara, from the Smithsonian." The young woman was speaking in a low, gruff whisper, as if she was afraid of being overheard.

"What is it, Lara?" Dinah asked. "What's wrong?"

"I need to see you. I need to talk to you about Mr. Whitfield." Lara stopped speaking, and Dinah heard muted wheezing, as if the girl was trying to hold back tears.

"What is it, Lara?" Dinah repeated, trying to keep her own tone calm.

"I need to meet with you," Lara said. "There's a Starbucks right next to the building you came to today. Do you know the one?"

"I can find it," Dinah promised. "When will you be there?"

"Six o'clock this morning. Can you make it?"

"Yes, of course. Is there any reason you can't talk at work?"

"Are you kidding?" Lara's voice suddenly went up several octaves. "They'll *hear* me. I can't talk there!"

"Okay, sure. Have you heard from Mr. Whitfield?"

"No! I think something has happened to him. I'm almost positive he's in trouble," Lara insisted. She paused, and then blurted: "I know why he was abducted and I know that they're going to kill him! You have to do something!"

"Are you. . . ?" Dinah didn't get the question out before she heard the dial tone in her ear. She immediately dialed Ferguson's number.

It took him a long time to answer, and when he did, he sounded like a grumpy grizzly roused from winter hibernation.

"It's Harris. I've just had a phone call from Lara Southall about Thomas Whitfield," Dinah explained in a rush.

"Lara Southall . . . is she the one with all that weird stuff on her eyes?" Ferguson asked sleepily.

"It's called makeup, genius," Dinah said. "Can you wake up, please? It's very irritating having to talk to someone who is still half-asleep."

He groaned and Dinah heard rustling as he lifted his heavy body into a sitting position.

"You could win Miss America based on personality alone, Harris," he grumbled. "Being so cheerful and bubbly and all."

"All right, Ferguson," Dinah said, rolling her eyes. "Lara didn't say much but she has more information for us. She wants to meet at Starbucks because she doesn't feel safe enough to talk at work."

Ferguson waited. "Is that all? That's the reason you woke me? To tell me we have a meeting with the secretary at a Starbucks?"

"I'm amazed sometimes that you ever made it into the FBI at all," Dinah retorted. "Don't you see the implications? If she is afraid to talk at work, then we may have a conspiracy among some of the influential people in this city."

Ferguson sighed. "Or maybe she's watched a couple of episodes too many of *CSI* and loves to be part of a bit of drama."

"We'll see. Be at Starbucks at six, the one next to the building we were in yesterday."

Dinah hung up without waiting for a reply. As she sat on the edge of the bed, she suddenly started to feel the effects of a hangover. Her hands shook as she placed the phone back on the night table, her stomach rolled uneasily, and her head pulsed with a steady pain right in the temples.

As she stood in the shower, hoping the warm needles of water would make her feel better, the final sensation from her dream hit her again.

*You can't do it on your own.*

She closed her eyes, thinking about the dream. It didn't mean anything, except in the most generic sense. She was searching for relief from the darkness that had overtaken her life. She was sick of living in the shadows. She yearned for light, perhaps even life.

\*\*\*\*

Dinah had almost left the house when she realized that she had left her gun in its customary location — underneath the pillow on her bed. Now that she was involved in an active case again, she was required to wear the gun.

She fastened the holster to her torso, the weight of the gun reminding her of her intense loathing of it, of understanding the damage that it could do. It had been bad enough for her to give up her role as an active agent and start teaching intense young FBI agents. Yet, on some nights when she had consumed several glasses of wine, she had begun to think of the gun as an ally. Sometimes she wondered if it wouldn't be the answer to her prayers, a way she could go to sleep and never have to wake up. Something had thus far restrained her from taking the ultimate step. But there were long nights when Dinah knew that it wasn't far away.

The streets were busy with young interns and staffers hurrying to their Capitol Hill jobs, even at six in the morning. Dinah felt illogically irritated by them, which was really brought on by her headache that wouldn't leave her alone, no matter how many Tylenol she swallowed.

When she arrived at Starbucks, she ordered the largest, strongest coffee on the menu. When Ferguson wandered in several moments later, he nodded at her by way of greeting and ordered the same.

Dinah desperately didn't want to talk about their conversation the night before, nor did she want him to realize that she felt like death warmed up. As soon as he sat down, she said brightly, "I knew Lara was lying to us!"

"Okay," agreed Ferguson, putting a great deal more sugar in his coffee than was healthy. "But I still think she's a little prone to drama."

"Are you trying to give yourself diabetes?" Dinah asked, raising one eyebrow at her partner.

"Yeah, funny, Harris." He scowled into the black coffee. "I got no sleep last night. I feel terrible."

Dinah was relieved that he was caught up in his own misery this morning and hadn't noticed her gray pallor and shaking hands. "Why is that?"

"Young kids and bad dreams," he said. "My youngest gets real bad nightmares. He crawls into our bed a couple of times a night. I wait until he falls asleep and then take him back to his own bed. Then there's your phone call. All told, I think I only got about three hours sleep."

"Yeah, I remember what it's like." Dinah chuckled wistfully.

Ferguson suddenly looked awkward and flustered. Then he looked around the Starbucks and down at his watch. "Where is she?"

Without waiting for a reply, he dug out his cell phone and dialed.

Dinah glanced at her watch. They had been sitting in the small café for 30 minutes.

Ferguson had started muttering under his breath as he dialed several numbers and hung up.

"I don't like this," he announced. "No one knows where she is. I got her address from your personal favorite, Catherine Biscelli. Perhaps we had better take a look."

Dinah felt her own sense of unease building as Ferguson drove them toward the young secretary's condo at Forest Hills. Traffic was still thick and it took them 40 minutes to arrive at their destination.

The neighborhood was quiet and the two agents approached the condo complex cautiously. Dinah was uncomfortably aware of the weight of the gun on her hip.

Ferguson took the lead and knocked sharply on the door. Both were hoping Lara would answer. Dinah felt almost positive this would not be the case.

A door across the hall clicked open and Dinah spun, her gun in her hands, adrenaline pumping and every nerve ending screaming.

"Oh my!" gasped the elderly lady who peered out of her door from behind owlish glasses.

Dinah exhaled slowly, lowering the weapon and willing her heart to slow down.

"Are you from the police?" the elderly woman asked, eyeing Dinah up and down with concern.

"Yes, ma'am, we're from the FBI," Ferguson replied. "Is there a problem?"

"I don't know," the woman said querulously. "I've been wondering whether to call the police all morning. Now that you're here, I ought to tell you and then you can make of it what you will."

"What is it?" Ferguson asked. He glanced over at Dinah, who was still recovering from the shock.

"Early this morning, I heard some thuds and bumps from that young lady's apartment. I thought it sounded like someone was moving furniture. Who would move furniture at five in the morning? Particularly that young lady, she isn't a very large girl, is she?"

"Did you hear voices or shouts?" Ferguson asked with great patience.

"No, I didn't. That's why I wasn't sure whether to call the police."

"Do you have a phone in there, ma'am?" Ferguson asked.

The old lady nodded earnestly.

"Could you please call the manager and have him bring up the keys to this apartment? We need to know whether the lady inside is okay."

The old lady was excited to be part of an FBI investigation and did as she was asked.

The manager arrived several moments later with a gigantic ring of keys dangling from one hand. He made a point of bad-temperedly demanding ID from each of the agents, and then reminding them that they were not to damage the apartment in any way. Dinah restrained herself from making a sarcastic comment regarding his sub-standard intelligence.

The agents took several moments to take in the one-bedroom studio apartment.

The kitchen was clean and looked as if it was rarely used. A small, round dining table stood adjacent to the kitchen, and it was being used for storage. Dinah couldn't see the surface of the table for the shoes, books, CDs, and shopping bags. The small living room wasn't much better, with two couches, a coffee table, and a TV. The coffee table was decorated with three half-melted candles, which probably accounted for the faint sickly sweet aroma in the room.

A doorway directly ahead of them was open.

Both agents had their guns out, and Dinah's felt cold and indifferent in her hands.

"Lara, this is the FBI. If you are able, please show yourself," Ferguson called.

There was no answer.

Dinah and Ferguson slowly approached the doorway, and Ferguson went in first, gun held straight in front of him. The bedroom was silent and messy, the dressing table cluttered with more makeup than Dinah had ever seen. Still more pairs of shoes littered the carpet.

While Ferguson checked the closets, Dinah entered the small bathroom. The blind was drawn, and the room was murky with shadows.

Then Dinah saw the still figure, curled into the fetal position in the shower cubicle, her head a bloody mess. She was dressed in a bathrobe.

"Ferguson!" she called, holstering her gun. She yanked open the cubicle door and knelt beside the motionless girl. Lara's black hair was stiff and coppery with dried blood. The entire side of her face was swollen and bloody. Dinah felt the girl's wrist for a pulse and found one, weak but steady. Lara was barely conscious, her eyelids fluttering.

Ferguson stood above them, calling 911 for the paramedics.

"Lara, can you hear me?" asked Dinah urgently. She took the girl's hand. "It's the FBI. You're going to be okay. We're going to take you to the hospital and you'll be just fine."

Lara moaned, a mewling as weak as a newborn kitten.

"Stay here," ordered Ferguson. "I'm going to check that the rest of the apartment really is empty."

Dinah squeezed Lara's hand and kept talking to her, hoping to keep her awake. She could hear Ferguson checking closets and any other places the perpetrator might be hiding.

Finally, the paramedics arrived and Dinah stood aside. The district police had now arrived and were questioning Ferguson and sealing off the apartment with crime scene tape. Dinah gave him a small wave. "I'm going to the hospital with Lara," she said.

Sirens blaring, she rode with Lara into the Metropolitan Hospital.

\*\*\*\*

Dinah was relegated to the waiting room while the ER doctors diagnosed and treated Lara. She remembered the last time she'd stared at the sterile wall of a hospital waiting room.

Last time she'd been sick with worry and numb with guilt, hoping desperately that death had not paid her a visit. The dread realization had already begun to sink into the deepest parts of her soul. Here she had the realization that death had called on her family.

She remembered the young doctor who had come from the ER, his face sad and drawn. She remembered thinking that doctors were the new soldiers of the 21st century, facing a battlefront every day without reprieve, dealing with the aftermath of human cruelty and selfishness.

He had shaken his head once. "I'm dreadfully sorry," he had said, and she knew that he had meant it.

Since that day, depression had been Dinah's cheerless companion.

She roused herself as a female doctor in her forties approached. "I'm Dr. Rae Fortune," she said. "You rode with Lara Southall?" The doctor was trying to ascertain Dinah's relationship with the patient.

"I'm Special Agent Dinah Harris with the FBI. My partner and I found Lara Southall and I rode with her because she is an important witness in one of our current investigations."

The doctor nodded. "The hospital has notified her parents."

"How is she?" Dinah asked.

"Not as bad as she looked, thankfully," Dr. Fortune replied. "Nevertheless she took a brutal beating. She has a compressed fracture of her left eye socket and cheekbone. I feared she had a skull fracture but she doesn't. She also sustained severe bruising on the left side her face and neck and there are a number of cuts — one above her eyebrow, which needed two stitches and one on her upper lip."

Dinah shook her head. "I see. Thank you for attending to her. May I see her?"

Dr. Fortune looked troubled. "Special Agent, I understand she may have vital information you need to obtain. However, I will warn you that if she begins to get distressed or upset in any way, I will terminate your right to see her immediately." The doctor stared hard at Dinah.

Dinah stared back. She didn't like it when others tried to intimidate her. At this point, Ferguson would have probably stepped in and calmed the situation. Then he would have made a smart comment about Dinah's ability to alienate every female she came into contact with.

When the stare finally broke, Dinah followed a doctor to where Lara was recuperating and approached the girl. Lara's face and neck were mottled purple and red with the bruising and her left eye was black and swollen shut. Her black eyelashes stuck straight up from the slit in her eye like spiky soldiers standing at attention.

"Lara, it's Dinah Harris from the FBI." Dinah spoke softly so that she didn't scare the girl. "How are you feeling?"

Lara turned to look at her visitor with her good eye. "Terrible," she said, her voice husky. "I have such a headache."

"Do you need me to get some pain relief for you?" Dinah asked.

"No thanks. I've just had morphine." Lara grimaced slightly. "I suppose you want to know what happened."

Dinah nodded. "Please take your time."

"I don't know what happened," Lara said, turning away from the agent slightly. "I spoke to you on the phone. Later I was about to have a shower when I felt something hit my face, on the left side. I fell to the ground and he just kept hitting my face. I curled up, trying to protect myself."

"Did you get a look at your attacker?"

"No. He came out of nowhere and I didn't even see what he hit me with."

"Did he speak to you at all?"

Lara paused for a fraction of a second. "No."

Dinah digested the lie for a moment. "I know you're scared," she said gently. "But this is very important. If he did speak to you, even if they were words that don't make any sense, it could still be crucial information."

"He was completely silent the whole time," Lara insisted.

"There was just one attacker?"

"Yes. At least I was only attacked by one person. I don't know if there were any others there."

"How long do you think the attack took?"

"It was over in a couple of minutes." Lara shuddered as she remembered. "It felt like an eternity."

"The attacker didn't tell you what he wanted?" Dinah asked.

"No."

At least the lie was consistent.

"What about the information you were going to tell Special Agent Ferguson and me this morning?" Dinah tried a different tack. "Do you want to share that with me now?"

Lara faltered. "It wasn't really important." She did not look at the other woman.

Dinah frowned. "It sounded important at two o'clock this morning."

"I'm sorry, I was overreacting. I am just so worried about Mr. Whitfield." Lara had focused on a point on the wall opposite her bed and wasn't moving.

Dinah sat on the edge of the bed and forced the young woman to look at her. "Lara, I know you're scared," she said gently. "I can help you if you're honest with me."

A solitary tear escaped from Lara's good eye. "You don't understand," she whispered. "I *can't*. I'm sorry."

A nurse bustled in the door and looked sternly at the pair, noting Lara's tears. Dinah took her cue to leave. She'd learned only one thing from the interview with Lara. Lara knew something important enough to be assaulted and threatened. The question was, what did she know?

**\* \* \* \***

Thomas Whitfield was in great pain.

He remained tied to the chair in the abandoned industrial building, and for the last half hour had been attended to by his abductor.

Thomas felt sure that his nose was broken and several of his teeth had been knocked out or broken. His face was sticky and warm with his own blood. There was a curious buzzing in his head, which felt too heavy for his neck. His vision had narrowed, the peripherals turning black over the course of the previous half hour.

His abductor had finally ceased the beating and stood in front of Thomas, shaking his head and breathing hard.

"Well, Thomas," he said with a smirk. "You've had plenty of time to think about what you want to do."

Thomas straightened, with great effort, to look his abductor in the eye. "You don't scare me," he replied. Around his missing teeth, it sounded like *You don schhhare ee.*

"You're stupider than I thought then," the abductor sneered. "First it was this nonsense that you wanted to tell Congress. That was bad enough, Thomas. Now, in your position, you tell me that you're not scared? You're not grasping the situation at all."

Thomas didn't reply. He simply didn't have the energy to argue.

"It's really simple," the abductor continued. "So you should get it. All you need to do is forget this load of baloney that you've been fixated on, forget presenting it to Congress, and forget all of your proposals. You will get out of here alive, and your job back, and you can continue on as if this had never happened at all. It's that simple, Thomas."

Thomas would have shaken his head if it didn't feel like it would fly off at any moment. "It's not that simple for me," he said. "I believe that what I'm doing is the right thing, and you can't threaten me or beat me so badly that I'll change my mind."

The abductor laughed incredulously. "You would exchange your life for some pathetic ideology?"

"I would," Thomas said. "For me it is truth, not ideology, and it is the greatest truth the world will ever hear. I will not peddle lies for one moment longer." As he spoke, a cloak of calm seemed to envelop him.

For the first time, the veneer of self-control left the abductor. His mouth twisted with anger and contempt, and he viciously kicked the chair in which Thomas was sitting. Thomas crashed to the floor with a thud that knocked the wind out of him and caused brilliant flashes of pain to radiate up his side like lightning. Momentarily, his world was plunged into darkness.

"You fool," hissed the abductor. He turned away from where Thomas lay groaning and paced in small circles. He seemed to take a few moments to control himself, and then picked up Thomas and the chair.

Thomas had never known such fear and pain, yet he felt strangely calm. He knew, in his heart of hearts, that everything would be okay. He had started to see human beings, even powerful ones, in a very different light in recent weeks.

"It's people like you," the abductor snarled, his teeth clenched, "that are turning this country into a pool of weakness."

He seemed on the verge on launching into a tirade, but he caught himself and waited for several beats.

"I won't give you another chance," said the abductor, his calm and controlled exterior back. "Your life amounts to what you say next: will you give up this nonsense that you've become obsessed with?"

"I will not," Thomas replied immediately. "In my soul, I know it to be the truth."

The abductor feigned sadness. "Then I can no longer help you or protect you," he said.

Thomas knew that the end of his life drew near. With some surprise, he found that it didn't bother him.

He thought about his wife, whom he'd only started to see — to really *see* — in recent months for the resilient, amazing woman she was. He thought about his children, who had both graduated from college and lived overseas. He thought about their smiles, their first words, their shrieking laughter from the pool. Fleetingly, he regretted that he hadn't shared the discovery of his life with them. He wanted them to know that he would be okay, that there would be no reason to grieve.

It was funny, Thomas thought, what flashed through his mind as death approached. He wasn't thinking of the accolades and awards he'd won as an anthropologist. He wasn't thinking about the various celebrities and heads of state he'd met while in the position of secretary. He wasn't thinking about the balance of his bank account or the value of his Georgetown house.

Instead, he thought of the things that life was really about — why had he only just realized this? The important things were his wife, his family, and most of all, his newfound joy and freedom.

The abductor moved closer to Thomas. He closed his eyes and waited.

When Dinah arrived back at Lara Southall's condo in Forrest Hills, she found Ferguson trying to coordinate the district cops and crime scene technicians and becoming increasingly flustered.

When he saw Dinah, relief creased his face and he jogged over. "How is Lara?" he asked.

"Not talking," replied Dinah with a sigh. "She was beat up pretty bad, and whoever did it had a pretty specific message for her. She'll live, but she's scared."

"Is it safe to assume that this all relates to Thomas Whitfield?" Ferguson mused. They both began climbing the stairs to Lara Southall's condo.

"Yes, genius, I would say so," agreed Dinah sarcastically. Ferguson ignored her. "Find anything interesting in her apartment?"

"Not really," said Ferguson as they arrived at the door to Lara's condo. The doorway was barred with crime scene tape, and the two agents ducked underneath it and stood, surveying the small living area. There was black fingerprint dust scattered indiscriminately throughout the apartment, which did nothing to detract from the general state of disarray.

"Let's start at the beginning," she suggested. "How did the attacker get in?"

Ferguson motioned at the door. "A skillful lock-picking instrument," he said. "The door itself is undamaged, but the lock was manipulated. When we take the lock apart in the lab, we'll be able to see the nicks and scratches on the metal where the tool has come into contact with it. It would have taken all of 20 seconds for someone who knew what they were doing to get in."

"No deadbolts or chains?" Dinah swung the door toward herself to look at the security. There was a deadbolt, but it too had been manipulated by someone who knew what they were doing. "Where do you get tools for lock-picking as sophisticated as these?" she asked.

Ferguson shrugged. "It's probably not that hard. Any locksmith would have these, but you could also get them off the Internet."

"I suppose dusting for fingerprints on the door is redundant," added Dinah.

"The techs did it anyway, although Lara has been living here for over two years. We would expect to find hers and the supers' and maybe the neighbors. To be frank, I would think if the attacker came armed with lock-picking tools, he would have been smart enough to wear gloves."

"Right. What about the rest?"

"No weapon found. There are no obvious signs of struggle or flight in the living areas, which suggests the victim wasn't attacked out here nor chased toward the bathroom. Initially, it looks like she was surprised as she was preparing to take a shower."

This was consistent with Lara's story, thought Dinah, so at least she was telling the truth about something.

"It looks like a very quick and efficient attack," continued Ferguson as they arrived in the bathroom. Blood had spattered the shower cubicle walls and more of it pooled around the drain. "He hit her and she fell to the floor. We didn't find blood anywhere else in the shower, so the cubicle is the primary scene. There was nowhere for her to escape to; she was essentially trapped in the shower cubicle at the attacker's mercy. If he wanted to say something to her at this point, she would have been conscious. Then he landed a few more blows and left as quietly as he came."

"So he was obviously very controlled and calm," Dinah said. "There seemed to be no anger or passion of any kind. He came and did what he had to do. Plus, he contained the scene in the bathroom. Was there any burglary?"

Ferguson shook his head. "Doesn't look like it. The victim's pocketbook and wallet were found, with credit cards and cash still present."

"Are you thinking professional hit?"

Ferguson considered this. "In the context of the abduction of Thomas Whitfield, it would be hard to believe anything else — particularly in the light of your early morning phone call." Suddenly remembering the phone call, he turned to Dinah. "Did she. . . ?"

"No," said Dinah. "I told you, she refused to talk. Weren't you listening?"

"If you're the one talking, then I tend to drift in and out," admitted Ferguson cheerfully. Dinah narrowed her eyes at him.

"I think it's obvious that Thomas Whitfield's disappearance is suspicious," Ferguson said. "The question is, is he still alive?"

The agents left the condo at Forrest Hills and decided to visit Thomas Whitfield's home in Georgetown. They were hoping that they would find some personal information that had been missing from his office at the museum. While Ferguson drove, Dinah started to feel tired. She hadn't been technically diagnosed as an insomniac. She felt sure, when she was honest with herself, that any self-respecting doctor would realize that the insomnia was a symptom of a deeper depression. Then the doctor would want to medicate and place her into therapy as quickly as possible. Dinah didn't want medication or therapy; for her, the pain was a deserved punishment for past transgressions. She found no relief in her fitful bouts of sleep and found herself thinking more and more about that final, endless slumber.

As is often the case with insomniacs, the sudden need to sleep could come at any time, and often at unwelcome times. Waves of exhaustion rolled across her and she lost the battle to keep her eyes open. She drifted into the heavy, quiet land of light sleep.

*You can't do it on your own.*

She was aware that she wasn't dreaming but recalling the vivid imagery of the previous night's dream. It had touched her subconscious and refused to let go.

\*\*\*\*

"Dinah, wake up!" She felt a hand shaking her arm lightly. She forced her eyes open and saw Ferguson looking at her strangely. The car had stopped and they were outside a graceful shingle-style, semi-detached complex with white-painted shutters.

"Sorry, didn't sleep very well last night," she said.

"No, you were mumbling to yourself," Ferguson said. "Something about doing it on your own. What were you dreaming about?"

Dinah hesitated. "Uh, I'm not really sure," she replied, truthfully. She desperately wanted to change the subject. "Is this the Whitfields' home?"

"Yup. Nice pad, huh?"

The two agents made their way up the path and onto the porch. As Dinah lifted her hand to push the doorbell, Ferguson suddenly grabbed her arm and put a finger to his lips. Then he pointed at the front door. It was slightly ajar. Both agents unholstered their guns and Ferguson pushed the door lightly. It swung open, and the agents crept into a living room furnished with floral armchairs and built-in bookshelves flanking the marble fireplace. Most of the books had been thrown to the tan hardwood floors and were scattered around, several with the covers almost entirely ripped off.

Ahead of the agents was an arched doorway, and Dinah could see the curved end of a staircase banister. They continued to tiptoe through the archway and into a relatively untouched dining room. Beyond this was an empty, galley-style kitchen, also largely untouched.

Ferguson tapped Dinah's elbow and pointed upstairs, indicating he would search up there. Dinah nodded and continued her stealthy progress. She could see that the back door, opening from the kitchen, was also hanging open.

Dinah found more evidence of a disturbance in the family room, where more books had been displaced, but by far the most damage was done in the study. The room looked like a tornado had touched down in there, sucked up the contents of the room, oscillated for several moments, then dropped everything back onto the floor. Two neat filing cabinets had been stored underneath the desk. All four drawers had been ripped out and the contents upended all over the floor. The desktop computer lay smashed amongst the paper. Computer disks were scattered across the floor.

Yet there was no sign of Mrs. Whitfield.

Ferguson materialized beside Dinah and said in a low voice, "Upstairs is clear, although there is a mighty mess up there."

"Same here. But is there a basement?"

The two agents found the door to the basement and crept down the short flight of stairs, each secretly glad the other was there. The basement was dark and musty, and the agents could vaguely see the washer and dryer and some household tools. Ferguson located a light switch, and the room was flooded with dim, murky light from the low-wattage, bare bulb swinging from the ceiling.

Then they saw Mrs. Whitfield. She was sitting in a chair backed up against storage boxes. Her ankles were tied to the legs of the chair, her arms were bound behind her, and her mouth was gagged. Her eyes were wide and terrified and stared at the agents imploringly. Dinah rushed over and immediately began loosening the binds, beginning with the gag. "Are you okay?" she asked. "Have you been hurt?"

"I'm fine," she croaked once the gag was free. "He didn't hurt me. He just took me by surprise, bundled me down here, tied me up, and messed around upstairs doing goodness knows what for what seemed like hours. I could use a glass of water though."

Ferguson went to find a glass and water from the kitchen. Mrs. Whitfield rubbed her wrists and ankles, trying to get her circulation moving again. When he came back, Dinah suggested, "Why don't you take us through exactly what happened."

"I was in the kitchen," said Mrs. Whitfield, after draining the glass of water. "I've been a bit jumpy since yesterday, because of — well, because of Thomas. I keep hearing noises. Anyway, I was in the kitchen, and I heard a noise from outside, in the back garden."

"What sort of noise?" interjected Ferguson.

"It was a screeching noise. There is a side gate." Mrs. Whitfield pointed to her left, apparently in the direction of the side gate. "If it's left unlocked, it swings back and forth and makes an awful screeching noise. It drives me crazy. Anyway, I thought I must've left it open so

I went outside to shut it. Almost the minute I stepped outside, I was grabbed."

"Exactly how did this happen?" Ferguson asked. In the partnership between him and Dinah, he had always been the pedantic one, questioning every tiny detail. He must've sensed Dinah's impatience, because he added, "Sorry to be a pain. There is no detail that is unimportant."

"I stood on the top step. The door had only just shut behind me and I was about to walk down the steps. A hand suddenly pressed against my face."

"From what direction?"

"I'm sorry, I really don't know. Could've been the right or the left. He lifted me almost off my feet and dragged me inside. I was struggling to get free, but he was too strong. Then he spoke to me."

"Did you get a look at him?"

She shook her head. "He wore a ski mask. He told me that he had a gun, and that I was to do exactly as I was told and I wouldn't get hurt. Then he released me and he took me down to the basement."

"Did he know the plans of the house?" Dinah asked.

Mrs. Whitfield considered this. "You know, now that you mention it, it seems that he did. He didn't ask me where the basement was. He just took me down there, tied me up, and gagged me. He didn't speak to me again." She paused. "Do you think that he's been here before?"

"It's a possibility," Ferguson said. "What happened then?"

"Well, I could hear him making a mess up there. Then he left and I started worrying about what would happen if nobody found me."

"He didn't come back down here at all?"

"No. Is he the person who took Thomas?" Mrs. Whitfield tensed as she spoke, seeming to steel herself against the answer.

"It certainly seems possible," answered Ferguson truthfully. In addition to being pedantic, he was also the master of the unique FBI language — noncommittal, taciturn, and unfailingly polite. "When you feel up to it, would you mind coming upstairs to check if anything has been stolen?"

The three of them made their way upstairs, where the damage to the living room and study made Mrs. Whitfield gasp and clap her hand over her mouth. She moved around the house methodically while the two agents went to the kitchen door where she was attacked.

Dinah noted that the kitchen was positioned in the back right-hand corner of the house and it would have been very easy for the attackers to hide around the side of the house until they heard Mrs. Whitfield close the back door.

Ferguson phoned the district police to send over a crime scene crew, while Dinah checked the side of the house for footprints or other preliminary evidence.

There was nothing.

"Nothing missing," reported Mrs. Whitfield from the kitchen.

Dinah came back inside and shut the door behind her. "Okay, that rules out robbery," she said. "Listen, my partner has asked the crime scene technicians to come and take fingerprints and look for other evidence. They'll be here shortly. In the meantime, I don't think you should stay here by yourself. Is there someone you can call?"

Mrs. Whitfield looked distressed. "I can't believe this is happening," she cried, tears welling in her eyes. "First Thomas disappears, and now this." She sniffed and Dinah waited for her to compose herself. "I'll call my sister."

Ferguson approached with his cell phone in his hand. "We gotta go back to the office," he informed Dinah. "I just saw crime scene turn into the street. Will you be okay, Mrs. Whitfield?"

She nodded miserably, her small frame hunched. Dinah wanted to hug and comfort her, but she didn't know what to say.

\*\*\*\*

"What's up?" Dinah asked as the two agents climbed back into the Crown and headed back towards headquarters.

"We've been summoned," Ferguson said, driving faster than was strictly safe. "By the boss." He suddenly held up a finger and turned up the volume on the radio. The hourly newscast was just beginning.

The secretary of the Smithsonian, Mr. Thomas Whitfield, has now been missing for 24 hours, and police say they have no new leads to his disappearance. Police refuse to confirm whether Mr. Whitfield may have met with foul play; however, it has been confirmed that there is some fear regarding his safety. In a related incident, Mr. Whitfield's personal assistant, Lara Southall, was assaulted in her condo in the early hours of this morning and taken to a hospital suffering head and facial injuries. She remains in the hospital and police are scouring her Forrest Hills condo for clues. Police will not confirm whether other staff at the museum are at risk; however, our sources close to the executive team at the museum confirm that the remaining staff are worried for their safety and are fearful that a serial attacker may be on the loose.

"A serial attacker?" groaned Ferguson. "Give me a break!"

"Guess that explains why the Special Agent in Charge wants to see us," Dinah said quietly. "Pressure's on."

Ferguson glanced at his partner. "Are you going to be okay?"

The panic and dread fighting for space inside Dinah's skull made her lash out at Ferguson. "I guess I don't have a choice," she snapped. "All thanks to you, since you decided for all of us that I was to be part of this investigation."

Ferguson absorbed the verbal attack silently as he found a parking space underneath the J. Edgar Hoover building. Dinah felt bad and wanted to apologize to her partner, but she couldn't find the words.

They both hurried in silence to the elevators and up to the Special Agent in Charge's office. The SAC, George Hanlon, was a classic law enforcement bureaucrat with a flair for politics, and his barely concealed desire to climb the ladder was well-known. George Hanlon was sharp and sarcastic, which Ferguson thought would be interesting, given Dinah's own ill temper.

They were ushered into the office almost immediately, where George Hanlon was staring out the window, his back to the two agents. Dinah looked at Ferguson and rolled her eyes. George Hanlon loved to assert his authority, even in the most petty of ways. He was a tall, skinny man, with a prominent Adam's apple and a nose that resembled the beak of an eagle.

Finally he turned around and eyed the agents. "Please sit down," he said. He waited until they had, then continued, "How is your investigation into Thomas Whitfield's disappearance going?"

"It's been 24 hours," said Ferguson. "But up until early this morning, we couldn't be sure that there was even a crime to investigate."

Hanlon watched his agent thoughtfully. "And now that you do know?"

"Crime scene haven't found any. . . ."

"Okay, what I'm hearing is excuses. I want answers," Hanlon interrupted. "The secretary of the Smithsonian does not simply vanish into thin air. He needs to be found, ASAP." He swung his chair around so that his back was to the agents. "And another thing," he continued in a soft, deadly voice. "Are you sure you're supposed to be here, Agent Harris?"

"I . . ." began Dinah but Ferguson nudged her and overrode her.

"I cleared it with both her supervisor and you," he said. "I wanted Harris to work with me on this case because she is simply a very good investigator."

"*Was*," corrected Hanlon caustically. "Frankly it doesn't show great judgment, Agent Ferguson, given the level of media interest and Agent Harris's previous mistakes."

"The circumstances surrounding that *mistake* were extraordinary," said Ferguson tightly. "As I'm sure you know."

Hanlon held his hands up in mock surrender. "All I'm saying, Agent Ferguson, is that the press has a nasty habit of dredging up the past and I'm warning you to be ready for it."

It was interesting and somewhat deprecating, thought Dinah, to have two people discuss her mental strengths and weaknesses as if she weren't there.

"The bottom line, in any case, is this: you'd better wrap this case up in the very near future or both of you will be looking for new jobs," continued Hanlon. He looked at Dinah directly as he added, "With or without nervous breakdowns in the field."

Dinah should have prepared herself for some level of malice from the SAC; in the absence of an ability to be a good leader, George Hanlon resorted to threats and taunts to assert his authority. Still, she was wounded to the quick by the man's words.

"I don't respond well to threats," she said, staring directly at George Hanlon. Ferguson could almost see the ire rising in her face, turning her cheeks bright red.

"Dinah . . ." Ferguson attempted to shut her down before she said something she regretted.

With great effort, Dinah pushed down the anger she was feeling and stood.

The two agents returned to their workstations, and Ferguson shot his partner a glance. Dinah knew that he worried that Hanlon's words would push her over the edge, and she deftly moved her internal mask across her emotions. Her exoskeleton, she liked to think of it, protecting the soft organs of hurt, grief, and remorse.

"He was pretty tough on you," Ferguson began tentatively. "Are you going to be okay?"

"I'll be fine," Dinah replied lightly. She stared at her computer screen, trying to signal that the conversation was over.

"Are you?"

"I said, I'll be fine! I don't want to talk about it," Dinah said. "Don't you have work to do?"

\* \* \* \*

In the country estate located in upstate New York, where the landscape had turned into a glorious mix of gold and auburn and sparkled in the late afternoon sun like jewelry in a showcase, two men met in an oak-paneled library.

The owner of the property, known locally as Mac, poured two snifters of brandy and took a seat in one of the antique King Louis wingback armchairs.

His visitor, known in the shady world in which he operated as Wolf, due to his ruthlessness, accepted the second snifter and also sat down.

"I presume you have taken care of the situation?" Mac asked, crossing his legs.

Wolf, who outwardly treated the other man with respect and a certain deference, inwardly thought him a vain old fool. Wolf could see the hair plugs from right across the room.

"It's over," Wolf answered.

"What," inquired Mac acidly, "exactly does that mean? Has the subject agreed to our conditions?"

"Not really," Wolf said, adding before Mac could insert another sarcastic comment: "We've had to implement Plan B."

Mac wrinkled his nose with distaste. "I see. So the secretary is dead?"

"He is," confirmed Wolf. He took a sip of brandy and grimaced. He would have much preferred the dulcet flavor of black-label bourbon.

"I find it puzzling that he simply didn't comply with our demands," Mac said. In truth, Mac didn't like being in the same room as a man he considered barely more than a trained orangutan.

Wolf shrugged. "Well, he didn't, so we were forced into Plan B."

There was a thoughtful silence as Mac swirled his brandy and considered this. "It creates a number of problems," he said finally. "What have you done with the body?"

"With all due respect, I don't think you really want to know," said Wolf, struggling to keep the disdain from his voice.

"Just reassure me that it won't be found," said Mac sharply. "Or that incriminating evidence will be found."

"I know what I'm doing," said Wolf. "It won't be found anytime soon, and we're being careful."

"I've been informed today that the FBI is involved," Mac said. "So this must never be traced back to you — or I."

Wolf nodded. "There's nothing to worry about."

Mac didn't quite believe him. Wolf was certainly good at what he did, which is to say he made for an efficient and dispassionate killer. However, Mac suspected he didn't have the vested interest in the outcome that Mac himself did.

"You may go," he said coldly. "I've wired the money to your account. I hope that this is all over."

Wolf allowed a smile, which was not at all cheerful. "It amazes me how many clients say that, and yet require my services year after year."

He let himself out of the country estate, leaving Mac to brood on the circumstances. Plan B had not been his favored method of solving the problem, but it was better than the alternative. He was confident that his own name wouldn't come up in any ensuing investigation, and if it did, he had no compunction in throwing Wolf to the wolves, so to speak. He chuckled, finished his brandy, and dialed a number.

"This is Perry," a reedy voice answered.

"It's Mac. We've succeeded in our plan."

The voice immediately warmed. "Excellent! So the secretary accepted our conditions?"

"I'm afraid he did not," said Mac. "We've had to remove him."

There was silence. "Please tell me that means you forced him to resign," Perry said.

"It means he's been *removed* from the face of the earth," said Mac bluntly.

There was a shocked gasp. "Why would you do that? I didn't — I mean, I never asked. . . . What were you thinking?"

"As I understood it, we both had our concerns regarding the incumbent secretary," Mac said. He was rather enjoying this. "I offered a solution to you, which you readily accepted. That makes you as culpable as I."

Perry gave a short, mirthless laugh. "All I wanted was scientific integrity! I didn't ask you to *kill* him!"

"The secretary made it clear he wouldn't preserve your scientific integrity," said Mac. "And so the next step needed to be taken. And so I think the words you are looking for are thank you."

"I — I — I can't condone killing," Perry said desperately.

"The thing is, Perry, I have evidence of you asking me to take care of the problem, and the problem was the secretary. As I recall, you used rather ambiguous language, and so a jury wouldn't have any difficulty believing that you actually meant to kill the secretary."

Mac waited for this to sink in.

Perry was making interesting choking noises on the other end of the phone. "I can't believe this!"

"Now you and I are tied together in this business," Mac continued. "And there are worse friends to have. But I can be a most difficult enemy and I would advise you to remember what I am capable of."

Perry accepted this in silence.

"Since you got what you wanted, you have no cause to complain. Therefore you will keep your mouth shut and follow my instructions. Do you understand?"

Perry swallowed with an audible click. "Yes."

"Excellent. Perhaps you'd like to start thinking of a replacement for the unfortunate Mr. Whitfield. I'll leave *that* up to you."

Mac hung up and allowed himself a broad smile. Perry's feelings about murder were of no consequence, he thought. Ultimately, Mac had achieved exactly what he'd wanted in the situation, and he'd gathered a few scapegoats along the way. Mac always succeeded.

It was late evening when Dinah and Ferguson arrived back at Thomas Whitfield's home. It was empty, Eloise Whitfield having gone to stay with her sister. It was time to get into the work that made up so much of an investigation that movies conveniently glossed over.

They tossed a coin and Ferguson lost, so he pulled on latex gloves and went to the trash. The crime scene technicians had wreaked their usual havoc, but their specialty was physical evidence — hair, fingernails, prints, foreign fibers or particles, and other evidence that would tie a perpetrator inexorably to his DNA or his environment. Finding clues about who may have committed the crime and why was left up to the agents.

Dinah started in the study. It was the messiest and would probably yield the most important information. Crime scene had taken the computer to check its hard drive. Dinah began to look through the paper littering the floor. It was mundane and time-consuming. She sorted the paper in two piles — relevant and irrelevant. In the relevant pile, she put bank statements, phone records, and correspondence. In the other pile, she put electricity bills, health check-up reminders, and charity donations. The best thing about this sort of work was that it utterly consumed Dinah, and she couldn't dwell on anything else.

She secured the two piles with rubber bands and went about replacing the books on the shelves. Every book she checked for exactly what the intruders had been looking for — loose leaf paper jammed between pages, cryptic messages penciled inside the front dust jacket, or anything that was out of the ordinary for a very ordinary bookcase. As she went, she wrote down the names of each book and its author in her notebook. Most of the books were scientific and business textbooks and therefore of very little interest to Dinah. Yet she dutifully copied it all down, knowing that the tiniest detail could mean a major breakthrough later on in the case.

"Hey," Ferguson said, appearing at the door and startling her. "I'm done with the trash. Found something interesting." He glanced around the study and shook his head at the mess.

"What is it?" Dinah asked absently.

"Cell phone. At the bottom of the trash can." Ferguson held it up, and then wrinkled his nose. "Man, I stink!"

"Yeah," agreed Dinah. "Can you try to stay downwind? Whose cell phone is it?"

"Thomas Whitfield's," said Ferguson, a note of glee in his voice. "I haven't checked, but hopefully there'll be text messages or some clue in the call register."

"Do you think they'd be that careless, given their attention to detail so far?" Dinah asked, her curiosity piqued.

"All right!" crowed Ferguson several moments later. "They've finally made a mistake. No text messages."

"Hardly surprising," interjected Dinah. "Thomas was not exactly part of the text message generation."

"*But,*" said Ferguson, with a momentary glare in Dinah's direction, "call register intact. Ready to write?"

Dinah copied down the lists of numbers from both calls received and made registers, in addition to how many times each number appeared in the register, and what date and time the calls were made and received.

While Ferguson sifted through the living room, Dinah had a quick look at the bank statements. Often large withdrawals or deposits were a good indicator that a person had been planning a so-called abduction. Sometimes they were indicators of other illegal activities that had contributed to the person's disappearance. In any case, large withdrawals and deposits often gave an investigator a little thrill of hope.

However, the Whitfield's bank statements appeared, at first glance, to be very routine. Thomas's salary was deposited each month. Regular withdrawals and payments were made during the course of the month. Checks were cashed on a regular basis.

Frustrated, Dinah stood and stretched, allowing her mind to wander. Why had Thomas Whitfield been abducted? What was there to gain by abducting him? Who had abducted him?

Dinah got the sense that the Whitfields were orderly, regular people, despite the disarray the house was currently in. While they were certainly comfortable, they were not obscenely wealthy; and in any case, a ransom request had not been received.

Who on earth could find Thomas Whitfield's existence a threat?

Ferguson reappeared in the study. "I don't know about you, but I need to get some sleep. Are you done here?"

Dinah gathered up the evidence and the two agents left the house in darkness.

As Ferguson drove her home, Dinah said, "I was just thinking to myself who would want to make Thomas Whitfield disappear? For all accounts, he was a normal guy living a normal life."

"He was high profile," Ferguson said. "Not many of us have direct access to Congress."

"Minor league high profile," corrected Dinah. "Not exactly an A-list celebrity."

Ferguson smiled. "What's on for tomorrow?"

Dinah pointed at the evidence bags held in her lap. "We've got phone records, bank statements, and cell phone numbers to analyze."

Ferguson groaned.

\* \* \* \*

Dinah slept fitfully, her dreams haunted by a vision of herself bound and gagged the way Eloise Whitfield had been and unable to struggle free. When she awoke in the early morning, her eyes were grainy and scratchy, as if she'd spent too much time at the beach on a windy day. She lay in bed, staring at the ceiling, waiting for her alarm clock to chirp, and tried to think of reasons to get out of bed and face another day.

She had hoped that becoming involved in another case would work as a form of therapy for her, that occupying her sharp mind and keen instinct for the unusual would keep her from dwelling on the despair that consumed her. She knew, two days into the investigation, that this wasn't working. In fact, she doubted that anything could erase the darkness that enveloped her world.

The alarm clock sprang into noisy action, and Dinah dragged herself from bed into the shower. The hot water did not ease her fuzzy headache. Just after getting dressed she thought about eating breakfast, but she felt very uneasy from lack of sleep and the thought of food made her stomach churn uneasily.

She put on the holster last and opened her front door.

A dozen bright lights immediately flashed, momentarily blinding Dinah and increasing the fuzzy headache to a full-blown roar. Confused, she let go of the front door and it clicked shut behind her.

When she could see again, a crowd of reporters and cameramen were crowded around her walkway, and now she became aware of the cacophony rising around her.

"Why were you brought back into active duty, Special Agent Harris?"

"Has the investigation into Thomas Whitfield's disappearance stalled?"

"Could this be the work of terrorists?"

*That was a particularly stupid question*, Dinah thought. She was still off-balance and utterly shocked that the media had found her so quickly.

"Can you confirm whether Thomas Whitfield is alive or dead?"

"Can you confirm whether there have been recent conflicts between Thomas Whitfield and the board of regents?"

"Do you think you can handle the case, given that your mental instability endangered the lives of others on your previous assignment?"

Dinah winced, shock draining the blood from her face. "What did you say?" she said in a voice that was barely more than a whisper.

The reporter who'd asked the question did not hear her, amidst the noise of the other reporters clamoring for Dinah's attention.

Dinah was frozen, her limbs locked into place. She stared at the sea of faces uncomprehendingly, her thoughts lost in that dreadful day.

Then she heard a familiar voice shouting above the rest. "Dinah! Get in, quickly!"

She roused herself and saw past the flock of vultures to where Ferguson had pulled the Crown up to the curb and was frantically motioning her to get inside the car.

Dinah pushed through the crowd, shoving past them as they pressed around her. After what seemed like ages, she finally made it to the car and Ferguson accelerated hard away from Dinah's apartment, the tires squealing.

Dinah slumped in the passenger seat, her heart still galloping like an out-of-control racehorse.

"You need to look at the paper," Ferguson said gently, pointing at the middle console.

As she took the *Post*, she noticed her hands shook uncontrollably.

The front page caused a wave of cold nausea to roll over her. A large picture of her had been taken with a telephoto lens, emerging from the Whitfields' home clutching the plastic envelopes of evidence.

The headline screamed, *DISTRESSED AGENT IN HIGH-PROFILE CASE.* With a mixture of disbelief, fury, and dread, Dinah continued reading.

An FBI agent with a history of depression, anxiety, and other mental health issues has been assigned to the high-profile case of the disappearance of the Smithsonian Institution Secretary, Thomas Whitfield. The FBI has defended the appointment of Dinah Harris, previously a Special Agent in Charge, to the case, citing her as being a competent investigator. However, Special Agent Harris was demoted twelve months ago and assigned to a lecturing job after a gang member extraction situation she was supervising disintegrated. . . .

Dinah threw the paper to the floor, disgusted. She couldn't bear to read any further.

"As soon as I saw that photo this morning, I thought the media might have followed you," Ferguson said. He was silent for a time, then added, "I'm terribly sorry, Dinah. I didn't mean for this to happen."

Dinah nodded, not trusting herself to speak.

They drove in silence to the J. Edgar Hoover building on Pennsylvania Avenue, Dinah trying to control the stormy mass of thoughts and memories inside her head. Ferguson began talking about the case, trying to distract her, but Dinah barely heard him.

The SAC, George Hanlon, was waiting for her at her desk, and she approached him with a sense of dread.

"A minute of your time?" he said, motioning to his office.

Ferguson shot her a look of concern and sympathy as she followed Hanlon, feeling like a mischievous child sent to the principal's office.

Hanlon pointed at the *Washington Post.* "I assume you've seen this?"

Dinah nodded.

"Is this going to compromise your investigative ability in this case?" he asked without preamble. In George Hanlon's world, individual feelings didn't matter. All that mattered was the current investigation and how quickly the agents would be able to wrap it up. This enabled Hanlon to call a press conference, get his face on television, and tell the world what an all-around great agent he was for taking care of the bad guys.

"I don't believe so," Dinah said. "Although I can guarantee that the media won't stop here."

"It's not a good reflection on the bureau," continued Hanlon. "It makes our agents look . . . flaky and maladjusted."

Dinah said nothing. Since Waco and 9/11, the FBI was particularly nervous about scandals.

"We can't afford another slip-up in the field. I need your assurance that you will handle this case professionally."

"You have it," said Dinah tightly. "As I've already told you."

Hanlon sighed. "I'm worried, Agent Harris, and I don't think you can blame me. I'd be much happier if you were teaching and Ferguson had chosen someone else to help him on this case. But if you are certain you will be able to cope with this case, including the media interest, then I'll allow you to remain with Ferguson. But you should know, I'll be watching you very closely."

"Thank you, sir," said Dinah, trying and failing to sound sincere.

Hanlon stared at her, brows furrowed, wondering whether to call her on it. In the end, he sat at his desk and motioned toward the door.

\*\*\*\*

While he waited for her, Ferguson had split up the bank statements, phone records, and the other evidence they'd gathered from the Whitfields' home and deposited it on Dinah's desk. He saw the thunderous look on her face and wisely chose not to say anything.

Dinah sat and resigned herself to a day of paperwork, which never happened in the movies. In the movies, there was always something exciting going down. Or there was a brilliant piece of evidence that led straight to the perpetrator.

She stared at the stack of credit card statements and felt strangely depressed by it. Sometimes she was struck by how marginal a human being's life could be — a fully functioning person, in a position of authority and prestige, reduced to the calls they made, the purchases completed, the tracking and analysis of the most boring daily routines. In the absence of the force of personality and individuality, everyone assumed the same bland personhood. In the end, it didn't matter who you were, reflected Dinah, everyone was the same at this level; everyone had to eat, go grocery shopping, and pay the bills.

The next hour or so blurred for Dinah as she checked every single transaction made. The Whitfields bought groceries, paid their phone and electricity bills, and dined out frequently at nice restaurants. Then she realized that a pattern of regular interstate travel was emerging. Over the past six months, Thomas Whitfield had purchased airline tickets on an increasingly regular basis. Prior to this time frame, there had been no airline tickets bought at all for a period stretching back at least two years. She tapped her chewed-down nails on the desk as she thought about what this might mean. Any change to a person's routine behavior, no matter how innocuous it might appear, could often hold clues to what Dinah had termed a person's secondary life — that secret, shadowy world kept close to one's chest where lived the gambling addiction, the drinking problem, the spousal abuse, any of the secrets a person didn't want the world to see.

Dinah rifled through the file they were building on Thomas Whitfield and found the schedules Lara Southall had printed out for them, which contained the secretary's movements over the last 12 months. She flipped through the schedule until she had the date of the first ticket.

There was no corresponding entry in Thomas Whitfield's calendar.

Dinah checked every single ticket Thomas had bought, and there was no explanatory entry in the calendar. Dinah frowned thoughtfully. Perhaps the tickets had been bought for family members or friends.

She called the airlines office for information and got a vacuous, indifferent female voice that spoke so slowly she instantly irritated Dinah.

"This is Special Agent Dinah Harris of the FBI," said Dinah, using an authoritative tone. "I require information regarding flight details for a person who has been abducted."

There was a long pause while the girl digested this. "Uh . . . I'm not sure I'm authorized to do that," she said finally. "Should I ask my supervisor?"

"Please do," said Dinah, relieved. She listened to light and inoffensive classical music interspersed with advertising from the airline while she was on hold.

After what seemed like a decade, the music was finally replaced with: "This is Lisa Atkinson speaking. How can I help you?"

"I need some flight details for a person whose abduction I am currently investigating," she said, then gave her badge number and the phone details so that the airline supervisor could confirm that she was indeed an FBI agent.

While Dinah waited for the supervisor to call back, she drummed her fingers on the desk impatiently and wondered if she had any wine left in the refrigerator at home.

The phone burst into life and Dinah answered.

Lisa Atkinson asked, "What flights are you concerned with?"

Dinah looked at the earliest statement. "The first is April 20, 1999," she said. "The flight was booked using a credit card in the name of Thomas Whitfield."

"Oh," said Lisa Atkinson, recognizing the name. "Do you have a flight number?"

"No, I'm sorry."

"Okay, this will just take a little while." Dinah heard the sounds of a keyboard being clicked rapidly.

"Okay, that was Flight 235 to Denver, Colorado," said Lisa, brightly. "Mr. Whitfield flew there on the 20th and returned to Washington on the 26th."

"It was definitely Thomas Whitfield traveling?" Dinah inquired.

"Yes, our passenger manifests are directly linked to the ticketing system."

Dinah wrote this down, thinking hard. Had Thomas Whitfield clearly gone to Colorado for vacation? If it had been a work engagement, it would have appeared in his calendar.

"Next date is March 1, 2000," Dinah said.

There was another pause while the computer waded through passenger manifests. "That flight was to Detroit, Michigan. He flew in on March 1 and flew out March 3," said Lisa.

Dinah discovered that Thomas Whitfield had also flown and briefly stayed near San Diego, California, in 2001 and Cold Spring, Minnesota, in 2003.

There was nothing immediately suspicious about these flights, but it was interesting that these quick trips had commenced suddenly, and none of them had appeared in his work schedule. Perhaps Thomas Whitfield had accepted a heavier public speaking workload.

Dinah thanked Lisa Atkinson and immediately dialed Catherine Biscelli, the director of public affairs at the Smithsonian Institution.

When Catherine picked up the call, after going through a switchboard and a receptionist, her voice was noticeably cool. "How can I help you, Agent Harris?"

"It's *Special* Agent Harris. I'm just checking some details of Mr. Whitfield's recent travels," said Dinah, recognizing there would be no small talk about the weather or football. "I want to know if they were work-related. I assume you would have access to Mr. Whitfield's daily schedules?"

"Yes, of course," Catherine Biscelli said, with a faint tone of derision. "I'm the one who vets all of his engagements. I was under the impression Lara had already given you a copy of the calendar. Doesn't it have the information you require?"

"While I appreciate the advice on how to do my job," replied Dinah acidly, "the information I need is *not* in the calendar and that is why I need your confirmation."

Dinah could imagine the other woman biting back several responses in the silence that followed. "Fine. What do you need?" Catherine said at length.

Dinah gave the other woman the dates and destinations of the flights Thomas Whitfield had taken. In spite of Catherine claiming to know Thomas's every move, she still had to look up the schedule on the computer to check. Imagine if all the computers went down, thought Dinah, no one would know anything.

"I'm sorry, there is no record of these trips in our schedules," said Catherine after a long pause. "They were not related to the work of the institution. Mr. Whitfield must have made them for private reasons."

"You're sure of that?" Dinah asked. "He wouldn't have attended a speaking engagement at the last minute or something like that?"

"Yes, *Special* Agent, I'm positive. If it's not in my schedule, it's got nothing to do with his work here. Is there anything else? I'm rather busy."

Dinah felt an instant surge of anger at the other woman's condescension. Also, she noticed that Catherine Biscelli had not once asked if the FBI had discovered Thomas Whitfield's whereabouts or whether he was okay. Dinah filed that bit of information away.

"That's all, Ms. Biscelli. I understand you are *very* concerned about Mr. Whitfield, as we all are. I promise to let you know the *minute* I have some relevant information."

There was a strained silence on the other end of the phone, and as she hung up, Dinah gleefully imagined the outrage on Catherine Biscelli's face.

Dinah rang Eloise Whitfield next on her cell phone.

"Have you found Thomas? Is he okay?" Eloise asked immediately.

"I'm sorry, I don't have any information for you in that regard," said Dinah. "I just wanted to ask you a question about Thomas's recent travels." She gave Eloise the dates and destinations. "Do you know anything about these trips?"

"Not really," said Eloise. "I knew he was going away, obviously, during those times. He said the trips were for a special project at work."

*Work doesn't know anything about them.*

"You didn't accompany him on any of these trips?"

"No, I didn't."

"Do you know if he traveled with anyone else?"

"No, I really didn't know anything about them at all. I assumed he went with people from the institution."

"I see," said Dinah, circling the notes she'd made. "That's all I needed to know. Thanks, Mrs. Whitfield."

Deep in concentration, Dinah stared at her notes until her eyes lost focus. Where would Thomas Whitfield be traveling, sans wife and the knowledge of his workplace, and why?

And what did any of it have to do with his disappearance?

\*\*\*\*

Jimmy Perez had just finished a sports magazine and was thinking about having a cigarette and closing up the yard when he heard three short, sharp blasts from the horn of a tow truck. He sighed and hauled his sizable girth to his feet. There would be no getting home early tonight or beating rush hour, he thought.

Jimmy leaned out of the window of his office, gave the tow truck driver a wave, and flicked the switch that would open the gates. The gates began to open begrudgingly, emitting an occasional grinding metal screech.

Jimmy stood in the yard of his auto-wrecking lot, a round, middle-aged man dressed in greasy overalls with black hair in dire need of a wash, and watched the truck drive in.

The car on the bed of the truck had once been a Chevy, a sensible family sedan. It now resembled a battered Matchbox toy car, the roof crushed in, the front and back panels crumpled. There was no division between the front and back seats; they were virtually on top of each other.

Jimmy shook his head. "What happened here?" he asked, always fascinated by the macabre.

"Nose-to-tail flip, landed on the roof," the driver said.

"Yeah? Anyone get hurt?" Jimmy was the kind of guy who would slow down on the freeway to get a nice, long look at a car accident.

"That's the weird thing, man," the driver said. "There was no one in it. Just this totaled car, sittin' on the edge of the road. Whoever was drivin' it must have got lucky and walked away." He shrugged. He didn't really care, one way or the other. His job was to drop the car off at the auto-wrecking yard and keep going. Rush hour was a great time for business. All those busy people trying to get home, thinking about work or what was for dinner and — WHAM!

"So where do you want it, man?" the driver asked.

Jimmy considered. There might be some salvageable parts left on the car, but all in all it was a pretty sorry looking thing. It wasn't even worth giving a once-over. He decided to crush it into a nice little cube.

He pointed to a nearby lot of recently acquired car wrecks and lit a cigarette while the truck laboriously groaned its way over to the lot.

Jimmy noticed that all four tires were blown and he shook his head again. *What a mess*, Jimmy thought. The guy who'd been driving it sure was lucky. He ought to buy himself a lottery ticket with that kind of luck.

Jimmy wandered toward the truck while the driver was messing with the hydraulics of the bed, lifting it to an angle so that the car could roll off the truck and come to rest on its blown-out wheels.

The driver jumped out of the truck and loosened the straps that had held the car in place.

"Ready?" he called to Jimmy. "I'm gonna let her go."

Jimmy acknowledged this with a wave.

The damaged car rolled off the back of the truck and came to a shuddering halt when it smacked into another wrecked car and the trunk came flying open.

"Hey, watch the merchandise!" called Jimmy, joking. The driver opened his mouth to reply when the odor from the trunk hit their nostrils at the same time.

Jimmy couldn't have explained the smell precisely, but it was a strong and belligerent odor, almost demanding that people take notice of it. He and the driver approached the trunk of the Chevy cautiously.

Inside the trunk was the bound form of a dead adult male.

The driver cursed under his breath while Jimmy almost inhaled his lit cigarette. Jimmy couldn't tear his eyes away and he felt bile rise in his throat.

The driver turned away, still cursing from the shock.

Jimmy dropped his cigarette from shaking hands. He felt light-headed and out of control, and for a brief, strange moment, he resolved never to slow down to look at a car accident again.

"He dead or what, man?" the driver asked in a reedy voice, clearly hoping that the figure inside the trunk would come to life, and soon.

"Yeah, I'm pretty sure he's dead," said Jimmy. He pulled his cell phone from his pocket and dialed 911. It took him several attempts because he was trembling so violently.

The operator immediately began to ask questions that were too hard. Had they checked the pulse? Were the airways clear? Had they tried resuscitation? She asked Jimmy to go back to the body and at least check for a pulse.

The thought of this made Jimmy feel cold and hot at the same time, but he went back to the trunk.

He wiped his free hand on his jeans and reached toward the still figure. He had trouble remembering how to take a pulse, but the emergency operator instructed him to place his fingers on the neck.

The skin was waxy and cold and felt like anything except how a human being should feel. It sent shivers down Jimmy's spine. "No," he said into his cell phone, "he's definitely dead."

While he waited for the police with the tow truck driver, Jimmy had the uncomfortable feeling he recognized the body. The thought was lodged deep in the recesses of his mind and wouldn't shake free. Given everything that had happened tonight, he decided he probably wouldn't remember who it was until 2 a.m. when he would awake with it as a single lucid thought.

Jimmy lit another cigarette. It was going to be a long night.

It was long past midnight — Dinah had long since given up keeping track of the time. Her mind was a whirling mass and it meant that she hadn't gotten any sleep. Instead, she lay staring at the ceiling, trying to force herself to relax, and failing miserably with every passing moment.

It was a dark and quiet night and Dinah was acutely aware of herself, a sensation new for her. She breathed in the stillness, existed in the darkness, and listened in the quietness. The night was drifting around her, and instead of hearing the clanging in her mind she heard a deep silence. She felt that if she could breathe deeply enough, the calm and peacefulness would seep through her pores, flow through her veins, and quiet her soul.

An insidious suggestion piped up in her brain: *isn't that what death would feel like?* How often had she imagined lying down, welcoming death, and succumbing to the eternal sleep? Could someone actually wish himself or herself to death? If you believed with your heart and soul that you had finished with this earth, that there was nothing endearing about this place anymore, could you literally give up the will to live?

*No, Dinah. Not yet.*

She closed her eyes and breathed, wondering what it would feel like to draw a last breath.

Her cell phone buzzed on the night table beside her, startling her. It was Ferguson.

"Ferguson? What's up?"

"We've found him, Harris," replied Ferguson, who sounded tightly wound. "We've now got a murder scene."

Although Dinah hadn't expected to find Thomas Whitfield alive, she had always hoped for a small miracle. A much larger percentage of her was relieved that they'd found a murder scene, because it meant a wealth of clues.

"Where is it?" Dinah asked, starting to pull on clothing haphazardly.

"An auto-wrecking yard down near the Potomac," said Ferguson. He gave her the address. "I'll meet you there?"

Dinah paused, rapidly counting the wine she had consumed earlier and the hours that had passed. "Could you pick me up?" she asked, feeling about two inches tall. She could almost feel Ferguson's frustration through the phone line.

"How bad are you, Harris?" he asked shortly. "The last thing we need is a mistrial because one of the lead investigators was. . . ."

"I'm not at all drunk!" interrupted Dinah, desperately trying not to hear the words Ferguson was saying. She had already had her integrity questioned once before; she couldn't bear for it to happen again. "I just don't think I should drive."

Ferguson sighed. "Fine, but eat something quickly and use some mouthwash." He hung up before she could reply, and she knew he was seriously hacked off with her.

Dinah finished dressing and did as Ferguson had asked, swallowing down two pieces of stale bread with peanut butter and rinsing her mouth twice with a foul-tasting, possibly noxious green liquid.

Ferguson sniffed at her as she climbed into the car. "Good," he grunted. He didn't speak as he drove, but that wasn't unusual. He didn't like to color her perception of the crime scene with his own opinions. He liked her to go in with a clean slate, to absorb the crime scene and surroundings, and to sense the clues speaking to her.

The auto-wrecking yard was several blocks from the Potomac and was currently awash with blue and red strobe lights. Dinah got out of the car and was struck by the cold — the air was close to freezing and it bit at her bones like a hungry vulture. A tight cluster of Washington Police Department officers, some uniformed and some plain-clothed, stood near the entrance to the wrecking yard.

A black man built like a linebacker spotted them and beckoned them over. He was the second level detective assigned to the murder from the police department, and his name was Samson Cage. Quickly he told the agents about the wrecked car being towed to the yard, unloaded from the tow truck, the trunk flying open, and the subsequent discovery of Thomas Whitfield's body. He pointed to the tow truck driver and the owner of the wrecking yard, both huddled together drinking instant coffee out of Styrofoam cups and looking decidedly weary and annoyed.

The car in which Thomas Whitfield had been found was cordoned off by bright yellow crime scene tape, and the forensic technicians were getting ready to go over the scene.

"Listen," Samson Cage said with faint embarrassment. "I know you have been operating on the premise that Thomas Whitfield was abducted and it was in your jurisdiction. Now that it's a murder, it'll fall into our jurisdiction. I'm happy to have you here, but I'm just warning you that my chief is probably going to feel that it's our case to solve, you know what I mean?"

Dinah rolled her eyes as she pulled the plastic protective clothing over her own — the booties over her shoes, white jumpsuit, hair cover — so that she didn't contaminate the crime scene with her own material. She hated the inter-departmental jockeying that went on between the police and the FBI — when jurisdictions overlapped, the police particularly resented the FBI getting involved. It was resentment that was ages old, but heightened since 9/11, where the police felt that they had sacrificed hundreds of their own in a tragedy that the FBI should have prevented.

"I've already thought about it," Ferguson said smoothly. "I think we'll want to set up a joint task force, since Thomas Whitfield is so high profile. Also, we have reason to believe that his disappearance and murder is politically motivated."

Samson Cage flexed his massive shoulders. "Whatever. I'll let you and my chief handle it. I take it you want the crime scene?" He gestured at Dinah, who was ready to go.

Ultimately, both agents knew that the murder would be handled by the FBI, but there was no point getting into a discussion about it with Detective Cage.

Ferguson moved off to speak to the tow truck driver and the wrecking yard owner. Cage helped Dinah through the yellow tape and then left her alone.

Dinah stood still for a moment, looking at the big picture, imagining the wrecked Chevy as a blank canvas, hanging in space on its own, yielding clues that possibly had nothing to do with this wrecking yard or even this city.

It was an average family sedan and had once been silver with black trim. The nose and grill were completely crushed in and down, so much so that the wheel arches had been compressed onto the blown-out tires. The steering column had been pushed right into the driver's seat. The roof had been crushed down and had imposed itself on the seat headrests. The back seats had been left relatively untouched. The trunk had been crushed inward, but not nearly to the same extent as the nose of the car. Both bumpers had fallen off, all four tires were blown, and the head and taillights were smashed beyond salvage. Dinah kneeled down and peered through the driver's side window to see inside the car. There were still some of the owner's personal effects inside the car. Dinah could see the rosary beads swinging from the smashed rearview mirror and a city directory hanging out of the glove box.

Dinah made several mental notes to herself: Who did the car belong to? Where had the killer obtained the car? How had he organized the car to be picked up by the tow truck driver?

She moved around to the trunk of the car and lifted the lid. The body of Thomas Whitfield had been unceremoniously jammed into the space left, and he lay on his left side, his wrists bound behind his back. His head was crusted with dried blood, so much so that the features of his face were almost unrecognizable. He was still dressed in the clothing he had gone missing in. Dinah tried to avoid touching the body, but she leaned closer to the body and looked around the trunk, searching for any clues. The crime scene techs would pick up most of the fibers, hair, and finer materials, but if Dinah could find any glaring evidence to direct the investigation, it usually meant a saving of days.

The trunk was otherwise bare, however. Dinah took some mental snapshots of the scene and backed away. The crime scene techs had set up their lights and equipment and were waiting to start.

Dinah walked under the yellow tape and started shedding her plastic protective clothing. Ferguson was waiting for her.

"How," he inquired, "does the secretary of the Smithsonian end up murdered in the trunk of a Chevy?"

## WASHINGTON, DC, 1996 — THOMAS'S STORY

Thomas Whitfield sat in the study of his Georgetown townhouse, researching his next article. There had recently been a discovery of several single-cell viruses that had mutated in response to the antibiotics being used to kill them. The world's media was worried about the "Super Bug," a virus that couldn't be killed. Thomas was more interested in the evolutionary ramifications of the discovery. It wasn't often that scientists could examine evolution in action, and he was excited about researching it.

"Hi, darling!" Eloise Whitfield poked her head around the study door. "Your article has been published!" She waved a copy of a journal in her hand.

Thomas grinned. This was his first published article, and furthermore, it had been published in the most prestigious scientific journal in the world. Eloise brought it over to him, and he looked it up. There was his name and photo in highlights, with a blurb about him.

Thomas Whitfield is a molecular biologist and anthropologist who has extensively studied the relationship between people groups and their environments. Mr. Whitfield has spent time with indigenous tribes in Canada, South America, Australia, and Micronesia.

As Thomas read his blurb, he felt a warm glow come over his face. Finally, he was getting the recognition he deserved after many years of hard work and research. He was currently a fellow on the staff at the Washington University, and this publication would lift him well above his peers.

"Congratulations, honey," Eloise said, her eyes glowing. "Why don't we go out to celebrate tonight?"

Thomas was too preoccupied. Now that one article had been published, he was pumped up to keep churning them out. "Sorry, maybe some other time," he said. "I need to keep working."

"You've been in here all day," objected Eloise, her elation at her husband's success starting to fade.

"Everything is flowing really well at the moment," Thomas said distantly. "I just want to make the most of it."

When Eloise left the room, disappointed and angry, Thomas barely even noticed. He was on a roll and time ticked by, unnoticed.

When the phone rang in his study, it scared the life half out of him. His mind still pondering viruses living and destroying a host body, he barely even remembered to say hello.

"Hi, Mr. Whitfield. I just wanted to congratulate you on your article," a male voice said. "It's excellent."

"Thanks," said Thomas, trying to place the voice.

"If you keep writing articles like that, your profile should continue to rise," continued the caller. "I can foresee television spots in a few years."

Thomas considered and then said, "Sorry, who is this?"

"Yes, let me introduce myself," agreed the caller. "My name is Damon Mason. I am the president of the Individualist Association for Scientific Integrity. Although it's not technically correct, we shorted it to IAFSI." He pronounced it *AY-fsee*.

"I'm sorry, I haven't heard of you," admitted Thomas, starting to wonder what relevance his caller and his association had.

Damon Mason chuckled. "I guess you wouldn't have. We like to keep a low profile. But we help our members be high profile."

"What do you mean?"

"Our association has members who are scientists or specialists in their field, are exceptional in their field, and who show an ability to further our cause. In return, we — that is, the board — offer increasing media profiles for members. This can lead to more publications in scientific journals, media spots, televised debates, and in some cases, even book deals."

Thomas started to listen harder. "Who have you helped so far?"

Damon named several scientists who regularly appeared on programs such as *Good Morning America, Sixty Minutes,* and *Fox and Friends.*

Thomas left the world of viruses completely behind at that point and began envisioning himself on television. "What is your cause?" he asked.

"I'd like to meet with you in person," Damon suggested. "I can tell you all about it and you can ask me questions."

Thomas agreed and a date was set.

\* \* \* \*

Thomas and Damon met at a tiny coffee shop, far away from where both of them lived and worked. Thomas wasn't sure what to expect from the other man. He had a mental image of a similarly scholarly figure like himself, but the Damon who walked through the door looked more like a lumberjack, with dark hair cropped short, a thick goatee, broad shoulders, and muscled hands.

They shook hands and Damon sat down opposite Thomas, unashamedly eyeing the other man up and down.

"It's nice to finally meet you," said Damon. "By that I mean I've done so much research into your scientific credentials that I feel as if I know you."

Thomas wasn't sure whether to feel flattered or disturbed. "Did you like what you discovered?"

"Yes, I was very impressed," said Damon. Had Thomas seen him in the street, he'd have thought Damon the least likely candidate to even understand the research Thomas had undertaken over the years. "I particularly liked your theory regarding the way humans and animals lived harmoniously for millions of years in their tribal cultures. The evolution of the human brain wasn't yet advanced enough to forget that they had once been animals themselves living in the same surroundings. Brilliant stuff. The next step, the civilization of man, is another rung on the ladder of human evolution."

"Yes, precisely," agreed Thomas. "It's a fine example of survival of the fittest — mankind is the dominant species on the planet."

"Perfect. Let me tell you a bit about IAFSI," suggested Damon as their coffees came. Surprisingly, the big man had ordered an espresso, and the tiny cup looked out of place in his big bear paw of a hand.

"We stand for the complete separation of church and state, to begin with," explained Damon. "And, not unexpectedly, the majority of our members are atheists. We are mostly scientists of one form or another, although we have a handful of members from other intellectual professions. We believe that we live in an age of reason and rationality and we want to break the shackles of religious fundamentalism that are holding this nation back."

"Okay," said Thomas.

"We have all kinds of scientific evidence for the questions that have plagued humanity for so long," continued Damon. "And mankind is intelligent enough to rule itself without relying on some God somewhere to ratify our decisions. Religious fundamentalism seeks to plunge us all back into the Dark Ages, when superstition ruled society. We want religion taken out of schools and workplaces, and to some degree, we've succeeded. But there is always work to be done, to combat religious fanatics who insist on cloaking scientific reason with their own brand of flawed logic."

"I understand," said Thomas. "Is that where the members come in?"

"Exactly. Our members write articles, appear in the media, and generally defend the principles of science in the public arena. This in turn raises their profile, which, of course, is invaluable to a scientist." Damon paused for a moment. "Of course, it's vitally important that before we accept you as a member, we understand where *you* stand. As your profile increases, you will be questioned about your beliefs."

"Okay," said Thomas. He drained his coffee and thought about it. He'd never actually given a great deal of attention to formulating his own ideas about God. "It's pretty simple really. I believe in evolution and I believe that science holds the answers to all of life's mysteries. I believe in what I can touch and see and experience. I find it difficult to believe in the concept of a God that I can't see."

"Good, that's perfect," said Damon enthusiastically. "You will note that many of our projects are scientific in nature. Let me explain. In schools you may have heard the debate raging around prayer in public schools and whether it should be allowed. Of course, we don't think it should. But when it comes to causes we publicly support, it's not one of them. We'd prefer to support the teaching of evolution in public schools. Whether people pray or not is not really our concern. What *does* concern us is children growing up believing in fairy tales about how we all got here when it's clear there is now a scientific explanation for it. Does that make sense?"

"Sure," said Thomas. "And I would agree. I don't think I'd feel comfortable talking about whether prayer is right or wrong. But I certainly wouldn't have any qualms in debating evolution." He paused while he drained the last of his coffee. "Who are your main antagonists?"

Damon laughed. "Have a guess — they're mostly from the Midwest. They call themselves young-earth creationists. In that regard, they take the Bible literally."

Thomas frowned. "I must confess, I don't know what a young-earth creationist is."

"Well, to start with, they are fundamentalist Christians," explained Damon. "They believe the earth was created by God in literally six days, as it says in the Bible. They also take the age of earth by adding up the genealogies in the Bible and so they say the earth is only about six thousand years old."

Thomas shook his head, dumbfounded.

"Sadly," continued Damon, "people actually believe them. They use dinosaurs and fossils and rock layers to 'prove' their theory. They're pretty vocal and have a lot of support behind them, particularly the conservatives."

"Amazing," said Thomas. "I can't believe they're taken seriously."

"Well, that's what we're here for," said Damon. "Can we count on you to join our cause?"

Images of published books, articles, television spots, and the title of *expert* were floating through Thomas's head when he replied, "Yes, absolutely."

## WASHINGTON, DC — PRESENT DAY

As the first pale threads of golden sunlight peered over the horizon like saffron filaments, the two agents drove directly to their office on

Pennsylvania Avenue from the auto wrecking yard. Dinah was keyed up about the discovery of Thomas Whitfield's body and eager to move forward.

"I've had a thought," said Dinah at length, her mouth full of glazed donut. "I really want to get the board of regents together today."

"Okay," agreed Ferguson. "But why?"

"It's something that has been bugging me," explained Dinah. "Don't you think it's weird that the FBI was called about Thomas Whitfield's disappearance in the first place?"

"Yeah, I guess so," admitted Ferguson. "But we thought he'd been abducted. Kidnapping is a federal offense."

"Right. But for the first few days we had a missing adult with no sign of foul play. There was no evidence of kidnapping. Yet we were still called. What would you do if somebody you knew had gone missing?"

"I'd call the police."

"Exactly. You wouldn't call the FBI."

"So what are you saying?"

Dinah pursed her lips. "I don't know yet. There just seems to be something off-kilter about it. I almost think that the person who first alerted the FBI knew what had happened to Thomas Whitfield before we did."

"Well . . . that person was Catherine Biscelli," said Ferguson thoughtfully.

They fell silent for a few moments, considering. "I'm just thinking aloud," said Dinah. "Don't put too much stock in it yet." She picked up the phone and called Catherine Biscelli's direct line. When the other woman answered, Dinah said, "Hello, this is Special Agent Dinah Harris."

"Yes, Agent?" Catherine said imperiously. "I'm rather busy here at the moment."

Dinah was silent for a moment as she was reminded of why she really didn't like this woman. "Thomas Whitfield is dead," she said after a lengthy pause, deciding not to bother with niceties. "He has been murdered."

There was a gasp at the other end of the phone. "Oh no!" she exclaimed. "How terrible. Do you know who is responsible for this?"

"We have some leads," said Dinah. "I need you to get the board of regents together immediately."

"Oh . . . well, that's going to take some time," said Catherine. "The board is made up of some fairly influential and busy people, as I'm sure you know. I'm not sure. . . ."

"I don't care how busy or influential they are," interrupted Dinah. "This is a murder investigation and I expect the board to cooperate with us fully. Otherwise I can charge you with obstructing the progress of an investigation."

"You surely wouldn't!" Catherine was outraged.

"Just get the board together and you won't have to find out," said Dinah. "I'll call you back in an hour to organize our visit this afternoon."

Dinah hung up before Catherine could reply. She turned to find Ferguson looking at her bemusedly. "You really don't like her, do you?" he said, shaking his head. "One of these days you're going to have to learn how to communicate with the human race again, you know that?"

"Yeah, maybe. Hey, you haven't told me about your conversation with the wrecking yard owner or the tow truck driver."

"Oh, right." Ferguson flipped open his notebook. "The wrecking yard owner wasn't much help. He pretty much saw the body in the car and that's about it. I was more interested in the tow truck driver. He received a call at about four o'clock this afternoon. It wasn't a client he knew — he normally receives calls from the police at the scene of an accident, or insurance companies. This was a random call. The car was found at the front of a property owned by a guy upstate. The guy was unhappy that the car had been dumped there and asked the tow truck to charge the owner of the car."

"So the person who owns the property doesn't own the car?"

"Right. He claims the car turned up the previous night. He waited all day for the owner to claim it."

"So the car was crushed up like that when it appeared on the property?"

"Apparently. The guy who owns the property doesn't recall hearing a car accident though. According to the local police, there is no record of an accident occurring in that vicinity over the past week. So I surmise that the car was picked up somewhere else and dumped, along with Thomas Whitfield's body, to avoid detection for as long as possible." Ferguson paused, flipping through his notes. "In fact, when you think about it, it's possible we would never have found his body. The owner of the wrecking yard says he was going to crush the car into a cube because there was nothing to salvage. If he had just crushed the car without the trunk popping open, the body of Thomas Whitfield would never have been discovered and we would never have been sure that a murder had even taken place."

"Yeah, that is lucky," agreed Dinah thoughtfully. "Have we put a trace on the registered owner of the car?"

"I'll do it now." Ferguson tapped at his keyboard, logging into the DMV site to search. The car was registered to an Ivan Petesky, of Foggy Bottom. Ferguson grabbed his keys while Dinah drained the last of her coffee.

He drove quickly, both agents consumed with urgency. Now that the body had been found, the next 24 hours were critical.

Ivan Petesky was a second grade teacher who was, by all intents and purposes, convalescing from a bad car accident. At his front door, Dinah rang a recently installed intercom buzzer.

"Hello?"

"Mr. Petesky, this is Special Agent Harris from the FBI. We'd like to talk to you about your car accident."

"There is a camera in the intercom," the muffled voice said. "Can you hold your ID up to it please?"

Dinah rolled her eyes at her partner but held her badge up. There were a few moments, and then there was a click as the front door unlocked. The two agents stepped inside cautiously, looking around the dim house.

"I'm down the hall on the right," the voice called out.

The two agents found themselves in a modified hospital room. Ivan Petesky was encased in plaster from his hip to his toe, a heavy neck brace and gauze wrapped around his head. Bright hazel eyes peered at them from beneath the bandage. He raised one free hand in greeting.

"Hi," he said. "Sorry about the nuisance. I just can't get up to answer the door as you can see."

"That's okay," said Ferguson, glancing around him. "Are you doing okay?"

"Oh yes," said Petesky cheerfully. "I've never been so glad to get out of the hospital, I can tell you. There is a nurse that comes around every day. I have to be honest, I can't really remember much about the accident."

"It's not really the accident we're interested in, per se," said Dinah. "We're interested in what happened afterward. But start from the beginning."

"Well, I'd just visited my mother in Pennsylvania, and I was driving home," said Ivan. "It was late at night, I fell asleep, and I hit a tree. Well, I clipped it side on, and the car rolled over a few times." Petesky laughed ruefully. "That's what I'm told, anyway. I don't remember a thing. I woke up in the hospital, covered in plaster. Broke my right hip and pelvis, and two ribs. I gave my head a good crack as well, but luckily I didn't have any injuries that were life-threatening."

"Do you know what happened to your vehicle after the accident?" Ferguson asked.

Petesky shrugged. "All I can tell you is what the insurance company told me. The car was towed to the insurance company holding yard, where they assessed the damage and what the payout would be, then took it to an auto-wrecking yard. I haven't seen it since the accident and I'm not sure I want to see it again."

Ferguson named the yard where Petesky's Chevy had yielded Thomas Whitfield's body. "Was it that yard the insurance company had it towed to?"

Petesky considered. "I don't think so. It doesn't sound familiar. I didn't think it was in that part of the city at all. You could always check with my insurance company though. I have the claim papers in the desk drawer in the next room." He paused. "Is there a problem? I sort of expected the insurance company to do some investigation of the accident, since it totaled the car. I didn't think they'd involve the FBI though."

"I'm sorry, I can't reveal any facts of the case to you," said Dinah. "I can tell you that we're not investigating you for insurance fraud. Do you mind if we take those insurance papers with us?"

Petesky waved his free hand again. "No, take it. The claim is paid and closed; the insurance company just sent me the papers as confirmation of the claim."

"Thanks for your assistance," said Dinah, while Ferguson began to dig through the desk in the next room. "We'll send the papers back to you when we've finished. I hope you recover well from your accident."

"Thanks," said Petesky, again sounding cheerful. "You know what? I am just happy to be alive."

Dinah imagined the teacher must have had more to live for than she, because she couldn't for the life of her imagine being happier alive than dead.

The late fall sun was at its zenith as Dinah and Ferguson reported for the worst duty their jobs called for — advising relatives of the deaths of their loved ones. Eloise Whitfield was staying with her sister, Mary, since her home at Georgetown had been ransacked.

Eloise's sister let them into the kitchen, where Eloise was making coffee, dressed in a housecoat. She glanced up, hope a tiny spark in her face. Without saying a word, Eloise saw the somber expressions of the two agents and realized that the news was bad. Dinah felt a helpless anger as the spark of hope in Eloise Whitfield was extinguished.

"It's bad, isn't it?" Eloise said, her lower lip trembling as she fought for control.

"I'm terribly sorry," said Ferguson, as gently as he could. "We found Thomas's body this morning."

Eloise sat heavily at the kitchen table, her face reflecting the pain of her world crashing down around her. Her sister Mary sat beside her with a box of tissues, her own face a mask of sadness. Dinah and Ferguson sat down and waited as unobtrusively as they could for the first, intense flurry of grief to subside.

Finally, Dinah said, "Mrs. Whitfield, I know this is very hard. I'm very sorry for your loss. But we still need your help to find the person who did this."

Eloise Whitfield sniffed. "I've told you everything I know."

Dinah nodded. "I know. I need to ask you some questions about Thomas's travels. They may provide an important link to what happened. We now know exactly where he went and I wonder if any of the places jog your memory."

"Okay." Eloise blew her nose and sat up straighter.

Dinah flipped open her notebook. "In April 1999, he flew to Denver, Colorado. He was there for an entire week. Do you remember what he was doing there for an entire week?"

Eloise shook her head, tears starting to well up again. "I'm sorry, I'm not. . . ."

"Wait a minute," interrupted Mary. "Denver in April — I remember that trip."

*We've been asking the wrong person*, Dinah thought in exasperation.

"*You* remember that trip?" Ferguson asked. "Why?"

"I remember it because you were both very upset," Mary said. "Eloise, you had just gotten out of the hospital and couldn't travel. I remember Thomas flew over there by himself."

"Oh no!" Eloise looked stunned. "How could I forget? Thomas and I lost our niece at Columbine!"

"In the school shooting?" Dinah asked.

"Yes! It was just awful. Rebecca was the only daughter of Thomas's brother," said Eloise. "Thomas was devastated. They lived here in Washington for over ten years and had only just moved out there. We had become pretty close in those years. Rebecca was like another daughter to Thomas."

"So what happened then?" Dinah pressed. "How did you find out?"

"I was still in the hospital, recovering from minor surgery," said Eloise. "Thomas had come to visit me. We were watching the news on the little TV they have in the room. As soon as they said the name of the high school, Thomas went white. I had no idea Rebecca was at that school. Thomas called his brother on his cell phone, but it was still chaos and they didn't know whether Rebecca had gotten out safely or not. An hour later, Thomas got the phone call that she had been killed."

She shook her head sadly. "I suggested he go out there for the funeral. He flew out the next day."

"He was very upset?" Ferguson asked.

"He was devastated," Eloise said. "We all were. Rebecca was incredibly bright and vivacious. I think she developed a special bond with Thomas because she was interested in science. She asked him all kinds of questions about where we all came from and that sort of thing. She wanted to be an astrophysicist, if you can imagine. Her parents bought her a telescope for her 13th birthday and she spent just about every night staring up at the sky. She really loved it."

She looked up at the agents from her memories. "Do you think the shooting had anything to do with what happened to Thomas?"

"It's difficult to say at this early stage," said Ferguson, with a glance at Dinah. "We're just gathering as much information as we can. You never know what eventually helps to catch the killer."

Eloise flinched at the final word.

"What about a trip he took to Detroit, Michigan, in February 2000? He stayed there for two days, rented a car, and stayed in a three-star motel."

Eloise thought about it. "No, I just don't know why he would do that."

"What about San Diego, California, in March 2001?" Dinah asked. "He flew in Monday night and out on Tuesday night. He rented a car and stayed in Santee."

There was another silence while Eloise chewed her lower lip thoughtfully. "No," she said finally. "I'm sorry."

"There was also a trip to St. Cloud, Minnesota, in 2003. He stayed at a little place called Cold Spring for a couple of days. Any ideas?"

Eloise shook her head. "I'm really sorry."

Dinah asked again. "Can you think of any reasons why Thomas would travel to Michigan, California, and Minnesota?"

Eloise and Mary chewed their lower lips in unison as they thought hard. *It must be a family trait,* thought Dinah, smiling in amusement.

Her son had chewed his fingernails like she did.

Her smile died.

"No," said Eloise at length. "I really can't think of anything. I have never been to Michigan in my life. I don't know a soul in California or Minnesota." She glanced at Mary, who shrugged and nodded. There was nothing else they could remember that would be of any help.

The two agents stood. Dinah knew when they left, Eloise would be left with the crushing sense of grief and loneliness that would never really leave her. They could walk away and turn their attentions to the case, but there was no escape for Eloise.

"We're very sorry again to have to bring you this news," Ferguson said. "We're doing everything we can to find the person responsible."

The two agents left the apartment and climbed back into the car. Dinah couldn't help but feel a nudge in the back of her mind — something that, if remembered, would link together vital clues in this case.

While Ferguson and Dinah drove back to the office, Ferguson received a phone call from the medical examiner to ask them to come to the morgue.

"Which examiner did the autopsy?" Dinah asked when Ferguson had finished on the phone.

"The head guy himself," said Ferguson. "Dr. Paul Campion. We can rest easy that it would be the most thorough autopsy possible."

"He's good?" Dinah asked, having been out of the field for a while and unfamiliar with the current batch of medical examiners.

"He's the best," said Ferguson. "I must warn you, he's one of those born-agains, though."

"A what? A born-again Christian?" Dinah asked.

"Yeah. Don't be surprised if he talks about it a lot."

"I don't care, as long as does a good autopsy," said Dinah as they pulled up in the parking lot of the medical examiner's office.

\*\*\*\*

Dinah had never liked the morgue. The cold, steel equipment and stark lighting served to enhance the atmosphere of indifferent death, in Dinah's opinion. Ferguson had once pointed out to her that playing harp music and having cheerful pictures on the walls wouldn't have been appropriate. Dinah had grudgingly agreed.

Dr. Paul Campion, the chief medical examiner, was in the front office talking on the phone when the agents arrived. It seemed that he was setting a date for an appearance in an upcoming trial. While they waited, Dinah studied him. He was a tall, thin man in his fifties with a full head of silvery hair. He had quick, dark eyes that looked intense, and an expression of contentment on his face. Here was a man, thought Dinah, utterly comfortable working with the dead.

When he was done, he looked expectantly up at his visitors. "Good afternoon," he said. "What can I do for you?"

The agents showed their badges. "Special Agents Harris and Ferguson," said Dinah. "We're here for the autopsy of Thomas Whitfield."

The examiner was silent a moment as he mentally catalogued his recent autopsies. "Ah yes," he said. "You're here to see Tyndale." He stood up and began to lead the way to the examining rooms behind.

"Uh, no, that's Thomas *Whitfield*," corrected Dinah.

"Yes, I got that," agreed Dr. Campion. "I give my patients a little nickname, you see. It helps to personalize them a little. It's just a little idiosyncrasy of mine."

While the two agents waited for Dr. Campion to don his scrubs and sanitize his hands, Ferguson asked, "So why the name Tyndale?"

"It's the cause of death," said Campion. "I'll tell you about it in a minute."

He led them to a steel table where the body of Thomas Whitfield lay, a green sheet pulled discreetly up to his chin. The blood that Dinah had seen on the body in the trunk had been washed off, but the bruising and swelling were clearly evident down the left side of his face.

"All right," said Dr. Campion briskly. "Let's begin with cause of death, shall we?"

He rolled the sheet down, exposing the Y-incision dominating Thomas Whitfield's torso. Dr. Campion pointed at the dead man's neck. The two agents leaned closer and saw what was a clear and deep ligature mark embedded in the skin of the neck.

"Death was caused by asphyxiation. Specifically, the victim was strangled using a length of rope, cord, or wire. You can see this from the ligature mark around the neck, but also because the ligature is quite high on the neck. The place of the wound indicates to me that the attacker stood behind the victim and pulled backward and upward at the same time. My guess would be that the person used wire."

"Why is that?" Dinah asked.

Dr. Campion gently moved Whitfield's head up so the agents could see the wound more clearly. "Apart from the fact that I found no fibers consistent with a rope or cord, the esophagus was crushed underneath the ligature wound. That would indicate to me that the weapon had little yield. Also, the wound is rather deep for a rope or cord to achieve."

Dinah nodded. "Okay. Go on."

"Death by asphyxiation is confirmed by the fact that we can observe petechiae in the eyes. This is generally caused by some trauma that results in this redness." Dr. Campion opened one eyelid to expose the broken blood capillaries that helped to confirm cause of death. "You will also see that the victim's lips are faintly cyanotic — that is, bluish purple in color due to the lack of oxygen."

Ferguson nodded. "And what about time of death?"

Dr. Campion made a face. "I really can't comment on time of death with any certainty. Generally speaking, I would say approximately 24 hours ago. I make this assumption based solely on the appearance of rigor mortis and hypostasis. I'll explain those in a minute. I can't be any more specific than that because I don't know whether the victim was killed indoors or outdoors, or how long he remained in those environmental conditions before being moved. Obviously, if he was killed and lay outdoors in below freezing temperatures, his body would cool much faster than if the murder happened indoors. I take it you haven't yet found the murder scene?"

Dinah shook her head.

"Then my rather generic time of death stands. Hypostasis occurs when blood ceases to circulate and sinks to the lowest part of the body. How the victim is positioned on the ground is evident through discoloration." Dr. Campion pointed to the torso and legs. "You can see the discoloration appears on the front of the torso and front of the thighs. This confirms my theory that the attacker stood behind the victim during the attack, then allowed the victim to fall face-first after death. The victim remained in this position for about two hours before being moved. I understand the victim was in a different position when he was discovered?"

Dinah nodded. "Yes, he was found in the trunk of a car on his left side."

"Hypostasis doesn't lie," said Dr. Campion, sounded enormously pleased about that fact. "Also, although most people find my next point disgusting, I must mention that there was no sign of any insect activity on the body. There were certainly no maggots, but I was surprised to find there were not even any eggs laid on the body. The cold temperatures overnight might explain it, but I would have expected some activity." He paused and looked at the agents. "Do you have any questions regarding cause of death or time of death?"

"No, you've covered it," said Dinah.

"Excellent, moving right along then," said Dr. Campion. "A study of the victim's internal organs yielded nothing of interest. No organic disease was present. The victim had no traces of alcohol or drugs in his system. He had not eaten recently. Nothing of real interest there. Are you happy to keep moving?"

The agents nodded.

"All right. Now, the victim did suffer a sustained, heavy attack before his death, and my first theory is that he was tortured. When the victim was presented to me, his head and face were covered with blood."

Dinah nodded, remembering that when she had seen the body in the trunk of the car, Thomas Whitfield's facial features had been almost totally obscured by dried blood.

"My first thought was that death may have occurred through some blunt force trauma to the head, given that head wounds bleed copiously. However, I found that the victim did not have any fractures of the skull although I found a small subdural hemorrhage on the left side of the brain. A hemorrhage of its size may have the killed the man, but it would have taken some days, if not weeks. Now, with the head wounds, I found that there were a large number of them, and that they were consistently very small and quite shallow. This is what leads me to believe that the attack the victim sustained in the head region was by a human fist rather than a weapon or tool of any kind. Usually a weapon or tool will cause some fracturing to the skull and, depending on its shape, open up large gashes in the scalp. It is my guess that the small cuts were caused by a ring or even a fingernail. It is a similar story on the victim's face, where you can clearly see bruising and swelling from the eye socket to the jawline. Now, I believe these injuries to be inflicted prior to death, due to the body's cellular reaction."

"Yes, the bruising," said Ferguson, nodding wisely.

"No, not quite," corrected the medical examiner. "A bruise is essentially a break in blood vessels that allows blood to escape into surrounding tissue. This can happen after death. The only way to tell whether bruising was inflicted prior to death is the number of white blood cells present. A body still alive at the time of injury will send white blood cells to help heal the wound, whereas if the victim was dead at the time of injury, we would find a lower count of white blood cells. As an aside, the victim has two recently cracked teeth and one recently missing tooth. The tooth itself is still at the site of the crime or has been disposed of by the killer." Dr. Campion looked up to ensure the agents understood.

"I also found two cracked ribs, with extensive bruising around the site." Dr. Campion pulled the sheet farther down and pointed to the left side of the body. "However, a small clue which you might find interesting. In the absence of tool or weapon marks, I did see what I thought was a shoe print in the bruise patterning. I've photographed it. I obviously couldn't tell you what type of shoe it would be, but there is no other consistent explanation for the pattern. Finally, all four fingers on his left hand were broken, all in roughly the same position, very recently." He paused for a moment thoughtfully. "Yes, I believe that is the full catalogue of injuries. Do you have any questions?"

"No, thank you," said Ferguson, sounding impressed.

"Excellent. Now, I did find some material underneath the victim's fingernails and on several areas around the body, mostly glued into place by the drying blood. It doesn't appear to be DNA material, but what it does look like is dirt."

"Dirt?" Dinah asked, mystified.

"Yes. I'll send it to the lab and hope that within the dirt, they can find some distinguishing characteristics," explained Dr. Campion. "That might narrow down for you the area where the victim was killed."

"Great, thanks," said Ferguson.

"Anytime, Agents. I hope you catch the person responsible," said Dr. Campion, leading them to the door. Suddenly he stopped, causing Dinah to bump into him.

"Oh! How forgetful of me. I have another small clue you might find helpful." He hurried back to the body of Thomas Whitfield, with the agents following, and held up the right hand of the body. "I found, written in very small characters, what appears to be a cell phone number."

Dinah peered closely at the hand. There was indeed writing in the webbing between the thumb and forefinger. The number would not have been visible in the normal position of the hand, and only became evident when the thumb and forefinger were stretched apart.

Dinah quickly copied the number down and thanked the medical examiner.

As they once again moved toward the exit, Ferguson asked, "So this Tyndale character was strangled with a wire too?"

Dr. Campion smiled. "Yes, he certainly was."

"What was his crime?" asked Ferguson curiously.

"Well, he dared to translate the Bible from Latin to English," said Dr. Campion. "In those days, the priests were the only ones with access to the Bible. The common man couldn't speak or read Latin and had to rely on the priests to teach them. The church was extremely corrupt and taught their congregations many things contrary to the Bible. Tyndale, and other sympathizers at the time, decided it was time the common man was able to bypass the corrupt teaching of the church and access the Bible themselves."

"I take it the church didn't like it and killed him?" Ferguson asked.

"Extraordinary, isn't it?" Dr. Campion shook his head. "Yet if it weren't for Tyndale and his sympathizers, we might still not have the Bible in the English language. Thank goodness for the Reformation."

They walked in silence to the front foyer. "Well, good luck with the case," said Dr. Campion cheerfully. "Please call me if I can be of any further assistance." He waved at them, and then disappeared back into the cold, steel bowels of the morgue.

The two agents walked back to the car, where Ferguson noticed Dinah staring at him.

"Well, I did tell you he was one of those born-agains, didn't I?" he said defensively.

\*\*\*\*

When Dinah checked her cell phone on the way back from the morgue, she found three missed calls from the formidable Catherine Biscelli. She had called an emergency meeting of the board of regents and it would be held at 4 p.m. sharp. She spoke in short, sharp, irritable bursts that reminded Dinah of the noise stiletto heels made on the sidewalk.

The agents drove directly to the main complex of the Smithsonian where the meeting would be held, arriving a half hour early. They immediately asked for Catherine Biscelli.

The Director of Public Affairs had her curly hair pulled back from her face with a headband, which served to make the planes of her face seem more angular and severe.

Ferguson took the lead. "Thanks for organizing the meeting so quickly," he said warmly. "We were just wondering if you could take us through who the board of regents are and what their roles are before we meet them."

Catherine Biscelli left the room and arrived back several moments later with an organizational chart.

"The head of the institution is the secretary," she said without preamble. "The board of regents is appointed by Congress and is responsible for the overall administration of the institution. The board reports to Congress on a semi-regular basis."

She flipped open the organizational chart to show the members of the board.

"The current members are Supreme Court Chief Justice and Chancellor Maxwell Pryor; the vice president of the United States, Charles Ransome; Senator Rosa Rubelli from the state of Massachusetts; Senator David Winters from the state of California; Senator John Buchanan from the state of New England; Congressmen Philip Constance, Peter Norfolk, and Tony Zullo from the states of North Carolina, Ohio, and Wyoming respectively; the CEO of the Washington Philharmonic Orchestra, Penelope Bright; Ken MacIntyre, the CEO and president of Seismic Corporation; Anne Dryzak, CEO of the Fidelity Trust Financial Group; Carlos Benes, president of Benes Logistics and Transport Corporation; and Carol Meyes, chairwoman of the charity Bravehearts." Catherine Biscelli stopped to take a breath.

Ferguson whistled. "Wow, there are some heavy hitters there."

"That's why the majority of the board will be joining us via tele-conference," said Catherine shortly. "It was the only way I could orga-nize this meeting."

There was a long silence as Catherine busied herself dialing in the conference number. Dinah watched the other woman through nar-rowed eyes.

"You know," said Dinah at length, "I'm really very surprised that you haven't asked about the circumstances of Thomas's death."

Catherine flushed. "There are some things I don't want to know," she said acidly, "if I am to sleep soundly at night."

The door opened and a tall, very thin woman with short gray hair, square glasses, and shockingly pink lipstick entered.

"Dah-ling!" she exclaimed, bestowing Catherine Biscelli with a fake air kiss. "Dreadful, isn't it? I *do* wish we could meet under more pleasant circumstances."

Catherine motioned toward the two agents. "These are special agents Ferguson and Harris from the FBI," she said. "This is Penelope Bright, from the Philharmonic Orchestra."

Penelope Bright offered a bony hand to shake. "I'd normally tell you that it's a pleasure to meet you, but it really *isn't*."

She was cut off by another entrance, this time a small, compact man with dark features and hair, a trim moustache, and an expen-sive suit. Catherine made the introductions again as Carlos Benes, the president of his own logistics and transport company. As the third and final delegate made her way into the room — Carol Meyers, a grand-motherly woman with wavy gray hair and a pleasant face — the tele-phone crackled into life as the remaining board members dialed into the conference.

"Thanks to all for making the time to be part of this meeting," Catherine began. "You are all aware that our secretary, Thomas Whit-field, has been missing for several days and we recently discovered he'd been murdered. It is because of this tragic turn that I introduce you to special agents Ferguson and Harris from the FBI, who will be handling the investigation."

Ferguson kicked Dinah under the table to warn her not to speak. "I'd like to reiterate Ms. Biscelli's appreciation for making the time to talk to us," he said. "The purpose of this meeting is simply to gather as much information as we can about Thomas Whitfield that might lead to his killer. If you have anything to say, could you please identify yourself first for the benefit of the group before speaking. Shall we proceed?"

There were no objections.

"Okay. Under what circumstances was Thomas Whitfield appointed to the position of secretary?"

"I can answer that. Chief Justice Maxwell Pryor speaking. I championed him and recommended him to the rest of the board," said a booming, deep voice. "The last secretary retired three years ago and I had started to look for replacements. I was looking specifically for someone with a scientific background. Thomas Whitfield had been getting quite a lot of press at the time for his anthropological work, and from what I could see, he seemed to be articulate and intelligent. I interviewed him and then the board interviewed him. We all agreed he was an excellent candidate and appointed him."

"Were there any disgruntled applicants who may have resented Mr. Whitfield's appointment?"

The chief justice barked a laugh. "No, it wasn't exactly a position that is advertised and applicants send in their resumes. No one can apply for the position unless invited by the board. In this instance, we didn't interview any other applicants."

Dinah wrote this down, thinking it was odd that Thomas Whitfield had been given the position with apparent ease.

"In case you're wondering," Maxwell Pryor continued, "our method is to invite applicants individually. If Thomas Whitfield had declined, we would have moved on to the next potential candidate. We didn't have multiple applicants at the same time."

"Okay," agreed Ferguson. "Was there any time during his serving as the secretary when he had trouble with any members of the public or press?"

"No," said Catherine Biscelli promptly. "Everything the secretary does and says is carefully controlled by my office. We handle his official duties, speeches, and media commitments." She paused and added condescendingly, "I think all of the board members will agree that the position of secretary of the Smithsonian is hardly a contentious or controversial one."

Ferguson, to his credit, didn't bite. Dinah knew she would have. "Does anyone know if Mr. Whitfield had any personal problems?"

There was a general mumble in the negative. "I can't speak for everyone," said Penelope Bright. "But my relationship with Mr. Whitfield was purely professional. He didn't come across as the sort of person who might confide his personal issues to just anyone. He seemed to be a very controlled, very private person." After a beat, Penelope said, "Sorry, that was me. Penelope."

There was another mumble of general consensus.

Ferguson tried a different tack. "Did any of you have any conflict with Mr. Whitfield?"

This time there were several definite denials. Ferguson glanced at Dinah. If there was conflict between members of the board and the secretary, nobody was owning up to it.

"Are any of you aware of any groups who may wish the Smithsonian harm?"

"This is Vice President Charles Ransome," said a smooth alto voice. "You can check with your terrorism unit. There are always fringe groups who wish to cause harm to American interests. I am not at liberty to speak about these on an open line. However, we have no specific intelligence relating to a threat against the Smithsonian at this time."

Dinah rolled her eyes at the uninformative politician's reply.

Ferguson added a few more questions but the board was unable to help. Dinah got the feeling that, like many professional relationships, nobody in the Smithsonian organization truly knew Thomas Whitfield.

Dinah couldn't shake the brief conversation she'd had with Lara, Mr. Whitfield's personal assistant, nor could she shake the sensation that the board of regents weren't being completely honest.

As the meeting adjourned, Dinah couldn't help but wonder if the death of Thomas Whitfield was part of something much larger — something that the board of regents were willing to lie to protect.

The question was — what was it?

\* \* \* \*

When Dinah arrived back at her desk, she found it increasingly difficult to concentrate. She had been awake for far too long and she decided to go home. She took with her the copies of Thomas Whitfield's credit card statements. She had to find out what was nagging the back of her mind. It must have been important.

Back at her apartment, over a strong coffee, she pored over the statements again. What on earth did Michigan, California, and Minnesota have in common? Was Thomas's trip to Colorado related in any way?

There were no unusual receipts at any of the places he'd visited — just motel rooms, rental cars, the occasional meal. Dinah couldn't get a feel for what Thomas Whitfield had actually been doing on his trips.

After a while, her head started to ache and her eyeballs felt rough and scratchy. She knew she would be too tired to make the link herself tonight but decided to give her computer a chance to solve the mystery.

She plugged in her laptop, and googled the three states. The results were enormous and too far-reaching, so she refined her search to the cities Thomas had flown into. Again, the results were too general. They ranged from official tourist sites to comments dredged up from a chat room somewhere in cyberspace.

Dinah finally tried the combination of cities and towns where Thomas had actually stayed in motels.

The minute the results came back, the link between all four trips was obvious. Dinah sat thinking about it for a moment, mentally kicking herself for not making the connection herself.

His first trip to Colorado had been to Littleton, where at Columbine High School two teenaged boys had killed 11 classmates and wounded 28, before taking their own lives. This had been where Thomas Whitfield's niece, Rebecca, had lost her life.

Apparently inspired by what he'd seen there, in 2000 he'd flown to Detroit, Michigan, and driven to the township of Mount Morris, where at the Buell Elementary School the youngest school shooter in history took the life of a six-year-old girl.

In 2001 he'd flown to San Diego, California, to visit the city of Santee, where at the Santana High School a 15-year-old boy had killed 2 and wounded 13.

In 2003 he'd flown into St. Cloud, Minnesota, to visit the city of Cold Spring, where at the Ricori High School a 15-year-old boy had killed two classmates, one of whom had allegedly been mean to him.

Thomas Whitfield had been visiting the sites of school shootings, including Columbine where he had been touched personally by tragedy. Had he been doing research for a new paper? Was he trying to understand what made a young person snap so violently and unpredictably? Was he trying to somehow assuage guilt over his own niece's death?

What relevance did these trips have to his own death?

Dinah was frustrated. She had made the link between the trips and found a common denominator. In the grand scheme of things, though, she had no idea what it all meant.

Still deep in thought, Dinah opened the refrigerator door to pour herself a glass of wine and discovered she didn't have any.

She sighed and picked up her keys. There was a liquor store about a block away, and although Dinah couldn't have felt less energized after her day, she decided to walk down to pick up a few bottles.

Outside, a freezing wind was busy beginning its first winter chore — stripping the trees of any leaves. Dinah tried to shrug herself deeper into her jacket to ward off the cold, but the wind was the sort to bite and tear at flesh with little regard for the clothes one might be wearing.

Behind her, the engine of a plain white van kicked into life and began to slowly cruise down the street, careful not to get too close to its quarry.

Dinah was preoccupied with the school shooting mystery. Although the shootings had garnered intense media scrutiny at the time, the fickle public had moved on. It appeared that Thomas Whitfield had not been able to move on — had the death of his niece affected him so greatly? Did he feel a compulsion to lend a sympathetic shoulder to the townspeople of a newly bereaved community? And, in any case, what did it matter? The perpetrators of those terrible crimes were either dead or apprehended. They were by no means sophisticated offenders.

Inside the liquor store, Dinah found her favorite white wine was discounted so she bought three bottles. To keep her mind from spinning its wheels on Thomas Whitfield, she envisaged the taste of the first sweet mouthful.

On her way home, she bent her head down because of the intense wind and didn't see the white van inching closer to her. She also didn't see the long, dark muzzle pointing directly at her from the window of the van or hear the clicks that were taken from only several feet away.

In fact, Dinah had no idea of the transaction that had just taken place and would only find out the following morning when, with a vague headache and dry mouth, she would pick up the morning paper and find a blown-up picture of herself on the front page of the *Post*.

By then, the rest of the city would have seen the picture of her walking against the wind in a thin coat carrying a bag full of alcohol. They would have read the headlines that screamed that the lead investigator in Thomas Whitfield's murder was a drunk. They would have read that it was not the first time she had showed poor judgment. They would read that, in fact, the last time she had showed poor judgment, she had been responsible for someone's death. They would read that in that sorry incident, she had been found to have an elevated blood alcohol reading and was immediately suspended. Why was it, the article queried, that the FBI tolerated drunkenness in their agents — worse, *promoted* agents with a history of alcohol abuse back into positions of authority? The article finished by demanding a complete overhaul of the FBI's policy with relation to agents caught abusing drugs and alcohol.

Dinah had once thought she had hit rock bottom.

What she hadn't realized was that it was possible to keep hitting rock bottom, over and over again, until the will to keep climbing back up was utterly vanquished.

The media circus was back in full force, camped in the streets around the FBI headquarters in their white vans. Dinah slunk in the back entrance and noticed the SAC, George Hanlon, watching her as she approached her desk. His arms were crossed over his chest and a frown creased his face. She knew what that look meant — George Hanlon was trying to decide whether keeping Dinah in the bureau was worth it.

Although it was early, there was no mistaking the spiky, peroxide hair that jutted up like a rooster's crop on the crime scene lab technician, Zach Booker, who was sitting at her desk with Ferguson, waiting for her.

"Hey, Zach," she greeted, trying to summon up a good mood. "What brings you here?"

Zach Booker did not fit the archetypal crime scene technician. His white-blond hair, year-round fake tan, pierced eyebrow and nose, and casual dress sense set him apart from his colleagues. What he lacked in appearance, he made up for in ability. Nothing escaped Zach's attention in the lab.

"Hey, dude," he greeted.

In spite of herself, Dinah smiled. "Hi, Zach."

Zach said rapidly, "I saw the article in the paper this morning. I just want to say that I think it blows, man. The whole lab thinks it blows."

Dinah was oddly touched by his show of support. "Thanks."

"Anyway," continued Zach. "What's the deal with all your crime scenes? Every time I turn around you guys have sent me another house or apartment or car to check out."

"And we still haven't found the big one, either," added Ferguson. "Still don't know where the victim was actually killed."

Zach opened a binder filled with reports and results and copious notes. "I've sent through the prelim results," he began. "I've got all the final results in now though. I'll start at the beginning. Security cameras at the institution take continuous footage and are saved on tapes every 24 hours. Clearly visible is Thomas Whitfield arriving the morning he disappeared, and there is absolutely no footage of him leaving again. Every person who arrived before opening hours who appeared on the tape can be accounted for — all of them are staff. Nobody on staff left early that day or had any unusual arrangements that might flag our attention. The tapes haven't been doctored in any way."

Dinah wrote down a summary of what Zach had said. "So how does the secretary arrive in the morning and not be seen since?"

"My guess is in the trunk of a car," said Zach. "The staff basement parking garage has security cameras but the staff elevator doesn't. The public garages and elevators all have cameras, and he definitely doesn't appear on any of them. Having said that, no car entered the staff parking area that didn't belong to a legitimate staff member."

Dinah glanced at Ferguson. Her theory of it being an inside job was starting to look less outlandish.

"The lab spent hours combing the footage for that day," Zach continued. "It wasn't easy, given the number of visitors to the museum each day. I originally thought that he could've popped up in the middle of a tour bus group or something, but I double-checked everyone's work. I am confident in saying that Thomas Whitfield did not leave the museum in plain view."

"Are there any exits in the building that don't have cameras?" Ferguson asked.

"No way, dude, I checked that out first," said Zach. "I gave you some brief information about his office. Totally wiped clean, which is really odd. His personal assistant, Lara Southall, arrived about 30 minutes after he did. So the abductors had 30 minutes to subdue and take Thomas, steal pretty much everything out of his office, delete the hard drive on the laptop, and wipe the place down. Lara was able to confirm that the attacker had taken his diary, organizer, blotter, stationery, computer disks, and calendar. You would've seen how empty it was when you were there."

"Would Lara have had access to his diary?" Dinah asked.

"Yeah, Thomas kept an electronic diary for work appointments and a paper diary for personal. Lara saw the paper diary from time to time but never saw what was written in it. Of course, when the laptop's hard drive was erased, she lost the records of his electronic diary, too. She can't access something that doesn't exist anymore, right?"

"So have you been able to retrieve the hard drive?" Ferguson asked.

"Here's another weird thing," Zach said. He licked his lips and Dinah noticed a new piercing in his tongue. "Let's say you buy an ex-government computer. The hard drive on that computer will have been erased with a standard issue, commercial grade deletion software. The average person who buys that computer doesn't know how to retrieve what's left on the disk, and furthermore, *can't*, because the type of software you'd need isn't commercially available. It's only available to law enforcement agencies, the defense force, Homeland Security, yada yada. You with me?"

The two agents nodded.

"Okay, so I use my special software to retrieve the disk's memory. I got nothing. After several attempts, it becomes obvious that my software just isn't gonna cut it."

"What does that mean?"

"It means that whoever deleted the hard drive has access to the type of software that should only be available to selected government departments and several very nasty hackers," said Zach. "I've had to send the laptop to the Department of Homeland Security. They have a system that can crack anything. It'll take more time. It gets you thinking though, doesn't it?"

Dinah couldn't have agreed more.

"Generally speaking, in his office, there was no evidence of any value. We didn't find any prints, fibers, hairs, or material that will be of any use. All I can say about that scene is that it's the absence of information that is interesting and possibly useful."

There was a pause while Zach moved his notes to the next scene and Dinah wrote furiously in her notebook.

"Now, I'm looking at the victim's house in Georgetown. They made more of a mess but were no less careful. The desktop computer in the study had its hard drive erased exactly the same as the laptop. Nothing of value was stolen. There was a wealth of fingerprints, but that's always going to be the case. We have run all the prints we found there — which could have been left by family members, visitors, the cleaner — but we haven't got any hits. So even if the attacker did leave a print behind, there is no record of him in the database."

It was a common problem, Dinah knew. Often the problem was not the lack of prints, but rather the onerous task of narrowing them down and hoping that one would result in a hit on one of the databases.

"The rope used to tie Eloise Whitfield to the chair was generic and can be found at thousands of hardware stores across the country. She was gagged with one of Thomas Whitfield's own ties, so there was really nothing to go on there."

"Do you have *any* good news?" Dinah demanded.

Zach smiled. "Actually, my dear, impatient friend, I do."

Dinah scowled at him.

"Two items of importance — Eloise Whitfield fought back, bless her, and we found DNA material underneath her fingernails. Again, no hits in our databases, but it's there for when you do apprehend someone. The second thing is that we found a very fine powder, concentrated in the areas where the intruders spent most of their time in the house. It's important because it seems out of place. We analyzed it at the lab and it turned out to be chalk dust."

"Chalk dust?" Dinah frowned.

"Yeah, the very fine dust that you get when you use a piece of chalk. It's odd because unless you are a schoolteacher or specifically have chalk in your house, it's not something that is commonly found in a person's home. Neither was Whitfield a teacher or had chalk in the house."

Zach flipped through his notebook and flicked the stud in his tongue absentmindedly as he did so.

"Okay, the Lara Southall apartment. We have the fingerprint problem again; there were hundreds of them but no hits. The lock had been picked pretty skillfully. The tool marks left behind would indicate someone in possession of both the tools and the knowledge to pick the locks quickly and quietly. The tools themselves aren't commonly available. They would generally be used by the locksmith trade. Unless you find the actual tools, though, it would be hard to try to trace them."

He flicked his tongue stud. Dinah began to get irritated by it.

"We know that Lara was attacked in the shower, probably from behind. There was no DNA material underneath her fingernails, indicating that she wasn't able to fight back. The whole scene was contained within the shower, so we didn't find any shoeprints or fingerprints in the blood itself. I would find it difficult to believe that the attacker didn't get some blood on his own clothes as a result, though. The most interesting thing is that we found the same fine chalk dust in the bathroom of Lara's apartment. Other than that, I don't have anything to report from that scene."

"So are we looking for a school teacher?" Dinah asked.

Zach shrugged. "I guess it would be within the realms of possibility. I can imagine the vice principal of my high school being quite capable of something like this. He was a mean. . . ."

"Let's get back on topic," suggested Dinah, cutting off Zach's enthusiastic reminiscing of his high school vice principal.

Zach gathered his thoughts. "The final scene was the trunk of the car in which Thomas was found. We found all the usual trace you'd expect to find there — gasoline and oil residue, for example. We found a large amount of dirt both in the trunk and on Thomas Whitfield's clothes and shoes. It's dirt that can be found anywhere around the city, but it did look like there was a high level of mineralization within the dirt. This would indicate that the dirt comes from an industrial or commercial setting rather than an urban one. We also found more of the fine chalk dust. Thomas Whitfield's hands were bound with a similar generic rope to the rope used on Eloise Whitfield.

"Here's an interesting clue — the DNA found under Eloise Whitfield's fingernails matches the DNA found under Thomas Whitfield's fingernails."

"So now we know for sure that the same person is responsible for both," said Ferguson. "Definitely no hits in the databases?"

"Nope," said Zach. "But it's there ready to nail the attacker when you find him. That's pretty much all I've got to report."

"So, in summary," said Dinah, looking back over her notes, "we've got computer hard drives erased with a program only available to a select few; DNA that doesn't match any known offenders; the same chalk dust found at three of the crime scenes; dirt from possibly an industrial part of the city; locksmith tools; a tooth of the victim found at the murder scene; and the fact that one of Lara Southall's attackers might have blood on his clothes. Am I correct?"

Zach nodded. "Yeah." He glanced at his watch. "Oh no! I'm late. I gotta go."

"Back to the lab?" asked Ferguson.

Zach grinned. "Nah, a lunch date."

"You can actually find a lady who wants to date you?" Dinah asked, only half-joking.

"Please," said Zach. "I've got to fight the *laydeez* off. See you guys around!"

The two agents looked at each other as Zach left in a hurry and Dinah shook her head.

"We do have one more thing you left out," said Ferguson. "We have that phone number found on Thomas Whitfield's hand."

Dinah made a gun from her thumb and forefinger, pointed it at Ferguson, and said, "Good point. Let's do it."

\*\*\*\*

The two agents found an interview office that was empty and used a conference phone on speaker to dial the number found on Thomas Whitfield's hand. The phone rang several times, and then a female voice said, "Hello?"

"Hello, this is Special Agent Dinah Harris of the FBI. . . ."

"Just a minute," the voice said. "I'll wake him up for you."

"No, I. . . !" objected Dinah, but the phone was dropped with a clunk. Dinah stared in bewilderment at Ferguson, who shrugged. Faintly, they could hear the woman calling for someone to come to the phone.

Several long moments ticked by, and then there was a rustling as someone picked the phone up. A man finally answered, "Hello? Is this the FBI?"

"Yes, sir, this is. . . ."

"How many did you get this week?" the man asked in a friendly voice, as if he knew Dinah quite well.

Dinah was taken aback. "How many *what* did we get, sir?"

There was a pause. "This *is* the FBI, isn't it? Who am I speaking to?"

"This is Special Agent Dinah Harris. Who am *I* speaking to and what did you mean when asked how many did we get?" Dinah used her sternest tone.

"This is Andy Coleman. I was asking how many death threats we got this week."

"Why would you be getting death threats?" demanded Dinah, still horribly confused.

"Because — look, I don't think we're on the same wavelength," Andy Coleman said.

*Obviously,* thought Dinah.

"Let me back up. I'm from the Genesis Legacy. We are a Christian apologetics organization and we get quite a number of death threats a week. We have a regular contact within the FBI, whom I speak to all the time about it. I assumed that's why you were calling."

"Christian what? What are you apologizing for?"

Andy chuckled. "We defend the truth and authority of the Bible. At this point in time, it is under major attack from many atheists and evolutionists. Think of the Richard Dawkins book, for example. Some people don't seem to like our ministry focus so we are in constant contact with the FBI."

"Who is your regular FBI contact?" asked Dinah.

"Agent Shannon O'Donnell."

Ferguson leapt up immediately and left the interview office to check the credentials of Agent Shannon O'Donnell.

"I still don't understand why you would get death threats," said Dinah.

"As I said, we're an apologetics organization and we pay particular attention to defending the truth of the account of origins in Genesis. That means that we believe the Bible's account of how the earth was formed, and how human beings came into existence. We believe that God created everything on the earth. We also believe that the true age of the earth is about six thousand years old. That puts us at direct odds with evolutionary belief, which believes the earth to be billions of years old, and that human beings evolved from single-cell organisms and that apes are our modern ancestors." Andy paused for a few seconds.

"Keep talking — I'm no closer to understanding how this gets you death threats."

"There are a lot of atheists, humanists, and secular scientists who take great offense at our message. There are a lot of people who hate the fact that we proclaim that God is the authority and that we answer to Him as our Creator. I am not told who the death threats come from specifically, but it is solely because of the work I do that I get them." Andy sighed. "Actually, it's not just death threats — I also get bomb threats."

Ferguson appeared back in the room and shoved a note under Dinah's eye. It read, "Agent S. O'Donnell confirmed from Cleveland field office. In regular contact with A. Coleman. Confirmed regular death threats — religious person. O'Donnell vouches for him."

"Right." Dinah shook her head in wonder. "So I assume you know Thomas Whitfield."

"Yeah, I sure do." Andy Coleman spoke of Thomas Whitfield in the present tense, Dinah noted.

"Then you know that Thomas Whitfield is dead," Dinah said flatly, waiting intently for Coleman's reaction.

There was a sharp gasp and then silence. "No, I didn't know," Coleman said finally. His voice was shaky. "What happened?"

"Don't you watch the news? It's been one of the top news stories over the past few days."

"I just got back from Israel," said Coleman. "I literally flew in a couple of hours ago. I have been away for nearly two weeks."

Dinah remembered the woman who had answered the phone had gone off to waken Coleman.

"What happened?" Coleman asked.

"Thomas Whitfield was abducted from his office three days ago. He was found murdered early this morning."

There was another stunned silence. "Oh, no. That's awful. Poor Eloise. Do you know who did this?"

"No, that's why I want to talk to you," Dinah explained. "Where are you located?"

"I am in Cincinnati," said Coleman. "I can't believe it."

"Sir, I want you to stay exactly where you are. We are coming down to talk to you, okay?"

"Yes, of course." Coleman sounded distant.

"Sir, do you have any idea why someone would want to kill Thomas Whitfield?" Dinah asked, almost as an afterthought, not expecting an answer.

There was a long silence. "Actually, Agent Harris, I think I do."

### WASHINGTON, DC, 1997 — THOMAS'S STORY

It began with Thomas's articles being published with a greater regularity, in scientific journals with a global distribution and lofty reputations. Even newspapers began to request short pieces and soon Thomas began to find it difficult to cram his writing obligations in between the classes he taught at the university.

Thomas didn't see the arm of IAFSI directly in his negotiations with the journals and press. However, everything went so smoothly that it was difficult for Thomas to think that he could have achieved this on his own. He knew that IAFSI had contacts in many parts of the community that were smoothing the way for him.

He was relaxing in his study late one night re-reading an article he had written about the correlations between the diets of early Neanderthals and apes. The diets had been very similar, proving that Neanderthal man had not yet completely severed their ties with their ape cousins and that the evolution of man was still in its infancy. The article had been published in *Nature* journal.

The phone rang next to him, startling him. "Hello?"

"Hi, it's Damon. I'm just reading your latest article about the whole diet thing."

"What do you think?" asked Thomas. He still felt absurdly proud when he had something published.

There was a pause, much longer than Thomas would have liked. "Look, it's a great article," said Damon at length. "It's accurate and precise and exactly what it should be."

"What's the problem?" Thomas asked, frowning. He had thought it was one of his best articles.

"Well. It's just that, it's very . . . scientific." Damon cleared his throat. "Which of course it's supposed to be, but you know, it's a bit . . . *dry.*"

"It's not a short story," said Thomas curtly. "It's a scientific article." He was confused. He thought he had been doing what IAFSI had asked him to do.

"Right. Well, I didn't mean it like that. It's not the way the article is written exactly, it's the content."

"Why don't you tell me exactly what it is you're trying to say," suggested Thomas. "I'm incredibly confused."

"Yes. Right. What I'm trying to say is: I wonder if there is any way to *add* to the article, in a very subtle way, that this proves there was no intelligent designer or creator? You know, you take the first step by saying evolution is science, and presenting the evidence. It would be great if you could take the second step and say that this clearly disproves the existence of a creator or designer." Damon's tone changed slightly, and Thomas immediately understood that he wasn't making a request exactly; it was more like a directive.

"You want me to be more anti-God in my articles," said Thomas flatly. "Is that what you're getting at?"

"I just don't want readers missing that second point, you know?" Damon said. "Even the most intelligent scientist might not get the second point unless it was spelled out."

"Okay," said Thomas, suppressing a sigh. "If that's what you want."

"Look, I know you're purely a scientist," said Damon. "But we have multiple areas of influence. You aren't the only scientist we're championing, you know."

Thomas knew this to be an understated threat, but a threat nonetheless. "I get it, trust me," he said. "I'll do as you ask."

"Great!" Damon's tone brightened. "I hope you're sitting down — I have some exciting news!"

"What?"

"Would you like to try television?"

Thomas felt a tremor go through him. "Are you serious?"

"We need someone to do a spot on *American Morning*," said Damon. "It'll be a quick spot, but we need an expert. I'm still getting the information on what the spot will be about, but are you interested?"

"Absolutely!" Thomas was almost speechless.

"Okay. I'll start to organize it then. In the meantime, I need you to brush up on what we've just talked about."

"What, the anti-God thing?"

"Yes. We need you to be crystal clear if you're going to be on television." Damon paused. "We wouldn't give this opportunity to just anyone, you know."

"You can count on me," said Thomas hastily.

"You'd better get to it," suggested Damon. "We never get much notice of these things and the program is likely to want you in only a few days."

Thomas hung up and stared moodily at the screen saver on his laptop. He'd always known, deep down, that it wasn't possible to get something for nothing. IAFSI wasn't going to give him all the opportunities they had without something in return. *What's the big deal, anyway?* he asked himself. They weren't asking him to espouse a view he didn't already hold. Anyway, he was going to be on television. The excitement of that alone soon dealt with any uneasiness he had about Damon's request.

"Are you nearly ready, honey?" Eloise asked from the doorway, startling him.

"Ready for what?" Thomas asked, glancing up at her. She was dressed up, wearing her best black cocktail dress.

"Tell me you haven't forgotten!" exclaimed Eloise. "We're going to the opera with Harold and Cynthia tonight."

"Oh." Thomas couldn't have sounded any less enthusiastic if he'd tried. "I'm really busy here. Did you know I've been asked to go on television?"

"We need to leave in 15 minutes," said Eloise sharply. "Are you going to be ready?"

"Can't you tell Harold that I've got the flu or something?"

"This is not about Harold. *I* want you to come," said Eloise.

"I'm sorry, honey. I've really got too much to do. I need to prepare for my television program."

Eloise clenched her fists at her sides and spoke through clenched teeth. "I've barely *seen* you in I don't know how long. Are you sure this is what you want to do?"

A more perceptive man may have realized that his wife's deceptively soft tone hid a much larger anger. But Thomas was too wrapped up in his impending fame. "Thanks, honey," he said cheerfully. "I knew you'd understand."

When Eloise left the house ten minutes later, she slammed the front door so hard the whole house shook.

Thomas barely noticed.

\* \* \* \*

The woman holding the makeup brush hovered near Thomas, trying to get in a few final swipes of powder on his nose. Thomas was going through his notes again, memorizing the important parts.

"Are you ready?" the carefully made-up and coiffed host asked, looking immaculate even though she'd been up since 3 a.m.

Thomas could only nod, hoping that when the interview went live, he would find his voice.

The *American Morning* introduction music swelled and the two anchors smiled professionally at the cameras.

"Welcome back to *American Morning*," said the host in her honeyed tones. "Our next guest is a well-known anthropologist, Thomas Whitfield, who is a prolific writer and has tenure at Washington State University. He is here to discuss the latest fossils found in the desert in central Africa, which are thought to be some of the most significant discoveries in recent times." She turned to Thomas, who forced himself to stop fidgeting. "Just what is so significant about these particular fossils, Professor Whitfield?"

"What makes this discovery so exciting," replied Thomas, relieved that he was speaking and that it made sense, "is that we have now found six species of sub-human fossils in the same area of Africa. All six species are different and seem to represent different links in the evolutionary chain of human development."

"So are these fossils the 'missing link'?"

Thomas smiled. "Not exactly. What I can say is that the discoveries of these fossils do provide continuity through time. What I mean by that is that we can see a steady progression of man's ancient ancestors from sub-human to human."

"Over what time period, Professor Whitfield?"

"We believe it to be over six million years, if we date all the fossils found in that particular area of Africa. Discoveries like these help to fill in the gaps about how our human ancestors made the leap from one species to another. We can see steady evolution of the shape of the skull, the appearance of sharper, carnivorous teeth, and height." Thomas paused. "Over the six-million-year time period, we see our ancestors getting larger skulls and, by default, brains; become taller and stronger, and turn from herbivores to carnivores."

"Is it possible that the two or more of the sub-species evolved independently of each other?" the host asked, looking down at her notes.

"Sure," agreed Thomas. "It's certainly possible. However, the qualifying evidence in this case is that each species gets stronger. Even if some of them evolved independently, the weaker species became extinct as the stronger species took over. It's one of the foundational precepts of evolution — survival of the fittest."

The host flashed a million-watt smile. "Thank you for your time, Professor Whitfield," she said, turning back to the camera. "After this commercial break, the results of our back-yard swimming pool survey are in!"

The mood on the set momentarily relaxed as the cameras stopped filming, and the crew rushed at Thomas, removing his microphone and ushering him off the set. The host and her co-anchor didn't leave their positions but shook Thomas's hand and thanked him for being part of the show.

Thomas left the studio, feeling elated. He'd gotten through his first live television spot pretty well, he thought. He'd managed to sound articulate and competent, and that was all he was worried about.

Seconds later, his cell phone chirped.

"That was great!" enthused Damon. "How do you feel?"

"Pretty good," admitted Thomas. "It wasn't as hard as I thought."

"She called you *well-known* and *prolific*," Damon went on. "That was perfect. I'm sure they'll ask you back."

"Really? Wouldn't they just get someone new?"

Damon laughed. "No. The networks like to get the same experts back time and time again. It helps build viewer trust. Do you know what I think will happen?"

"What?" Damon's excitement was infectious.

"I'm seeing regular spots on *American Morning*. And then I'm seeing a televised debate!"

"What, like the presidential candidates do?"

"Right! It's never really been done before, but I think we can pull it off in this climate," said Damon, sounding like he was starting to talk to himself. "Yes, it's coming together, Thomas. I'll talk to you later. I just wanted to tell you how great you were!"

As Thomas walked to his car, he felt it was time to congratulate himself. It was all starting to come together — the published articles, tenure at the university, television appearances. His profile was rising, the money was starting to pour in, and he was regarded as one of the most proficient scientists in his field.

It was perfect. It was what life was all about, wasn't it?

As Dinah stood, gathering her notes from the phone conference with Andy Coleman, Ferguson held up his hand to stop her.

"Just a moment," he said. "While we're in here, I want to make another phone call."

"Who to?" Dinah asked curiously.

"A phone number I got from Thomas Whitfield's phone records," explained Ferguson. "I spent last night reviewing them and checking against numbers we know — like Whitfield's family and friends. There was a particularly high call rate from Whitfield's cell to this particular number."

"Haven't we been through the call records already?"

"Yeah, but there's something about this one I have a hunch about. Eloise told me he was a work colleague, but I haven't found him in any of the personnel at the Smithsonian. I want to know exactly what kind of colleague we're talking about."

Dinah sat, and while Ferguson found the number he wanted to dial, she rang the administrative assistant who sat on their floor and asked her to book flights to Cincinnati.

Ferguson dialed and then a male voice answered, "Hello?"

"This is Special Agent David Ferguson from the FBI. To whom am I speaking?"

There was a pause. "This is Damon Mason."

"The reason for my call, Mr. Mason," continued Ferguson, "is the investigation into the murder of Mr. Thomas Whitfield. Your name, more specifically, your cell phone number, has come up in the course of our investigations."

"The investigation of *what*?" Damon Mason sounded aghast.

"The murder of Thomas Whitfield," repeated Ferguson. When he got no response, he prodded: "You have seen the news reports that Thomas Whitfield has been murdered, haven't you?"

"Yes, of course," said Damon. "I'm just . . . anxious that my name has come up, I suppose."

"Obviously you knew Mr. Whitfield. There are a number of dialed and received calls between your cell phones. What was the nature of your relationship with Mr. Whitfield?"

"Well, it's hard to explain. I suppose I gave him career advice."

Ferguson glanced at Dinah with a skeptical look on his face. "With all due respect, Mr. Mason, why would the secretary of the Smithsonian need career advice? It would seem Mr. Whitfield had quite a secure position."

"Yes, that's certainly true," agreed Damon Mason. "I met Thomas some years ago while he was a university professor. I had some experience in the media and he was interested in lifting his public profile. I organized television appearances and that sort of thing for him. When he became secretary, he didn't really need me anymore, but we still kept in touch."

"Still asking for advice?"

"In a manner of speaking. Despite the fact that he was the secretary of the Smithsonian, Thomas wasn't really media savvy. Sometimes he'd ask advice about a press release or public appearance."

"Do you work for a public relations company or something?" Ferguson asked.

"No, I'm an independent consultant," said Mason.

Ferguson pursed his lips. "Are you shocked that Thomas Whitfield has been murdered?"

"Yes, of course!" said Mason, sounding outraged. "I can't imagine who would want to hurt him."

"Mr. Mason, we're going to want to speak with you in person," said Ferguson. "Are you located in DC?"

"Yes. I work from home."

"I'll give you another call shortly to organize a time to see you," said Ferguson. "It will probably be in the next day or so. Will you be around?"

"Yes, absolutely. If there is anything I can do to help you find whoever did this to Thomas, I'm glad to help."

Ferguson thanked him and hung up. He looked at Dinah, who was in pensive thought.

"What do you think?" he asked her.

"I think," said Dinah, standing up again, "that I hope either Andy Coleman or Damon Mason knows what happened to Whitfield."

The two agents returned to their desks. The administrative assistant handed Dinah a printed receipt. She had booked the agents on a flight to Cincinnati, leaving that afternoon at three o'clock.

Dinah called Andy Coleman's number. This time, he answered.

"Hi, it's Special Agent Dinah Harris again. We're flying down to see you this afternoon. We'll want to speak with you as soon as possible," explained Dinah. "I wanted to make sure you'd be around."

"Yes, of course I will," he said.

Dinah took his address and hung up. Ferguson was staring at the pile of paper and files stacked on his desk that made up the Whitfield case so far.

"What are you thinking?" Dinah asked.

Ferguson shrugged. "I'm just wondering how a media consultant, creation scientist, and a school shooting tragedy will solve Whitfield's murder." He paused and looked at his partner. "Because that's really all we have, isn't it? Does it make sense to you?"

"Not really," said Dinah.

\* \* \* \*

Mac was currently sitting in the back of a limousine, drinking a whiskey on the rocks, being driven to the airport. He was preoccupied, having seen the newscasts that had splashed the murder of Thomas Whitfield all over the country.

Mac was extraordinarily self-sufficient and composed, but this latest turn of events had nettled him. He'd been assured by Wolf that the body wouldn't be found, yet it had been. His instructions had been to make it look like an accident, yet when the wrecked car had been discovered by police, the body was in the trunk, of all places, thereby immediately ruling out the possibility of an accident. If he himself had been in charge of disposing of the body, he would have at least buckled the body into the front seat to create a more believable scene.

It was just like anything else, Mac thought, if you wanted to get something done right, you'd better just do it yourself.

He drained his glass and made a mental note to himself to take care of Wolf. He'd never intended for the goon-for-hire to outlive this operation, anyway. Wolf knew too much and that was the only excuse Mac needed to get rid of him.

Mac was, after all, in a distinguished, high-profile position; his face was well-known all over the country; and his reputation was as pure as new snow. He fully intended to keep it that way.

His cell phone chirped while Mac was considering another whiskey. "Yes?" he answered.

There was no mistaking the panicky tones. "It's Perry. The FBI is coming."

Mac waited a beat. "Suppose you start from the beginning," he suggested, not bothering to keep the contempt from his voice. "What exactly is the problem?"

"The FBI wants to speak with me. I've just finished speaking to them on the phone," said Perry. "They want to see me in person!"

"I see," said Mac. "I'm still not clear on what your problem is." He looked longingly at the whiskey bottle.

"The *FBI*, Mac. I'm scared to death. Do you think they know what happened?"

Mac had often over the years been irritated by people who flew into hysterics over the tiniest thing. "Perry, I have already spoken to the FBI," he said. "It's no big deal. Of course they're going to want to talk to you."

There was a beat of silence. "You've spoken with them already?" Perry asked. "What did you say?"

"That I was appalled, that I was saddened, that I would do anything to help find the person responsible," said Mac. "You know, the usual sort of thing people say when they find out someone they know has been murdered."

"Did you say anything about me?" There was a gasp as a new and horrible thought occurred to Perry. "Did *they* say anything about me?"

"Of course not. Despite what you seem to think, this whole debacle does not revolve around you."

"How can you be so calm?" Perry wailed. "I don't know what to say to them!"

Mac was thoroughly disgusted. "Stop being a princess," he snapped. "Tell them as much of the truth as you can. It'll actually sound believable. Got it?"

"Tell me what you said," begged Perry. "Where were you when they spoke to you?"

Mac tried to tamp down his temper. He took several deep breaths before replying, "The FBI demanded that the board of regents gather for a conference, which we did. They asked us if we knew anybody who might want to hurt Thomas Whitfield. They asked if we knew of any conflict in Thomas Whitfield's life. They asked about his history with the Smithsonian. In all honesty, they were very innocuous questions."

"Okay," said Perry, sounding as if he were trying to digest this. "Okay."

"Try to calm down and think about information that is of public record," advised Mac. "Or information that could easily be discovered. Do not lie about anything of this nature. If they find out you've lied once, they'll turn the spotlight onto you. Just try to be intelligent about it."

"Yes," said Perry. "Right. Okay. Intelligent."

Mac smiled slyly to himself as he inquired, "And you *do* have an alibi for the period in question, don't you?"

"What?" Perry sounded like he was on the verge of panic once again. "You didn't mention anything about an alibi. The FBI didn't ask *you* for an alibi, did they?"

"No, they didn't." Mac felt a delicious thrill of anticipation before he slid the metaphorical knife into Perry's ribs. "But then, I am who I am, and you are who you are, and I don't need an alibi." It was always satisfying, thought Mac, to remind certain individuals that there was a class system in operation in this country, and that he was many rungs higher on the class ladder.

There was silence on the other end of the line, and when Perry spoke again, he was calm. "You know, you might want to think about the fact that you need us as much as we need you."

Mac scowled. "What are you talking about?"

"I'd really hate to withdraw our support from you and put you in a tough situation." Perry's tone was sly and Mac hated it. He swallowed back several retorts, because much to his chagrin, Perry was right.

"Of course. I understand," Mac said smoothly. "I don't want to jeopardize our relationship."

"Then you better cut that 'I don't need an alibi' rubbish," Perry said harshly. "I may only be one person, but IAFSI is far bigger than all of us and it is under my control. You would do well to remember that."

"I think what we all need to do is remember each other during these proceedings," suggested Mac. "I'll make sure you are protected, and you make sure I am protected. What do you think?"

"That's precisely what I was thinking," said Perry, "but the trouble is, you weren't sounding so enthusiastic a few moments ago."

"My mistake," said Mac. "Don't worry, Perry. I know we need each other. I won't forget that."

"Good. Please keep me updated if the FBI contacts you again." It was an order, not a request, and it made Mac burn with anger. However, he kept his voice cool and calm.

"Of course. Anyway, must go." He hung up without waiting for a reply.

With hands shaking angrily, Mac poured himself another whiskey. Perhaps he needed to think more carefully about whether Perry was a liability. It was true that Mac needed IAFSI, and he had never been able to forget that fact. However, with or without Perry, IAFSI would continue to thrive. If Perry should happen to meet with an unfortunate accident, Mac's support would not be in danger of being cancelled. In fact, the only danger could possibly come from Perry remaining alive.

The man was clearly unused to dealing with these occasional, admittedly distasteful necessities and was in danger of falling apart. Any FBI agent worth his or her salt would dismantle Perry in about two seconds flat. The question was, would Perry then start singing about who else was involved in this operation?

*Almost certainly.*

Mac downed his drink and dialed another number.

"It's Mac," he said when his call was picked up. "I need to get in contact with Wolf."

\* \* \* \*

Dinah and Ferguson's flight to Cincinnati got in at about 6:30 that evening. Both agreed to eat dinner in the hotel's restaurant before questioning Andy Coleman. Dinah went up to her room to freshen up beforehand.

In the bathroom, she splashed water on her face and combed her hair. The dark circles underneath her eyes were now permanently etched into her complexion and her eyes were red. She was wearing a black pants suit that had fit perfectly a couple of years ago but now was baggy around her hips. She stared into her own eyes in the mirror for several moments and did not like what she saw there.

Ferguson was waiting for her in the restaurant dining room. He handed her a menu and announced, "I'm having the chicken-fried steak."

Dinah smiled. "Yeah, you look malnourished to me." She looked pointedly at her partner's torso, which was beginning to strain at the shirt he was wearing.

Ferguson just laughed amiably and sat back in his chair, waiting for her to choose. Dinah wasn't hungry — she was rarely hungry and only ate out of necessity — but she spent a lot of time looking at the wine list.

Ferguson noticed and watched her. Dinah felt him watching her, took one last, longing gaze at the bottle of Australian riesling, and went back to the real menu. Dinah closed her eyes briefly and imagined the cool, dulcet tones of the wine in her mouth.

"Would tonight be one of the first in a while where you would not have any alcohol?" inquired Ferguson suddenly.

*Here we go,* thought Dinah wearily.

"I don't know," she said. "I don't really keep track." She kept her tone light and airy, as if the subject was of little concern to her.

"I'm willing to bet that it is," Ferguson continued, much to Dinah's chagrin. "I think it's been a long time since you went to bed sober and had a good night's sleep."

Dinah spent a few moments hoping for a hotel fire or some other emergency that would get her out of here. "There's a difference," she remarked, "between someone who has a few drinks with dinner and someone who gets wasted every night."

"Is there? I'm not sure there is a difference — both exhibit an inability *not* to drink every night."

"I fail to see that this is any of your business," said Dinah coldly.

The waitress who appeared with their food noticed the tense atmosphere, put down the plates quickly, and left.

"It certainly is my business," said Ferguson. "You are my partner, in whose hands I place my life every day."

Dinah dropped her fork on her plate with a clatter, and the people around her looked over and stared. His words, like a poison-tipped arrow, had found their way directly to her heart. "Is that what this is about?" she asked quietly. "You're afraid I'll screw up again and get you hurt?"

Ferguson considered his next sentence very carefully. "No. To be frank, I'm worried more about you than me. You will get slaughtered in the media, quickly followed by the agency, if you so much as fail a breathalyzer test. You know that. You can see it happening as we speak. They follow you to take pictures of you buying more alcohol. Why do you keep flirting with danger?"

Dinah stared at him. "Do you have any idea," she asked, "what it's like to wake up every morning and wish that you hadn't?"

"No," said Ferguson truthfully. "But do you think alcohol is the answer?"

"I don't know, Einstein. Why don't you tell me what the answer is?"

"What about therapy? You could get medication," suggested Ferguson.

"I don't want therapy and I don't want medication," snapped Dinah. "The pain I feel reminds me that I'm alive and I shouldn't be."

"You think *punishing* yourself will help you?" Ferguson shook his head. "You. . . ."

"Excuse me, folks," the maître d' interrupted, wringing his hands and looking flustered. "Is everything okay here?"

"Yes. Sorry," said Ferguson, his eyes not leaving Dinah. "We'll keep it down."

The maître d' gave a strange little bow and hurried away. The two agents ate in silence, Dinah hoping that the subject was dropped, and Ferguson trying to figure out a way to bring the subject back up.

Finally Ferguson asked, "Please tell me that you haven't thought about doing anything stupid with your service pistol."

Dinah wasn't sure how to answer. The truth was, she had thought about it. In fact, she didn't know what was stopping her, except a strange feeling that the time was not yet right. How would she explain that?

"I'm not going to do anything stupid with my pistol," she replied.

Ferguson added, "Because no matter how bleak you think the future is, please remember that things will always get better. There are people who care about you."

Dinah pushed back her chair and stood, anger bubbling. "How would you know?" she demanded. "You have no idea what my life is like. You have no right to judge me or my actions. Just leave me alone!"

She threw her napkin down and left Ferguson sitting at the table, looking miserable. She was glad that the elevator was empty, and when it stopped several floors below her room and a happy-looking couple with their arms wrapped around each other tried to get on the elevator with her, she glared at them until they decided to wait for the next elevator.

In her room, she feverishly searched the mini-bar until she found the little bottle of Russian vodka. She tossed the contents down her throat, feeling the slow burn all the way to her stomach, and lay on the bed until the anger subsided.

When Ferguson rang her cell phone 15 minutes later to enquire whether she would accompany him to Andy Coleman's house, she was calm and composed.

And slightly drunk.

\*\*\*\*

Andy Coleman and his wife lived a little way out of the city, on a quiet, wooded property with a little pond at the front of the house. The two agents took a rental car out to the property. Ferguson glanced at his partner, probably wondering if she had consumed alcohol in her room. Dinah refused to look at him and stared out of the window until they arrived.

The Colemans were waiting for the two agents to arrive, standing on the porch under the light watching as the rental car drove slowly up the drive.

It was a mild night compared to the chill of DC, but the Colemans had lit the fire in the living room, and it was very warm as Andy Coleman ushered them toward a large couch. Andy was a tall, thin man with a shock of graying hair that looked always in need of a cut. He had dark, sharp eyes and several days' worth of stubble on his cheeks. He wore khaki chinos and a short-sleeved plaid shirt that was buttoned to his neck.

After the formal introductions had been made, Andy sank into an ancient armchair that creaked alarmingly. "You don't know how sorry I am to hear about Thomas Whitfield's death," he said. "It's a tragedy."

"Can you tell us about what you've been up to over the past few days?" said Dinah, ignoring the small talk that most other agents would use to put their interviewee's at ease.

Andy blinked at her abruptness, but replied, "Sure. I think I mentioned on the phone that I had been to Israel for the past two weeks. I've been lecturing to the Christian church in Jerusalem. While I was there I took the opportunity to trace the footsteps of Jesus and other biblical history."

"Yes," said Dinah, wanting to stay on the subject and not meander down the path of history. The effects of the alcohol and the warm room were making her feel uncomfortably hot, and she felt sure her face was bright red. "When did you get back from Israel?"

"This morning," said Andy. "I flew into Cincinnati at about six." As he finished speaking, his wife came into the room with mugs of steaming, hot coffee and plates of sweet cookies. She sat down with them at the table.

"Did you go to Israel, too?" asked Dinah.

"Yes, I did," said Sandra. She was noticeably shorter than her husband, pleasantly plump with short, curly blond hair and large blue eyes. She exuded a very motherly, capable air. Dinah could imagine her slapping away an over-eager hand reaching for the cookies as they came out of the oven. Sandra continued, "We left two weeks ago Monday and arrived back this morning, as I overheard Andy tell you."

Sandra spoke with a strong accent that Dinah couldn't place. The only indication that she'd been living in Cincinnati for a fairly long time was the way her *r*'s were softer and rounder.

Andy noticed her curiosity. "She's Australian," he said. He sneaked a glance at his wife. "I was down there a lot when I was younger. A friend of mine took me to the beach there — a glorious beach, white sand as far as the eye can see, the bluest water. Out of the waves came this beautiful blond girl with a surfboard. She was the coolest girl I'd ever seen. I was entranced."

Sandra shook her head and blushed. "I don't get out on the surfboard much anymore."

*Isn't that lovely,* the sarcastic commentator in Dinah's head remarked. *Now can we get back to the topic of murder?*

Ferguson seemed to sense Dinah's impatience, and he interjected smoothly, "Speaking of your life's work, Mr. Coleman, can you explain more of that for us?"

"I'm a creation scientist," Andy said. "What that basically means is that I believe that this earth, this universe, and everything in it — including you and I — were created by God. I believe that the account of how this happened, our origins, is clearly documented in the Book of Genesis, in the Bible. I believe the Bible is an accurate history book in addition to being the inspired Word of God, and, therefore, that the world is probably about six thousand years old. What I *don't* believe is evolution — that a group of molecules, over millions of years, evolved into many different life forms and has eventually led to humans inhabiting the earth. I don't believe that the universe is millions of years old and I don't believe the big-bang theory."

Dinah and Ferguson glanced at each other. "Right. So you fly in the face of all known scientific discovery and ignore all the evidence?" asked Dinah sarcastically.

Andy didn't take offense; in fact, he looked amused. "Not at all, Agent Harris. The evidence that evolutionists use and the evidence I use is exactly the same. I have evidence of fossils and dinosaur bones, just as they do. The difference is how these items of evidence are interpreted. You should also remember that the idea of evolution is just that — an idea, and one that hasn't been proven."

Dinah threw Andy some bait. "What about natural selection? Hasn't that been proven?"

Andy's eyes glimmered amusedly. "Ahh, the old classic raises its head again."

"Classic?"

"Creationists are constantly accused of rejecting natural selection. We do nothing of the sort. Natural selection happens in this world. Species die out because of weather changes, or predators, or other influences, while other species survive. That's part of natural selection and as such has only ever been observed within a kind, whether animal kinds or even plant kinds. Evolutionists believe natural selection is one of the driving forces that eventually establishes new and different kinds — for instance, dinosaurs evolving into birds. Natural selection is not capable of such a major change. And anyway, no one has ever observed such large changes to change one kind into a totally different kind. It's much more plausible to explain natural selection in terms of biblical history that tells us that God created each kind after its own kind. The implication here is that kinds remain stable, even though there can be great variety within each kind."

Dinah didn't feel like arguing. "Okay, so is this why you get death threats?"

Andy seemed quite blasé about it. "Yeah. I get death threats from people who don't think I should talk about God, the Bible, and science all in the same sentence. It normally amounts to people who do not want to answer to an authority other than themselves. Rejecting God's authority is what the Bible describes as 'sin.' I am a scientist who believes in God's authority because the evidence confirms it."

"And is this how you came into contact with Thomas Whitfield?" Ferguson asked.

"Yes," said Andy. "We were on opposite sides of the argument, and we came up against each other pretty regularly. As secretary of the Smithsonian, he was a staunch advocate of evolution and the big-bang theory." Andy smiled wryly. "And he had the good fortune to have mainstream society on his side. It's widely accepted that we evolved from apes, because that's what we're taught in schools and universities right across the country. That's in spite of the fact that evolution can't be proven and requires faith just like Christianity does. In that way, evolution is really a religious belief."

"So you and Thomas Whitfield were enemies then? On opposite sides of scientific thought?" Ferguson asked, wondering if he was on the right track. Could religious fundamentalism have led to Thomas Whitfield's death?

"Actually, no," said Andy. "We became very good friends because we ran into each other so much. Aside from the fact that we didn't agree with each other, we had a lot in common. We both had close families and pride in our children's endeavors. We spoke about our kids all the time. I might add that becoming friends with someone in his position is not normal. Many evolutionists and I are polite toward each other, but we aren't friends."

"So when was the first time you met Thomas Whitfield?" asked Ferguson.

Andy sat back in his creaking armchair. "Well," he mused. "I remember it pretty clearly."

## NEW YORK CITY, NEW YORK — 1998
## — THOMAS'S STORY

At 5:20 p.m. Andy Coleman found himself in the green room at NBC studios in New York City with a tiny and efficient woman brushing powder on his face while directing other assistants around the room with military precision. Andy didn't dare move his head in case he brought down the wrath of the makeup woman upon his head. He had caught a flight from Cincinnati early that morning and instead of feeling tired, he felt buzzed. In several moments he was due to face live television for one of the most controversial issues to grip the nation in years. His opponent in the debate would be the prominent anthropologist Thomas Whitfield. The two had built up fairly decent reputations in their own fields of interest, and this was bringing them into more frequent conflict.

While he was made to look presentable for the television audience, Andy prayed for eloquence and wisdom. He was deep in concentration and was startled when someone behind him tapped him on the shoulder.

"Hi, Andy, we meet again!"

Andy turned and found himself looking at the familiar features of Thomas Whitfield.

"Hi, Thomas," he replied. "Are you here about the MacLeod case, too?"

"Yeah. Looks like they enjoyed our last debate so much they've invited us back for another round," said Thomas. In his television makeup, his skin was too dark and his eyebrows and eyelashes almost looked blond.

A pretty blond production assistant poked her head around the door to the green room. "Let's go, guys!" she called.

Thomas and Andy stood and meekly followed the assistant to the set, where the host of the show sat with a helmet of sprayed silver hair and a distinguished expression. He shook hands with his guests, had makeup applied, and then it was time to go on the air.

"Welcome back to the show," he began in his impressive baritone. "We now move on to an issue which has gripped the country since earlier today, when the Supreme Court threw out the appeal of a teacher who had been removed from his high school biology classroom for teaching creationism or, as he calls it, 'intelligent design' in his classroom. To discuss both sides to the controversy, I have with me the renowned anthropologist Thomas Whitfield, and the president of the Genesis Legacy and creationist Andrew Coleman."

The television cameras panned to each of the guests, and both Andy and Thomas tried to appear both pleasant and knowledgeable.

There was the briefest of pauses, and then the host continued, "Professor Whitfield, I'll begin by asking you, are you happy with the outcome of the Supreme Court's decision?"

"Yes, I am," replied Thomas smoothly. "The Supreme Court has upheld one of the most fundamental elements of our Constitution — that of separation of church and state. The premise of the separation of church and state is that the government, represented in this instance by the government school, does *not* have the right to impose religion on the students of the school. Thus I believe that the ruling was absolutely correct."

"What is your reply, Mr. Coleman?" The anchor turned to look at Andy.

Andy had practiced what he was going to say on the plane. "I disagree with the decision because it was based on an incorrect assumption. The assumption, that Professor Whitfield has already mentioned, is that the courts believed Mr. MacLeod was forcing his religious beliefs on his students. Actually, he made no mention of the Bible, of God as Creator, or any other religious precept. He simply truthfully explained to his students that evolution has not yet been scientifically proven — which it hasn't — and encouraged his students to think critically about the evidence that clearly points to design."

"What do you say to the criticism that Mr. MacLeod was an outspoken Christian and that his intention, however subtle, *was* to indoctrinate his students?" the host asked.

"Everybody in this country has the freedom to choose his or her own religion, and to speak about his or her beliefs," said Andy. "In that regard, Mr. MacLeod was exercising his freedoms afforded by our Constitution. There has never been any question that Mr. MacLeod taught the curriculum of the biology course diligently and at no time taught alternatives to evolution nor spoke about his own personal views. I would like to make clear a fundamental point. If you teach evolution, you teach about a past event you cannot prove. The same is true if you teach about creation. Creationists refer to a book that claims to be an historical account of origins and consider the evidence in the light of that claim. Evolutionists claim that there is no accurate historical account and look at the evidence according to their own assumptions about the past. At the very least we should be presenting both views to students if we are interested in education. At the moment we are simply indoctrinating rather than educating children. We give our children no platform of education to allow them to decide upon. At the moment there is no freedom of choice in the classroom — students are taught only one concept, which is evolution."

"If that's true, Mr. Coleman," interjected Thomas, "if the teacher was in fact teaching all alternatives to evolution, then why didn't he speak about all of the other religious theories about how we all got here? Why didn't he also teach the Muslim and Hindu teachings about the beginning of life? That is truly religious freedom without bias. The truth is that he didn't, and the reason he didn't is because he is a Christian, and he wanted the students to learn about Christianity."

"Mr. Coleman, what relevance does Christianity even have in a high school biology class?" the anchor asked.

"I want to make it clear that when we talk about science in this regard, we need to differentiate between observable science and origins science. Observable science consists of theories that are testable in a laboratory setting in the present. Origins science is quite different because it happened in the past and it's unobservable and unrepeatable. What the teacher, Mr. MacLeod, was correctly pointing out was that evolution requires faith, just like any religion. To believe a creationist's version of events, we also require faith, but contrary to popular belief, it's not a blind faith. It's a faith that is confirmed on the basis of biblical historical accuracy being confirmed by evidence and scientific observation. Therefore, both points of view do deserve to be spoken about as legitimate theories on the origin of life in a high school science class, and Dr. Whitfield well knows that the Judeo-Christian account of origins is the only other account of origins with a historical record detailed enough to test on the basis of observational science."

"Mr. Coleman, am I correct in saying that you and your colleagues are proponents of an earth and human race created by God, and that the earth is only about six thousand years old?" The anchor tried, and failed, to keep an incredulous look off his face.

"That's correct," confirmed Andy. "Furthermore, I believe that everything on this planet was created by God, including plants and animals. I believe that there is astounding evidence in the complexity of life to prove the existence of a Designer. I simply cannot agree that the diversity of life on this planet was the result of random chance. Finally, I would like to add that the Bible states exactly what happened at the beginning of the world, and that nobody — modern science included — can disprove it. In fact, the evidence overwhelmingly confirms its historical accuracy."

Thomas made a noise of disgust. "That's what I'm talking about. These Christians would have you believe that the Bible is as valid as a science textbook in a classroom." He shook his head. "What I don't understand is why you can't be happy with teaching your Bible stories in religion class, and leave science out of it."

"Is the evolution model so weak that you would want to suppress any alternatives being taught?" demanded Andy. "That's what it looks like to me."

"Professor Whitfield, *is* evolution a scientific fact?" The anchor stepped in once more to take control of the discussion.

"Of course it is," replied Thomas. "The scientific community at large, which includes biologists, geologists, chemists, physicists, anthropologists, and so on, have accepted evolution based on sound scientific research. We have evidence of evolution with the presence of fossils, bones, footprints, skeletons, and other displays you might find in museums all around the world. Evolution is actually foundational to all other types of science! The simple fact is that evolution has eliminated the need for humans to believe in God altogether, and Christians simply don't want to believe it."

"You know as well as I do that none of those fossils or bones prove that evolution is correct," said Andy, staring straight at his counterpart. "It's how you interpret them that makes a difference. Those same items of evidence, considered in light of biblical history, also show that the earth is very young and that most fossilized remains found throughout the world could be explained by a single catastrophic disaster, namely a worldwide flood. This eliminates the need for millions of years, which is the backbone of the evolutionists' case for their theory. It simply doesn't work unless you add millions of years."

"By worldwide flood, Mr. Coleman is referring to the great Flood as told by the Book of Genesis in the Bible," said Thomas contemptuously.

"Gentlemen, although I get the feeling this discussion could run into many hours, we've run out of time. Could I have your final thoughts on this court case?"

"Separation of church and state," said Thomas quickly, "and therefore, church and education, is a fundamental precept of our Constitution. If you want your children to learn about religion, send them to church."

"Teachers should have the freedom to teach their students to think critically and expose the flaws in *any* concept posed to them during their education. Evolutionists have transformed our science education into evolutionary indoctrination. It is a *theory never proven and so not a fact,* despite what Professor Whitfield would have you believe." Andy wanted to say more but knew that he would be cut off by the host who was even now signaling for a commercial break.

The anchor thanked both of his guests and was immediately surrounded by powder brushes.

Andy and Thomas were whisked off set and found themselves together again in the green room. The viewing audience might not see any further debate, but both men knew that the argument wasn't over — not by a long shot.

\*\*\*\*

Neither of them spoke as their makeup was removed.

Finally Thomas said, "You know, I respect the passion with which you argue your case and the strength of your beliefs. But I do think you Christians are holding onto the past. Science has replaced the need for God now."

Andy digested this for a moment. "Then why," he asked, suddenly feeling enormously weary, "do you even care what I believe or how many people I tell? Why does it matter to you and your fellow atheists if I believe in God? There really is not one reason why you should even care. If we are all here because of random chance from a cosmic bang that happened in a vacuum, there really is no reason to care about anyone's belief. We live, we die, we get eaten by worms."

"I care because it's scientific discovery that pulled our ancestors from the misery of the Dark Ages and propelled us into enlightenment. I care because science has been able to lengthen life, improve the quality of life, and eliminate superstition. We live in a civilized society because of science." Thomas rubbed his temples. "I think it's time you faced facts. We live in a post-modern era, where human freedom and self-determination have become the new religion."

"Firstly, Thomas, much of the scientific discovery that pulled us out of the Dark Ages was from Christian men that believed the Bible. Take Isaac Newton, for example. Second, can't you see you've just replaced one religion with another?" countered Andy. "For if, as you say, I can't prove the existence of God, you certainly can't *disprove* the existence of God, either. You have never proven an alternative. Therefore, your willingness to believe or disbelieve in God comes down to one thing

— faith. And where there is faith, there is religion. As much as you will hate to admit it, Thomas, atheism and evolution *is* religion."

There was silence for a few moments. "Can I ask you a question?" Andy asked at length. "Because I am truly interested in the answer."

Thomas shrugged. "Okay."

"Why is it so offensive to you to even consider whether there is a Creator?" Andy took a bottle of water and took several sips.

Thomas answered, "I believe in advancement — not just scientific advancement but social advancement. That good ol' gospel religion suppresses mankind's freedom. To me, its oppressive and its fictional and you guys want it to be a part of mainstream education."

"True freedom can only be found in truth. Please remember that. You know, one of the first questions I am asked when I talk to the public is, 'If there is a God, why is there so much suffering in the world?' People correctly don't see a lot of good in this world. The difference between you and me, Thomas, is that I can offer them answers and hope based on authoritative truth. I know that you don't accept that truth, but I also know you have never really looked to see if it's authentic. You spend more time denying it. No truth, no hope."

"*Misguided* truth and *misguided* hope," muttered Thomas.

"Now we're just back where we started. Why would an atheist care? If there is no God, and I've got it all wrong, then why is it a problem to offer people hope and make their lives more meaningful, before we all turn to dust?"

Thomas glanced at his watch. "I guess I dislike people being deceived. And you know what? God or no God, it's a gamble I'm willing to take."

Andy grabbed his bag and stood. "That's a pretty big gamble, Thomas. A gamble with odds you don't understand and eternity at stake."

Thomas looked like he wanted to argue but instead said, "I've got a plane to catch. See you later, probably at the next debate, I would guess."

"I'll be there," promised Andy. He sat back down at the small dressing table and closed his eyes. *I can't do this on my own strength, Lord. Not my strength, but Yours.*

## CINCINNATI, OHIO — PRESENT DAY

By the time Andy Coleman had finished his story, it was well after midnight and Dinah was beginning to feel the effects of a long day. Both Colemans, who were still jet-lagged, looked even worse than she felt. The agents agreed to come back the next day to continue their discussions.

On the way back to the hotel, Ferguson asked, "Can you see Andy Coleman wanting to kill Thomas Whitfield?"

Dinah considered. "Ordinarily, I would say no. But when you add religion to the mix, who can say what people are capable of?"

"You think God ordered a hit on the irreverent atheist Thomas?"

"Perhaps, though I wouldn't have put it quite so crudely," said Dinah. She frowned as her cell phone suddenly burst into life. She glanced at her watch as she dug it out of her bag. "Who on earth would call at a quarter to two in the morning?" she muttered.

"Hello?"

For an instant, all Dinah heard was quick breathing, like the person on the other end had just finished a sprint. "Hello, is this Dinah Harris of the FBI?" a familiar female voice said.

"Yes, it is. Who is this?"

"It's Lara Southall."

Dinah gaped, then motioned at Ferguson to pull the car over. "Lara! Where are you? Are you okay?"

"I'm fine," said the girl. "But I don't want to say where I am." She paused. "I'm sorry it's so late."

"Don't worry about it, Lara," said Dinah. Ferguson had yanked the car onto the shoulder of the road and bunny-hopped it through a series of potholes. "What can I do for you?"

"I wanted to tell you what I know about Thomas Whitfield," said Lara. She sounded tired and sad. "I heard that you found his body."

"Yes, we did. He has been murdered."

Lara sighed. "I feel absolutely horrible that I did nothing that may have prevented it. I didn't talk to you because I was scared."

"I understand," said Dinah gently. "They got to you in a bad way."

"I don't know much, but I hope it'll help," said Lara. "I know that Mr. Whitfield and the board of regents were at each other's throats. I know that Thomas was under a lot of pressure."

Dinah glanced at Ferguson, who was watching the one-sided conversation intently.

"Do you know why they were at each other's throats?"

"No, I don't. I just know that they argued with him all the time, and several times Thomas told me that he sometimes thought they wanted him gone."

Dinah's ears pricked up. "Gone? As in dead?"

"No," said Lara, "I mean, as in no longer in that position. He thought they wanted him to resign. But he didn't want to resign. I also know that the board held quite a number of meetings without Mr. Whitfield there. I remember thinking that that was unusual. The only reason they should meet under normal circumstances would be to discuss the museum, and the secretary would be a part of that."

"Was there anyone in particular who argued with Thomas frequently?"

Lara thought for a moment. "I remember Justice Maxwell Pryor was usually the spokesman for the board. So he would have been the one communicating to Mr. Whitfield the most."

"And you don't know what any of the arguments were about?"

"No, I don't. I just know that the arguments were getting progressively longer and more heated, and they occurred more often, too."

"Did you observe any threatening or abusive behavior toward Thomas from Justice Pryor or any other board members?"

"Not directly. I believe any argument was over the phone. Mr. Whitfield would come out of his office looking anxious, so that's when I knew he'd had an argument. Since I was the one who patched the call through to him, I knew who the caller was who'd upset him. It was always Justice Pryor. That's pretty much all I know. I wanted to tell you because straight after I'd reported Mr. Whitfield missing, Justice Pryor rang me directly to warn me to tell the police — or you guys — that there were no problems between the board and Mr. Whitfield. I asked him why, and he said it was because it would waste the police's time in investigating a harmless difference of opinion instead of looking for the real culprit."

Dinah raised her eyebrows at Ferguson, hoping to convey her excitement at the information Lara was telling her.

"You've done very well," she said. "That's all extremely helpful. Are you up to talking about what happened to *you*?"

Lara sighed again. "Unfortunately, I can't really remember," she said. "The doctor told me that's not unusual with a head injury like mine. I remember taking a shower that night, right before I went to bed. I go to the gym after work and I don't like going to bed all sweaty and gross. The next thing I know I wake up in the hospital feeling like I'd been hit by a bus." She paused. "But I did get a phone call when I got home from the hospital."

"From who?" Dinah asked.

"I don't know," confessed Lara. "It was a male voice, and I didn't recognize it. He basically told me not to talk to the FBI anymore. He said that if I did, the next time I would be killed." Lara stopped speaking for a moment as her voice caught. "So I obeyed him. But when I heard that Mr. Whitfield had been murdered, I wanted to speak to you one last time."

"Thanks, Lara, you have been incredibly helpful," said Dinah. "And I know that it can't have been easy for you. Do you feel safe where you are at the moment?"

"I do," said Lara hesitantly. "But I'm going to keep moving around until I hear that you've caught whoever did this."

"We'll find them," promised Dinah. "I won't rest until we find them." She hung up and turned to Ferguson, who was practically tearing his hair out wanting to know about the conversation.

"That was Lara," said Dinah. "She came through for us. And we've caught the board of regents in a *big* lie."

\* \* \* \*

The two agents managed to snatch four hours of sleep before meeting each other in the hotel's restaurant for breakfast. Dinah was momentarily shocked to see how old Ferguson was getting — his skin seemed more sallow in the morning and the dark patches under his eyes more pronounced. Judging by his reaction to *her*, though, she supposed she didn't look much better.

Because Ferguson was watching her, Dinah forced down some scrambled eggs and toast, although the last thing she felt like was food. Ferguson heaped his plate with bacon, sausage, hash browns, and fried eggs.

"It's amazing that your heart can find the strength to keep beating," Dinah remarked. "If it were me, I'd have given up a long time ago."

Ferguson was too busy inhaling his food to reply. As Dinah sat back with her coffee, her cell phone buzzed.

"Hello?"

"Dude, it's Zach from the lab," came a cheerful voice.

"Hi, Zach," Dinah said. "What's going on?"

"I found some further information that might interest you," said Zach. "I've just analyzed the dirt found on the victim's body that the medical examiner sent over."

"Oh, right. What did you find?"

"Calcium carbonate!" said Zach excitedly.

"Though I appreciate your excitement," said Dinah dryly, "I have no idea what that means."

"It means that I found a large amount of trace within the dirt that is chalk dust," said Zach. "Now, the dirt is common to the area. I know that because dirt itself has characteristics such as volcanic activity, the level of minerals in the soil and the like identify it as belonging to a certain geographical area. The addition of calcium carbonate, or chalk dust, is not a natural occurrence unless there is a limestone deposit nearby. We don't have limestone quarries or deposits anywhere near Washington, so my conclusion is that the chalk dust came to be in the soil by human intervention."

"Okay, I'm with you," said Dinah.

"So then I started to wonder — where would a person get chalk dust and carry it around on themselves apparently without even realizing? And also how would that person transfer relatively large quantities of it into the soil?"

"A school teacher?" suggested Dinah. "We've already talked about that. It doesn't explain how it gets into the soil."

"Right. So I did a bit of research. Guess what I found?"

"Don't keep me in suspense, Zach," said Dinah, rolling her eyes.

"I found a factory on the outskirts of the west side of DC that manufactures chalk," said Zach. "Isn't that interesting? Now, if soil samples taken from the body of the victim match the soil samples of a very particular area of the city, then I would say you would find the murder scene pretty quickly. Furthermore, since we keep finding calcium carbonate on items which the attacker has touched on associated crime scenes, then I would say that at least one of those attackers spends a good deal of time in or around one of those chalk manufacturers."

Dinah felt another thrill ripple up her spine. "Have I ever told you how special you are?"

"You haven't," said Zach, laughing. "My mother tells me all the time. But wait, there's more!"

"An extra three types of cheese?"

"I may have done a little snooping on these chalk manufacturers — there are two of them, by the way," Zach went on. "I was curious about who owned them, for example."

Dinah went very still. "And?"

"Well, I think this name will be familiar to you. Both of them are owned by one Mr. Kenneth MacIntyre, president of the Seismic Corporation."

Dinah racked her brains. The name was familiar, but where had she heard it? Then she had a light bulb moment. "The board! Ken MacIntyre is on the board of regents of the Smithsonian!"

"Top marks, Special Agent," said Zach.

Dinah's mind had gone into overdrive. "Is there anything else you want to share?"

"Nope, that's it. That's enough, isn't it?"

Dinah hung up and grabbed Ferguson's wrist with excitement.

"What?" he asked, around what looked like an entire sausage stuffed into his mouth.

Dinah explained the situation. "We have to get back to DC to talk to this MacIntyre guy, and also Justice Pryor. There is something bad going down here."

"What about the Colemans?" Ferguson asked. "We're not done with them yet."

Dinah didn't reply but dialed the Colemans' number on her cell phone. When Andy Coleman answered, she said without preamble, "This is Special Agent Harris from the FBI. We have several urgent leads in Washington that we need to follow up and will be returning there today. I need you to come with us."

There was an infinitesimal pause. "Okay. I want to help in whatever way I can."

Dinah hung up and burst into action, with a flurry of calls to the airline, packing her things, and calling for a cab.

Poor Ferguson didn't even get a chance to finish his breakfast.

Dinah and Ferguson barely had a chance to drop their overnight bags at the office before heading out again. Ferguson spent the whole trip whining about his empty stomach, and that it was well past lunchtime. They were headed to the chalk factories that Zach had pointed them toward, and Dinah had a buzz of anticipation that couldn't be dampened by Ferguson's grumbling.

Outside, it was crisp and clear and cold, with not a cloud in the bright blue sky. The winter sky on sunny days always looked like someone had taken a giant brush and scrubbed the vast surface, Dinah thought, leaving it squeaky clean.

"We're here," announced Ferguson, breaking into Dinah's reverie. In front of them, two identical gray industrial buildings rose into the sky like monoliths. Both were taped off by yellow crime scene tape, indicating that the crime scene technicians that Zach had organized were already there.

## Chapter 11

The agents ducked under the tape and entered the first building gingerly. They knew how important it was not to contaminate the scene with their own bodies, and they didn't know as yet where the valuable evidence might be found. So they stood just inside the door until Zach spotted them and jogged over, still wearing his plastic protective clothing. He shook their hands. Today his eyebrow ring, nose ring, and lip ring were all in the shape of tiny barbells and he had notches carved into his eyebrows as was the current trend.

For all his piercings, tattoos, and multitudes of lady friends, Dinah had once seen tears slipping silently down his cheeks as he worked at the murder scene of a young teenage girl.

"What's up?" Zach greeted them.

"How long have you guys been here?" asked Dinah. Zach gave them both latex gloves and plastic booties to cover their shoes.

"About an hour and a half," replied Zach, waiting for Dinah and Ferguson to get ready. He spoke somberly, morphing into his serious professional persona. "We've found some interesting things. We've done most of the inside, but haven't started on the outside of the building yet."

"Have you found anything new that we should know about?" Ferguson asked.

"At this stage, nothing new," said Zach. "What we've found more or less confirms some of the assumptions we've made to date."

He started walking, and the agents followed. The front of the warehouse was an enormous, cavernous room where most of the heavy work was done. Zach perfunctorily explained what happened in this room — the limestone quarried would be transported here, and then pulverized, first through large machines with gaping jaws, then through smaller machines that reduced the limestone to pebbles. The limestone pebbles were washed to eliminate impurities, then a process called wet grinding, carried out in rotating steel drums, crushed the limestone until it was a very fine powder. The powder would then be washed and dried, ready for shipping.

"We didn't find anything useful in this part of the building," said Zach. "We found a lot of chalk dust, many shoe prints, and thousands of fingerprints." He grinned. "A sheer cacophony of evidence is how we term it in the lab."

Ferguson nudged Dinah. "A sheer what?" he whispered.

Dinah glanced at Zach, who had overheard and rolled his eyes. "It means there is so much evidence that it is useless," he explained.

"Sorry about that," Dinah said. "My partner here left high school in the tenth grade, and sometimes it shows."

"Hey, I'll have you know I went to college and. . ." began Ferguson indignantly.

"*Joking*, Ferguson," said Dinah, shaking her head.

They arrived at a series of offices behind the main hall, some of which were double size and used as storerooms.

"The offices are used by the administration staff and the foreman," said Zach. "The storerooms are used — well, to store things, obviously. Nothing of interest in the offices, but take a look here." He opened the door to a large storeroom that had crates stacked against the walls but was empty in the middle. The concrete floor was coated in chalk dust.

"There was nothing obvious here," said Zach, "but when we sprayed luminal, the floor lit up like a Christmas tree." He pointed to the middle of the floor. "There was also some blood spatter on the walls. I know that the victim in question was strangled, but there was evidence here of quite a severe beating. I can say that because the pattern of blood is star-shaped, which indicates drops of blood falling with a degree of force. There was no pooling of blood."

He faced Ferguson. "For example, if I punched Ferguson in the mouth and split his lip" — Zach mimed the punch — "the blood would continue in the direction of the punch. It would eventually fall to the floor in an elongated drop, as if the blood was trying to continue its journey. If I stabbed Ferguson, the blood flow would be immediately downward, in pools, due to the large quantity of it. Does that make sense?"

The two agents nodded.

"Also, we found a tooth under one of the crates," added Zach. "If I remember correctly, the victim's autopsy showed that he had lost a tooth recently. So I'm pretty certain that when we get the blood and tooth back to the lab, we'll be able to confirm that it belongs to your victim."

"So this is the murder scene," said Dinah, looking around the drab concrete room.

"There is certainly evidence to indicate that the victim suffered a beating in this room," agreed Zach, "and although I couldn't say this is 100 percent accurate, I would guess he was strangled here too. I say that because there was a great deal of chalk dust found on his body, particularly where he had bled around the head. If you can imagine the victim being beaten, then strangled and then dropped to the floor. Chalk dust will immediately adhere to the drying blood on the facial injuries. That's exactly where we found chalk dust on the victim."

"Zach!" shouted a voice from the back of the property. "We found something outside!"

The three of them quickly made their way into the bracing cold, into the small plot of earth at the back of the building. Three crime scene technicians, blinding in their white plastic coveralls, were gathered in a tight bunch.

"What is it?" Zach asked.

One of the technicians, a middle-aged woman, said, "We found a stain on the dirt that looked like blood, and the testing confirmed that it was blood. We also found a perfect shoe print over here. And we found what looks like human hair, short in length." Dinah could see that the three separate items of evidence were isolated from each other with string and measured with rulers lying lengthwise. Another of the technicians was photographing each item individually.

"So perhaps the victim was then dumped out here," theorized Zach. "He may have lain here for a while as they cleaned up inside or decided what to do next."

"That would explain why there was little insect activity," added Dinah excitedly. "Even though he lay outdoors, it's too cold for insects at the moment, particularly at night. It may have even slowed down decomposition."

Zach nodded and flicked the stud in his tongue. "Listen, I'll send this back to the lab to confirm the blood, hair, and tooth."

"In the meantime," Ferguson said, looking at Dinah, "I think it's time we had a little chat with one Mr. Kenneth MacIntyre."

\*\*\*\*

Kenneth MacIntyre worked in a large glass and steel structure in downtown DC. His company, Seismic Corporation, occupied the whole building. The agents were surprised to find that it was not an open building. The front doors were locked and manned by two security guards, whose job apparently was to screen guests.

Dinah flipped open her badge. "Special Agent Harris, FBI," she said. "We would like to see Mr. MacIntyre."

"Do you have an appointment, ma'am?" one of the guards asked, which instantly annoyed Dinah.

"No. What happens with the FBI is that we turn up to interview people. Sometimes they know we're coming, sometimes they don't. Whether you like it or not, we're going to see Mr. MacIntyre in about ten seconds."

The guard stared at her. "Mr. MacIntyre might not be available."

Dinah sighed and turned to the other guard. "Sir, you may wish to telephone whoever is in charge and tell them that your friend here has been arrested." She reached for her cuffs.

"What?" exclaimed the first guard. "Just give me a minute, and I'll call up to Mr. MacIntyre's office."

Ferguson just shook his head in bemusement.

A few moments later, the agents rode the elevator to the top floor, where Kenneth MacIntyre occupied the whole floor. As soon as they stepped off into a large atrium, his secretary looked up, visibly shaken.

"Excuse me," she said, standing up. "You shouldn't be here. There is no appointment in the diary. How did you get in?"

Both agents continued to bear down on her, showing her their badges. "We're with the FBI, ma'am," said Ferguson, trying to be a little gentler with her than Dinah had been with the guards.

"No, this isn't in his schedule," said the secretary, wringing her hands. "This will ruin his entire day! You really shouldn't be here. Oh dear." She stared at the phone on her desk, obviously wondering whether to invite the wrath of her boss by announcing his unexpected visitors.

She was saved by a large wooden door swinging open behind her, and a short man entering the atrium.

"It's okay, Cheryl," he said. "They're FBI agents. Could you organize coffee and pastry? Please make sure we are not interrupted."

"Yes. Right. Certainly." Cheryl still looked confused and upset at this unexpected turn of events.

Kenneth MacIntyre ushered the agents into his office. Dinah and Ferguson sat on two trendy, egg-shaped visitors chairs while MacIntyre sat behind his massive mahogany desk. His office was huge, and in addition to the desk and chairs, contained two Chesterfield couches and a wing chair in reddish brown leather, a wall of built-in bookcases, a marble-topped bar that looked fully stocked, and a treadmill. Behind MacIntyre, ceiling-to-floor tinted glass afforded him an impressive view of the city, White House, Capitol building, and beyond.

Dinah studied the rather inauspicious man. He was short, probably only about 5'5", with black hair combed straight back from his forehead and held in place with a greasy sort of gel, and eyes that were almost black. Everything about him screamed money — he was wearing an expensive-looking wool suit, Italian leather shoes, diamond cuff links, and a Rolex.

"Well," he said, clearly starting to squirm a little under Dinah's scrutiny. "I must say, you are welcome to call ahead before you come down to see me."

"Yes," said Dinah, "but we like to surprise. So what is it your company does, Mr. MacIntyre?"

Kenneth cleared his throat while he adjusted to the line of questioning. "Well, in a nutshell, we search and drill for new oil and gas sites using seismic technology," he said. As he spoke, he flicked a heavy gold pen between his fingers incessantly. "It is often sensitive work. As you would be aware, any new oil field could potentially be controversial and spark an international incident, so we have to be careful. That's why the building is locked and guarded."

"I see. And what about your sideline business interests?"

Kenneth MacIntyre looked puzzled. "What do you mean?"

"We know that this company is not the only thing you own, Mr. MacIntyre," said Dinah.

MacIntyre smiled and stepped up the speed at which he flicked the pen between his hands. "I own in excess of 15 properties and businesses in the DC area alone," he said, with what Dinah could have sworn was a smirk. "So was there a particular one you wanted to discuss?"

Dinah *loathed* being patronized. "Your chalk factories," she said shortly. "We want to talk about those."

"Okay," agreed MacIntyre, unperturbed. He leaned back in his chair, trying to affect a relaxed air. "What about them?"

Dinah studied him closely as she said, "Have you been out there recently?"

MacIntyre thought for a moment. "No. I have managers who run them. I really only go out there if there is a problem."

"Then nobody has informed you about the most recent problem?"

"No, what problem?" MacIntyre truly looked mystified.

"When was the last time you saw Thomas Whitfield?" Ferguson took over.

The sudden change in topic caused MacIntyre to pause for a few moments while he changed gears.

"I haven't seen him since the last board meeting, which was in September," he said. Perhaps the reality of having two FBI agents in his office, both of whom were starting to be distinctly unfriendly, was starting to dawn on him. He backed his chair away from them, put his pen down, and interlaced his fingers so tightly his knuckles became white.

"What happened at the board meeting?" Ferguson pressed. "Any arguments?"

"No, our board meetings are always very civilized," replied MacIntyre.

"What do you usually talk about?"

"Usually just the program of the museum over the coming season," said MacIntyre. "You know, what displays we're going to have and so forth. We talk about the budget. We talk about any issues that may have cropped up. It's just your run-of-the-mill board meeting."

"So you are telling me that there were no arguments or disagreements of any kind either at the board meeting or since?"

"That's correct."

"Do you know why we found human blood at your chalk factory?" Dinah interjected.

This clearly rattled MacIntyre. "You found *what*?"

"Human blood and a human tooth, at your factory," said Dinah. "While you're thinking about it, perhaps you could also tell us why we found chalk dust from *your* factory on the body of Thomas Whitfield?"

MacIntyre rolled his chair even farther back, looking aghast. "I have absolutely no idea what you're talking about!"

"Here's what I'm talking about," said Dinah, leaning closer to MacIntyre. "I'm talking about the fact that Thomas Whitfield was murdered at your factory. I know that because your chalk dust was found on Whitfield's body and his blood was found at your factory."

"And *I'm* talking about the fact that despite you claiming not to have argued with Thomas Whitfield before he disappeared, I know that you did," added Ferguson. "I know that the board as a whole was very unhappy with Thomas Whitfield. So my question to you is this: what did he do to wind up beaten and murdered in your warehouse, Mr. MacIntyre?"

MacIntyre stared at the two agents in horror. Then he swallowed, and both agents heard his dry throat click. "I think I would like to speak to my lawyer," he said finally.

Ferguson shook his head. "You should know this, Mr. MacIntyre. I don't care who you are or how many properties you own or even if you lunch with the president every week. I know that Thomas Whitfield died on your property and that you had something to do with it. You can talk to your lawyer any time you want, but you're gonna go down, and we both know it."

There was heavy silence in the room as MacIntyre processed that. He seemed, to Dinah's watchful eye, to be having a monumental struggle within himself to keep his emotions under control. It was at this precise time that Cheryl chose to enter with a tray of coffee and pastry. "Coffee!" she announced brightly.

MacIntyre stood, not taking his eyes away from Dinah and Ferguson. "My attorney will be contacting you," he said tightly. "In the future, you will direct any questions through him. You will not speak to me in person again. Please get off my property immediately."

Cheryl's mouth dropped open in astonishment. Ferguson sighed and shook his head as he rose from the chair. Dinah kept her eyes on MacIntyre as they backed out of the room. MacIntyre's face was alive with muscle tics, but his body was as still as a stone.

"You know what bothers me the most?" Ferguson commented as they took the elevator down. "Their stories are all exactly the same, like a bunch of well-trained robots. It's like *A Brave New World* or something."

"It may be new," muttered Dinah. "But it's certainly not brave."

\* \* \* \*

Ferguson clambered behind the wheel of the car, sucking in his ample girth to fit into the seat. "Back to the office?" he asked. "We need to check that the Colemans have arrived."

"Okay," agreed Dinah. She tapped her fingers on her pants leg and then added, "I've been thinking about Lara all day. While you drive, I'm going to check up on her."

While Ferguson pulled out into traffic, she scrolled through her call register and dialed the cell phone number that Lara had called her from in the middle of the night. It rang a few times, and then a male voice answered, "Who is this?"

Dinah frowned. "Who is *this*?" she demanded.

"This is the police. Please tell me your name and relationship to Lara Southall immediately," the authoritative voice said.

Dinah gasped. "Lara! Is she okay? What happened?" She looked wildly at Ferguson and then remembered. "Sorry. This is Special Agent Dinah Harris of the FBI. Lara Southall is one of our witnesses. What on earth has happened? Where is she?"

"I can't speak to you over the phone, ma'am. I suggest you come to her condo as soon as you can." He hung up.

"Oh no!" groaned Dinah. "Lara went back to her condo. There are police there."

Ferguson understood and changed the direction of the car. "Is she okay?"

"I don't know." Dinah felt sick. She drummed her fingers on her leg and wondered why Ferguson was driving so slowly.

Once again, the condo at Forrest Hills was surrounded by DC police and yellow tape. Red and blue lights flickered across the stucco walls.

Dinah found the captain in charge standing on the front lawn of the building, talking to a bunch of frightened occupants. She flashed her badge at him and he moved away with her. His badge said his name was Rocky Dubois.

"What's going on?" Dinah asked, frantic at the activity.

"I'm sorry, Agent Harris. She didn't make it," Dubois told her.

"She didn't *make* it?" Dinah was overwhelmed. "What happened to her?"

"The building super got a complaint that there was water dripping from Lara's apartment through the ceiling to the one directly underneath. He knocked and didn't get an answer, but he could hear water running inside. He used his master key to get in and found her in the bathtub." Rocky Dubois pointed over to the super, a man Dinah had already met.

"And?"

"She'd been dead for some time. Her throat had been cut and she was lying in a bathtub full of water, both faucets still running."

Dinah was horrified. "What have you discovered so far?" she asked.

"The front door has obviously been manipulated," Dubois said. "Both locks bear some significant damage. There was no sign of robbery or assault. We have crime scene people in there at the moment trying to lift some evidence."

"There won't be any," muttered Dinah.

Dubois eyed her curiously. "I assume this is somehow tied into the Thomas Whitfield murder."

Dinah sighed. "She was a witness. In fact, she was beaten badly recently due to the fact that she spoke to us. Can we go in to see her?"

Dubois shrugged. "Be my guest."

Dinah and Ferguson took the elevator up to Lara's apartment in silence. Dinah could feel the elation she'd experienced over the past few days with the breaks in the case start to crumble away.

The apartment looked much the same as the last time the agents had been there. Dinah studied the locks on the front door for a few moments. Last time, they'd been picked very carefully with a minimum of noise, to ensure that the occupants of both the building and the apartment wouldn't hear anything. This time, Dinah felt that the locks had been almost wrenched free from the door with great emotion. Perhaps Lara's killer had been enraged with her decision to talk to the FBI, particularly after being explicitly warned.

The bathroom contained several crime scene technicians, going through the room carefully and slowly, looking for evidence that might lead to the identity of Lara's killer.

The body of the young woman was obscured by the shroud the crime scene workers used to give the victim some dignity. Dinah could see the water in the bathtub, however, and could see that it was heavily stained with blood. The floor was soaked and squished underfoot as the technicians moved slowly around the room.

Dinah was saddened by the latest development. Lara had been murdered because she chose to tell the truth. Ferguson, too, was very quiet.

"We're going to the Smithsonian," said Dinah, her voice tight with anger. "I'm fed up with the lies. Those lies" — she pointed to the shrouded body of Lara Southall — "have led to the death of this young woman and that is completely unacceptable to me."

Ferguson didn't need to be told twice.

\*\*\*\*

The rage was all-consuming. Dinah's entire body was moved by it, as if she were an amplifier at a rock concert. Ferguson glanced at her as they climbed back into the car.

"Do you want to take a moment before we go back to the museum?" he asked.

"No," said Dinah, keeping her voice calm with a great deal of effort. "I'm fine."

Ferguson complied and turned the car toward the Smithsonian Institution. The sun was low in the sky, sinking fast as if it were ashamed to show its face over such a world where young women met their death alone at the hands of another.

The institution was rapidly emptying of people as the agents arrived. Dinah wasn't in the mood for niceties and strode straight past Catherine Biscelli's secretary and threw open the door.

Catherine Biscelli looked up, startled. When she saw Dinah standing in the doorway, her face turned cold. "To what do I owe this *pleasure*?" she asked. She didn't look at her visitors but continued to type on her computer.

Dinah felt freshly enraged with the other woman's indifference. She yanked out the power cord from the back of the screen and the screen fell dark.

"*Excuse* me," snapped Catherine, getting to her feet. "What do you think you're doing?"

Dinah glared at her. "I'm investigating a murder," she said. "Except now it's not just Thomas Whitfield. Another of your colleagues has been found dead."

Catherine froze. "Who?" she whispered.

"This may come as a surprise to you, but I think you know exactly who it is." Dinah watched Catherine Biscelli's face carefully. "And I wonder if you have another person's blood on your hands."

Catherine sank into the desk chair. "I can assure you," she said quietly, "that I did not have anything to do with the murder of this person, whose identity I don't even know."

Dinah shook her head and leaned over the desk. "The problem is that I know you are lying. You've been lying to me all along and frankly, I'm sick of it."

Catherine shook her head. "I haven't, I swear! I. . . ."

"Then you'd better explain to me why an independent witness has confessed that there was a great deal of friction between the board and Thomas Whitfield, and yet you insisted to me on several occasions that there was no such tension." Dinah spoke in an even tone. "And you'd better think about your answer. Because if you lie to me again, I *will* arrest you for obstruction."

Catherine gaped at her, lost for words.

"Do you attend the meetings between Thomas Whitfield and the board?" asked Dinah.

"Yes, of course I do," agreed Catherine.

"What is normally discussed at such meetings?"

"Well . . . just general business," Catherine said. "Any day-to-day operations issues, presentations, and displays planned for the museums, Mr. Whitfield's schedule."

"And why would any of that create friction that we've been told about?" Dinah demanded. "There must have been at least one contentious issue."

Catherine sighed. "There wasn't any friction at the meetings," she repeated.

"Fine," snapped Dinah. "You've left me with no choice. I am now going to read you your rights. You have the right to. . . ."

As she spoke, she pulled the plastic cuffs from her belt, approached the diminutive woman, and pulled both hands behind Catherine's back.

"Wait," interrupted Catherine. Dinah let go of her hands and waited, still standing in close proximity. Catherine paused, appearing to compose herself.

Under Dinah's gaze, she added, "Look, the only thing I do know about is some e-mails."

Dinah nodded, encouragingly.

"I know that Mr. Whitfield received some e-mails that upset him a great deal," Catherine explained.

"How do you know that?"

"I came into his office to prepare for an upcoming press conference," Catherine explained. She stared down at her desk. "When he looked up at me from his computer, he had tears in his eyes. Of course I asked him what was wrong."

She paused, and Dinah resisted the urge the shake the next tidbit of information from her.

"He asked me whether I'd ever gotten an e-mail that had questioned my integrity," Catherine continued at length. "I told him that I hadn't, but that if he was receiving slanderous e-mails from members of the public he should inform me and that I could release something to the press denying it. I remember he just looked at me for a long time and then finally said that the e-mails weren't from members of the public, but from within the Smithsonian."

"Did he say from whom?" asked Dinah, thinking about the computer hard drive that was with the Homeland Security lab in an attempt to have its contents restored.

"No, he didn't. I suppose I was trying to drag the information out of him without asking him outright. I did suggest that we could look at taking disciplinary action against a staff member if that was who was hassling him. He just laughed and said that wouldn't work."

"Did he say why it wouldn't work?"

"No."

"What do you think that meant?" Dinah pressed.

"At the time, I thought he meant that whomever had sent the e-mail was too powerful for disciplinary action." Catherine stared at her hands.

"Why did you not tell me this when we first spoke to you?" Dinah asked. "You don't know how important this might be."

Catherine flushed. "I didn't think it was relevant. It was just an e-mail."

"I'll decide what's relevant and what's not," said Dinah frostily. "That's my job, and that's why *I* ask the questions." She paused, deep in thought for a few moments.

"So you never discovered the identity of the writer of that e-mail?" she asked.

"No."

"And you have no idea of the specific content of the e-mail?"

"Other than what Mr. Whitfield told me, no."

"So as far as you know, someone questioned Thomas Whitfield's integrity, which upset him. The only other thing you know is that Thomas Whitfield believed the writer of the e-mail to be above any disciplinary action of any kind."

"Right."

"Did you ever suspect anybody of having written the e-mail? A board member, for example?" questioned Dinah.

"No. It's not really my place. If Mr. Whitfield had needed my help, he would've asked for it."

*Unless he believed you had something to do with the e-mail,* Dinah thought as she stared at the other woman.

Although Catherine had finally started to talk, Dinah couldn't shake the feeling that the head of public affairs was still holding back important information. There was something about her story that didn't ring true. Why would she bother to hide an e-mail — rather bland in the context — if she truly wanted to help Thomas Whitfield? It just didn't make sense.

"Can you tell me who has been murdered?" Catherine asked. She looked a little pale.

"Lara Southall." Dinah continued to watch the other woman carefully.

Catherine seemed to turn even whiter and turned away. "That's awful," she murmured.

"Yes, it is," agreed Dinah. "And what would be worse is more people dying before I get the truth out of you."

"Well, I told you all I know," said Catherine somewhat testily.

"I certainly hope so, for your sake," said Dinah. "The other thing I need from you is Maxwell Pryor's contact details."

Catherine opened her mouth to object but Dinah shook her head. "Don't," she warned. "Just give them to me."

Catherine Biscelli's entire face darkened but she complied.

"Thank you," said Dinah, keeping the sarcasm out of her voice with superhuman effort. "I'm sure we'll be in touch again."

Dinah and Ferguson let themselves out.

Ferguson shook his head as they walked back to the car. "That woman can't help but lie," he commented. "I'm willing to bet my next meal that she gave a snippet of truth to satisfy you, but that the real truth is still out there."

"You're willing to bet your next meal?" Dinah said in mock wonder. "That's a pretty big bet, Ferguson. Can you afford to lose?"

The two agents were exhausted and agreed to call it a night. When Dinah arrived home, her apartment was dark and cold and supremely uninviting. Without turning any lights on, she poured herself a glass of wine and sat in the living room. She was bone weary and yet a restless energy coursed through her veins. She felt like she was in some doctor's office waiting in anticipation of a painful procedure. She couldn't sit still; she wanted to leave but knew she couldn't; she couldn't concentrate on anything except what was coming. Yet she couldn't identify exactly what it was she was waiting for. Was it the end, perhaps?

She drank a second glass as she sat in the dark room. In a fit of sudden resolve, she knelt beside a storage box and opened it.

It was her — *their* — music. Their lives had revolved around music. They met in a tiny, smoky club where an unknown garage band had been belting out something that was truly awful. Dinah had endured the first three songs, then stumbled out the door. Luke had been right behind her.

"Did you find that as insufferable as I did?" he'd asked her with a winning smile.

"You didn't like it?" Dinah had replied, dryly. "I thought their first song, "Roadkill," was sensitive and poignant. And "I'm Gonna Punch You" was a particularly thought-provoking social commentary."

He laughed, they clicked, and they went down the road for coffee.

Now on her third glass of wine, she pulled out each CD and experienced a flood of memories with each. There was *Throwing Copper*, the live CD they'd played incessantly when they first met. Luke would roll down the windows of the old Cadillac, and they would sing at the top of their lungs while the wind roared past them, flicking their hair into their eyes.

There was Green Day's "Time of Your Life" that became their college graduation mantra. It had been a tough summer. Luke had accepted a job in a law firm in Richmond, Virginia, while Dinah went to DC. He'd packed his Cadillac with everything he owned and left the following weekend. As Dinah watched the car drive toward the horizon, she was seized with a sudden panic that she'd never see him again. Instead, she went to the nation's capital and tried to cope with nightly phone calls. They shuttled back and forth every weekend and worked like maniacs during the week to try and forget their loneliness.

They'd been apart for ten months when Luke took her away to Vermont. He played her an old favorite U2 song, "All I Want Is You."

Luke took her hand. "My happiness is with you," he'd said softly, "and nowhere else. I don't ever want to be apart from you again. Will you become my wife?"

She looked at him in wonder. "Of course," she murmured, embracing him, whispering a promise that would haunt her. "We'll never be apart again."

Their wedding waltz was to the Righteous Brothers' "Unchained Melody." She cried as they danced — shuffled, really; Luke wasn't a dancer — and Luke had held her tighter in alarm.

"What is it?" he whispered fiercely.

"I don't want this moment to end," she said. "It's too perfect."

"It won't," he promised. "This is what our life together will be like. As long as we have each other, we can face anything."

He was true to his word. When her parents died within six months of each other, he'd held her up at the funerals when she'd wanted to collapse, made her cups of hot tea, lain beside her, stroking her hair in silent empathy while she cried.

He was with her when they found out she was pregnant. In the heights of their ecstasy, he whooped around the room like a little boy. He read every fatherhood book he could lay his hands on and whispered to her stomach, sweet nothings to his firstborn. When she gave birth to a tiny boy with a scrunched little face that made him look like an impossibly old, wise man, they named him Samuel, and he played Creed's "With Arms Wide Open."

Kneeling in her living room, Dinah realized she was crying silently, the tears slipping down her cheeks with ghostly caresses. She put the CDs back in the box and edged backward, toward the couch.

*How could I have let my world leave me?* she wondered. She knew now that Luke and Sammy had been her everything, and yet she had let them go. What would she give to hold her precious son just once more? When her parents died, she had certainly felt grief and loss. There had been many things she wished she'd told them — how she loved them, how she would never stop needing them. Yet, after a period of time, she began to live again — perhaps differently, in a way that would make them even prouder were they still alive.

But when Luke and Sammy left, a large part of herself had gone away too — the part that was a mother, a wife, a worthwhile person. The void in her was bottomless. The elements of basic living — eating, sleeping, breathing — became infused with a pain she didn't know existed. She struggled with buying groceries because there were so many memories: how she would buy chocolate with macadamia nuts, even though it was ridiculously expensive, because Luke loved it, how Sammy loved to gnaw on juicy plums until his chin and fingers and hair were red, how she would buy a surprise dessert to treat them every Sunday night.

She struggled to pay bills simply because Luke had always done it. She struggled to cook for one person, because she had always cooked for three. She struggled when strangers asked politely whether she had any children. *I am a mother!* she wanted to scream. *Just because he's not here with me doesn't mean I'm not a mother.*

She now knew, too, that it was impossible to have the meaning of her very existence ripped away from her and expect to keep living. It just couldn't be done.

And so the decision was made clearer in her mind. Once a foggy possibility lurking in the black area of the mind that most people don't ever look into, it now became crisply clear. She couldn't keep looking through music and photos and those tiny little baby shoes and feel like her life was worth living. Simply, it just wasn't.

Dinah felt calm and composed. She finished the bottle of wine and allowed herself to think of what she would do.

That night, she went to bed feeling more tranquil than she had in a very long time.

Perhaps it was because she knew the end was near, and that the interminable pain would soon be over.

Perhaps it was because her only wish of falling into the darkness forever was about to come true.

\* \* \* \*

When Dinah stumbled out of bed the next morning, with a pounding head, fuzzy mouth, and rebellious stomach, she silently cursed herself for drinking the whole bottle last night.

Ferguson raised his eyebrows at her as she straggled to her desk. Despite brushing her teeth several times, using almost a whole can of body spray, and putting eye drops in her bloodshot eyes, Ferguson remarked, "Harris, did you hit the bottle again last night?"

Dinah ignored him. "Aren't we supposed to see the guy from the atheist lobby group today?"

"Yes," replied Ferguson. "But I think he might pass out from the fumes coming off your body."

"Well, what are we waiting for?" Dinah asked, rolling her eyes. "Let's go!"

"I might drive, though," said Ferguson, as he stood and they walked to the elevator. "I'm pretty sure you'd still be over the limit."

"Okay, enough already!" Dinah swatted his arm. "I get the message."

Ferguson just looked at her and didn't say anything. He didn't need to. *You don't get the message at all — you continue to drink and come into work hung over or worse, still drunk. So when are you going to clean up your act?*

The headquarters of IAFSI was located in a small office block downtown. Damon Mason met them in a small reception area and took them into a multi-purpose office. He was an incongruous man — he was very tall and broad and would have been at home on a football field, but was softly spoken and clearly nervous at having two FBI agents in his office.

"So, tell us about what you do here," suggested Ferguson, once Mason had brought coffee.

"Well, this is the headquarters of IAFSI," began Damon Mason. He had a habit of entwining his fingers repetitively as he spoke. "IAFSI stands for Individualist Association for Scientific Integrity. Broadly, we seek to further the cause and protect the integrity of pure science. As a result, we also represent atheism, because we believe that scientific reason has abolished the need for the human race to superstitiously believe in God. That's what the 'individualist' part of our title means — to pursue independent thought or action."

"Independent from who exactly?" Dinah asked, frowning.

"From the church, the government, religion," said Mason. "Science has struggled against religion for hundreds of years. The church used to execute scientists for suggesting that the world was round and not flat! Yet despite all the odds, science has managed to survive, and even flourish, because certain scientists decided to pursue individual reason rather than accepting what the church told them to do."

"It's not the Spanish Inquisition anymore," commented Ferguson.

"That's true," agreed Mason. "Now of course the biggest problem we have are Christian fundamentalists denouncing evolution. Our struggle now centers around trying to keep science *in* schools and religion *out*, working for the separation of church and state, and influencing public policy to ensure we live in a society not dominated by religious dogma."

"Are you involved in politics then?"

"Yes, we also support politicians who agree with our mission. We're not lobbyists. We prefer to develop relationships that are mutually beneficial."

"In what way do you support them?" Dinah asked.

"We help fund election campaigns, for example," replied Mason. "We use our networks to raise awareness of the candidate, and hopefully influence people to vote for that candidate."

"And in return, you get someone in a position of power who supports your agenda," guessed Dinah.

Mason shrugged. "Nothing illegal about that."

Dinah thought about that for several moments and filed it away for future reference. Something about what Mason had just said resonated with her, but she couldn't determine exactly why just yet.

"So how did you meet Thomas Whitfield?" asked Dinah.

Mason blinked. "The organization decided he would be an individual we'd like to sponsor," he said. "Several years ago, Mr. Whitfield was gaining prominence as an anthropologist and had published some excellent articles. I contacted him and met him to decide whether we should pursue sponsorship. He was an excellent candidate, and therefore I began to work very closely with him."

"What do you mean, sponsor him?" Dinah pressed.

"By and large, the scientific community fades into the background of society," explained Mason. "People know they're there, but they don't know what they're doing or why. Occasionally one of them will be on television or in the paper. The organization wants to promote scientific endeavor, through the media, to show people that science is the savior of mankind."

"Why did Thomas Whitfield make a good candidate?"

"He had very good credibility," said Mason. "He was a thorough researcher. He was articulate and well spoken. He could speak to people in simple terms. In short, he was the sort of person who could engender trust in the general population, and who would be very successful in furthering our cause."

"If he was already having articles published and rising in prominence and so forth," Dinah interjected, "why would he need to affiliate himself with your organization?"

"We are a nationwide organization," said Mason with a smile. "We have thousands of members from all walks of life. Some of our members are in the media and other powerful positions, and therefore we could offer Mr. Whitfield a variety of media opportunities. For a scientist, to be able to talk about his research in the public arena was a tremendous opportunity. We felt he would be a natural doing television appearances, and he was. Everyone loved him. He could talk about a complex scientific finding in the simplest of terms that anybody could understand."

"Did you require him to mention your organization as part of the deal?" Ferguson asked.

Mason shook his head. "No, we prefer to stay out of the limelight. In any case, we didn't *require* of him anything. It was a mutually beneficial arrangement. We had a scientist in the media spreading our message and he enjoyed talking about his research to such a large audience. There was nothing sinister about it at all." Mason laughed nervously.

Dinah frowned. "Why would we think there was something sinister?"

Mason's laughter dried up quickly. "Well, you know, you're FBI agents. Don't you see something sinister in everything?"

There was an awkward pause. Damon started to squirm under Dinah's flinty gaze.

"How did Mr. Whitfield end up as the secretary of the Smithsonian?" Dinah asked at length.

Mason looked rather proud of himself. "It was perfect timing, actually," he enthused. "It was a very exciting time. We were certain he'd have great influence."

The agents waited as Mason gathered his thoughts.

### WASHINGTON, DC — 1999

Thomas Whitfield had barely struggled awake on a rare Saturday morning when he had absolutely no commitments and nothing to do except sleep in, enjoy a leisurely breakfast, and read the paper. It was raining heavily and Thomas thought there was nothing better than the sound of rain on the roof.

At least, he had nothing to do except for the insistent pounding on his front door.

"Who on earth could that be?" Eloise wondered, hastily pulling on a robe while Thomas hunted for his own.

Damon Mason stood outside his front door, soaking wet.

Thomas opened the door and ushered him inside. "What are you doing here?" he asked.

Damon Mason shook himself out of his jacket, and Thomas was reminded of a large dog shaking the water from his fur after being in the rain.

They sat in the family room and Eloise brought in coffee.

"Normally I would have waited until Monday," said Mason. "But the news is so exciting I couldn't wait. What would you say if I told you that a high-profile position at *the* most prestigious museum has become vacant?"

"I would assume you're talking about the Smithsonian Institution," replied Thomas dryly.

"Exactly. Can you imagine yourself as the secretary of the Smithsonian?" Mason asked. His excitement was infectious. "You will be in charge of leading a renowned museum and research center which attracts *millions* of visitors each year. You will have an annual budget of over $900 million. Can you believe that? The best part is the research and scientific investigation programs that are undertaken there."

Thomas did indeed know that the research program at the Smithsonian was enviable. For a scientist, having the freedom and funding to engage in these activities was akin to heaven. Being in charge of the research activities was even better, like being in charge *in* heaven.

But Thomas didn't want to get ahead of himself. "Wait a minute, how did the vacancy arise? Has it been advertised yet?"

"The last one resigned," explained Mason. "He was in his early seventies and it was getting to be too much for him. This is an important opportunity. The last secretary did a pretty good job, but he was a businessman and administrator and had been his whole life. His main passions were to balance the budget and have an organized desk. So if we could get a scientist, like yourself, into the chair with a passion for science and knowledge, then I think the institution would move ahead astonishingly. Given that the media are already quite comfortable with you, I think you could improve the profile of the Smithsonian as well."

Thomas looked at the other man thoughtfully. Obtaining the position of secretary of the Smithsonian would legitimize his entire scientific career. He would no longer be the scientist that sometimes appeared on television but whom nobody really knew. He would be the key speaker, he would be respected for his position as well as his achievements, and he would no longer have to duke it out on silly televised and radio debates.

"I'm very interested," he said finally. "But tell me, what's in it for you?"

Mason knew the question was coming. "You know what's in it for me," he said cheerfully. "Being in that position will give you the authority to espouse your beliefs that science is the answer. People will believe you."

"So continue with what I've been doing already?" Thomas asked.

Damon raised his eyebrows. "Right. Except this way, you're in a respected, unique position and you can help steer the activities of the research programs, with the approval of the board, of course."

"The board?"

"Yeah, the board of regents. It's a group of people who oversee the running of the place," explained Damon. "Not unlike a board of directors in a company. They report to Congress periodically and help you to get funding from the government on an ongoing basis."

"Who is on the board?" asked Thomas.

"Who *isn't* on the board," replied Damon, chuckling. "Only the vice president of the United States. There are several senators and congressmen; a Supreme Court judge, the heads of some large philanthropic organizations, and some businesspeople. It's a heady mix of power. They're the sort of people who can get things done."

Thomas was already envisioning the stratosphere of funding and prestige he would occupy as the secretary of the Smithsonian.

"So what do I need to do next?" he asked.

"Meet the board," said Damon, "for an informal chat. We'll see how they like you and how you like them."

A sudden thought struck Thomas. "How do you know about this before the position is even advertised?"

Damon smiled enigmatically. "I think I told you when you first joined IAFSI that we have members all over the country. Many of our members prefer to do our work quietly, without broadcasting to the world that they belong." He chuckled again. "Certainly our members who are elected officials and have constituents who might find their membership offensive would never even mention it. But there are some on the board of regents who are members of IAFSI, like you."

"Who in particular?" Thomas asked curiously.

Damon shook his head. "I swore I'd never tell anyone who they were, and I won't break that promise. Suffice to say, if you become secretary, you'll find out who they are pretty quickly. Just don't expect them to broadcast it." He sighed ruefully. "So, shall I arrange for you to meet the board?"

"Absolutely!" exclaimed Damon.

**\* \* \* \***

The meeting was organized for the following Tuesday. Thomas hadn't been so nervous in a long time. He discarded three shirt and tie combinations before he was happy. He polished his shoes. He combed his hair and fleetingly realized that he was losing more hair by the day.

He tried to eat breakfast. Eloise watched him over the kitchen table.

"What's wrong?" she asked finally.

"I don't know. I guess I'm just not that hungry," said Thomas, pushing the bowl of cereal away. He drummed his fingers on the table. He got up and sat back down again. His skin seemed too small for his body.

"Do you know what today is?" Eloise asked quietly.

Thomas looked at her impatiently. "Of course I do. Why do you think I'm so tense? It's my interview at the Smithsonian today." He glanced at his watch. "And I've got to go."

He jumped up, kissed Eloise on the cheek, and checked out his reflection in the hall mirror.

"Bye! Wish me luck," he called as he closed the front door.

Eloise didn't reply but stared at the kitchen clock. This time, she couldn't bring herself to cry.

"No," she said to herself. "Today is our 20th wedding anniversary."

Finally, Thomas stood at the end of Independence Avenue, looking down the National Mall. In the distance, the Capitol building rose from the horizon majestically. Clusters of people moved across the manicured green lawns between the buildings that made up the institution. It was a surreal feeling, Thomas thought, to survey the Mall and wonder if perhaps one day he'd be in charge of it.

He made his way to the castle, the main building where the offices were located. A young lady who was volunteering at the information center showed him to the boardroom where he would meet with several members of the board. While he waited, he drank in the atmosphere of the place. He felt an almost mythical air of solemnity that this was where important truths were communicated to the public, where secrets of the great civilizations were celebrated, where the ingenuity of mankind was commemorated. To be a part of that would be an honor and a privilege. Suddenly, Thomas knew that he *must* have the position of secretary and that he would do whatever it took to have it.

A secretary finally showed him into the boardroom, where the members of the board of regents sat around a long, polished table. As they introduced themselves, Thomas couldn't help but feel impressed and a little overwhelmed. The vice president of the United States, the chief justice of the Supreme Court, several congressmen and women, and several senators!

The Chief Justice, Maxwell Pryor, seemed to be in charge. After introductions, he suggested, "Why don't you tell us about yourself?"

Thomas launched into an explanation of his anthropology career, his studies of indigenous populations, the articles he'd written, and the research he'd championed. As he finished, he wondered if it would be enough.

"As you may be aware," Maxwell Pryor said at the end of Thomas's speech, "the purpose of the Smithsonian Institution is to distribute truth to the people. We like to think that we can provide understanding and reason to this country. What are your thoughts on that?"

"The very reason for all of my research," said Thomas, "is to promote our understanding of the human race and how we evolved. I firmly believe that we cannot know where we are going if we do not know where we came from."

Several members of the board nodded their heads. "One of our requirements for the secretary this time around," continued the chief justice, "is to appoint somebody who can speak knowledgeably about scientific matters in the media. You may know that fierce debate rages between the scientific community and religious groups at the moment. How do you think you will handle that particular controversy?"

"To be honest, I already have been dealing with it," Thomas replied. He searched the faces of the board members in front of him for their reaction to his words. "I've already been involved in radio interviews and television appearances, including debates, arguing on that very topic. I think I'm experienced enough to handle that aspect of the position."

Again, several board members nodded. "What, in brief, did your arguments convey?" Maxwell Pryor asked softly.

"Broadly, that *science* is the answer to many of society's problems," said Thomas. "To anyone closely interested in history, we can see that religion is the *cause* of many problems and not the answer. And so I find it quite concerning to think that religious groups want to exert any power in our society. Science has eradicated many diseases, provided treatment and comfort for many other diseases, vastly improved our life expectancy and infant mortality rates, and provided us with many creature comforts previously unavailable. Science is the savior of mankind, because *science* will allow us to live as long as we wish, disease- and degeneration-free. Personally, I look forward to that day."

Chief Justice Pryor glanced at his fellow board members and allowed a small smile. "Excellent, Professor Whitfield. It is certainly clear where your loyalties lie." He allowed the room to digest that cryptic remark before continuing, "Professor, we must advertise the position openly to be fair, and therefore we will conduct interviews with other applicants. However, thank you for your time today. You did an excellent job."

Thomas stood and shook hands with the chief justice. On his way home, he felt the light-headed excitement of anticipation.

Three weeks later he received a phone call from Chief Justice Pryor. "Congratulations! You are the new secretary of the Smithsonian."

After Thomas hung up, he let out a shout of excitement. He raced around the house, trying to find Eloise so that they could go out to a celebratory dinner.

He didn't find Eloise. He instead found a note, saying she had gone to her sister's house.

Thomas frowned for a few moments and then shrugged. He didn't have time to wonder about the hidden messages contained within that note.

He had to prepare for his new life as secretary of the Smithsonian Institution.

Dinah hadn't sat at her desk in days and it showed. Her e-mail inbox was overflowing and her phone was flashing with messages she would have to deal with at some point. The very first message turned out to be the most important — Zach at the forensic lab.

"My favorite FBI agent?" Zach answered his phone.

Dinah let a beat go by. "You are really a very strange person," she commented.

Zach chuckled. "Yeah, I know. How's the investigation going?"

"Well, you know," Dinah sighed. "Nobody will talk to me."

"That's surprising," said Zach. "What with your gregarious personality and all."

"What's surprising," rejoined Dinah, "is that you even *know* the word gregarious, let alone how to pronounce it."

"Yee-oww!" howled Zach, thankfully away from the phone so that he didn't rupture Dinah's eardrum. "You're hot, girlfriend!"

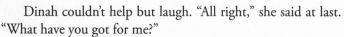

Dinah couldn't help but laugh. "All right," she said at last. "What have you got for me?"

"Just some confirmation," said Zach. "The tooth and the blood were matched to Thomas Whitfield, according to samples taken from the autopsy."

"Great. Now do you have any idea who took him there, beat the living daylights out of him, and killed him?"

"No," admitted Zach. "I'm good, but even I can't conjure up this killer."

Dinah hung up and relayed the news to Ferguson.

"We'll go back to MacIntyre," suggested Ferguson. "He may have lawyered up, but we still might be able to shake him a bit."

"What about Maxwell Pryor?" Dinah added. "We need to talk to him about his arguments with Thomas Whitfield and why he warned Biscelli not to talk."

Ferguson pulled out his cell phone and dialed the number Catherine Biscelli had given them. After a brief conversation, he hung up and announced, "Chief Justice Pryor is in chambers this afternoon, but he'll meet us after his session. In the meantime, let's swing by MacIntyre's joint."

This time, the guards standing outside the front doors of the glass and steel headquarters of Seismic Corporation didn't argue when Dinah and Ferguson held their badges up. Nor did Cheryl, MacIntyre's secretary, who sat guard in the atrium, say anything as the agents walked into the large office of Kenneth MacIntyre.

MacIntyre, who was on the phone, glanced up at them and motioned them toward two egg chairs. A mixture of fear and resignation flitted across the businessman's face. MacIntyre finished his conversation, then without acknowledging the agents, buzzed Cheryl.

"Please send up Jeff Downing," he instructed her.

He then rubbed his temples with his hands. "What can I do for you this time?" he asked, a weary note in his voice.

"Bad news for you, I'm afraid," Ferguson told him. "The forensic evidence we found in your factory definitely belongs to Thomas Whitfield. So I need you to tell me about that."

Kenneth MacIntyre just shook his head and sat in silence. It didn't take Dinah and Ferguson long to figure out why. Only a few moments later Jeff Downing burst into the room, and it was apparent that he was MacIntyre's lawyer. He was a tall, austere man with graying hair at his temples and stern blue eyes. "I hope you haven't asked my client any questions in my absence," he said, sitting next to MacIntyre and eyeing Dinah and Ferguson up and down as if they were a deadly contagious disease.

"We were just wondering why a murdered man's blood and tooth were found at your client's factory," Ferguson said pleasantly. "Rather odd, we thought. Leads us to the next question: what was your client doing early last Tuesday morning?"

Kenneth MacIntyre leaned forward and murmured in his lawyer's ear. Downing smiled. "He was hosting a breakfast seminar for several of his top suppliers," he said, a note of triumph in his voice. "He was there until ten o'clock, with about 30 people who can vouch for his whereabouts. What else do you need to know?"

"Why would the secretary of the Smithsonian's blood be found at your factory?" Dinah asked. "And why was he murdered there?"

"I can assure you," Downing replied, "just because the unfortunate victim died there doesn't mean my client had anything to do with it. I know he's already told you that he rarely goes there and that he has on-site managers who oversee the operations there. I really don't see the relevance."

"Its *relevance* lies in the arguments we know your client and our victim had immediately prior to his death," Dinah said bitingly. "Why won't he talk about that?"

Downing smiled condescendingly. "An argument between adults hardly means a murder will follow, even if such an argument did occur. If Mr. MacIntyre tells you there was no argument, then you'd better believe that there wasn't."

"I'm afraid I don't believe him," snapped Dinah, losing what little patience she had for smug, well-paid Washington lawyers. "As I don't believe him when he tells me he doesn't know anything about Thomas Whitfield's death."

"I see. So you have physical evidence that my client was at your murder scene?" Downing asked. If it were possible, he sounded even more patronizing. "Hair? Fingerprints? Fibers?"

There was an uncomfortable silence. Dinah and Ferguson both knew that they didn't have a single specific item of evidence linking MacIntyre to the crime scene.

"Ah," said Downing smugly. "Just as I thought. You seem to have a very circumstantial case. A murder was committed at my client's premises, which is horrible, I'll grant you. But my client has an alibi and you don't have any physical evidence. That's an awfully shaky case."

"I'll want a list of your employees who work at the factories," said Dinah shortly.

Downing smiled again. "Certainly. Once you hand over your subpoena, I'd be glad to help you out."

"If your client is innocent, there shouldn't be a problem in handing over a list of employees," Ferguson commented. "Unless he's afraid one of them will talk."

"Nevertheless, I appreciate the law for what it is," replied Downing smoothly. "And the law stipulates that you must provide a subpoena. Was there anything else?"

"No," said Dinah coldly. "But I can assure *you* that you'll see more of us. We want the truth and if I have to move heaven and earth, I'll get the truth."

The lawyer just looked at her, unimpressed. "Of course," he said mildly. "We're on the same side, Special Agent."

Dinah could have hit him.

\*\*\*\*

Maxwell Pryor, the chief justice of the Supreme Court, was in chambers when Dinah and Ferguson arrived at the court building. It gleamed whitely in the pale sun, the Corinthian columns imposing. As they passed under the banner, EQUAL JUSTICE UNDER LAW, Dinah felt a sense of kinship with the purpose of this grand building. Its purpose, the mandate of protecting this great nation with justice available for all, enshrined the doctrine of all men and women being born equal. It formed the cornerstone of an egalitarian society, where your birthplace was not as important as your work ethic; where your measure of contentment was limited only by the scope of your dreams; and where the hope of a new life was sweet and tangible.

But there was no place on earth, reflected Dinah, where you could outrun your past or forget how it molded you.

The chief justice's associate, a young, balding man who seemed to be trying too hard to copy the mannerisms of the judge, showed them into a small office and left with an air of superiority.

The agents knew that they couldn't very well barge in on the judge like they would any other person, and it chafed on Dinah. She bit at her nails, tapped her foot, paced, drummed a pattern with her fingers on her leg, and twisted her ponytail until Ferguson finally glared at her.

"If you want something to do," he said, "you could call the office and organize a subpoena for the employee lists of Kenneth MacIntyre."

Dinah did just that, and as she was finishing the conversation on the phone, Chief Justice Maxwell Pryor appeared, still wearing his billowing black robes.

"Special Agent Ferguson, Special Agent Harris," he said, sounding harried and out of breath. He was tall with a hooked nose and prominent cheekbones. "I came as soon as I could call a small break."

"Thank you for meeting with us," Ferguson said, immediately taking charge. Dinah knew that he had concerns with her abrasive interviewing style, which probably wouldn't have worked with Pryor.

"As you can probably guess," continued Ferguson, "we are here to talk about Thomas Whitfield's case, and also by connection, the Lara Southall case."

"What a simply dreadful situation," said Pryor, shaking his head mournfully. "To lose these wonderful employees so violently in such a small space of time is astounding; a terrible coincidence."

Ferguson paused. "I'm afraid the FBI doesn't believe in coincidences," he explained. "We are treating both murders as being related."

The judge looked shocked. "How awful! On what grounds?"

The agents knew very well how the two deaths were connected but weren't about to divulge to a possible suspect. "That's what we're trying to find out, sir," said Ferguson. Dinah noted his courtesy. She probably would have said something like "none of your business."

"So what we're trying to find out about, specifically, is the source of conflict between the board of regents and Thomas Whitfield," added Ferguson.

Predictably, Pryor said, "I'm sorry, I don't know that there ever was any conflict."

Ferguson waited a beat. "Some of your colleagues on the board disagree with you, sir." That was, perhaps, the tiniest of white lies.

Pryor raised his eyebrows. "Really? Well, that's certainly news to me. What have they told you?"

Ferguson was not about to aggravate the lie with details he didn't have. Instead, he said, "How is it that you were not aware of this conflict?"

The chief justice drew himself up importantly. "I certainly do not involve myself in any petty squabbles, if indeed there were any," he explained loftily. "Therefore it is entirely possible that I simply didn't know about them. I am sure that were there any major problems, I would have been told."

Dinah sighed loudly, conveying her impatience. The board was a tight-knit little group, she conceded. She was getting rather sick of the same old story they insisted upon regurgitating. Pryor glanced at her in annoyance.

"I'm afraid we have it on good authority that you were aware of the conflict," Ferguson said. "And that not only were you aware of it, but that you were one of the instigators and that you were heard frequently arguing on the phone with Thomas Whitfield."

Pryor actually looked flabbergasted. "I have never heard such garbage in all my life!" he thundered.

"Did you have occasion to speak to Thomas Whitfield outside of normal working hours?" probed Ferguson. "And by calling his home?"

This calmed the judge down. He seemed to be thinking, then said, "Of course I spoke to him outside of hours. However, I must insist that I argued with Thomas Whitfield very rarely. There may have been the occasional small problem, as there is with any professional relationship."

"Well, you see, Judge Pryor," interjected Dinah smugly, "we are interested in why you have gone from having no idea of any group conflict to admitting personal conflict with Thomas Whitfield."

Ferguson shot her a warning glance while Pryor barely deigned to acknowledge her.

"What were these occasional small problems about?" Ferguson asked, trying to get the judge back on track.

"They were so minor that I don't recall," snapped the judge. "And I have to get back to court." He stood and gathered his robes about him. "Ought I obtain an attorney?"

"If you feel you need one," Ferguson advised.

The two agents were left alone in the office.

"I was thinking," said Dinah slowly, "as we walked into this building about equal justice under the law. Do you think equal justice extends to the chief justice of the Supreme Court?"

Ferguson shook his head. "I'm not so sure."

\* \* \* \*

Thomas Whitfield was due to be laid to rest the following morning, and both Dinah and Ferguson were eager to attend the funeral. Their interviews with the board of regents were not going well, the Colemans were busy settling into the city after their trip from Ohio, and it would be more productive than battling the heap of e-mail back at the office.

It was cold and crisp, the sky a pale and frosty blue.

The memorial service was held at the Georgetown Presbyterian Church. Dinah and Ferguson arrived early and sat at the back, watching the mourners straggle in. Most seemed to be rather scholarly looking ladies and men in the same age bracket as the Whitfields. Dinah saw several members of the senior staff at the Smithsonian and several members of the board of regents.

Ferguson nudged her at some point. "Who is that guy?" he whispered, nodding at a tall, skinny, vaguely familiar man. He was in his early thirties with black hair and pale skin and he was dressed casually, unlike most of the other mourners. He seemed to be alone and he sat on the edge of one of the pews and scanned the church continuously.

Who *was* he? Dinah definitely had seen him before, only recently, but she couldn't put her finger on his identity. Her brain whirred into overdrive, mentally comparing his face with everyone they'd spoken to in relation to Thomas Whitfield's death, but frustratingly, she couldn't place him.

Finally, Eloise Whitfield appeared, flanked by two young women, whom Dinah assumed to be her adult daughters. All were dressed well but they couldn't hide the puffy dark patches or the blank shock that still masked their eyes.

Eloise Whitfield paused at the entrance, and her eyes touched on Dinah's. She gave the briefest of nods, acknowledging the agents' presence and somehow conveying her approval that they search for answers even here, at the funeral.

The minister waited for the family to sit, then began the service. He was, rather surprisingly, a young man with a pleasantly open face and compassionate smile. Dinah had always thought of ministers as the strict, forbidding type she had occasionally encountered in her childhood.

"Friends, we are gathered here today to remember and celebrate the life of Thomas Whitfield," the minister began. "Some of you may be surprised to hear me say that today ought to be a celebration, so let me say it again. Today *is* a celebration of his life rather than mourning for his passing. You see, dear friends, when one believes that death is not the end, but the beginning of a glorious new life, we can be full of gladness. The Lord God promises us that eternal life can be ours, and not to fear death. The Lord tells us in Revelation chapter 21 verse 4 that in eternal life, He will wipe every tear from their eyes, and there will be no more death or sorrow or crying or pain. All these things are gone forever."

The minister paused, and Dinah felt a bolt of melancholy slide down her spine. *What a world that would be*, she thought. *No more sorrow or crying.*

"God's greatest desire for every one of us is that we should join Him in eternal life when we die," the minister continued. "He asks us to call him Abba, Father. He longs to have a relationship with you that is as close as a father is to his own child. He says in the Book of Isaiah, 'For I hold you by your right hand — I, the LORD your God. And I say to you, "Don't be afraid. I am here to help you." ' What a wonderful promise, dear friends. The Lord God loves you each so much that He promises to hold your hand wherever you go in this world, and promises also to take you with Him into the next world, a world free of death and suffering."

Dinah sighed. In that world, Luke and Sammy would not have gone away, and she would be whole again.

The minister saved a special smile for Eloise and her daughters. "I tell you truthfully that Thomas Whitfield is this day with his Heavenly Father in a place free of the terrible injustices we see around us today. Thomas Whitfield found the truth of life and death while he was still with us, and the reward is heaven for all eternity. You may wonder how you might find this truth for yourself. You see, God created a perfect world for us to live in, yet we rejected Him and wanted to go our own way. He created you and I with free will to choose for ourselves how we would govern our own lives. Some of you might think you are doing that pretty well. Some of you might think you've done a terrible job."

*I'm definitely in the "terrible job" category*, thought Dinah ruefully.

"The truth is, we all have gone our own way and made our own choices, and along the way, done bad things. It is clear that none of us is perfect. You might have told a white lie. You might have stolen something. You might harbor hatred in your heart for someone. The Bible says in Romans chapter 3 verse 23 that everyone has sinned, we all fall short of God's glorious standard. Now we have a problem. We have rejected our Creator and indulged in all kinds of evil. So how is it that a perfect God and an imperfect person may be reconciled in heaven? There is only one answer, and His name is Jesus, God's one and only Son. He came to earth, both fully man and fully God, as a sacrifice. You have heard the story of the crucifixion of Jesus. It is more than just a story, friends, it is history. Jesus did die on the Cross, but it is so much more significant than that. He bore the punishment, the wrath of God, for all the sins committed by you and everyone else. Jesus rose from the dead on the third day, conquering death forever to prove that we need not fear death again. We were all like prisoners on death row, when Jesus took our place in the gas chamber and gave us a full pardon. He invites you to take the pardon, give thanks for this incredible free gift, and change your life forever. And not just change it here and now, but for all eternity."

The minister paused again, his eyes roaming the congregation.

"I wish for you the certainty that Thomas Whitfield had, in knowing that a new life awaited him beyond death. I wish that same peace and freedom from fear for you all. There is nothing any of you could do to save yourselves; it has all been done for you by Jesus. All you have to do is receive His offer of salvation. This means that you are sorry for your old life and your sins, and that you want to live the rest of your life with God as your Master."

Dinah felt a strange sense of irony. She wasn't scared of death. She was looking forward to it, as an instrument of release, but she hadn't given much thought to what would happen after death. She had been raised as a nominal Anglican; that is, she'd been to church about four times in her whole life. She supposed that somewhere in the back of her mind, she did believe in some sort of God, more as a distant and shadowy puppeteer, occasionally checking in with earth to see if it was still there. The concept of a loving, fatherly God was a completely different proposition. *Perhaps,* she thought, *I'll check that out properly before I take the final step.*

It no longer alarmed her to think so calmly and rationally about life and what might lie ahead for her.

\* \* \* \*

It was late in the afternoon, the pale sun sinking regretfully behind the horizon as the two agents left the funeral service and arrived at the FBI headquarters. Ferguson was impatient and irritable because he couldn't place the tall, skinny guy they'd seen at the funeral. Dinah was absorbed in her own thoughts, thinking about the message the minister had given.

Both of them were snapped rudely from their thoughts upon exiting the elevator. Their boss, the Special Agent in Charge George Hanlon, was waiting for them.

"You two," he snarled at them. "In my office, now." He stalked off, while Dinah tried not to smirk at his balding patch and the sweat stains under his armpits.

Ferguson, guessing at her thoughts, nudged her with a warning look.

Dinah hissed, "Well, how am I supposed to take him seriously?"

The two agents sat in his office with the door closed and waited for the haranguing to begin.

"I got a call from Chief Justice Maxwell Pryor this afternoon," he began ominously. "You better have a good explanation for what happened."

"He is a suspect in the death of Thomas Whitfield," began Dinah, ignoring Ferguson's silent plea in his eyes to keep her mouth shut. "Just the same as every person who has been connected with Mr. Whitfield up until his death. We are obviously aware of the fact that he is the chief justice, but nobody is above the law." Dinah added, after a beat too long to be anything but insolent, "Sir."

George Hanlon glared at her. "I am well aware of your contempt for authority, Agent Harris," he said sharply. "And since you appear to be well-versed in the law, then perhaps you've heard of a small concept called the presumption of innocence."

"Sir, I can assure you that we did not accuse him of anything," Ferguson intervened hastily. "We have reports regarding serious conflict between the board and Thomas Whitfield that none of the board members want to tell us anything about. We feel it may be crucial in finding out why Thomas Whitfield was murdered, and therefore a step closer to finding out who did it. We simply asked Chief Justice Pryor if he knew anything about it."

"And?" Hanlon raised his eyebrows.

"He said that he didn't," admitted Ferguson. "However, this directly conflicts with other reports we've been given. So I'm afraid that we do not believe him. And we would have to question why he would lie to us."

"Is it possible that Pryor really does *not* know anything about the conflict, and that the other reports you have been given are false?" Hanlon asked, still scowling.

"I don't believe that is the case," replied Ferguson stubbornly.

Hanlon heaved a sigh. "Then you must know the shaky ground on which you tread. You simply cannot barge into the chambers of the chief justice of the Supreme Court and demand answers from him. Whether he is truly a suspect or not, I'm sure he now has a fine attorney who won't let us within ten feet of him." He stood, turned his back on them, and stared out his window. "I'm calling you off him, immediately. If you must investigate him, do so at a distance. The fact is that he is also a part of the justice system in which we all work, and we need him to be on our side. Now you'll have to get some actual evidence instead of harassing confessions out of people who know better."

"With all due respect, *sir*," Dinah said, implying that she felt no respect toward him at all, "there simply isn't a lot of evidence to find. Both murders have been thoroughly professional. So that leaves us with only one option — to talk to people until we find out the truth."

Hanlon turned to face the agents and anger flared in his eyes. "Agent Harris, you are one warning away from being taken off this case," he snapped. "You are rude and insubordinate, despite the fact that I am doing you a favor even letting you be part of this investigation. Not only that, you are bringing disgrace on the bureau *again* by the way you live your life. I don't know why the bureau didn't just terminate your employment in the first place."

Dinah stood, her cheeks flaming. "Are you done?" she demanded, not trusting herself to enter an argument with him.

"Actually, not quite," replied Hanlon, trying to remain eye-to-eye except that she was half a foot taller than him.

"Well, I'm done listening to you," Dinah said coldly. She left the office, slamming the door behind her. Her colleagues, momentarily stunned, looked up at her, saw the storm clouds circling her face, and wisely went back to work.

Dinah left the office, having no stomach for more work. On the way home, she envisaged several entertaining ways George Hanlon might meet his death.

What eventually cheered her up was the thought of the cool, dulcet tones of the bottles of wine in her fridge, helping her to forget.

A cold sleet fell as Jane Morrissey walked briskly down the street. It was well after midnight, and she was aware that she shouldn't be walking around on her own at such an hour, even in a neighborhood like this one with bright street lamps. She had been volunteering at the homeless shelter all night, serving bread rolls and vegetable soup to the masses of poor souls who had nowhere else to go. She was tired but felt almost euphoric, the natural high that came from helping others.

Usually she caught a ride in with one of the other volunteers, but he had the flu. Tonight she had driven to another volunteer's house and parked there instead. She wasn't too concerned except for the biting cold. She turned the collar of her jacket up around her ears and jammed her hands farther into her pockets. Jane noticed that the residents had put their trash bins out for collection the next morning, and their presence obscured the view onto the street of where she had parked her car. She wasn't very good at things like remembering where she had left the car. Everyone she knew had accused her of being a dreamer at some point.

She passed a row of little shops, which collectively used a commercial Dumpster and had wheeled it out to the curb. Jane stopped next to it as it gave her some relief from the sleet, and looked up and down the street, searching for her little Ford.

Finally she spotted it and took a step forward. As she did so, something brushed her cheek and caused her to gasp in fright. She jumped and looked over her shoulder, expecting to see somebody — perhaps a homeless bum — but didn't see another soul. She glanced at the Dumpster and saw something hanging out of it at about head height and breathed a sigh of relief. That must have been what touched her. But her heart didn't stop hammering at a thousand miles an hour, and she leaned closer to the object that had brushed her cheek.

It was a white-white human arm, the blood flow long since ceased, the tips of the fingers and the fingernails blue.

Jane shrieked, then tried too late to muffle the sound with her hands. She had touched and hugged countless unwashed and diseased people at the shelter, but never a dead person.

Wait, she thought. Perhaps the person wasn't dead. Perhaps the person just got his arm caught and the rest of him was alive and kicking. Gingerly, she reached out and felt for a pulse at the wrist of the arm. The skin was waxy and cold and she couldn't feel a pulse.

Digging through her handbag, she found her cell phone and dialed 911. Then she sat at the curb, hunched against the cold, and waited for the show to begin.

It didn't take long — an ambulance and a police car with lights blazing arrived less than ten minutes later. Jane stood and waved them over.

The paramedics also felt for a pulse and glanced at each other. Jane guessed that the look meant whoever was in the Dumpster was dead. She shivered.

It took the two paramedics and a police officer to lift the heavy Dumpster cover. It made a horrific screeching noise that echoed up and down the quiet street. Standing on a little ledge that ran around the outside of the Dumpster, about halfway up, the two paramedics checked the remainder of the body for any sign of life.

When they began hauling him over the side of the Dumpster, it was apparent that there was no life. The body was male and his entire upper torso was covered in blood.

The two uniformed police officers took Jane aside so she didn't have to watch and asked her to go through the events of the evening. Jane recounted her short story. She couldn't help but stare as the body was loaded onto the paramedics' stretcher. Suddenly, she felt a jolt of recognition as she looked at the body and gasped.

"What is it?" one of the cops asked her.

"That person . . . I think I know who it is!" Jane exclaimed. "Could I see a bit closer?"

She approached the stretcher tentatively and tried to ignore the queasiness in her stomach. While there was a great deal of blood, the face of the body was remarkably untouched. Jane took in the square jaw and dark hair.

She nodded. "Yes, I do know who that is," she said. She tried not to retch. "It's Damon Mason."

"Thank you, ma'am," said the police officer. "Is he a relative of yours?"

"No," said Jane. "He is the president of an association of which I'm a member."

"Which association is that?" the cop asked, writing in his notebook.

"The IAFSI, Individualist Association for the Freedom of Scientific Integrity," explained Jane.

"I'm very sorry for your loss, ma'am," the cop told her. "We'll be contacting his next of kin, and we'll probably ask one of them to do the formal identification at the morgue. In case we need you, we'll call. Can I take down your cell phone number?"

Jane nodded and gave it to him, the shock starting to wear off and the reality starting to sink in. The person she had found dead in the Dumpster was someone she knew! And the fact that he'd been left in a Dumpster could only mean that he had met a violent end.

Jane shook her head in disbelief.

Who would want to kill Damon Mason?

\* \* \* \*

Dinah was up early the next morning and made herself a pot of strong black coffee. As she drank the first cup, her cell phone rang. Trying to ignore her fuzzy head, she saw that it was Ferguson.

"Morning," she greeted him, trying to sound more alert and chipper than she actually felt.

"Hey, Harris. We've got another body," Ferguson said gravely.

Dinah felt her heart sink. "Really? Who is it?"

"Our favorite atheist, Damon Mason."

The news threw Dinah. "What?" she exclaimed. "Why? That's out of left field. What happened?"

"He was found by a woman coming home after volunteering in a homeless shelter," reported Ferguson. "Who just happened to be a colleague of his at IAFSI. It looks like his throat was cut, just like Lara Southall, and then tossed into a Dumpster."

"Let me guess, no fingerprints or DNA or anything useful to speak of?" Dinah asked, already knowing the answer.

"Nope. I'm definitely thinking that these hits are professional," Ferguson said. "They're just so tidy."

"Wouldn't a professional use a gun though?" Dinah countered. She drank more coffee and actually started to feel more human.

"Maybe not," said Ferguson. "Guns can be traced. We have ballistics to help us link crimes. Anyway, I'll see you at the office?"

"Sure," said Dinah. She gulped down the last of the coffee, poured herself a second cup, and thought about whether she should eat breakfast. She decided against it and left the apartment.

Traffic was reasonable along the beltway because it was still a little too early for the rush hour commute, and Dinah arrived before Ferguson. The floor where she and Ferguson worked was starting to fill, except George Hanlon's office. While Dinah waited for her computer to boot up, she started thinking about the connection between the Smithsonian, IAFSI, and Andy Coleman.

It was clear that Thomas Whitfield had a close relationship with IAFSI. They had helped him, early in his career, to publish in well-respected scientific journals. They had obtained for him coveted media spots in television and radio. They had made him the resident "expert" to whom the media turned when they needed a scientific opinion. As a result, Thomas Whitfield's profile grew brighter and brighter. In fact, he grew so well known that he was given the Smithsonian secretary position without any real competition. It was easy to see why Whitfield had agreed to the partnership between himself and IAFSI.

But what was the payoff for IAFSI? They had to be getting something out of it, too. Dinah was willing to bet all the wine in her refrigerator that IAFSI wasn't doing it out of the goodness of their hearts. There had to be a payoff.

The trouble was, Dinah couldn't work out what IAFSI got out of the deal.

Then there was Andy Coleman, IAFSI's natural mortal enemy. The two were locked into a fierce battle between evolutionism and creationism, with Thomas Whitfield the mouthpiece for IAFSI. Andy Coleman seemed to be of the belief that it was this battle that had killed Thomas Whitfield. Surely Andy Coleman wasn't so right wing as to be militant? Dinah pursed her lips. Perhaps Coleman had gotten sick of the constant arguments with Whitfield and decided to take him out?

That didn't explain why Lara Southall and Damon Mason were killed. They had both been murdered after speaking to the FBI, but Lara Southall had never met or spoken to Andy Coleman and wouldn't have been able to incriminate him in any way. Damon Mason made a more likely victim in Dinah's Coleman theory, so why wait so late to get rid of him? And why would the board of regents be so cagey about the alleged conflict with Whitfield? Why would the crime scene of Whitfield's murder be at a site owned by one of the board members?

There were too many holes in the theory for Dinah to seriously consider Coleman as the perpetrator. What about the other side? What if IAFSI had gotten rid of Whitfield because he wasn't living up to his end of the bargain? Damon Mason had stumbled across the plan, threatened to talk, and been killed as a result. Although that was a reasonable theory, it didn't explain why Lara Southall was murdered because again she didn't have any connection to IAFSI. Nor did it explain the board members' reluctance to talk, or the crime scene at MacIntyre's factory. Again, there were too many holes for that theory to be taken seriously.

Dinah sighed in frustration. That left the board of regents and their mysterious conflict. She was more convinced that she simply had to get to the bottom of what the conflict was about.

A sudden rap at her cubicle wall startled her. Ferguson waved with one hand and stuffed a doughnut into his mouth with the other.

Dinah gave him a wave, still preoccupied.

Ferguson got the message and left Dinah alone. She stared at her computer screen and wondered if there might be an obvious material connection between the board of regents and IAFSI or Coleman.

Dinah entered the bureau's broad database search function and typed in the organization's full name. The search, similar to a Google search, would bring up every mention of IAFSI in the media, on websites, and on blogs, similar to a microfiche search at a library.

The results of the search were massive, and Dinah began to methodically scroll through, taking short notes. There was mention of IAFSI in many scientific journal and magazine articles; apparently IAFSI was a big advertiser and supplier of information regarding the articles. IAFSI was quoted on many subjects, including genetic engineering, hereditary disease, anthropology, molecular biology, and so on.

They sponsored a large number of seminars, and often the keynote speakers were members of IAFSI. The seminars, as Dinah looked through the material, seemed to be aggressive in style. The subjects were similar, but each speaker devoted a good deal of time within his or her speech to criticizing the opposition — the fundamentalist Christians. Every seminar, without exception, focused a great deal of time on pointing out the weaknesses in the creationist argument and denigrating the creationists in general. Was this one of the requirements IAFSI had of its speakers? Dinah wondered. Perhaps part of the agreement was that they would sponsor you, if in return you adhered to their agenda. What had Mason called it? A *mutually beneficial* relationship.

IAFSI was also active in the social and charity scenes. They sponsored golf days at exclusive country clubs, they hosted charity balls and dinners, and they held award nights for high achievers in the scientific field. Dinah read through a number of newspaper articles about the events and found a similar theme. For the money they spent, IAFSI got airtime. Their favorite charity cause was hereditary and degenerative disease — they threw all manner of events for cystic fibrosis, for Lou Gehrig's disease, for Parkinson's disease. At each event, an IAFSI speaker would present a short seminar on the disease, its treatment, and how IAFSI and the scientific community at large were trying to overcome such diseases. In each speech, the speaker would disparage other community groups — usually ethics and Christian groups — for hampering their efforts. They concluded by urging the guests to support IAFSI endeavors and to vote for politicians who supported them.

*Ah, here's the rest of the truth,* thought Dinah. *They're lobbyists too, if you are of the correct political persuasion.*

Dinah began to flip through the pictures that accompanied the newspaper and magazine articles. Not surprisingly, there were many featuring Thomas Whitfield with the recently deceased president, Damon Mason. Many pictures included prominent atheists. Still other photos displayed politicians, past and present, usually thanking IAFSI for their support of funds and votes among their members.

Then Dinah stopped and stared hard at a familiar face, standing next to Damon Mason, shaking his hand at yet another black-tie function.

It was the now senator from California, David Winters. He was publicly thanking IAFSI for vigorously campaigning with him and funding much of his election campaign. It was the very same David Winters who was on the board of regents at the Smithsonian.

Dinah didn't know what it meant, other than the fact that she had found a tenuous link between the board and IAFSI. She kept going through the pictures, searching for names she knew. Finally, she found another.

This time, the event was hosted by IAFSI to thank their financial supporters. Dinah remembered that for all of the events IAFSI held, and there were many of them, someone had to be picking up the tab. And there he was, amongst a group of them, a certain Kenneth MacIntyre.

Another link between the board and IAFSI, and now this latest link extended to include Thomas Whitfield's death. Kenneth MacIntyre, benefactor and friend of IAFSI, member of the board of regents, and owner of the factory where Thomas Whitfield died.

It was still circumstantial, Dinah knew, but too coincidental to be disregarded. She needed to find out more, but she was running out of people to talk with.

She stood and found Ferguson, once again munching on a sugary treat.

"Let's go," she said. "I'll tell you about it on the way."

**** 

The Colemans were staying in a residential hotel to the south of the city, away from the tourists. There was no view of Capitol Hill, nor was it within walking distance of any of the other monuments in the city. The Colemans were simply setting up camp, where Andy would wait to speak to the FBI and continue his work for his Genesis Legacy organization.

Andy and Sandra welcomed the two agents into the small living room. They made small talk for a few moments, Andy explaining that he had conducted some speaking engagements up here.

Then Dinah asked him to continue telling about the growing relationship with Thomas Whitfield. They settled back as Andy began.

## WASHINGTON, DC — 1999

Thomas Whitfield arrived home to a dark, empty house after a particularly long day. He ambled aimlessly from room to room calling his wife's name. After several minutes, he began to feel worried. Eloise was *always* here. Where on earth was she?

He switched on the kitchen light and looked at the little calendar Eloise kept on the refrigerator. It was the only way the two of them could keep track of each other. Thomas was often away or had long days, and Eloise filled in her lonely stretches of time with her sister and friends.

He found the date and his stomach dropped. Eloise was in the hospital! How could he forget? It was a simple procedure, one that required an overnight stay only, but it had utterly escaped him. Frantically, he closed up the house and drove to the George Washington University Hospital, remembering to pick up a bedraggled bunch of flowers — the only ones left — from the hospital florist.

Eloise was eating an early dinner and watching a rerun of a daytime soap when he burst into her room. She gave him a half smile, as if she knew he'd forgotten. He made a show of kissing her and asking how she felt, bustling around the bed, offering to fetch more pillows.

She said finally, "Thomas, just sit down. I'm fine, everything went well."

He sat, realizing how tired he was. They watched the television companionably in silence for a while, and then Thomas's cell phone startled them both.

"Thomas!" Eloise hissed. "You're not supposed to have your cell on!"

"It's Billy," he said. It was unusual for his brother to call him. Normally they left it up to their wives to arrange get-togethers. William Whitfield was a high school history teacher in Colorado.

"Hello, Billy," he answered his phone. Instantly, he knew there was something wrong. Bill was crying.

"What is it?" he asked, suddenly apprehensive.

"It's Rebecca," Bill choked. "Have you seen the news?"

Thomas immediately changed the channel. "No, what happened?"

The footage on the news and Bill's story echoed each other in a terrible way. Two students at his daughter Rebecca's school had come to class with a gun. They had opened fire during a bloody rampage and killed 11 students and injured 24, before turning the gun on themselves. Rebecca had been one of the 11 who had died in the gunfire.

Thomas felt the life being sucked right out of him. Beside him, Eloise grabbed at his hand, asking, "What? Thomas, what is it?"

"I'm so sorry, Billy," he said finally. "I'll come out to see you, help you with things." There was silence as both men digested what things would be involved in burying a 16-year-old girl.

"You don't have to do that," said Bill, his voice thick.

"I want to," declared Thomas. "I loved her, too."

"She — she wanted to be a scientist . . . just like you," sobbed Bill. "She was doing great in physics and chemistry . . . she would have been. . . ."

Thomas felt tears well in his eyes. "Oh, Bill. I'm so terribly sorry. I'll come out as soon as I can. I'll call you back with my flight details."

When Thomas hung up, he looked desolately at his wife, lying in a hospital bed. Eloise had guessed by the conversation what had happened and looked stricken.

"Is it Rebecca?" she whispered.

"Yes," said Thomas. "She's . . . gone." He pointed mutely at the television, unable to articulate the gruesome details.

"You must fly out there and see them," Eloise told him. "Don't worry about me. My sister can pick me up tomorrow. You should be there for them."

"Are you sure?" Thomas asked. "I don't want to leave you here either."

"I insist. This is nothing compared to what Bill and Emma are going through. You must go!"

So Thomas found himself catching the very next flight to Denver that he could find. His brother Bill and his wife, Emma, met him at the airport. Rebecca had an older brother, Evan, who was currently in Canada and was also flying in at the earliest opportunity.

Thomas didn't know what to expect, but Bill and Emma both looked completely ravaged by what had happened. Bill's eyes were dead and hollow, and in the past few hours his skin had gone a sickly gray color. Emma looked no better, and she was shaking.

Thomas embraced them both and tried to comfort them. What could you say at a time like this?

Bill drove the three of them directly to the school. It was after seven in the evening now, and bitterly cold. The shooting had happened nine hours earlier but the high school was frenetic.

The police had cordoned off parts of the school with yellow crime scene tape, mostly for recording purposes, as there was little doubt as to the perpetrators. There were lights on in some of the buildings, and Thomas wondered if they were cleaning crews, getting rid of the blood and bone. At the school fence, a memorial had been set up. A mound of flowers, cards, photos, and drawings had been placed there, and it was ever growing. Small clusters of people stood at the memorial, some crying and some quiet and still in disbelief at what had happened.

"We spoke to the police chief," said Bill quietly. They stood at the memorial where a photo of Rebecca fluttered in the chill wind. "The guys who did it roamed around the school at will. They went into the library and asked questions of each of the victims before executing them. It was like . . . like they were trained killers." Beside him, Emma cried into her hands. "They were cowards, they hit kids who didn't know what was happening. It only ended when they shot themselves."

Thomas couldn't think of anything to say so he stood with his arm around his brother.

"I guess you were right all along, Tom," Bill said. "How could we do this to each other? We are nothing but animals. Yet you guys think we've evolved into a higher form. I don't call this a higher life form." He chuckled bitterly. "I think you guys have got it wrong. I think we're *de*volving, getting worse every day. We're just a bunch of vicious brutes."

Thomas didn't have a reply.

## LITTLETON, COLORADO — 1999

Thomas spent a sleepless night in the guest room. He didn't think his hosts were sleeping either; he heard them moving around all night, speaking in hushed whispers.

At breakfast, they resembled a small contingent of zombies — all were ashen with fatigue, their spirits numbed. Nobody could stomach anything to eat, so Emma made some coffee and they sat at the kitchen table drinking coffee in silence.

"There's a memorial service at our church later," Bill said finally. "You are welcome to come with us."

"Yes, of course," agreed Thomas. So they dressed somberly and drove to the Baptist church. The service was for all the victims of the shooting, and Thomas was surprised to find that this included the dead gunman. It was a community still reeling in shock, and the congregation was quietly mourning as the service began.

There were several hymns, which Thomas remembered from his childhood. Then the minister of the church stood and said, "I would like to introduce to you a special speaker today." His voice was soft and serious. "I asked him to speak because he has lectured a great deal on the subject of suffering and grief. My hope is that his words will provide you with some comfort at this time."

There was no ceremony or pomp, but Thomas was still astonished to see Andy Coleman take his place behind the lectern.

"First let me begin by expressing my sincerest condolences," Andy began. "This is a terrible tragedy and I can assure you that you are all in my prayers." He paused and the sound of soft crying was clearly audible.

"I hope today that I can give you some measure of comfort," he continued. "I suppose the biggest question many of you have is how could God let something like this happen to our kids? Why couldn't He have protected our children? Isn't God supposed to be a God of love? In fact, I know that many of you are probably angrily asking these very questions of God. Do you think God dropped the ball? Do you think God was a bit busy somewhere else and forgot to check in on your kids?"

There was silence. Thomas glanced around the church and saw rapt faces drinking in the words. Personally, he felt uncomfortable. He could debate it intellectually without pause for thought, but religion that was raw and emotional was a little too unsettling. He looked sideways at his brother and saw the intent expression on his face, too. Thomas knew that he would just have to sit through it.

"I came here tonight to answer a question. How could a loving God allow death and suffering? This is a question that does have an answer, but if you tonight are looking for me to take away your pain, I can't. We all are going to feel deep hurt, grief, loss, and anger whenever we see tragedies such as the one that has occurred here. When God created this world He made a statement at the end of each day. He saw that it was good. At the end of the creation week, God proclaimed that it was 'very good.' You know if God saw something that was very good, it must have been perfect, because He is a perfect God.

"But when we look around us, we definitely do not see a perfect world. This tragedy is a very painful reminder of this fact. We live in a world that is dominated by bad news. We turn on our televisions and hear of tragedies and disasters. I can tell you that nothing is any worse than what we have just seen here. God created for us a home in this world vastly different to the present one we are living in. Something huge happened.

"We can point the finger at God in anger about this change in our world, but we would be missing the point about why the world is like this. The truth is not always easy to hear, but it can help us with a sense of understanding."

"At the end of creation, God warned our first parents, Adam and Eve, that disobedience to His one and only rule would result in the tragedy of death. Humanity actually had the choice to live in the reflection of a glorious Creator in a perfect, joyful, and fulfilling life that would never end.

"But you know what? We ruined it. Adam and Eve directly disobeyed God's command and immediately had destroyed the perfection that God had created. So here is your first answer — we live in a world with death and suffering because it is no longer perfect. And the reason for that is because we all have disobeyed God's commands. We reject God and choose our own kingship over His authority. Because we sinned, we created an environment where what was once perfect now experiences suffering and death as normal. We were warned, but we rejected our Creator's warning."

Andy glanced around at the congregation. "That leads us onto the next question: do you think God cares about your suffering? Does He even love you? I know He does. I know He does because He sent His Son to earth to suffer on our behalf. Despite the fact that we disobeyed God, He still desperately wanted to bring reconciliation. In order to do that, He needed to punish the wrong things we were doing because He is a perfect, holy, and just God. So He sent His precious Son, who suffered unspeakably and died on the Cross to make that payment of justice on our behalf. God poured out His wrath and punishment on Jesus for every wrong thing that's ever been done. Can you imagine watching your own child go through so much pain, but then also to take out your anger on them? God did it because He loves us so immensely. And He promises over and over again, throughout the Bible, that He will never leave us and that He will always be with us, and He makes an even more amazing promise. If you truly believe that you do wrong in the eyes of God, and you accept that Jesus sacrificed Himself in your place, then you will live with God for eternity in heaven! Life on this earth may be full of grief and sadness, but you can look forward to eternal life with God in heaven.

"We live in a world of tragedy, but God offers us an eternity of hope. Hope based on His truth.

"None of us will ever be able to cope with tragedies like this. This is because God tells us that death is our enemy. Death is an enemy, but Jesus Christ conquered death! I hope that you can somehow realize that God does love you and care about you, and that you can lean on Him at this terrible time."

Andy paused and gathered his thoughts. "There is much more I'd like to tell you, but I don't have time. If you want to talk to me after the service, I would welcome it."

Thomas endured the rest of the service, remembering why he had eschewed church long ago. It was just a bunch of meaningless words, designed as a crutch for people who were suffering. He watched at the end of the service as people shook Andy's hand and thanked him and hugged him. As the church emptied and people went home, Thomas waited.

Andy did a double take when he walked up the aisle and found Thomas sitting in semi-darkness.

"What on earth are you doing here?" he asked, astonished.

Thomas stood and shook his hand. "My niece," he said. Nothing more needed to be said. He sat down, with Andy in the next pew.

"Thomas, I'm sorry. I am surprised to see you here. Was the message I shared helpful to you?"

"Andy," said Thomas wearily, "you know I'm an atheist. I don't believe in that pie-in-the-sky stuff."

"I know. So how are you handling all this?" Andy asked.

"You know what? Tragedy's always been there," said Thomas. "Through evolution, the weak have died and the strong have survived. I would say that many of the atrocities in the world have been caused by people who didn't know right from wrong. It's just our human nature. Some of us are good. Some are bad."

"I don't buy that argument at all," rejoined Andy. "How does an atheist explain right and wrong? Where do you think the concept of good and bad comes from, if there is no absolute authority?"

"It's up to each individual to determine right and wrong, in conjunction with societal acceptance," said Thomas. He suddenly felt enormously weary. "I don't think any atheist or Christian would agree that society condones what happened here."

"Perhaps we shouldn't have this argument now, Thomas; you must be in dreadful suffering. Would you like to talk another time?" Andy asked in concern.

"It's okay, Andy; I stayed here to listen to you. Go ahead and answer. Surely neither Christians nor atheists condone this tragic event."

"Certainly not. But what if the kids who did the killing firmly believed that they were right in their actions? Where does a society get *its* value system from?"

Thomas didn't reply because in actual fact, he didn't know.

"I'll tell you where," said Andy. "Our society got its values and morals from Christianity, and therefore from God. That's why we think killing and stealing is wrong. That's what the Bible teaches!"

"In answer to your original question," said Thomas, trying to take control of the conversation, "there is no answer. I don't think that filling people's heads with fairy tales does them any favors."

"Right, because we evolved by random chance and because there is no meaning to life since we are born, then we die, and then nothing. Am I right?"

"I guess so," said Thomas.

"Well," said Andy, "I feel enormously sorry for you. I don't know how you cope during stress or trauma if you accept that miserable outlook on life as truth. I can't imagine the despair you must feel when you think that we must suffer through this life, and then die. What's the purpose? You must think everything is utterly meaningless!"

Andy stood while Thomas sat in silence. After a while, he said, "I've got to go, Thomas. I'd be really happy to keep talking to you about this rather than debate you on TV."

"Maybe," mumbled Thomas.

Andy gave him a brief pat on the back as he strode by and out the doors of the church.

For the first time in his life, Thomas couldn't get past a tiny nagging worry in the back of his mind. *What if I've got it all wrong?*

*What a week*, Dinah moaned to herself as she locked the door to her apartment late Friday night. The living area was dark and empty, and Dinah resolved to set it up nicely before she made her final decision.

The refrigerator was noticeably devoid of food but was well stocked with wine and vodka. Dinah wondered if she should eat. She glanced down at her pants that hung loosely on hipbones that were beginning to protrude. Perhaps she would order a pizza.

Once that decision was made, she sat on the couch and turned on the television for background noise. In front of her was a recently opened bottle of the finest New Zealand sauvignon blanc. Piled next to her were photo albums, ones she hadn't looked at in years.

When the pizza arrived, she began to look through the albums. She had one motive in mind — these albums would spur her into decisiveness. She knew that she couldn't look through these photos and continue to want to live.

Dinah began at the wedding album, with Luke in a starched suit and her in a white dress, as they faced the cameras with joy. Dinah remembered how she had felt in those days. Her future with Luke seemed to stretch on forever, like a golden beach that caressed the horizon. Sure, she knew there might be problems — everyone faced hard times. She felt confident facing them all with Luke.

The next album contained a number of holiday snaps: skiing at Aspen where they'd maxed out their credit cards and laughed at the rich people who took themselves too seriously; taking a cruise to Alaska; lying on the beach in the Bahamas. There were photos of Dinah the day she was accepted into the FBI academy, wearing a brand-new FBI cap and flak jacket.

Dinah took a long drink and ate a slice of pizza, lost in memories of training down at Quantico, the recruits pushed physically and mentally to get rid of the ones who wouldn't make it. Dinah knew she'd make it, and go even further than that. In fact, she knew she could reach the very heights of the bureau because she was smart and hardworking. And she had fulfilled her dream — she was the agent they spoke about in hushed whispers around the water cooler. Now she was barely hanging on, a disgrace and embarrassment to the bureau. They still spoke about her around the water cooler, but with concealed laughs instead of awe.

Dinah drained her glass.

Next came the most painful albums of all — where Sammy had joined their family. There was the very first one, where a tiny wrinkled newborn baby lay in the arms of his exhausted and proud mother. There were countless photos of Sammy smiling for the first time, sitting up for the first time, playing with his new fluffy mobile, standing, walking, his first birthday. There were photos of his toothless gummy grin, the silly Superman suit they'd found somewhere, his blue eyes that could see straight to your soul, his chubby little arms and legs.

Dinah realized she was crying. She touched Sammy's little face, frozen forever in time staring with bewilderment at the candle on the cake, and whispered, "Mommy misses you." The void in her heart ached unbearably.

She couldn't bear to look at more. She closed the album and knew that looking at the albums had achieved what she had wanted. It had galvanized her into action.

Dinah finished the bottle of wine and took her service gun from its holster on the bedside table. Back on the couch with a fresh bottle of wine, she stared at its cool lines. She had never viewed the gun as more than a trusty tool to use on the job until the last year or so. During the last 12 months, it had seemed to her to be an option; more than that, it seemed to be a solution. It would be easy and it would be over in seconds.

Still, the thought of the sheer violence of a gun made her a little uneasy. It would be messy and undignified. If it went wrong, the results could be catastrophic. She finished her glass of wine and stared at it. Here was another option, she realized. She could drink a couple of bottles of wine and take some sleeping pills. If it didn't work, she reasoned, she would wake up with her stomach pumped and a pounding headache.

The important thing, Dinah thought, was not to decide how she would do it right away. First she needed to put into action a plan. There were several other things she wanted to do first. She wanted to write letters to Luke and Sammy to apologize for not being stronger. She wanted to assure Ferguson that it wasn't his fault. She wanted people to know that you couldn't lose your whole family and be expected to live. It was worse than a broken heart. Her spirit had been shattered and her soul destroyed.

Dinah stood and the world spun. She was well past drunk, she realized as she staggered to her bedroom. On the whole, she was pleased with the night's work.

She had a plan and it would culminate with blessed release from this world.

**\* \* \* \***

Dinah suddenly woke a second before the alarm clock shrilled, and for a moment she couldn't remember where she was. She stared into the darkened room, and slowly it came back to her. First, the memory of deciding between the gun and the wine, and second, the formulation of her plan to end her life. Instead of feeling dread or horror at the thought, she felt relief. It was time, she realized, to move forward and make the hard decisions in life.

Dinah stood and the room spun crazily, in tune with the turmoil in her stomach. She waited for it to pass and knew that she was still slightly drunk. She took a long, hot shower and felt marginally better, then made herself a tall, strong coffee. At the hall stand, where she picked up her pocketbook and fastened her holster, she looked at herself in the small mirror.

Her eyes were bloodshot and puffy, with dark circles. Her skin was pale, almost gray, and her face was so thin that she looked gaunt. She looked awful, she knew.

She strode to her car and spent several seconds fighting back nausea before she drove away. The drunken feeling was slowly dissolving into a shocking hangover. Blood pulsed in her temples, causing pain to radiate throughout her head.

Dinah had to fight to concentrate on the road. Three or four hours of sleep — particularly after consuming so much wine — were not enough; her eyes were heavy and her mind jumbled. If she had a car accident now, she knew she would be over the legal limit and her career, lingering as it was, would be swiftly terminated.

She arrived without incident at the medical examiner's office and saw that she was 20 minutes early. Ferguson had not yet arrived. Dinah decided to rest her aching head on the steering wheel and relax for a few moments.

The next thing she knew, she was woken by a sharp rap on the car window. Ferguson peered in, his face creased in a frown. She plastered a smile on her face and got out of the car.

"Morning," she said brightly. "I got here early and decided to catch up on a bit of sleep."

Ferguson opened his mouth to say something and then stared at her suspiciously. "Dinah," he said at length, "you absolutely reek of alcohol. Have you been drinking this morning?"

"This morning? No, of course not!" Dinah protested, wondering if 2 a.m. counted as "this morning."

"Did you drink last night?" Ferguson pressed.

"A little," admitted Dinah. "Look, I'm fine. I just didn't sleep very well, okay?"

Ferguson looked entirely unimpressed. "If you'd only had a little, you wouldn't have such a bad hangover and you wouldn't have alcohol oozing out of your pores," he snapped. "In fact, I'm willing to bet that you're still drunk because you can't even focus properly."

"Look, I'll be fine," said Dinah. Deep shame began to rise in her and spread deeply, like butter on hot toast. She should not have let Ferguson see her like this. "Just leave. . . ."

"Is everything all right, folks?" inquired a voice behind them. Dr. Campion, the medical examiner, stood with a briefcase and a red and white bowtie peeking out from behind a heavy coat.

"Dr. Campion, good morning!" said Ferguson. He added, by way of explanation, "We got here a little early."

Dr. Campion nodded, looked over at Dinah, and didn't say anything for a few moments. "Well," he said finally, "sorry to keep you waiting. I assume you're here about Damon Mason?"

"Yes, that's right," agreed Ferguson as they followed the medical examiner into the building. The receptionist had just arrived and bustled around, snapping on the lights and checking the heating. The two agents trailed Dr. Campion meekly into the steel morgue, where the sharp smell of formaldehyde could not mask the unmistakable, underlying stench of dead bodies. Dinah's stomach trembled as she and Ferguson soaped their arms and hands and put scrubs on over their clothes.

Dr. Campion found the locker he was after and wheeled out the body of Damon Mason. Mason, who was large in life, seemed shrunken in death. He had been cleaned during the autopsy and now looked remarkably like he was sleeping, if it weren't for the large red gash across his neck.

Dinah began to sweat. The smell and the sight of Mason's body, which ordinarily wouldn't have bothered her, caused an awful fluttery lightness in her stomach.

"There is certainly one very defining feature of the bodies linked to your case," Dr. Campion said as he consulted his notes. "The deaths are very clinical and thorough. I would probably even term it as professional."

"Why is that, Doctor?" asked Ferguson, shooting a glance at his pale and silent partner.

"People who are used to killing other people," explained the doctor, "particularly noticeable where a firearm isn't used, is the lack of hesitancy and tentativeness in the wound. Secondly, there are only enough wounds to cause death. Typically, an inexperienced killer will have a few attempts. He's not sure where to cut, for example, or how deep. So there are usually several distinct marks on the victim. Where the murder is born of rage or passion, the killer won't stop at a simple neck wound: he'll continue to stab or cut until his emotions are satisfied. In this case, we have neither situation. It seems to be the cool, detached method of someone who is an experienced murderer, and an emotionless one at that." He pulled the sheet down, and the two agents could see there were no other marks on Mason.

"Right. And the deaths of Lara Southall and Thomas Whitfield could be similarly classified?" asked Ferguson.

Saliva poured into Dinah's mouth and she knew she was in trouble.

"Exactly," confirmed Dr. Campion. "Now, if we move along to. . . ."

"I've gotta go," Dinah said suddenly as vomit rose in her throat. She stripped the scrubs off in record time and ran from the morgue.

She made it to flowerbeds just outside the building before she could no longer hold it back, and threw up violently. Her stomach was empty of anything except fluid and she didn't stop retching until it was completely empty. She waited, still bent over with her hands on her knees. She heard someone's footsteps behind her and recognized Ferguson's shoes.

"I'm okay," Dinah said, before he could say anything.

"You need to go home," Ferguson said, in a tone that brooked no argument. "I'll take it from here."

"Really, I'm fine," protested Dinah.

"You are *not* coming back into the morgue," snapped Ferguson. "That's final. I would suggest you don't go into the office either, because Hanlon will sniff you out in five seconds and have the best excuse he'll ever need to fire you. So go home."

The thought of sitting in her empty apartment was somehow worse than being publicly sick. "What about the Colemans?" she suggested. "I could visit them."

Ferguson sighed. "Whatever. Just don't go to work and don't come back here. I'll talk to you later." He turned and walked away, his shoulders stiff with anger.

Dinah stared at the blacktop and knew her humiliation was complete.

\* \* \* \*

If Andy and Sandra Coleman were surprised to see Dinah on their doorstep, they hid it well. If they were shocked to smell the sharp alcohol cloud that followed her in, Dinah didn't notice. Perhaps the fact that Sandra immediately made a pot of strong coffee was a hint, but by this time Dinah was sitting back on the living room couch and welcomed it.

Dinah briefly massaged her reeling head and then tried to gather her composure. "Firstly," she began, "I need to warn you, in absolute confidence, that Whitfield's contact at IAFSI, Damon Mason, has been found murdered."

Sandra had brought in a tray with coffee and overheard Dinah's words. She shot a worried look at her husband, who was shaking his head. "What happened?" Andy asked.

"Without going into gory details, suffice it to say that we believed he was killed for talking to us," Dinah said, taking a sip of coffee and almost scalding her tongue. "There seems to be a pattern emerging, and I need to remind you that you may also be in danger."

Andy nodded. "Yes, we'll keep that in mind. Doesn't it seem strange to you, though, that the murder victims are all on the other side?"

"What do you mean?" Dinah asked, trying the coffee again.

Andy glanced at his wife. "Special Agent Harris, the scientific community in this country isn't a large one. We all know each other and what each of us stands for. One of the problems with such a tight-knit community is that there is an expectation that all will follow the status quo. There is no room for tangential thinking. There is certainly no room for challenging or questioning the senior scientific authorities. I am a prime example of what happens when one does challenge the established thinking."

"Go on," said Dinah, intrigued.

"I have two science degrees," said Andy, "both from prestigious universities. I have studied and published more than many of my contemporaries. But I am consistently and publicly written off as an uneducated quack, trying to line my own pockets. I will never be published in any of the major scientific journals because I don't subscribe to *their* way of thinking. I will never be offered tenure or a doctorate at the mainstream universities because I have challenged and rejected the accepted scientific theories. I will be publicly exiled pretty much for the rest of my life. I will always be an outcast within the community I serve, because I think differently than everyone else. And it's not just me. I have people in my organization who are qualified in quantum physics, astronomy, geology, molecular biology, chemistry — all the major disciplines of science, and the same thing has happened to them."

"Okay, but why?" Dinah asked, frowning. "Isn't science supposed to be a field where you question and challenge? Isn't that how scientific discoveries are made?"

"You're right," agreed Andy. "But the scientific community has some powerful alliances with some hard-line groups, such as IAFSI. In return for their support, IAFSI requires that any scientific thinking that does not agree with them be shut down. IAFSI is motivated by their own beliefs, and they want everyone else to have those beliefs, and they use the scientific community to help achieve that goal."

"I don't mean to sound rude," said Dinah. "But that sounds like religion to me."

Andy nodded. "Again, you're exactly right. It is a religion, a fundamentalist religion, much like the one I'm accused of being associated with. If you watch the evening news, you will know how strident they are in trying to wipe out any reference to Christianity within schools, courthouses, and the government."

"Humor me a little," said Dinah. "Why would they care?"

"Because they don't like being challenged or questioned," replied Andy. "Christianity is their biggest threat, and they hate it, particularly in the educational environment. You know, as a Christian I am often labeled as a fundamentalist, but neither I nor my organization have ever advocated that creationism exclusively be taught at schools or universities. Yet that is exactly their aim. They do not want young people to question what they are taught, and the best way to achieve this is to ensure that young people never hear an alternative viewpoint. My organization would be happy if both viewpoints were taught as explanations for the origins of the universe, because it would be pretty clear which explanation is most reasonable and rational."

"Okay," said Dinah. "So you're telling me that IAFSI and the scientific community are powerfully aligned, and that they are actively trying to destroy or alienate any streams of thought that differ from theirs. But does this extend to murder? That's a pretty big leap."

Andy shrugged. "I don't know. All I'm saying is that the people associated with that alliance have a pretty bad mortality rate right at the moment."

"Does IAFSI have any influence politically?" asked Dinah.

"They try to keep it all pretty secretive," replied Andy, rubbing the stubble on his cheeks. "But over the years I've gathered that IAFSI does fund certain politicians. I've heard rumors that they contribute to election campaigns and that sort of thing, on the understanding that the particular politician will support their views."

Dinah nodded. "And what I want to know is, what does it have to do with Thomas Whitfield? What happened after you met with him in Colorado?"

"He started following me," said Andy with a wry smile. "By that I mean, every school shooting tragedy that happened after Colorado where I would be speaking at a local church, we'd meet. It was the only time we could have a frank one-on-one discussion."

"What did you talk about?"

## MOUNT MORRIS, MICHIGAN, 2000
### — THOMAS'S STORY

This time, the student responsible for killing a fellow student was just six, the youngest in United States history. He had arrived at class with his father's gun and killed a six-year-old girl. The township was shocked. What do you do with a six-year-old boy who has just become a murderer?

Halfway through Andy's sermon at the Baptist church, he noticed a familiar figure, who had tried to hide behind a hat and sunglasses, but who was still clearly Thomas Whitfield.

Afterward, they drove separately to a 24-hour diner on the freeway, where the coffee was bad and the food greasy enough to instigate an immediate heart attack, but where no one from their respective organizations would find them.

"Well, Thomas, I must admit this is a surprise," said Andy, after they'd been served a pot of terrible coffee. He had been doing a lot of traveling of late, however, and was glad for the caffeine.

"My family is having a bad time," admitted Thomas. "You remember that my niece was killed in Columbine? It's been nearly a year and we're all still trying to come to terms with it. It's been pretty hard." Thomas didn't mention that his brother Billy had told him he often drove around the city looking for a good place to commit suicide. Or that his sister-in-law, Emma, was drinking pretty heavily now. Or even that he himself, who could once explain everything according to the unvarying laws of nature, was badly shaken by an event nobody could explain.

"My guess would be that you don't have any hope," said Andy softly.

Thomas considered this. "You know, you might be right."

Andy weighed his words carefully. "The reason I say this is not because I want to preach. My family and I have had some terrible things happen to us too — the sickness and death of loved ones that didn't make any sense at the time. The only reason I think we could accept it is because we have hope in God."

"I guess I understand what you're saying," said Thomas. "But doesn't that validate my argument that people use religion as a crutch?"

"You know what? Just humor me for a moment," suggested Andy. "In your honest opinion, do you think I'm stupid?"

"No, I certainly don't! I've debated you enough to realize that you are far from stupid," said Thomas with a rueful grin.

"Do you think I would put blind faith in God, severely affecting my reputation and career and earning capacity, if such faith contradicted what I've learned as a scientist?"

Thomas was silent for several beats. "I don't know," he admitted. "That's what I've never understood."

"I can tell you the answer, I wouldn't," said Andy as the food arrived. He bit into a pastry. "I have a brain very much like yours — it's rational and logical. I don't have a lot of understanding of feelings and emotions. What I found while I was at college was not that the Bible contradicted science, or the other way around. In fact, what I found was that the Bible *confirmed* science. In fact, I tried to find holes in the Bible, and I couldn't."

Although Thomas had several answers on the tip of his tongue, he waved at Andy to continue.

"Here's why: we look at the same evidence. You use fossils and rock layers in your evolution arguments; I use the very same fossils and rock layers in my creation arguments. The problem lies not with the evidence, but with the human interpretation of that evidence. You approach each fossil with the desire to fit it into evolution somehow, and I approach each fossil on the understanding that it confirms biblical creation and the Flood of Noah's day."

"Okay, so how does the Bible directly confirm science as we understand it today?" challenged Thomas.

"Okay, let's look at one of the first verses in the Bible itself," suggested Andy. "In Genesis, we read that God created every living thing according its kind. We would rightly interpret that to mean that the dog kind, or family, will always produce dogs, though there could be different species or varieties within the dog kind. The same would be true of the cat family, elephant family, and human kind. The evolutionary concept is that all these different kinds evolved over millions of years, from one kind into another, until human beings came into existence. Supposedly, natural selection and mutations and other mechanisms are the driving forces behind all this. If I look at this from using observational science and apply what we know about genetics, then the evolutionary concept has a great number of problems.

"In genetics, mutations only operate on the information that is present and never lead to brand-new information that would be required for molecules-to-man evolution. Most mutations are detrimental anyway. Let me just ask one more question: is there a single example where brand-new information has been added into DNA?"

Thomas knew instantly that he had no answer but tried valiantly to think of a way to negate the argument. Eventually, he shook his head.

"Back to your original question," continued Andy. "I am not filled with despair when bad things happen, because I believe in God and His book, the Bible, which says that He has ultimate control of this world. I believe that our life span of 70 or so years pales in comparison to the eternity that follows. I believe that what we choose to believe determines what happens to us after we die. I don't believe that we are all here by way of a random accident, or that there is no purpose to our lives, or that there is nothing after death."

"Listen, I appreciate what you're saying," said Thomas. "But I'm not the sort of person who believes in God just because you tell me I ought to."

Andy broke into a wide grin. "I couldn't agree with you more," he said. "Let me leave you with one more thought then — something you and others who've chosen to believe the idea of evolution have often said to me. It's that religion is not compatible with science, and an example of this is that the Church vehemently believed that the earth was flat for many years. It was science that finally corrected that myth, wasn't it?"

"Yes, absolutely," agreed Thomas.

"Actually, the Bible is the source of truth. The Book of Isaiah in the Bible, written hundreds of years before Christ, mentions the circle of the earth. Not the flatness or squareness of the earth, but the *circle* of the earth. The Bible was, and always has been, totally correct. It's the people who get things wrong. So that's one more example of science corresponding with the Bible."

They sat in silence for several moments while Thomas absorbed this. He had a thousand questions and arguments and challenges for what was being said, but he couldn't help but realize that he'd never actually given any credence to what Andy had been saying over the past several years. Yet he couldn't deny the plausibility and intelligence of the man's case. This, of course, gave rise to a disconcerting possibility.

*What if Thomas was wrong?*

When Dinah arrived rather sheepishly but sober to work the following morning, Ferguson seemed to be over — at least temporarily — his anger with her. He beckoned her with an excited expression on his face.

Dinah had been expecting a lecture at the very least but was relieved to avoid the difficult conversation. As she followed her partner into one of the small conference rooms, she glanced over at the glass enclosure where George Hanlon had his office. He was standing behind his desk, staring at her. Dinah suddenly realized with a shudder that he knew about the previous day's incident.

Zach was sitting in front of a laptop almost bouncing with excitement. "We've done it," he crowed. "Well, in all honesty, *I* didn't do anything. The dudes at Homeland Security did it — but we finally have Thomas Whitfield's hard drive!"

## Chapter 16

Dinah and Ferguson crowded around the screen. Dinah momentarily forgot about her career issues. "What happened?" she asked. "I mean what was so difficult about retrieving it?"

Zach was booting up the programs and while they waited, he explained that the hard drive had been erased with a program far more sophisticated than was commercially available. Most commercial deletion programs were low level, getting rid of data that the common person could no longer find. They were used when computers were resold or reused or generally cleaned up. Other computer programs existed that could recover that data relatively easily. However, organizations such as the military, certain sensitive government departments, NASA, the FBI, and the CIA used far more powerful data deletion programs, wherein the data could be recovered only by programs developed by the same organizations, who didn't allow the general public or corporations access to such programs. His lab, Zach continued, routinely used their recovery programs in investigations. In this particular case, the deletion program was so powerful that the only organization with technology advanced enough to recover the data was the Department of Homeland Security. This didn't bode well for the investigation, Zach warned. Somebody with access to such a deletion program was likely to be either extremely powerful or influential or both.

"Computer systems," mused Dinah. "Ken MacIntyre would probably have access to some reasonably high-level computer systems given his connections in government."

They sat in silence, digesting this fact, while the computer finally whirred to life. Zach had carefully gone through the computer's hard drive to discover what had upset Whitfield's abductors so much. Whatever the perpetrator had attempted to delete didn't amount to much — one PowerPoint presentation and a Word document that looked like the associated speech.

"That's it?" Dinah wasn't impressed. "This is what they were trying to hide?"

Zach shrugged as the PowerPoint presentation appeared on the screen. Silently, the three read. It was apparent that Thomas had intended to present it at the meeting before Congress at which he'd failed to appear. Suddenly, the *reason* for his death became bizarrely clear. The secretary of the Smithsonian Institution, one of the most famous natural history museums in the world, no longer believed in evolution. He had become a Christian and now wanted to introduce creationism into the museum as an alternative explanation to the origins of man. He would no longer be available for debate where he would espouse an evolutionary viewpoint. He questioned the accepted dating methods of fossils and natural phenomenon. His vision for the museum included equal presentation of evolution and creationism. It was time, he argued, to disallow the religion of atheism to dominate scientific thought.

Dinah had to reread the presentation to ensure she understood it. Was it possible Thomas Whitfield was murdered because he'd converted from an atheist to a Christian?

"Okay, let me try to understand this," Ferguson said, thinking aloud. "Whitfield had the most recent part of his career sponsored by IAFSI, which is one of the more prominent atheist organizations in the country. He was their poster boy in public debate. How upset would IAFSI be to learn of his conversion to Christianity?"

"Upset enough to kill him?" queried Dinah. "It's such an extreme measure."

"What about the board at the Smithsonian?" continued Ferguson. "The museum might be neutral, but I've been there and I can guarantee you that they do not acknowledge creationism as a valid explanation for the origins of man. So presumably the board would also be pro-evolution?"

"It would certainly account for the high levels of tension and conflict between Whitfield and the board," agreed Dinah. "Again, would they take the extreme measure of killing him?"

"Maybe they gave him some warning," theorized Ferguson. "He refused to back down on the Christianity thing."

"So what do you think about Lara Southall and Damon Mason? Why were they killed?"

"Southall is easy — she was killed because she knew about the conflict between the board and Whitfield, and she was about to tell us why. I would think Damon Mason was killed for the same reason — because he would potentially talk to us." Ferguson nodded as he spoke, as the pieces of the puzzle clicked into place.

"So there is a connection between the board and IAFSI, but we still really don't know what it is."

"Right. More correctly, we don't know *who* that connection is."

They sat in silence, both thinking hard.

"So the crux of the matter is that Whitfield converted to Christianity," said Dinah at length. "They took extraordinary lengths to hide it — by wiping the hard drive and killing Southall and Mason."

"Now we've worked out perhaps why the three of them were killed," added Ferguson. "Now we have to work out *who*."

Zach whistled long and low. "Good luck to ya, dudes."

\*\*\*\*

The main building of the museum was full of school children and tourists, all oblivious to the drama unfolding in the background of the famous institution. Once again, Dinah and Ferguson ignored Catherine Biscelli's hapless secretary and threw open her door. She was on the phone and looked up, startled. Within seconds, she hung up her phone and sprang to her feet behind the desk. Her flinty eyes glared at them.

"What do you think you're doing?" she demanded. "I've had enough of you storming into my office every five seconds!"

"Really?" shot back Dinah, unable to keep the snarl out of her voice. "We've had enough of your pathetic lies. You have done nothing but hinder our investigation since it started, and despite your best efforts, we finally know the truth."

Catherine kept her expression extraordinarily bland, but her eyes glanced away. "What? Do you know who killed Mr. Whitfield?"

"I'll ask the questions, thank you," snapped Dinah. "Now sit down and think very carefully about your answers. If I find any hint of a lie, you'll be charged immediately with conspiracy to commit murder. Do you understand?"

Catherine tried to maintain her dominating glare but finally sank down into her chair. It was probable that she remembered Dinah whipping out the plastic handcuffs last time she tried to resist the FBI agent's requests.

"We know that there was an enormous source of conflict between the board and Thomas Whitfield," began Dinah. "We know it stems from his decision to convert to Christianity and his desire to present within the museum creationism as an equally valid explanation to the origins of man. Does this sound familiar to you?"

Catherine seemed to be debating within herself. Finally she conceded: "Yes."

"In fact, on the morning Thomas Whitfield disappeared, he was going to present his ideas regarding creationism to Congress, hoping to get approval. Did you know about that?"

"Yes, I did."

"Did the board of regents know that he was planning to do that?"

"Yes, they did."

"So Thomas Whitfield did not try to hide that he was a Christian and that he wanted to change some of the museum to reflect that?"

"No, he didn't. The board had already declined his request."

"So by attempting to obtain approval from Congress, Whitfield was effectively going over the heads of the board?"

"Yeah, I guess so."

Dinah glanced at Ferguson, who looked troubled.

"I suppose the board didn't really like that, did they? After all, Whitfield was deliberately flaunting their authority."

"No. Theoretically, the museum is responsible to Congress, so any member of the board, which includes the secretary, can petition Congress."

"So which member of the board had the biggest problem with what Whitfield was doing?"

"I don't. . . ."

"Catherine, don't start lying to me now!" Dinah noticed that the other woman was actually starting to sweat.

"I'm not, I swear!" protested Catherine. "The board closed their meetings to everyone except members. I wasn't privy to much of what went on at those meetings."

"But you *did* know about the conflict, so someone must have been passing information to you."

"Yes, that's true."

"So who was that?"

Catherine swallowed hard. "Justice Pryor."

Dinah glanced at Ferguson again. "Okay, so what was he telling you?"

"He didn't tell me much. He only told me what Mr. Whitfield wanted to do and that the board disagreed. Specifically, I was to monitor everything Mr. Whitfield attempted to tell the press. He said the board had decided that the public didn't need to know that there was a difference of opinion here until it was resolved by Congress. He was worried that Mr. Whitfield would try to rally the fundamentalist Christians on his side."

"Did he ever mention anything that might make you think he or the board would try to harm Whitfield?"

"No, absolutely not!" declared Catherine. "I can tell you I was just as shocked as anyone when I found out he had been murdered."

"So who has been telling you not to talk to us?"

Catherine massaged her temples and sighed. "Justice Pryor."

Dinah shook her head in amazement. "Doesn't that strike you as odd? I would have thought a man in his position would know how important it is to cooperate with the law."

"I know a lot about public relations," said Catherine wearily. "I don't know much about the law. He told me that Mr. Whitfield's death had nothing to do with the Christianity thing. He said that if it got out it would be blown out of proportion and would give the conservatives more media time. He said eventually the real culprit would be found and in the meantime not to drag the museum's name through the mud."

Dinah sat back and thought about this. There was a great deal of circumstantial physical evidence linking Kenneth MacIntyre to the murders — the use of his factory in the crime and chalk dust being found on every dead body that had turned up in the course of the investigation. But there was nothing to link him personally: he had an alibi and his support of IAFSI didn't necessarily amount to murder. On the other hand, there was absolutely no physical evidence linking Justice Maxwell Pryor to the murders, yet he was the one behaving as if he had something to hide. Dinah sighed in frustration. If she could somehow combine the two, she would have the perfect suspect.

Dinah leaned forward. "Listen, Catherine, I want you to tell me something. You must admit that there is something particularly nasty happening within these four walls. I want your personal opinion on exactly what is happening. Do you think this is simply a fight between the evolution and creation camps, or is it deeper than that?"

Catherine took her time to answer. Her forehead was starting to shine with sweat and she twisted her lower lip between her teeth. Finally she said, "I don't know exactly what happened to Mr. Whitfield or Lara, and I don't know exactly why they were killed. I can tell you this — if you look at the history of this museum and the people who have worked here, you will notice that anyone who has dared to mention Christianity or creationism has immediately been fired or publicly smeared or both. I don't know who is behind it and I don't really understand why, but I do think it might just be as simple as evolutionism versus creationism."

Dinah sat back, her mind spinning. Catherine Biscelli might be abrasive and assertive, but she was by no means stupid. If that's what she truly thought was behind the deaths of Whitfield and Southall and even Mason, then perhaps she was right.

The war between creationism and evolutionism had just turned particularly nasty.

\*\*\*\*

When the two agents emerged into the crisp sunlight, Dinah discovered she had several missed calls from the lab. On her message bank, Zach had left several excited voicemails.

Dinah held up her hand to halt Ferguson's progress, and called Zach.

"I found a mistake!" he crowed when he answered the phone. "He finally made a mistake!"

Dinah felt a surge of adrenalin. "What? Who made a mistake?"

"I found a fingerprint in the belongings of Damon Mason," reported Zach. "A fingerprint, in blood, on Mason's watch clasp. It's as clear as day. It's beautiful."

Dinah closed her eyes briefly in relief. "Did you find a match?"

"Sure did! It belongs to a Peter Ivanov, who was once an infantryman in the army," said Zach. "I've faxed a copy of his papers to your office."

The name didn't ring any bells with Dinah. "So is he anyone we should know?" she asked. "Did you get any hits?"

"I'm afraid there are no outstanding warrants on him and no prior convictions," said Zach. "That's about as far as I got. The lab is getting further and further behind so I've only done the preliminaries."

"Okay, great! Thanks for that." Dinah hung up and motioned to Ferguson. "Come on, there's a fingerprint; it's at the office."

Ferguson didn't bother asking what she was talking about.

At the office, the fax was waiting on her desk. Ferguson and Dinah examined the identification photo and Ferguson snapped his fingers. "He's the guy from the funeral," he exclaimed. "I saw him at the funeral."

Dinah stared intently at the photo and knew she'd seen him before too, from somewhere other than the funeral. The hair color was slightly different and the clean-shaven face was much younger. Dinah flipped through the lists of suspects and witnesses they'd spoken to throughout the investigation. And there it was. The same man listed as Peter Ivanov in the army identification kit was also a person they'd spoken to by the name of Ivan Petesky. The biggest difference was that when they'd spoken to Ivan Petesky, his body had been encased in plaster as the result of a car accident.

"I know who he is," she told Ferguson. "It's Petesky, the supposed second grade teacher. We spoke to him about the wrecked car in which Thomas Whitfield's body was found. Do you remember? He was covered in plaster head to toe!"

Ferguson remembered. "And I saw him only a few days later at Whitfield's funeral, no plaster in sight. He was walking around just fine. I just didn't recognize him."

Dinah groaned. "Why did we assume that stupid car accident actually happened?"

"Well, it probably did," conceded Ferguson. "We just didn't check that Petesky was *in* the car accident."

"Who encases themselves in full body plaster to convince the FBI they've been in a car accident?" grumbled Dinah.

"Someone who needs to cover up the fact that he's a killer," replied Ferguson moodily.

Dinah knew how he felt. They had accepted Ivan Petesky's car accident story on face value and fallen for a clever disguise. They were supposed to be smarter than that. "Do you think he's just a killer? Or do you think he's a professional?" Dinah asked.

"Up until five seconds ago, I thought he was a second grade teacher!" Ferguson glared at the computer screen. "I don't think we even know where he taught."

"We'll have to run the usual traces on his real name," said Dinah. "I'll ask Zach to put a priority on it. But I have a hunch that if he is a professional, he'll have disappeared a long time ago. There won't be any social security numbers or recent addresses or teaching records."

"So if he's a pro, who hired him?"

"That's the million-dollar question, isn't it?" Dinah thought hard for a moment. "Is it possibly Justice Maxwell?"

"Or Kenneth MacIntyre?" added Ferguson. "This is so frustrating. Either of them have the means to hire a professional killer. Suddenly MacIntyre's alibi looks a little too convenient."

"Kenneth MacIntyre is somehow involved — his factory was used as the murder scene, and there is chalk dust all over every single body we find. Yet Maxwell Prior is the one cautioning everybody in the museum not to talk to us and essentially asking them to lie." Dinah pursed her lips. "What if they're *both* involved?"

"A joint conspiracy?" Ferguson was silent as he mulled over the idea. "That may actually be a possibility. What I still don't understand is why? Why would Whitfield's conversion to Christianity threaten either of those men?"

"And it didn't just merely threaten them — it induced them into such a state to kill him, and anyone else who might talk about it," added Dinah.

"And also we can't just pressure or threaten Maxwell Pryor into talking." Ferguson socked his fist into his other hand in frustration. "We've effectively been hamstrung!"

Dinah considered. "That's true, but we could always try it with MacIntyre. We've gotten no orders to keep away from him."

Ferguson nodded. "And let's do it on our turf this time. We'll bring him in and make him sweat."

"Excellent," agreed Dinah. "I love making suspects sweat. Do you think a judge would give us a warrant to search Petesky/Ivanov's home?"

"Well, we have his fingerprint on a murdered victim," conceded Ferguson. "I don't see why not. I'll contact a judge tonight. Hopefully tomorrow morning we can search and question this guy."

"Imagine encasing your entire body in plaster just to convince us that you'd been in a car accident!" Dinah shook her head in wonder.

"To be fair, it wasn't a bad idea," Ferguson said. "It also helped to hide his identity for a long time because we didn't have a sharp image in our heads of what he looked like."

"True," agreed Dinah. "But now I think I've seen it all."

\* \* \* \*

For the first time that winter, snow threatened the city. Evening rush hour was atrocious as commuters took a look up at the bleak sky and tried to get home. It took Catherine Biscelli twice as long to get home to her Wesley Heights house, and the temperature had dropped to well below freezing by the time she eventually made it inside her home. Once there, she turned the heat up, changed into sweats, and turned on the television. Dinner could wait a few moments, she thought, while the tension of the drive home drained from her body. It had been a hard day, she reflected. Being caught in the middle with her superiors on one side and the FBI on the other was not at all enjoyable. Even someone as glib as she had difficulty keeping her story straight.

She found some old *X Files* reruns and settled in to watch. She was comfortably ensconced when there was a sudden knock at the door.

Exasperated, she went to the door and looked through the peephole.

"What on earth are you doing out in the cold?" she asked, unbolting the door and allowing her visitor inside. "Come into the warm."

"Thanks," said her visitor, shaking the sleet off his shoulders. "It's threatening to snow now, I'd say."

"Do you want a drink?" Catherine asked. "I can make some hot chocolate."

"Sure, sounds good." Her visitor glanced around the apartment, and while Catherine slipped into the kitchen to make chocolate, he quickly checked that the bedroom and bathroom were clear before he settled on the couch.

Catherine reappeared with two steaming mugs. "So what brings you here?" she asked.

"The boss is a little worried about the FBI investigation," he replied. He took the mug but didn't drink it.

"I thought the FBI was supposed to have backed off by now," Catherine said.

"What do you mean by that?" her visitor asked.

"I didn't realize they'd be so . . . unrelenting," explained Catherine. "That woman agent barges into my office every second day demanding to know about one thing or the other."

"So what do you tell them?"

Catherine laughed. "Well, there's not much to say. They know about Mr. Whitfield's conversion to Christianity. They wanted to know if that was the source of the conflict between him and the board. I guess they're trying to work out why that's such a big deal."

"How did they find out about the Christianity thing?"

"I don't know. They already knew by the time they appeared in my office this morning."

"What else did you tell them?" The visitor leaned forward on the couch.

Catherine drained her mug. "I think that's about it. I don't really know anything else. Why? What's going on?"

"The boss just wants to make sure it's contained. He doesn't want it to turn into a circus."

"Do you know who actually killed Mr. Whitfield?" Catherine asked, starting to feel uncomfortable.

Her visitor ignored the question. "Do you know that we listened to your conversation with the FBI agents this morning?"

Catherine stared at him. "What do you mean?"

"We've listened to every conversation you've had with them in your office," continued the visitor. "Just to make sure you haven't over-stepped the mark."

Catherine was beginning to realize she might be in a bit of trouble. "You *bugged* my office?"

"The boss is a little . . . paranoid."

Catherine glanced around her, trying to estimate how long it might take to get to the phone. Her cell phone was in her handbag that she always stashed in her bedroom. The wall phone was a lot closer, in the kitchen.

"You neglected to mention that you told the FBI agents about what happens to other scientists who get it into their heads that Christianity is a good idea." The visitor leaned close to Catherine. "Why would you say that? Why would you want to confirm their suspicions?"

Catherine shrank away from him. "I . . . I didn't . . . think . . ." she stammered.

"Well, Catherine, that's a problem. We are happy to have you around if you know how to keep your mouth shut. But it would appear that you *don't* know how to keep your mouth shut."

"I do! I just didn't know. . . . I swear I won't talk!" Catherine edged away from her visitor and eyed the front door. How long would it take to sprint through the door to get help from a neighbor?

Her visitor seemed to sense her thoughts. "I'm sorry, Catherine. You know we can't let this go on, don't you?"

Catherine stared at him in horror. "What . . . do you mean?" she whispered.

Her visitor stood and Catherine suddenly knew what was planned for her. For a fraction of a moment, she debated whether to run or fight. She turned and moved quickly toward the door, but in a moment she felt a gloved hand wrapped around her mouth and another arm lifting her from the ground.

Catherine tried to kick out at him, claw at him, bite him, but he was much stronger and bigger than she, and it made no difference. She saw that he was headed to the bathroom, and with complete clarity, saw that there would be no escape.

Snow began to fall at about eight o'clock that evening, at about the same time Dinah had nearly finished her first bottle of wine. Snow always brought back bad memories. Sammy had been born in the middle of a snowstorm in January and seemingly, as a result, had been a snow bunny. He had never been happier than when he was making snow angels or snow men or being pulled in his sled by Luke, his high-pitched squeals of laughter filling Dinah's heart. They had planned to take him on a skiing trip when he was just a little older, knowing that in no time he would have been zooming between their legs at breakneck speed. She and Luke had tried to fit a skiing trip into their schedules and finances at least every two years. There was nothing better than the crisp air, nose numb from the cold, and the crunch and swish of the snow as the skis cut into it in a lazy S down the mountain.

She wondered what it would be like to lie down in the snow and go to sleep. The thought of going to sleep knowing that she didn't have to wake up the next morning and face another day was appealing. Dinah eyed the next bottle of wine. Her strength of resolve not to drink to excess was weak at best, and she knew it slipped away with each passing moment.

Before she knew it, she'd uncorked the bottle and poured another glass. A tiny voice in her head begged her to stop, but the alcohol was too seductive. The pleasure she got from swallowing each mouthful was the greatest positive emotion she had experienced in some years. It numbed the despair she felt at even being alive.

Dinah had almost finished the second bottle when she slipped into the heavy, dreamless slumber of a drinker on the couch.

She was awakened suddenly by the shrill ringing of her cell phone. Dazed and disoriented, she sat up, and the memory of the evening's drinking session flooded back to her. She dug around for her phone and finally answered it.

"It's me," said Ferguson, his voice tight and terse. "We've got another body."

Dinah was still struggling to return to reality. "What? Who is it?"

"Catherine Biscelli was found in her apartment by her sister. Can you meet me there?"

"Uh . . . yeah, sure. What's her address?" Dinah's senses were dull, and she knew it was because she was still drunk.

After she'd hung up, she tried to assess herself. She tried to walk to the door and knew that she was stumbling. She made her way to the bathroom and splashed some water on her face. Her eyes were bloodshot and heavy-lidded.

*I'll be okay,* she told herself, *I'll just concentrate on talking clearly and walking straight. No one will know.*

She decided to catch a cab to the scene, and she had the driver pull up a block away from the patrol cars. She didn't want Ferguson to know that she couldn't drive, because he would know exactly why.

Ferguson was already inside the apartment, standing back while the white-suited crime scene technicians searched for evidence.

"So what happened?" Dinah asked, standing slightly away from her partner in the pretence of staring into the bathroom.

"It's a similar story," Ferguson reported. "She was taken into the bathroom, laid in the shower, and her throat was cut. There looks like a head injury that would have subdued her. It's a very clean scene." He looked resigned. "I'm guessing that we won't find any evidence."

Dinah just nodded, not wanting to speak more than strictly necessary. Then a question occurred to her. "How did the killer get in?" She was pleased with her steady pronunciation of the sentence and didn't notice the odd look Ferguson gave her.

"No sign of break-in at all," he said. "It would appear that she actually knew him and let him in."

"Do you think she was killed because she talked to us?" Dinah asked.

"That's my first guess," agreed Ferguson. "Otherwise it's an awful coincidence, and you know I don't believe in coincidences."

The supervisor of the crime scene technicians appeared from the bathroom. "You guys can come in now."

Ferguson gestured for Dinah to head to the bathroom first. Dinah warned herself to concentrate on walking. She had done pretty well, she thought, until she stumbled at the doorway to the bathroom and grabbed the doorjamb to steady herself. She could almost feel Ferguson's eyes burning a hole in her back.

Dinah focused on the shower. Catherine Biscelli's body lay in the shower cubicle, and it was clear that the killer had turned the faucets on above her. The majority of any blood and evidence had washed down the drain and had left a remarkably "clean" scene, as Ferguson had termed it. She tried to concentrate on the scene, but her brain was dull and slow.

After a few moments, Ferguson suggested, "Let's go outside for a bit."

Dinah complied, following him back downstairs and out into the freezing air. She was glad he hadn't followed her because she knew she was swaying and stumbling despite her best efforts. Finally, when they were out of earshot of the uniformed cops, Ferguson hissed at her, "What do you think you're doing?"

"What do you mean?" Dinah played dumb.

"Look at you!" Ferguson was clearly disgusted. "You've turned up here so drunk you can barely walk. You absolutely reek of alcohol. Are you so stupid to think that I wouldn't notice?"

"I . . . I . . . didn't. . . ." Dinah was shocked by the vehemence of his tone.

"You're talking like you're underwater," continued Ferguson. "The poor crime scene techs inside the apartment nearly collapsed when you walked into the bathroom. I swear I think I'm getting drunk just smelling the fumes coming off you!"

He paused for a moment and then widened his eyes in horror as a thought flashed into his mind. "Oh no, please *please* tell me you didn't drive here tonight!"

"Cab," mumbled Dinah, her face flushed.

Ferguson was somewhat relieved. "I told you when you fell asleep outside the medical examiner's office and then proceeded to throw up in the middle of an autopsy that you had gone too far. Now you've gone even further and done *this*. This is an absolute joke. It's a disgrace! *You're* a disgrace!"

"I . . . didn't think . . ." Dinah tried again.

"What?" demanded Ferguson, his face almost purple with anger. "You didn't think that even though you are an FBI agent in the middle of an active investigation that you might be called to a crime scene in the middle of the night? Is that what you thought?"

He glared at her, waiting for a response.

As sad as it was, it was the truth. Dinah hadn't thought about the fact that she might be called to a murder scene. And would it have mattered even if she did? The need to drink was powerfully strong. She nodded.

Ferguson digested this for a few moments, then shook his head. "You need to go home, Harris. I'm sick of looking at you in this state. If you come into the office in the morning, there better not be any sight of a hangover or I'm going to recommend to Hanlon myself that you be fired on the spot."

He started to walk off, then wheeled around, his tirade not yet spent. "And another thing: I supported you and vouched for you when everybody else thought you were a lost cause. All I wanted was to help you do something you used to love. I wanted you to feel the old spark and thrill of the chase again. And you've let me down so badly that I wonder why I thought it would ever be a good idea. You know what? I think I was wrong; I think you *are* a lost cause."

His fury finally depleted, he turned and walked away from her. Dinah stared after him, an enormous lump rising in her throat.

He was absolutely right, she realized, in calling her a lost cause. If *she* no longer believed in herself, why should anyone else?

\* \* \* \*

The story broke the next morning and it was front-page news.

A photographic team had been following Dinah for days, it seemed, and two huge photos appeared beneath the headline that screamed: FBI Agent Drunk and Disorderly!

The first photo was a headshot of Dinah, asleep in her car with her head resting on the wheel, her mouth slightly open. The caption underneath read: *Agent Harris attends the autopsy of a high-profile murder.* The second photo was from the previous night, stumbling down a curb as she flagged down a cab to leave the site of Catherine Biscelli's murder. The caption beneath read: *Agent Harris at the scene of last night's murder.*

The ensuing article embellished the details. It began by explaining that Dinah Harris was currently working on the Smithsonian murders, despite the fact that she was regularly arriving at work in a drunken state. It wondered if FBI standards had sunk to such low levels as to let an agent with an obvious alcohol addiction work on active cases. It wondered whether the public realized that they were being "protected" by a drunk agent with a firearm. What if, in a drunken state, Agent Harris shot at the wrong person and your son or daughter died as a result? Shouldn't the public require more from its law enforcement personnel?

It went on to helpfully point out that this was not the first time Agent Harris had been embroiled in controversy. In fact, Agent Harris had been reprimanded, demoted, and reassigned following a tragic incident. At the time, the article helpfully explained, she had been the Special Agent in Charge of a small, specialized, highly trained group of negotiators. Their primary focus was the extraction of high-ranking gang members from their respective gangs. They used words rather than force to encourage gang members to turn and inform on their gangs, and then they would set them up in the witness protection program. They had had an unusually high success rate due to Agent Dinah Harris's uncanny ability to connect and negotiate with the gang members. Former gang members described how they trusted her completely in spite of their long-held suspicion and hatred of law enforcement. They were literally entrusting their lives to her, and she never let them down.

There had just been the one time, where she had promised protection to an 18-year-old boy who had joined the gang as a 10-year-old child. He had upheld his part of the bargain, informed Harris's team of all he knew of his gang. He had arrived at the designated safe meeting place ready to enter witness protection, his gang by now very suspicious of him, but the FBI had failed to appear. Several days later his body had been found in an industrial area, horribly mutilated and tortured. Harris had suddenly and spectacularly failed.

The internal inquiry subsequently held by the FBI was a closely guarded secret. At the time, the press believed that the FBI had acted swiftly in trying to protect their star agent for reasons the media had never been able to unearth. Rumor had it that Harris had been drinking heavily on the night the gang member was supposed to be picked up by the FBI, and that she had entirely forgotten about him.

Yet here she was, resurfacing as an active agent on a high-profile case. Surely, the article trumpeted, the public must have absolute faith in the personnel assigned with protecting them! Now look at her: passing out on the job, stumbling down the curb after being sent home from a murder scene. It was unacceptable. The FBI must take action now and weed out agents who were not living up to its lofty standards.

In the midst of a thumping headache and frequent bouts of nausea, Dinah read the article in horror. After dashing to the bathroom to vomit, she re-read the article carefully. The horror dwindled away only to be replaced by dread. This was surely the final nail in her career coffin. There was no way George Hanlon and his superiors would let this article slide. The FBI had taken too much of a media battering over the past several years to allow a single agent to drag its name through the mud again. She would be sacrificed on the altar of law enforcement reputation.

But didn't she deserve it? As a new recruit ten years ago, if Dinah could have seen what she would eventually become, surely she would have been horrified. Back then, she would have been the first to agree that alcoholic agents had no place in the FBI.

*Is that what I am?* Dinah reflected, shocked. *An alcoholic?* The word conjured images of homeless, unshaven, middle-aged men, clutching half-empty bottles of cheap booze, propped up on a park bench. She hadn't considered that it would apply to her. She just needed a drink or two to relax after work! And who wouldn't need a drink after everything she'd been through? She'd lost her family, her very heart and soul, and their space in her life had been replaced by a chasm of despair and hopelessness. The void yawned so deeply within her that even she knew not where it ended. It gruffly demanded her attention. Dinah had found that wine had fed the chasm reasonably well, but even she knew, deep down, that she had to drink more and more to achieve the same level of equilibrium.

She put her head in her hands. The desolation bubbled inside her and it threatened to choke her. It was at these very moments that she began to crave relief from the relentlessness of it, and perhaps the reason she had thought about achieving final release.

Just because it was too much for one person to withstand.

\*\*\*\*

Dinah arrived at the office the following morning, reasonably alert and refreshed. She had slept for most of the previous day, recovering from both the binge drinking and lack of sleep. Late in the afternoon, Ferguson had called, letting her know that she was required at Hanlon's office at nine sharp the next morning. His tone was cool and distant, and Dinah knew that she had finally lost her greatest ally.

An insidious thought had crossed her mind as she'd dressed in a black pants suit that was now a full size too big for her. What if she just had one or two drinks to settle her nerves before going in to face Hanlon? Dinah was dismayed at the depth of her dissoluteness. She was about to lose the final part of her life that had any meaning, and all she could think about was the next drink. Could the disgust and contempt for herself become any worse? She didn't think so.

George Hanlon, the Special Agent in Charge, was waiting for her with Ferguson. As soon as she exited the elevator, the two of them escorted her to her boss's office. Dinah refused to make eye contact with either of them.

When they were seated, Hanlon shook yesterday's newspaper and glowered at her. "I suppose you've seen the article about yourself," he began ominously.

Dinah swallowed and nodded, not trusting herself to speak.

"Well, is it true?"

Dinah stared at Hanlon's hairy forearms. The hair extended all the way down his hands and fingers, and for some reason, they irritated her.

"Yes, sir. It's all true." She lifted her chin and stared at a spot above Hanlon's head.

Hanlon nodded and pursed his lips. "I see. So you *did* pass out at the medical examiner's office, throw up in the garden, and arrive at the most recent murder scene drunk?"

"Yes, I did." From the corner of her eye, she could see Ferguson standing at the side of the room, clearly not wanting to take sides. Dinah had never felt so lonely.

"How long has this been going on?"

Dinah felt her old resentment rise. "How long has *what* been going on? Arriving drunk at crime scenes? I can assure you, that's only happened one time."

Hanlon stared at her. "Now is not the time for sarcasm, Agent Harris. I hold your future in my hands and I suggest you wrap your mind around that before you start with the comments."

Dinah resisted the urge to roll her eyes.

"I want to know how long your drinking has been a problem." Hanlon couldn't take his eyes off the pictures in the newspaper of Dinah, and she could see the contempt in his eyes.

"I don't know," she said honestly. "I don't know when it became a problem. All I know is that it started when . . . you know, when everything happened."

Hanlon nodded. "I suspected as much. Listen, Agent Harris, what would you do if you were in my position?"

Dinah shrugged. "I really don't know."

"Well, my superiors have made it pretty clear to me what I have to do. You must realize that the bureau can't tolerate this sort of behavior and the exposure it creates." Hanlon gestured at the newspaper.

Dinah sat still, waiting for the torturous moment to be over.

"Agent Harris, you're relieved of all duties effective immediately. You will no longer take part in any active investigations and will hand over any relevant materials to Ferguson. You will hand in your firearm and badge to me." Hanlon did a pretty impressive job of looking impassive while he delivered his speech. Inside, Dinah knew he must be gloating.

Her humiliation complete, Dinah complied. She slid the gun and badge across his desk. She still didn't dare look at Ferguson.

"Harris, as a gesture of goodwill, the bureau would like to offer assistance with rehabilitation," continued Hanlon, obviously feeling more confident the further he got into his soliloquy. "We're happy to provide counseling, treatment programs, whatever you need."

Dinah found the idea so ludicrous she almost laughed out loud. Rehabilitation? What was the point of rehabilitating a person who was determined to die?

"Are you done?" she asked, standing, sick of the scene, but mostly sick of herself. "I want to go now."

Hanlon shrugged. "Okay, Harris. What about rehab?"

"Don't bother," she snapped. "I don't want to be a burden on the bureau for a moment longer."

"Harris, it's a great idea," chimed in Ferguson. "I think you should consider it."

"Oh, *now* you speak up," retorted Dinah. "Thank you both for your touching concern, but I think it's best if we just part ways for good." Inside, she wanted to scream, *Stop looking at me with those eyes full of pity!*

Hanlon and Ferguson seemed to sense her desperation, because they both fell silent. Dinah left as quickly as she could. While she waited for the elevator, which seemed to take several centuries, she could imagine the eyes of her former colleagues watching her. *Look at the great Dinah Harris*, they would say to each other. *Look how far she's fallen. She's nothing but an unemployed, hopeless alcoholic. Who would have thought?*

When she arrived home to her small apartment, she sank down on the couch. She felt too numb to cry or feel angry. It was over, she knew. There were no threads remaining, however tenuous, linking her to this life. She had no husband, no child, and no job. There was no longer a solitary reason for her to get up in the morning. The time was finally right.

It was time to end the aching hurt in her heart, her head, her soul.

\*\*\*\*

Now that she'd made up her mind, Dinah felt a strange calm descend upon her. She began to set the scene.

She pulled out the biggest photos of Luke and Sammy she could find, framed pictures she had previously been unable to look at. She traced the familiar lines of their faces — the still-baby roundness of Sammy's cheeks, the wisps of dark hair, the deep blue of his eyes that she could've fallen into. She touched the spiky ridge of Luke's hair, combed carefully forward because he was sure he was balding; the smile that melted her heart, the eyes that looked into her soul and somehow found nothing wanting.

But it was the essence of her family, the thing photos couldn't capture, that Dinah most clearly remembered — Sammy's gurgling laughter, Luke's complete and utter adoration of his son, Sammy's obsession with the Wiggles, Luke's fierce protectiveness of her.

And she'd let them all down. She hadn't been able to protect Sammy, despite the fact that it should have been her sole focus. What else should a mother do but protect her toddler son? She hadn't been able to save Luke, despite swearing to hold him close on their wedding day.

Dinah stared at the pictures and felt the darkness that lived within her heart overwhelm her. She couldn't bear to look into the despairing chasm that gaped within her, knowing she would find hopelessness. Now she was too numb to even cry.

She was ready. Dinah settled into the cushions, propping her beloved pictures around her. A full bottle of sleeping pills and the biggest bottle of vodka that she'd been able to find in the liquor store she propped against another cushion on the other side. She cracked the seal on the vodka and took one full mouthful. It burned down her throat and made her eyes water, but she savored the feeling, for it represented the first step on her final journey to eternal bliss.

*Do you know what comes after death, Dinah?*

The thought seemed to come from nowhere, and unsettled her. She had never thought about that, seeking only release from her current life. She took another mouthful of vodka. What did happen after death? It was the greatest question in life that nobody could really answer. It was a question that couldn't really be answered until you'd actually been there — and then you couldn't come back to tell everyone about it.

Suddenly the doorbell rang. It startled Dinah and she jumped to her feet.

"Dinah? It's just me, Sandra," her caller yelled through the door.

Dinah was torn between not wanting to be rude to Sandra Coleman and wanting to be left alone. Finally, she relented and opened the door.

"Hi," she said weakly. Sandra stood holding an enormous casserole dish that was actually steaming.

"Hi, Dinah." Sandra Coleman smiled at her warmly. "I come bearing gifts." She gestured with the dish.

In confusion, Dinah stood aside and allowed the other woman to enter. Sandra found a kitchen bench and placed the hot dish down. "It's my famous Moroccan chicken," she called.

"Oh, thanks," said Dinah, sitting back down on the couch. While Sandra was in the kitchen, Dinah quickly sneaked a mouthful of vodka. "You didn't have to do that." She was embarrassed. Did she look so pathetic that people now felt the need to feed her?

Sandra sat opposite her in the armchair. "I read the newspaper every day," she offered. "I thought they were being a bit harsh. Nothing cheers me up like a big plate of my favorite food."

Dinah nodded and wondered how to get Sandra out. "Well, thanks," she said. "I really appreciate it."

Then she realized that Sandra wasn't looking at her. She was looking at the vodka bottle and sleeping pills, still in full view on the edge of the couch. Dinah realized, with a sudden shock, that Sandra had just discovered what she was about to do.

"I must confess, I've been wanting a plate of that chicken ever since I made it," confessed Sandra. "I'll just serve it up. What do you think?"

Even if Dinah wanted to refuse, she couldn't think of how to do it. "Okay," she agreed. While Sandra was serving two plates of Moroccan chicken, Dinah took another mouthful of vodka. She was starting to feel a pleasant buzz and relaxation. She was even starting to think that perhaps she would just keep drinking even if Sandra did see her. It was her house, why couldn't she do what she pleased?

Sandra reappeared and Dinah tasted the chicken. It was truly excellent, exotic and spicy without being too overwhelming on the taste buds. They ate companionably in silence for a while, until Dinah had cleaned half her plate and wondered how she could sneak another mouthful of vodka. Finally, the desire for it overcame her need for decorum in front of her guest, and she quickly downed another shot when she thought Sandra wasn't looking.

While Sandra cleaned the dishes in the kitchen, Dinah got further reprieve and downed several more shots. Surely her guest would leave in a minute.

When Sandra re-entered the living room, she sat down on the arm-chair again and looked squarely at Dinah. "Tell me, what were you planning to do here tonight?" she asked.

Dinah tried to look shocked. "What do you mean?"

"Please, let me be blunt. I've only known you a short time, but you appear to me to be extremely depressed. And you're self-medicating with alcohol."

Dinah expected the other woman's words to be judgmental, but they were strangely soft and compassionate.

"I don't know what you've suffered," continued Sandra, "but anyone would surely be negatively affected by the recent media cover-age. Nobody would blame you for that."

Dinah nodded. That was true, the media criticism was harsh and unfair. No wonder she was self-medicating.

"You seem so alone," added Sandra. "I sense a great sadness within you and it troubles me that you have no support to help you. I want to help you."

"You don't understand what I've done," blurted Dinah. She felt confronted and uneasy by Sandra's words, but yet the spark of some-thing — was it hope? — had suddenly been lit.

"I promise you, I don't care what you've done," replied Sandra. She leaned forward and touched Dinah's arm. The human touch startled Dinah. "It is not my place to judge you. In any case, I think you are your own worst judge."

Dinah didn't know how to reply. She was skilled at pushing people away and isolating herself.

"Please, at least give me a few days," asked Sandra. "I know what you want to do." She gestured at the sleeping pill bottle. "Don't do that until you give me a few days to help you. Will you at least give me that?"

Perhaps the alcohol had dulled her fight instincts, but Dinah yielded. What were a few days anyway? She knew what she wanted to do, and she was determined to do it. If she had to put up with Sandra for a few days beforehand, so be it.

Sandra helped her to bed, then returned to the living room. Quietly she poured out the remaining vodka and threw the pills in the trash. Then she lay on the couch with a pillow and blanket, stared into the darkness, and prayed until sleep overcame her.

Dinah began to surface from a deep sleep into wakefulness. She had been having a dream that mirrored her intentions from the previous night — she was sitting on the couch, bottle of pills beside her and vodka bottle in her hand. In her dream, instead of Sandra being there to take away the bottle from her, it was someone she couldn't see. She became aware of the living room being suffused with warmth and kindness, and suddenly her hand let down the bottle of its own accord. Then words sprang into her mind: "Dinah, I love you." The words shocked her to her core. She didn't know anybody left in her life who loved her. The compassion she sensed in those words lit a desire to know more about this faceless person.

Suddenly she awoke. She was disoriented, the dream's tendrils still drifting over her, and a residual of the warmth she'd felt in her dream lingered. Then the events of last night came flooding back, and she realized that she should really be dead. Then she smelled bacon being fried in the kitchen. Sitting up in bed, she ran her fingers through her knotty hair and tried to sort out her confusion. Yesterday she had been determined to kill herself; in fact, she had been halfway along the path to actually doing it. Today, a combination of Sandra's presence and the dream she just had tilted her intentions. Now she didn't know what she was going to do.

Dinah took a hot shower, hoping to kill off her emerging hangover, and then followed her nose to the kitchen, where the smell of frying eggs had joined deliciously with bacon.

Standing in the kitchen were Sandra and Andy Coleman, Sandra cooking on the stove and Andy at the toaster and pouring juice.

"Good morning," said Andy cheerily. "Thought I'd pop in and find my wife this morning. Hope you don't mind."

"Not if you're going to cook breakfast," replied Dinah, trying to match his level of joy.

The three of them sat at the kitchen table together to eat breakfast, a disconcerting feeling for Dinah. She was not used to eating much, let alone eating with others. In a sharp moment of clarity, Dinah realized the extent to which she had isolated herself.

"Actually, I'm here to continue to help with the investigation," Andy said. "I wanted to show you some information I've got on the Smithsonian's past history."

Dinah dropped her eyes. "Oh . . . haven't you heard, Andy? I'm not part of the investigation anymore."

"Well, maybe not officially," replied Andy. "But you already know so much that it makes sense to tell you everything we know and then you can decide what to do from there."

Dinah shrugged. It wasn't as though she had anything better to do. "Okay, what have you got?"

"Well, somewhat unsurprisingly, the Smithsonian has a history of discriminating against staff members who profess Christianity," began Andy. He moved an article across the table toward Dinah. "This article was written by a senior researcher from the institution, and was published in an independent scientific journal."

Dinah glanced at the title of the article. "Irreducible complexity and reproduction," she read. "I have no idea what that means."

Andy briefly grinned. "It's one of the most obvious reasons that evolution doesn't work," he said. "The article talks about how mammal reproduction is so complex that there is evidence of design within it. He doesn't actually mention God or creation or the Bible, but suggests the possibility of an intelligent designer having something to do with the origins of life."

"Right," said Dinah. "So what's the problem?"

"Evolutionists and atheists vehemently deny any involvement of an intelligent designer, whether it be God or anything else. They assert that all living things are related to one another through common ancestry from earlier life forms that differed from them. Evolutionists call this 'descent with modification,' and it is still the most widely used definition of evolution, especially with members of the general public and with young learners. You would have heard the idea — life began as a single-celled organism millions and millions of years ago." Andy sighed. "They believe our most recent ancestors are from ape-like creatures — that over millions of years gradually underwent changes evolving into what we know as modern humans. To evolutionists, humanity is no more special than any other animal or organic matter. If there is even a hint of acceptance that there could be a creator God who is a Supreme Ruler, atheistic evolutionists will go into the strongest mode of defense. The idea of evolution asserts that there is no need for God anymore and really, what they call science is their new religion."

"So what you're saying is that if you don't agree with the evolutionists, there could be a problem?"

"Absolutely; furthermore, there is evidence that it *is* a problem," agreed Andy. "The senior researcher who wrote this article was immediately fired, discredited as a scientist, and labeled a 'fundamentalist Bible basher' by his former colleagues. A large-scale e-mail campaign was circulated throughout the institution and into the wider scientific community, which was essentially full of lies, and goes so far as to call him a creationist." Andy laughed. "What an insult."

Dinah was confused. "Would a scientist who allows for intelligent design have a major problem with being called a creationist?"

"Certainly some would," Andy replied. "Scientists who allow for intelligent design are not necessarily religious at all. They are simply willing to admit what the evidence shows — that there is too much complexity in life to legitimately consider everything happening by chance. An intelligent designer could be anything — even an alien — and this is a long way from belief in a biblical Creator. But evolutionists make their own connection to creationism. I suppose they think that there is a chance that intelligent design conclusions could lead to a consideration of the Bible."

Dinah frowned. "I didn't realize the evolutionists were so radical."

"It goes further than that. The researcher demanded an independent inquiry into his firing, which he felt was unfair. As a result of the inquiry, it was found that the widespread discrediting and character assassination were carefully orchestrated by senior members of the Smithsonian and the most prominent evolutionist-atheistic lobby group in the country."

"IAFSI?" guessed Dinah.

"Exactly right. In fact, the inquiry found that IAFSI has so much power in the scientific community that it can stop peer-reviewed articles from being published in the major journals if it thinks the article questions evolution at all."

Dinah's mind whirred into action. "So if they're willing to fire and discredit an unknown staff member for daring to suggest the possibility of intelligent design rather than evolution, what would they be willing to do to the well-known secretary who had become a Christian?"

"Not just a Christian," added Andy, "but a full-fledged young-earth creationist Christian."

"What do you think happened to Thomas?" Dinah asked.

"I have no doubt he was killed by the Smithsonian and IAFSI," said Andy promptly. "I read and edited the presentation he wrote to Congress, trying to establish an alternative point of view with regard to the origins of life within the institution. The scientific aspect of the report was even peer reviewed by four of the top creationist PhD scientists, just to be sure that it was scientifically flawless. He knew that the institution would be extremely unhappy with what he was planning to do, and he was willing to lose his job over it. I don't think either of us realized they would be willing to take his life."

They all sat in contemplative silence for several moments.

"So what happened when Thomas decided to convert to Christianity?" Dinah asked.

## COLD SPRING, MINNESOTA — 2003
## — THOMAS'S STORY

This school shooting was starting to sound horribly familiar. A 15-year-old boy had killed two classmates, one of whom had had been "mean" to the shooter. Apparently, this was becoming enough to cost a life these days. The community lapsed into shock and confusion.

Again, Thomas sought out Andy and they met in a tiny cafe after Andy had spoken to a large Baptist church in the area.

"I'm glad you're here," Andy said. "The police have found some information relating to the shooter's state of mind on his Facebook site." Andy slid some printouts across the table.

Thomas read, "I will prove that I am the STRONGEST and FITTEST of my species by eradicating those weaker who I see as unworthy of life. They are disgraces of the human race. I am the strongest animal and I will decide who LIVES and who DIES!"

"Is that how most evolutionists think?" Andy inquired.

"No, of course not!" Thomas felt shocked by the words of the shooter. "This is awful."

"I have to tell you, that even though you do not think this way, he was being totally consistent with evolutionary principles. I think this is *exactly* how evolutionists view the world when they allow logical conclusions." Andy stirred creamer and sugar into his coffee. "Isn't one of the strongest principles of evolution that there is no ultimate meaning to life or God-directed purpose?"

"Yes, we do. Science has replaced the need for humans to believe in God," said Thomas.

"So you understand then that if people no longer believe in supreme authority, and they no longer believe that they have a purpose for their lives, and they don't even believe that there is 'right' or 'wrong,' then ultimately they will do whatever they want," explained Andy. "It's clear to me that this shooter believed he was doing the right thing. So how can you, as an evolutionist who believes exactly the same thing, judge him? In fact, he practiced exactly what you people preach."

Thomas was silent.

"In fact, why would you be upset at all? We are all just random accidents, the result of millions of mutations and chemical reactions. Right? This is just another reaction in an animal. You don't get angry when a lion kills a gazelle, so why would you be upset because a human kills another human?"

"Well, because it's wrong to do that," Thomas blurted.

"No, you can't use that argument," corrected Andy. "If you don't believe in God, and therefore have no ultimate basis for any difference between right and wrong, how can you say anything is absolutely wrong?"

Thomas stared at the table, trying to think of a reply.

"I'll tell you why *I* think this latest school shooting is wrong," continued Andy. "Because God clearly tells us throughout the Bible that the murder of other human beings is wrong. That is why cultures that have a Christian heritage still include this law in their criminal codes. While I am deeply saddened, I am not shocked that such things happen, because I believe that we live in a world ruined by sin and that mankind is capable of all kinds of evil. What amazes me is why evolutionists and atheists are shocked that such things happen.

"Really, I would have thought you'd be happy that incidents like this seem to confirm your belief that we are nothing but accidental animals," Andy went on. "But to confirm this as evolutionary behavior actually doesn't condemn the behavior because it should be normal evolutionary behavior that is applicable to all evolved beings. Only God says it is a result of sin and is evil and wrong."

Thomas was troubled by Andy's words.

"Did you know that Jeffrey Dahmer, one of our worst serial killers, believed evolution as truth? He said that basically, if there is no God, then there is no point in modifying behavior to within socially acceptable ranges. He felt the need to be a mass murderer, and if he's not accountable to God, then why shouldn't he be allowed to do whatever he wants? If he, as a human male within our kind, is stronger than another human, then isn't he free to take a weaker life if he chooses? That's just survival of the fittest, isn't it?"

Thomas objected: "Come on, I know for a fact that even *you* believe in natural selection."

Andy nodded. "Yes, I do, with the following qualification: I believe we can see natural selection at work when we find long-haired dogs native to cold climates, and short-haired dogs native to hot climates. It is rational and logical to believe that short-haired dogs in cold climates might struggle to survive and would die out over time. A true understanding of natural selection within God's ordination of kinds certainly does not justify murder or violence of any kind, or even racism."

Thomas absorbed this information for several moments. "Okay, I can understand your arguments there," he said at length. "But I've just never been able to take God seriously. Science has the answers for so many problems. Look at what we've achieved in the medical field."

"You know I'm a scientist, right?" Andy asked. "Believing in God and being a scientist are not mutually exclusive. And while I agree with you that science *has* found answers for many things, it falls short many times. For example, can science explain why that young man put on a mask and gunned down his fellow students? Can science explain why a husband and father would leave his wife and children after 20 years of marriage, or why a young lady with potential to be anything she wants to be continues to shoot heroin into her veins despite the knowledge that it'll kill her? Science can't really explain the essence of our *humanity*, our spirit and soul. But God can explain all of those things, because He formed you with His own hands, breathed life into you with His own breath, and watches over you even today."

"I've never believed there to be a God so personal," admitted Thomas. "If I've ever thought about a God, it's that He's up in heaven somewhere, occasionally looking down to see if we're all still here. I certainly don't think of Him as caring about *me*."

"He most certainly does. He knows you better than you know yourself, and yet He still loves you more than you can imagine." Andy grinned. "I say 'yet' because even you would have to admit you have *some* flaws."

Thomas smiled briefly. "How do you know that?" asked Thomas. "I mean, how can you say with all certainty that you know God loves us?"

"Well, the Bible tells us that many times," Andy said. "But there is one particular event in history which absolutely clinches it. When I tell you that I, along with other Christians, believe the human race to be sinners, what do you think?"

"I've heard the term. I suppose I think it means none of us are perfect."

"Right. None of us are perfect, and the reason for that is because the first man and woman, whom you can read about in Genesis, disobeyed God's commands. They were created perfect, you see, in a perfect world, completely at one with God. But they ruined it, and the world has never been the same since. We're all born into sin and there is nothing we can do to escape this state. We are in constant rebellion, if you like, against God. That is why we see murder, robbery, adultery, child abuse, lying, and deceitfulness all around us, and why we indulge in it ourselves. It's like we can't help ourselves. That's because we can't escape who we are — less than perfect."

"Okay, so if we've messed everything up so bad, why does God let it go on?" Thomas asked. "Why didn't He just end it all?"

"Well, because of His enormous love. Picture this: our Creator God, just having created a beautiful, perfect world complete with two perfect people, is disobeyed and rejected by those very people. You would almost expect a fit of rage, destruction of everything, and then sitting in the corner of the universe wondering why it all went so horribly wrong. The opposite is true: despite Adam and Eve having failed Him, He could not turn off His love for them — or us — any more than you could stop loving your own kids. So now we have a problem. We have a God who is both perfect and loving. He can't tolerate our sin, but He loves us too much to simply wipe us out. So what can we do about that?"

"I expect that most people would say that living a good life was enough," said Thomas. "You know, working hard, being good to your family, having a decent set of morals."

"The answer is, actually, there is nothing you can do," replied Andy. "Based on God's commands in the Bible, if you've ever told a lie, if you've disobeyed your parents, or maybe cursed at someone, then you've fallen into the category of sinner. The truth is, nobody can possibly live up to the perfect standard of God. So God, in His great love, decided to do something about it Himself. There needed to be a way where God could punish sin, once and for all time. But He needed to do this to Someone who had never sinned. It was up to God Himself, once again, to provide the Person upon whom His anger and punishment would be inflicted. And so He sent His Son, Jesus Christ, to earth to fulfill this requirement for the sinless blood of a spotless lamb. He lived among us, here on earth, in a fully human form. He was tempted and mistreated, just like we are. He dealt with those who treated Him cruelly with love and compassion. He did not seek revenge. He did not call down legions of angels to destroy those who might kill Him. His purpose was greater. You see, when Jesus died upon the Cross, He not only suffered a physical death, He also suffered the outpouring of wrath and judgment of God for every sin that mankind has ever committed, and will ever commit; not because He deserved it, but because *we* deserved it. Can you understand it? Jesus, who is God, bore our punishment rather than allowing us to suffer it ourselves. And the shedding of His perfect blood was the final covering necessary."

Andy paused, gathering his thoughts. "Then He rose from the dead three days later, in victory over death. He is powerful enough to defeat death, which is why Christians do not have to fear death. We know that the God who loves us enough to sacrifice Himself upon the Cross, and who defeated death, will raise us up in life. That is why we do not believe, as atheists do, that there is nothing after death. We believe that there is eternity after death, and that the decisions you make here on earth will determine where you spend eternity. If you acknowledge and believe in Jesus, the Son of God, if you understand yourself to be a sinner who cannot be worthy in God's eyes but cling to the power and love of Christ's sacrifice on the Cross, then you can be sure you will be with God in heaven. If you don't, God will grant your wish — you will not have to spend eternity with Him, but will spend it in hell."

Thomas was transfixed. "But how do you *know*? How do you know for certain?"

****

Thomas was determined to stay in Minnesota until he'd heard the end of the story. He met up with Andy the following morning over a hot breakfast. He'd lain awake all night, thinking about the things Andy had said, not only the previous day but also through the years that they'd debated and argued the subject. He'd thought about the arguments he'd used to refute Andy. To his own surprise, he was beginning to open his mind to a different way of thinking.

"So last night, you asked me how I knew for certain all of the things I've told you up to this point," Andy began. "And I know the standard answer of 'because the Bible says so' is not going to satisfy you."

"No, I'm afraid it wouldn't." Thomas tried to articulate how he felt. "I know that Christians believe the Bible, but I've never understood why. I mean, why do you not accept that it could be wrong?"

"You know what? I'm really glad you are questioning me on that," Andy said. "It's easy for Christians to believe what they do without *ever* understanding why they believe it. I think it's important for us to understand why we believe it, for it truly deepens the awe and appreciation for God. Here's why I believe the Bible is absolutely the truth, given to us by God. The ultimate argument is that the Bible claims to be the word of God. It claims authority and it claims to be totally accurate. The onus is on the critics to prove if it is wrong because this claim is special. If the Bible is God's Word, claims contained therein are from God. I have never — not once — found evidence that does not support the historical accuracy of the Bible that leads me to see its authenticity in its message about not only the history of this world but also the history of Jesus as our Savior. In fact, I have not found a scientific avenue yet that hasn't supported the claims of biblical authority including geology, astronomy, biology, anthropology, or any other area."

Thomas interjected, "But aren't there many critics who have disputed that? Archaeologists and others?"

"Many critics of the Bible claim that it is outdated and unreliable, and base these arguments on archaeological discoveries. For example, the critic Ferdinand Baur claims that the New Testament wasn't written until late in the second century A.D., a time period during which myths and legends about Jesus had been exaggerated and idealized. Actually, there have been many documents discovered, such as the Chester Beatty Papyri, dated A.D. 150, that confirm the accuracy of the New Testament and bridge the gap between the time of Christ's life and existing manuscripts from later dates. Furthermore, this type of evidence leads to the belief that the books of Jesus' life, the gospels, were produced within one generation after His death and Resurrection, allowing little time for folklore and myth to exaggerate the details of His life since people were still alive who had been with Him."

Andy stopped to eat bacon. Still chewing, he continued. "Another famous archaeologist, Sir William Ramsay, had always taught that the New Testament, particularly the Book of Acts, was not written in the first century as is claimed, but rather in the second century and was therefore unreliable. However, during his research into the history of Asia Minor, he spent some time examining the Book of Acts and finally came to the conclusion that the author was a historian of the finest rank, that the facts were meticulous in their accuracy, and that it was a book of absolute reliability.

"Of course, critics today still argue that over the past 2,000 years, the Bible has to have been changed from its original form and, even if it once was accurate, that it couldn't possibly continue to be accurate today."

"Exactly. That's what I've always thought." Thomas's eggs were cold and he pushed his plate away.

"Well, that's a valid argument. None of the original manuscripts are still in existence, so we would have to ask the question, how reliable and consistent are the copies that we have? This is true not only of biblical manuscripts, but any document. For example, Aristotle wrote his poetics in 343 B.C., but the copy we have is dated 1,400 years later, and only five of these copies exist. We have nine copies of the first century historian Josephus, which were written some 1,000 years later than the originals. Yet the reliability and accuracy of these early writings aren't criticized.

"Compared to Aristotle and Josephus, there are *5,600* biblical manuscripts, far more material than any other ancient book. In 1975, 200 biblical manuscripts were discovered in the Sinai. All confirm that the New Testament has been preserved throughout the centuries with remarkable purity. In fact, Sir Frederic Kenyon, director and principal librarian at the British Museum, has said of these early copies of biblical manuscripts that the last foundation for any doubt that the Scriptures have come down to us as they were written has now been removed. So I think it is safe to say that we can trust the accuracy of the Bible as it stands today."

"I understand that point," conceded Thomas. "But how do you know that the original authors were themselves credible? I mean, couldn't the Bible be the result of a madman's ramblings? There is a great deal of it that doesn't make a lot of sense, as I recall."

"Absolutely." Andy rubbed his hands together enthusiastically, bacon forgotten. "I can't tell you how glad I am that you're asking these questions. We would then apply the test of internal criticism, which aims to determine whether the original written record was of itself credible. The author of such records must have been present to the events, both geographically and chronologically. For example, the best people to record the history of American society in the 21st century are ourselves, because we both live in the society we are chronicling and during the relevant time period. Biblically speaking, there are six eyewitness accounts of the life of Jesus Christ, one of whom is Luke. Luke has been acknowledged by both liberal and conservative scholars alike to be an extremely accurate historian, and the other five eyewitness accounts are very close to Luke's account of Christ's life. Furthermore, many of the eyewitnesses contained within these accounts were hostile and would have needed no encouragement to challenge the validity of the writings if they were inaccurate. Finally, we can obtain corroboration of the biblical transcripts through external sources, such as the Jewish historian Josephus and the Roman historian Tacitus. Both of *these* gentlemen are accepted universally as being reliable in their relation of history during the time of Jesus. Josephus specifically refers to Jesus Christ in his writings as being the martyred leader of the church in Jerusalem, and that he was a wise teacher who had a large and lasting following of believers despite being crucified under the reign of Pontius Pilate. Now, Josephus *wasn't* a follower of Jesus during this time and in fact was sympathetic to the Romans, so you wouldn't expect more than a basic account of his life. What's interesting is that historically, his account and the biblical accounts are very similar. Secondly, Tacitus refers to Christians being persecuted during the time of Nero. Tacitus was wholly unsympathetic to Christians but still records the success and spread of Christianity based on Jesus, who was crucified under Pontius Pilate. He also reports that a large number of Christians were willing to die rather than recant their Christianity."

Andy paused to drink his coffee.

Thomas nodded slowly. "So let me see if I have gotten this straight: if you apply the standard tests of historicity to the early biblical manuscripts as one would to the manuscript of Aristotle, Josephus, and Tacitus, the results are overwhelmingly in favor of the Bible being an accurate historical record, relatively unchanged throughout the centuries."

"That's right," agreed Andy. "The question for you is: *if* the Bible is accurate and reliable, what are you going to do about the message it contains?"

There was silence for several moments.

"I don't know, Andy," admitted Thomas at length. "But you've given me a lot to think about. I can at least promise you that I'll give it some serious consideration. I can tell you that I have one major hurdle to taking this all a lot more seriously."

"Oh? What's that?"

"If we can go back to the evidence that we both use to support our arguments: every time you look at evidence you start with the Bible. Your belief flavors everything you find." Thomas watched Andy intently, waiting for the answer.

"You're talking about a presupposition, Thomas, and you have them as well," Andy replied easily.

"How can you say that? For us, evidence is all we have. We don't have an underlying belief system."

"Actually, Thomas, I can prove your presupposition. Let me give you an example question. How do you determine how old a rock or a fossil is?"

Thomas looked relieved to be asked such an easy question. "Radiometric dating, of course. See, no presupposition."

"Actually, there is. Radiometric dating works on the basis of estimating the age of rocks from the decay of their radioactive elements, right?"

"Yes, we measure the half-life of elements such as polonium and uranium. We can then extrapolate the calculation to determine the age of the rock. No presupposition still," Thomas said confidently.

"Not quite. Your calculations rely on three critical assumptions. The first is the initial condition of the rock sample — something you couldn't possibly personally observe. The second assumption is that the amount of the radioactive elements in the sample has not been altered by any other process. As scientists, we must admit that rarely do conditions in the natural world remain constant. Thirdly, you assume that the rate of decay has remained constant since the rock was formed. These assumptions are, in effect, your presupposition. You know that different circumstances can dictate release rates, but you have not presupposed that any of these circumstances could have been a factor. Your presupposition is that current conditions are exactly as they have been in the past."

Thomas was impressed. "I see your point. You are telling me that when I consider that the present is the same as the past, that is a presupposition."

"Precisely. We both have starting points. The difference is that my presupposition, the Bible, never changes. I have not yet seen any evidence to place my presupposition in conflict. It seems when there is a conflict with your starting point, you just change your presupposition. That doesn't seem consistent, does it?"

Andy drained his coffee and continued, "Look at what was discovered at Mount St. Helens. We know that rocks were formed as a result of the volcanic eruption in 1980. In 1997 dating tests were performed on a rock sample using radiometric dating. The results of the tests claimed that the rock could be up to 2.8 million years old! We know that this cannot be true. Therefore, this is a good example of the failing of your presupposition. So how am I supposed to believe any of your other claims of rocks and fossils being millions of years old when I know that the dating methods you use are seriously flawed?"

Thomas was considering Andy's response. "Andy, you really do have some great points. This is the first time in my life that anyone has been able to get me to really consider God. I truly will give it some real thought and we'll keep in touch."

"My God is an awesome God," said Andy as they stood. "You can't run from Him forever. He knows exactly where to find you."

## WASHINGTON, DC — PRESENT DAY

Dinah sat lost in thought for several moments.

"So he became a Christian," she said at length. "We know that because we found his presentation to Congress. Somewhere along the line, he seriously irritated some fundamentalist atheists."

"Right," agreed Andy. "We live in a culture that considers science as holy as religion because, whether they acknowledge it or not, evolutionism requires an incredible amount of faith, and they won't stand for anyone questioning their beliefs. If you can find out who is the most strident atheist in that organization, I think you'll find the killer."

All three of them pondered that thought in silence and were startled when there was a knock at the door. Dinah was surprised to find Ferguson standing on the step, a dusting of snow on his shoulders. She was not surprised to find Ferguson eating a chocolate and jelly doughnut.

"Hey," he greeted as he shrugged out of his coat. He nodded toward Andy and Sandra. "I thought I'd come and see how you were doing."

He didn't meet Dinah's eye, and she knew what he was getting at — how bad had her bender been? He was clearly relieved to see her standing alive and sober and probably even more relieved to see the Colemans with her.

"I hope everything has settled down at the office," Dinah said. "Did Hanlon reassign you a new partner?"

"Settled down . . . you could say that," said Ferguson, dropping his heavy frame onto the couch. "The investigation is not considered active. I have been moved on to other cases."

Dinah stared at him. "Are you serious?" How could the investigation be deemed inactive? There were four reasonably fresh unsolved murders, all of whom were linked and one of whom involved a high-profile victim.

"I'm afraid so — Hanlon dropped the news right after you left," confirmed Ferguson.

"Don't you think that's a little weird?" Dinah's mind was whirring into action.

"More than a little," agreed Ferguson. "That's why I'm here. I have to make some pretense of investigating these other cases so I simply can't devote the time I'd like to this case. But you can, off the record and unofficially."

Dinah shook her head. "Ferguson, I've been fired from the bureau entirely. I have no badge, no gun, and no authority. How am I supposed to make people talk to me?"

"You usually find a way," replied Ferguson dryly. "Listen, all I'm asking for is your mind. I can keep gathering information under the radar, but I don't have time to brainstorm. That's where you come in."

Dinah considered this. "Okay, what do you have for me?"

Ferguson produced several sheets of paper, with headshot photos. "Here's the list of employees of the Smithsonian," he began. "Guess who's on security staff?"

Dinah waited. "Who?"

Ferguson pointed at a familiar face. "One Mr. Ivan Petesky or Mr. Peter Ivanov, whatever his real name is. Only he's adopted a different alias in this case, Mr. Paul Petranov."

"Imaginative," murmured Dinah.

"Right. So I tell Hanlon this yesterday. I think we have a good case to obtain an arrest warrant and grill his Russian butt. I think he's our killer, acting on the orders of someone else. He's definitely got the hallmarks of a seasoned, military-grade, professional killer. Hanlon finally agrees with me, and gives me authorization to go to a judge for a warrant. I got one from Johnson late last night, was ready this morning to make the bust." Ferguson then whipped out the morning newspaper with a flourish. "Look at this."

It was a tiny article, almost an afterthought. The caption read: *Cessna down over Atlantic, all feared dead.*

Dinah read the article. At midnight last night, a privately owned Cessna took off from Boston, carrying the pilot and two passengers. Radio contact was lost an hour after take-off, the plane disappeared, and a search would be resumed in the morning to look for wreckage and survivors. However, it was feared all three had died.

One of the passengers was Petesky/Ivanov/Petranov.

Dinah's heart started pounding. "You *can't* be serious!" she exclaimed. She stared at Ferguson. "Are you thinking what I'm thinking?"

"For the first time in history, probably," admitted Ferguson. "So here's what I need you to do. This needs to be untangled. We've got four murders, the victims somehow caught in a Smithsonian/IAFSI scheme. The first victim is beaten and killed in a factory owned by one of the board members of the Smithsonian. The second and fourth victims are warned not to talk to the FBI by another board member. The killer is shadowy ex-military who has conveniently disappeared right around the time he's due to be arrested. The FBI suddenly closes the case. There is a puppet master, Harris, and I want to know who that is."

"Who on earth would have that much power?" Dinah asked, astonished.

"Here are some safe assumptions, I think," said Ferguson. "It's almost certainly a board member of the Smithsonian, acting with some level of collaboration with other board members. There has to be a connection to IAFSI. There may even be a link to the bureau. It's just going to take some heavy-duty time and research to make it all clear."

"Do you know what you're saying? All of the members on that board are high-ranking politicians or business people. We're suggesting one of them has organized four murders, followed by the disappearance of the actual murderer, just to avoid some conflict over Christianity and evolution! That is almost unbelievable." Dinah chewed her fingernails, her mind whirring with the possibilities.

"Actually, it's not," chimed in Andy Coleman. "If you remember, the first time I spoke with you, I thought you were my usual contact within the FBI. I get so many death threats and bomb threats that my security is permanently monitored. It would take only one of these people to succeed in business or politics, assume some power, and establish their personal agenda. It would only take a little patience."

"Aren't *you* worried?" Dinah asked him. "Given your beliefs and the fact that you're speaking to us, surely you have to be worried about your own safety."

Andy shrugged. "I've got a choice. I could always be worried about my safety, or I could get on with life. I believe in God, so I believe that He's got everything under control as the Bible tells me."

"But you're not worried about dying?"

"Not at all. I've always thought heaven would be a pretty nice place."

*Remarkable,* thought Dinah. Neither of them cared about dying — but for Dinah, the concept was fraught with pain and despair, while Andy was relaxed and trusting.

Dinah wondered how she, too, could achieve the same frame of mind.

Dinah made herself a strong coffee and plugged in her laptop. She was reasonably sure that due to bureaucratic inefficiency, the bureau would not yet have cut off her access to their computer systems and she wanted to make the most of it. The Colemans waved goodbye, seemingly satisfied that their charge was stable, at least for the moment.

The trail started with Ivan Petesky/Peter Ivanov. Dinah started at the beginning of what they knew about him: that he had been an infantryman. She pulled up the military records and found that he had enlisted in the marines in the early 1980s, and had served in Beirut in 1982, giving him his first taste of war. Participation in the invasion of Panama followed in 1989 and a tour of the Gulf War in 1991. At this point, Petesky joined the Delta Special Ops and reports of his activities became non-existent. Dinah couldn't find any further information until he resurfaced in 2000, honorably discharged.

Dinah frowned. The information, sketchy as it was, seemed to suggest that Petesky had received extensive specialist training throughout his two decades within the armed forces that would easily translate into an ability to skillfully kill unsuspecting civilians. It would explain why Thomas Whitfield, Lara Southall, and Catherine Biscelli had allowed the killer into their offices and homes — they would have known him and trusted him as a fellow member of staff at the Smithsonian.

Still the million-dollar question hadn't been answered — who was instructing him? He was a trained marine, used to following orders.

Dinah went back to the beginning of her search, when Petesky had enlisted in the marines. Perhaps she could find a common thread between his time in the military and his employment at the Smithsonian.

She found the answer during Petesky's tour of the Gulf in 1991. For several moments, she sat in shock, wondering if she was mistaken. It was so ludicrous that it almost made her laugh, yet it fit so beautifully that, deep down, Dinah knew she was right.

Dinah's thoughts were interrupted by a light tap at the front door. As she stood to open it, it slowly swung open and she realized that she hadn't locked it after the Colemans had left earlier that morning. Still fixed on her discovery, Dinah barely looked up, assuming it was Ferguson or the Colemans.

The sudden sensation of a much bigger person in the room finally caught Dinah's attention. He was dressed from head to toe in black and he trained a Magnum Desert Eagle handgun on her chest.

Dinah's jaw dropped. "You! I thought you. . . ."

Ivan Petesky grinned. "Dead? Yes, so does everyone else. It's much more convenient."

Dinah rapidly inventoried the weapons available to her. She had been forced to hand back the standard-issue Glock when she'd been fired from the bureau, and although most agents had a personal backup weapon, she had never thought to obtain one. The thought of even the Glock in the same house as Sammy had made her feel ill.

"What do you want?" Dinah asked.

"I want you to come for a ride with me," said Petesky. "We've got some things to sort out."

"I see. You think you can just order an FBI agent around?" Dinah demanded, fear giving way to anger.

Petesky laughed. "Don't you mean an *ex*-FBI agent?"

His smug demeanor irritated Dinah. "Why don't we trade? I'll come with you if you answer a few questions for me."

"That's an interesting proposition, but here's the thing: the one with the gun gets to control the person without the gun. So you can forget about your proposition. I suggest you come with me before I feel compelled to take out your right kneecap." Petesky smiled pleasantly.

"All right, no need to get nasty," conceded Dinah. Her mind was whirling, trying to think of ways to escape this situation.

Petesky gestured with the gun for her to walk in front of him through the door and down to a waiting black Towncar with smoked black windows. He pressed the gun into the small of her back as he pushed her into the back seat of the car.

"Where are we going?" Dinah demanded. "And do you really think there won't be people looking for me within the hour?"

"Who?" sneered Petesky. "Your FBI colleagues? They laugh behind your back. You're nothing more than a joke to them."

Dinah didn't reply, knowing he was probably right. Her heart sank.

"So was it during your time in the Delta Special Ops when you learned how to garrote someone with a piece of wire?" she asked.

This time, Petesky's smile was distinctly unpleasant. "Among other things."

"I'd have thought you'd be better trained than to simply cut someone's throat," goaded Dinah. "How amateur."

His facial expression didn't change.

"I must say, it's dedicated of you to get into plaster from neck to toe just to convince us you'd been in a car accident," continued Dinah. "Whose idea was that? Little bit dramatic, though, don't you think? I would've thought a cast on the arm would be enough."

Petesky aimed the gun at her knee. "You are getting on my nerves. Shut up, or I'll take out your right kneecap first."

Dinah crossed her arms across her chest, stared out of the dark window, and wondered if anyone would ever see her again.

\*\*\*\*

The trip wound through downtown DC. Dinah stared out of the window to keep track of where they were going. As she did so, a nasty thought struck her: if her assailants didn't care if she knew where she was being taken, they probably didn't intend for her to remain alive. Dinah's palms began to sweat. *Think!* she screamed at herself. *You're an FBI agent; surely you can think of some way to get out of this!* But her mind remained blank, paralyzed by fear.

Petesky sat in silence opposite her, the gun aimed at her without wavering and with inscrutable eyes. Dinah spent the time trying to connect the remaining pieces of the puzzle and trying to allay her fear.

Finally, the car stopped and Petesky motioned at her to get out. Dinah obeyed and found herself in the warehouse district of the city, outside the chalk manufacturing plant of Kenneth MacIntyre. It was here that they'd found the crime scene for the murder of Thomas Whitfield, and soon, presumably, Dinah Harris. Dinah glanced around her, trying to gain an understanding of her surroundings. The district around her was dark and quiet; there seemed to be no other people around to whom she could run or shout to obtain their attention.

Petesky seemed to anticipate her thoughts and reminded Dinah of his presence by pressing the gun against her spine. "Just walk forward," he growled. "Nobody will be able to help you here."

Petesky guided her into the warehouse, past the cavernous plant floor, through to the offices located at the back of the building. Dinah looked for one thing only — doors that exited to the outside. However, it was clear that like many industrial buildings, there were few ways to get out other than the front and back doors.

Finally, they stood outside the door of the main administration office. Petesky motioned her to open it and enter. Dinah did so and crossed the threshold into a threadbare office containing a cheap desk and chair, computer, and phone. Behind the desk sat the master puppeteer, the one who had orchestrated all four deaths.

It was the senator from California, David Winters.

He smiled at her. Dinah glared back.

"Please, take a seat," he invited, pointing at a pair of decrepit plastic chairs. His tone indicated that there wasn't much of a choice.

"Well," he continued, "you are a surprise package, I must say. You've caused us no end of trouble, which was rather unexpected."

"I *am* an FBI agent," Dinah replied tartly.

The senator laughed. "Come on, let's be honest. We all know that you *used* to be a highly effective agent. Vodka has taken its toll now though, hasn't it?"

Dinah flushed. "What were you expecting, that I couldn't do my job?"

David Winters shrugged. "More or less. That's what *I* was told to expect."

"Who told you that?"

Winters smiled as he stood and pulled out a paper bag from underneath the desk, from which he took a bottle of bourbon and an acrylic tumbler. "I think I'll leave that until later." He poured himself a shot of bourbon. "Would you like a drink?"

Dinah heard the mocking tone. "No thanks."

"There's a first time for everything, isn't there? *You* turning down alcohol, I mean."

"Do you have a point?"

"Actually, I do." Winters suddenly turned serious. "Your investigation into this matter is over."

"No, it isn't," shot back Dinah. "There are four people dead. That isn't the kind of thing I'm willing to sweep under the rug."

"It's my understanding that you've been fired from the bureau, effective immediately." Winters swished the liquid in his tumbler and then downed it in a smooth motion.

Dinah didn't reply. She didn't want to mention Ferguson, whom she knew would continue to investigate.

"And let's face it, who would believe a discredited drunk?"

Dinah decided to change the subject. "So you met your little slave over there in the military?" she said, gesturing over at Petesky. "I know that you were his commanding officer in Delta Special Operations forces in the Gulf War."

"My military record is public," said Winters, pouring another shot of bourbon. "I have a long, distinguished career that helped me immensely in my political campaigning. The country loves a war hero."

"What was it about Petesky that made him stand out?"

Winters smiled. "He kills without impunity. It's rare to find a man so thoroughly without a conscience."

"So you took him under your wing?"

"You could say that. You might also say that I helped him *develop* his skills."

"And you helped him develop his torturing skills as well?" Dinah asked sarcastically.

Winters laughed. "He doesn't need any encouragement in that area, I can assure you."

"So why? Why do four people have to lose their lives at your orders?"

"Let's start with the most recent, shall we?" Winters drained his drink. "Sure you don't want a drink?"

Dinah shook her head.

"Well, Catherine Biscelli was asked not to mention certain conflicts within the institution," said Winters.

"How much did she know? She gave all kinds of grief."

"Of course she did — she knew how to do her job. She really knew nothing. Originally, she was told that the board of regents and Thomas Whitfield were having some conflicts and to keep it out of the media. When Whitfield disappeared, we told her not to mention anything of the conflict to the investigators. We also told her that eventually the heat would cease and that the FBI would lose interest."

"That's all she knew? She was killed because she mentioned there was conflict between the board and Whitfield?" Dinah asked skeptically.

"We would have preferred it that nobody knew about it." Winters shrugged. "I'm nothing if not thorough. I don't leave loose ends."

"What about Damon Mason from IAFSI?"

"He was a different proposition altogether," admitted Winters, leaning back in his chair with his hands clasped behind his head. "He knew everything. In fact, we nicknamed him Perry, you know, after the detective Perry Mason because he was always sniffing around. He was horrified when he found out what Whitfield was proposing to do. He organized meetings with the board of regents and wanted to know what we were going to do about it. I took charge, told him I'd take care of it. At the time, he didn't know we were going to kill Whitfield if he refused to back down, but Mason took the news pretty well. His main concern was that this Christianity nonsense would be kept out of the Smithsonian."

"Why would he care so much? Does Christianity pose such a threat to evolution that you would take such drastic steps?"

"Fundamentalist Christianity is a stain on our society," said Winters, a sudden snarl in his voice. "It's hypocritical and repressive. It takes away personal freedom and independent thought. It promotes scientific ignorance."

It was a similar refrain to what Damon Mason had told Dinah and Ferguson during their interview with him.

"So he seems to me to be on your side. Why would you then get rid of him?"

"Unfortunately he lacked the discipline required." Winters was silent for a few moments. "Murder is a means to an end for myself and Ivan, but Mason actually had some moral objections."

"How ironic," commented Dinah dryly. "Atheism and morals — about as far apart from each other as you could get. So he was killed because he was about to tell us what happened?"

"He couldn't be trusted. He seemed to be crumbling under the pressure of what he knew and your repeated threats of throwing him in jail. So we took the easiest option."

"What about Lara Southall? Just another innocent victim?"

"A similar situation to Catherine, I'm afraid. She didn't know much about the conflict between the board and Whitfield, but she was in the unique position of being close enough to Whitfield to know that the conflict was more than insignificant. And we weren't sure what Whitfield had confided in her in the days leading up to his disappearance. So we warned her, then we finished the job. She was explicitly told not to speak to you."

"So the problem with all of those three victims is that they had big mouths?"

"Right," sighed Winters. "Civilians have no capacity to follow orders. Sometimes I think I'd prefer it back in the army."

Dinah shook her head in amazement. "You can't control people, you know. A second ago you were bleating on about personal freedom and now you're wishing you could make people do what you want. That sounds a bit inconsistent to me."

Winters laughed. "I see you haven't killed *all* your brain cells yet."

Dinah was silent for a few moments, then asked, "So what about Thomas Whitfield?"

Winters poured himself another drink. He leaned back in the chair and lifted the drink in the air in a mock salute to Dinah. "I can certainly see why this stuff can be addictive. I can't really blame you for that."

Dinah clenched her jaw and waited.

Finally, Winters said, "Well, Thomas Whitfield really brought this on himself. He was hired specifically for his scientific background, and for the direction we wanted the institution to take. We wanted someone who would staunchly defend the principles of science."

"Someone who was an evolutionist, you mean," interjected Dinah.

"Yes, to be blunt. He was a member of IAFSI and had been an evolutionist all his life. We thought he was a safe bet."

"So what happened?"

"He started hanging around that irritating Coleman fellow," said Winters. "He ended up being completely brainwashed. We didn't know he would be so easily influenced. Of course we watched them go head to head in the debates and so forth, but I didn't count on them actually *liking* each other. Eventually they ended up being friends and Whitfield actually converted to Christianity. That would have been barely tolerated, but he wasn't content to leave it there. He wanted to include in the Smithsonian exhibits that advocated creationism as a credible alternative for how the world began. Can you believe it? He discussed it with the board, and obviously we were not happy. We've been fighting against creationism for many years."

"Of course. In spite of your outward declarations of personal freedom of thought, speech, and religion, you really don't want anyone to practice any religion except atheism, right?" Dinah said mildly. "That doesn't sound like freedom of religion to me; that sounds like religious persecution."

Winters glared at her. "That's not true! Science is the one remaining area where religion can't sink its insidious claws. Yet Christians think they can exert control over it as well. We just want the scientific arena kept out of the religious debate."

"Isn't it true that science can't prove either the big-bang theory nor evolution because they can't be duplicated in the laboratory? That's hardly science," countered Dinah. "In any case, why do you care so much? Does creationism pose that big a threat to you?"

"Have they converted you, too?" demanded Winters, his face darkening. "It's typical for them to take a pathetic drunk under their wing."

"So the board declined to allow creationism to be exhibited at the Smithsonian?" Dinah asked, ignoring the spiteful jibe.

"Right, but Whitfield refused to take no for an answer. So he began lobbying Congress. As you know, there are many conservative Republican idiots who would side with him on this issue, and if it got to the point where Congress actually agreed with him, we wouldn't be able to do anything about it." Winters finished his drink and began pacing the room.

"I still don't get it. You have one of the most powerful positions in our country and in all the matters of national leadership, yet you have exposed yourself to multiple murders on the basis of scientific beliefs. It doesn't make sense to me, *sir*," Dinah responded with sarcastic disdain.

Winters stood, glaring at Dinah, his face red with anger. "Do you really think that going back to primitive religious beliefs is going to allow us to advance humanity? First you will allow creationism as a recognized viable alternative to evolution and then you break down everything that we have worked for in a humanistic and secular society. A society with a religious conscience will take power away from women's rights and family planning; it will isolate relationships to an archaic institution of marriage and take away sexual freedom. They'll bring morality into the search for medical cures, outlaw embryonic stem cell research and other major research. This nation has had a conscience before and it stunted human progression for years. Religion is a step back to the Dark Ages and the one thing that will solidify the religious position is any kind of scientific acceptance of a Creator. And *you* — you interfere, looking for the horrible murderers, and you have no idea of the regression that society will get by giving power to those you are protecting. These deaths are collateral damage — no more. We have been working for a liberal society of human order and freedom of human choice, and the drastic effect of claiming some fairy tale god as our authority is *not* going to happen on my watch." Winters must have suddenly realized he was ranting and took a deep breath, adjusting his tie. "Rhetoric aside, I was simply upholding my end of the bargain."

Dinah took a guess. "Your mutually beneficial relationship with IAFSI?"

"Whether I agree with them or not, I need them." Winters stood facing the wall contemplatively. "My family left me with a number of assets and a huge load of debt. I have no access to the type of cash needed to fund a senatorial campaign."

"So IAFSI agreed to fund your election campaign in return for selling your soul?" Dinah smirked.

"Not just the last election campaign — I am not sold as cheaply as that." Winters narrowed his eyes. "I want to be president. IAFSI agreed to fund *all* my campaigns, including the presidential one. In return, I was to support their ideology and use my position to ensure that conservatives are kept away from the halls of power, which of course includes the secretary of the Smithsonian."

"That still seems like a pretty big risk for IAFSI," commended Dinah. "You may not continue to be re-elected."

"They chose me for a reason," boasted Winters. "Apart from the fact that I am eminently electable, I come from a liberal state. As long as Californians continue to agree that religion represses human progression, re-election is not a problem. In the meantime, it was IAFSI's job to use their networks to drum up support for me in other states in preparation for a shot at the presidency."

"And once there, you can use your increased power to pass all sorts of legislation that the Christians would adamantly oppose," speculated Dinah. "So in return for their ongoing cash, they ordered you to sort out the problem with Whitfield. They didn't realize how far you were prepared to go, but they continue to support you nevertheless. What happens if they find out you were behind Mason's death?"

"They won't," Winters said. "I want to be president too much to let that happen. You shouldn't underestimate me. I do not leave loose ends."

Dinah smirked at him. "So Whitfield was a loose end, something for you to clean up?"

"We warned him off first," said Winters. "I'm not totally barbaric."

"How did you do that?"

"First, just with words. We threatened his job, his reputation, and his salary. I suppose it was during this time that Lara Southall and Catherine Biscelli picked up on the conflict between him and the board. But he wouldn't listen. He was determined, he said. The media would have a field day. Finally, on the day he was due to give his submission to Congress, we organized a little side trip for him."

"That's the day he disappeared," added Dinah. "How did you get him out of the building without the security cameras picking up on it?"

"Ivan is the head of security. He can doctor any of the digital recordings he wants," boasted Winters. "We had to increase the pressure on Whitfield to let the whole creationism thing drop, so we used some physical force. Just a few ideas we'd picked up in the army."

"So you brought Whitfield here and tortured him, trying to get him to agree to re-convert back to his evolutionist origins?"

"Right," agreed Winters blithely. "But he still wouldn't give in, so we eventually killed him."

Dinah took a moment to digest this — Winters spoke of the murder of Thomas Whitfield as though it was no more substantial than a discussion of the weather.

"Let me get this straight — you killed four people simply to ensure that creationism doesn't find its way into the Smithsonian; to ensure that IAFSI continues to support you financially so that you can become president?"

Winters looked steadily at her and simply smiled. "You don't win wars by being timid."

Scarily, the senator appeared to be entirely without reason.

"What about Chief Justice Pryor?" Dinah asked. "What does he know about this?"

"Not much, but even if he'd started to guess at what had happened, he owes me too much to open his mouth." Winters snorted. "You see, there's a man who knows how to keep his mouth shut."

"Why does he owe you?"

"The appointment of the chief justice is made by the president. Pryor desperately wanted to become the chief justice, and we equally wanted a liberal on the Supreme Court bench. So we appointed him, despite the fact that we had to pass over several much more experienced judges to do so. It was an unpopular decision at the time, and Pryor has never forgotten it. Wisely, he didn't ask any questions and simply tried to make sure that the argument stayed out of the media."

"And away from us," added Dinah. "He told the staff not to mention the conflict between the board and Whitfield to the FBI."

"Well, he's a wise guy, like I said."

"And he's totally behind your humanist agenda?"

"You bet. In fact, he and others are working on new vilification laws right now. I will have great pleasure introducing them to the Cabinet."

"What type of vilification laws?"

"Christians are soon about to be breaking the law for their draconian ranting against our modern society. We're positioning their Bible teaching on this as 'hate crimes.' Soon they won't be able to proclaim their anti-gay or pro-life dogma without answering for it in a court of law. It's the legal muzzle we've all been waiting for and we're not going to let some moralistic scientist open a platform for them to stand on. The churches in America are weak because they have no consistent backbone, but creationism tends to inspire them to really take their Bibles seriously, and that could give them just what they need to stop the liberal advancement of our culture. Most churches have accepted either evolutionary teaching or other progressive ideas and attempted to fit them into their Bible, ultimately taking any foundation they have to argue against the vilification laws. They no longer are a voice of authority and I am not about to let them have one. Neither is Pryor, even though he wouldn't be particularly in agreement with my more aggressive but very necessary methods." On the edge of another rant, Winters pulled himself short.

"And Kenneth MacIntyre? He also seemed to be involved."

"No, he was the guy we set up to take the fall," corrected Winters. "It was clumsy and ill-planned, but we thought throwing the majority of the evidence his way would be enough for you to concentrate on him, even if you couldn't ever arrest him."

"So he knew nothing?"

"He knew less than nothing. His companies take up most of his time. He comes to board meetings, ignores everybody, doesn't say anything, and then leaves. Sometimes I think he barely knows what it is the institution actually does."

Dinah frowned. "You keep saying 'we' and I know that there has to be more people involved in this. Who else knows about this?"

Winters grinned. "Oh, you're gonna love this when I tell you. You're right, of course, there is one more person who assisted me. Can you guess who it is?"

"No," snapped Dinah. "Just tell me."

"I can do better than that, I can bring him right out." Winters gestured over her head, and Ivan opened the door to allow a fourth person into the room.

Dinah turned around and when she saw him, her jaw hung agape in shock and confusion.

Winter's co-conspirator was none other than her former supervisor and Special Agent in Charge, George Hanlon.

**\* \* \* \***

"Well," said Dinah contemptuously. "I always thought you were a slimy little snake."

George Hanlon smiled and accepted a drink from Winters.

"Since when did you care about the politics of evolution and creationism?" she continued.

Hanlon shrugged. "I don't, to be honest," he replied. "I care about my promotion to the position of assistant director."

"What did you have to do?" Dinah asked, although she already knew the answer. "Apart from sell your soul, I mean."

Hanlon shrugged. "I've been friends with Mac here for over 30 years. He told me about the problem he was having with Whitfield. I told him about how being a SAC was boring and I wanted to move up the chain. So we reached an agreement."

"What agreement?"

"Funny enough, it involved you. If I could arrange for an investigation to either not incriminate anybody or, alternatively, incriminate the wrong person, then I would get my promotion. I thought about how I could achieve that, and I immediately thought of you."

Dinah knew what was coming and remained silent.

"I chose you because of your past history of messing everything up," gloated Hanlon. "I knew about your alcohol addiction, and I knew that if you came too close to the truth, I could ruin you and your career quite easily. Luckily, you did it yourself."

Dinah sat in misery. Her weaknesses had been used by Hanlon and Winters on purpose to achieve their goal and ultimately kill four people.

"Who is going to believe you, Harris?" Hanlon taunted. "You are nothing but a drunken misfit, too washed out to even do your job. The media thinks you're a joke."

Dinah knew that it was true. She had single-handedly destroyed her own credibility. She hadn't realized that she had any capacity left to feel more pain, but the realization of what she had become caused a new pain full of regret and disappointment.

"Tell me, Harris, why do you think we've told you everything?" Winters asked mildly. He gestured at Petesky, who was still standing behind her. "It's not to satisfy your curiosity, although I'm glad we could help you in that regard. Unfortunately, your depression will become too much for you and you will take a lethal dose of alcohol and drugs. It's a tragic end to a career that was at times quite brilliant."

Dinah would have smiled, if the fear choking her would have allowed it. Did any of them have a clue as to how close she'd come to doing it for them?

"So why not just do it before? Why bother bringing me here?"

Hanlon gave a sinister smile. "Information is king, Harris. We wanted to talk to you to see if you divulged anything we should be worried about, particularly in relation to Ferguson."

"He doesn't know anything about this," Dinah angrily retorted.

"Well, we will ensure that he doesn't." Hanlon motioned Petesky again.

She noticed from the corner of her eye that Petesky was fixing a drink, including sprinkling ground-up pills liberally into the liquid.

"You don't need to do that," she said quickly. "As you pointed out, I have no credibility and nobody would believe me even if I did try to reveal what you've told me. I know how to keep my mouth shut. There's no need to do anything drastic."

Winters smiled. "Didn't I just spend the last half an hour explaining that it has been the big mouths of people that couldn't be trusted that put us all in this mess in the first place? I'm sorry, you're too much of a liability. As I said, I don't leave loose ends."

Petesky glided to her side and handed her a drink. It was almost 100 percent vodka, and despite the circumstances, Dinah could feel the power that alcohol had over her.

"You will drink it," said Petesky.

"I won't," retorted Dinah. A sudden and powerful realization hit her: *I don't want to die!*

"She's always had a stubborn streak, Wolf," commented Hanlon. "But we know you can handle it."

Winters drained his drink and stood. "Yes, we'll leave you to it. Goodbye, Dinah. I truly am sorry that it's come to this, but I'm afraid that's reality. I really don't like to hang around for the messy parts, so I hope you'll excuse me." Hanlon waved arrogantly at Dinah and followed the senator toward the door.

At the door, Winters turned and said to Hanlon, "You can stay here and make sure the job is done." His tone brooked no argument, and Hanlon meekly obeyed.

"Now," said Petesky. "I don't want to have to hurt you, but the truth is, I can hurt you terribly without leaving any marks. So I think it's best if you just do what I tell you to do."

Dinah clenched her jaw, clamped her teeth together, and shook her head.

Petesky pushed a finger into the soft, tender gristle just underneath her ear. Stabbing pain shot through Dinah's jaw and head, and her mouth fell open involuntarily. Fluidly, Petesky poured the liquid into her open mouth, and although Dinah tried to spit it out, the gag reflex in her throat meant that she swallowed the majority of it.

When they had finished the first glass, Petesky grinned at her. "There, that wasn't so hard, was it?"

Hanlon watched, a slightly sick expression on his face. Perhaps he'd never realized the impact his selfish choice had on their chosen victims, and was only now being forced to accept it.

Petesky spent the next half hour inventing ways that Dinah might be forced to drink the lethal combination. Gradually, Dinah could feel her senses fading and her resistance slipping. She was drifting into the dark, quiet place that she had dreamed about for so long, but she realized now that she wanted to live.

*God!* she cried desperately as the room spun and her vision narrowed. *If You're there and You truly care about me, please don't let me die! I need You to help me. I'm sorry for what I've done, I'm sorry for everything.*

And then she knew nothing as the darkness overcame her.

\* \* \* \*

Dinah floated in a mirage, hazy with streaks of light. She felt weightless and strangely out-of-body. *I must have died,* she realized. She was rather disappointed; where was the white light leading her home? Where was the rich and kind baritone of God welcoming her to heaven?

Instead she sensed a person leaning over her, possibly shaking her where her arm would normally be. The light gradually became stronger, and then her other senses started to kick in.

"Dinah! Wake up for me. Come on, Dinah!"

Dinah struggled to wake from the fog she was lying in. Was she alive after all? Eventually her eyes began to focus on an unfamiliar face leaning over her. Finally she realized where she was — in a hospital, with a doctor staring at her.

She tried to speak, but her tongue remained a furry slug in her mouth and wouldn't move.

"She's awake!" proclaimed the doctor. "Young lady, you are very lucky indeed."

Dinah frowned and tried to convey her confusion without words.

Then a familiar face joined the doctor, who was now shining lights in her eyes and taking her temperature. Sandra Coleman grasped one of Dinah's hands.

"Thank You, God," she said fervently. "Oh, Dinah. You don't know how glad I am to see that you're awake."

Dinah tried to speak again. "Wha . . . ?"

"Vital signs are good," announced the doctor, finishing his checks. He turned his attention to Dinah. "You've had your stomach pumped, so you are going to feel a bit tender for a few days. You'll stay here until you've regained your strength and your eating habits have returned to normal. Then I'd like you to book into the outpatient psychiatric clinic attached to this hospital. We don't take murder attempts lightly." He looked at Sandra. "I'll be back later. Let the nurses know if you have any questions."

Dinah looked at Sandra in confusion, and then pointed to the water glass next to the bed. Sandra helped her drink it, and the dryness in her mouth was relieved. Then Dinah saw the large head of Ferguson appear, also hovering over the bed.

"What happened?" she asked thickly.

Sandra sighed. "Ferguson is what happened. Thank God for Ferguson."

"You can thank me later, Harris. I was coming to see you and happened to catch sight of the Petesky fellow putting you into a car. You weren't looking overly happy at the prospect. So I followed you out to the industrial precinct and called for backup. Imagine my surprise when we burst into that room and found you passed out, with Petesky and Hanlon standing over you. They were intending to take you back to your apartment, where it would look like you had taken the overdose yourself."

"Did you arrest Hanlon and Petesky?" asked Dinah eagerly.

"We certainly did. It's caused no end of fuss in the media. This hospital is crawling with journalists, hoping for a bedside interview with you."

"After the way they've treated me?" Dinah exclaimed. "I don't think so. I never want to talk to one of them again." She paused, thinking. "Do you know what happened with David Winters?"

Ferguson shrugged. "The senator? There was no one else around at the time. Why?"

"Because he was involved, too!" Dinah struggled to sit up but didn't have the strength. "He was there only moments before Petesky tried to jam sleeping pills down my throat. He's the one who set it all up. I did some research just before Petesky arrived at my door. Petesky served under Winters in the Delta Special Ops. He explained it all to me — how they were unhappy with Whitfield wanting to introduce creationism into the museum and he set it up to have him killed. IAFSI ordered him to fix the problem with Whitfield because they have been funding his election campaigns, and he wants to be president and they've promised to fund that campaign, too. He arranged for Petesky to kill Southall, Mason, and Biscelli, too, because they all talked and he didn't want us to find out his level of involvement." Dinah stopped to catch her breath. "What did Hanlon and Petesky say?"

"They're not talking," said Ferguson thoughtfully. "I don't know what evidence we'll be able to find to implicate Winters. If Hanlon and Petesky don't corroborate your story, it'll be you against him in a court of law. And to be honest, I don't think you'd win."

Dinah was disheartened. Again, she was reminded of the power of the senator and her own self-imposed credibility problems.

Ferguson stood. "I'll look into it," he promised. "But don't get your hopes up. If there is no physical evidence, and Hanlon and Petesky don't talk, I'm not sure I'll get a judge to agree to indict him. He's a senator, not just some schmuck off the street."

Dinah nodded, her mind whirling. Hadn't Winters boasted to her that he didn't tolerate loose ends? She was one of the biggest loose ends in the whole case.

Ferguson left and Dinah and Sandra sat in silence for several moments.

"Listen, Sandra. I know now that I don't want to die," Dinah said suddenly.

Sandra grinned and grasped Dinah's hand. "I'm so glad to hear you say that," said Sandra. "And what about your . . . you know, alcohol problem?"

Dinah hesitated only a moment. "I know I need to do something about that as well."

Sandra let go of Dinah's hand, looking vastly relieved. She pulled up a chair close to the side of Dinah's bed.

"Can you tell me what happened?" she asked. "I know you carry great pain within you. Are you able to tell me about it?"

Dinah considered. She had never trusted anyone enough to open her heart. Yet the woman sitting before her had saved her life only hours before. She supposed if anyone deserved her trust, it was Sandra Coleman.

B elieve it or not," said Dinah bitterly, "I used to be a very good FBI agent. I used to work with gang members, getting them to leave their gangs and set up a new life, and learning about the way the gangs worked in the process. It was important work, I thought. I threw everything I had into it. And I suppose my family suffered in the process. I was married to Luke and we had a little boy, Sammy. He was nearly two." She thought of his golden wispy hair and cheeky smile and the pain assaulted her once again. The emptiness of her heart never ceased to shock her.

"Luke was my first and only great love," Dinah continued. "We met at a concert that was terrible, so we left and went for coffee. I don't even know how to explain the bond. We both loved music; in fact we measured milestones by the music that was around at the time. He was smart and funny and good-looking and I couldn't bear to be apart from him. We were really happy for a time, our little family."

She paused as her throat tried to close. The funny thing was that now she was having difficulty remembering the line of his jaw and the exact shade of his eyes and she hated herself for it.

"Once we had Sammy, Luke wanted me to cut back on work and spend most of my time with him. And that was my plan, too. But I was caught up with work — I was too busy saving the lives of these gang kids and my own family was slipping away. I know now that I wasn't doing the right thing. Sammy needed me, but I thought he would always be . . . there; I didn't know I didn't have much time."

And how would you know that you didn't have any time left? She thought of their lives as a long, intertwined braid with many years ahead of them. She had watched Sammy's personality develop over the two short years they'd had together, and she had looked forward to seeing his first day at school, whether he loved sports, his first girlfriend. What she had lost was so much more than a son. She had lost her hope.

Dinah struggled on. "Luke was right and I should have listened to him. I wish I had listened to him. I was too engrossed in myself and my career to notice what was happening: that they needed me."

Sandra could see the distress, still raw, on Dinah's face. "You can't change the past," she said gently.

"I didn't listen for such a long time. Luke got sick of repeating himself. I was working long hours — well, you've seen the odd hours we have to work sometimes. Finally he laid down an ultimatum. He told me to choose between my family or my job, that I couldn't have both."

Dinah sighed, wishing for the thousandth time that she could turn back time.

"We had a big fight that night. I hated being told what to do, being an independent woman. But if I'd just listened to what he was saying — it all could have been so different. I said some horrible things. I told him that I didn't need him and not to drag Sammy into it, that he was overreacting." Her words had been like tiny arrows, too hard to take back once they'd been fired. She remembered his wounded eyes as each arrow found its mark.

"Then Sammy woke up because he heard our shouting and came out, crying. It was already a stressful situation and then he started to scream. I couldn't take it and I yelled at them both to stop it and be quiet. It only made things worse. I remember Luke's eyes became really flat and cold, like I had crossed a line. The way he looked at me — it was horrible, like I wasn't worthy of motherhood anymore. He told me to go to bed, and he was going to take Sammy for a drive to calm him down. That was the last time I saw them."

A lump rose in Dinah's throat and it took great effort to say, "My last memories of them are the cold hurt in Luke's eyes and Sammy so upset his little face was red from screaming."

Sandra put her hand on Dinah's arm in comfort.

"They didn't come home. I went to bed, thankful for some peace and quiet, and I didn't wake up until about midnight. I hadn't heard them come home, so I got up to check. The house was too quiet, it didn't feel right. I thought perhaps Luke had decided to sleep on the couch but the house was empty. Sammy wasn't in his bed, Luke was nowhere to be found. I remember that a cold shiver went down my spine right as the phone rang. It was the police, calling to say that there had been an accident. Luke and Sammy had collided head-on with a semi-trailer. The driver had fallen asleep momentarily and the truck crossed the lines and hit our car. They didn't stand a chance."

Dinah's tears flowed freely. "I had to go to the hospital and identify them. The horror of that is something I can't even think about. It is too deep; too painful. They were dead, and my whole life had died with them."

"Oh, Dinah, how awful," said Sandra, tears in her eyes. "I'm so terribly sorry."

"I don't remember the funeral. I felt as if it wasn't real, that I was an actor in some tragic romance movie. I vaguely recall people being there around me, but I couldn't tell you who they were. I barely even reacted when the caskets were lowered into the ground. I couldn't believe they were in them. I went home and lay in our bed, staring at the empty side where Luke always lay. That was when I realized that he would never lie next to me again, that I would never be kept awake by his snoring again, that I would never again be awakened by Sammy in the early morning, wanting to snuggle in bed with us." Dinah could no longer speak and she dropped her head into her hands, as her sobs wracked her frame.

There were so many things that she couldn't verbalize to Sandra: that the numbness of her heart terrified her; that death didn't sever the bonds of love yet didn't allow her to practice it; that their ghosts still haunted her when she saw other boys Sammy's age; that guilt is so huge and encompassing that it chokes the will to live.

"That is why," Dinah said, finally, "I have spent the last 12 months wanting to die."

\* \* \* \*

Sandra nodded. "Please, go on."

"I went back to work too soon," Dinah continued, when she was able. "I wanted something to occupy my mind so that I *couldn't* think about Luke and Sammy all the time. If I stayed home, I probably would never have gotten out of bed at all. But things had changed — I was tired and distracted and . . . well, you read what happened in the newspaper, I'm sure."

"Everyone makes mistakes, Dinah," Sandra said.

"Except that my mistakes lead to people dying," replied Dinah bitterly. "I had let down my family and they were dead. I had let down a boy who wanted to escape his gang and have a chance at a normal life and he was dead. I felt like I had the touch of death." Dinah closed her eyes and tried to compose herself. "I was given a research and teaching position where I couldn't do any damage. It was humiliating."

"When did you start drinking?" Sandra asked.

"A few nights after the funeral," Dinah said, after considering. "I couldn't sleep. I found that if I had a few drinks before I went to bed I slept better. Plus, I hate being awake — all I think about is how I could've done things differently. And drinking made me feel numb."

"Is that how you feel now?"

Dinah frowned. "I don't know . . . I suspect I'll always crave it, but before, I didn't really care. I was planning to . . . you know, I didn't want to be alive. But now I do and I don't want to live the same life. Things have to change."

"Why did you think suicide was the answer?"

"I didn't want to feel pain anymore. I was sick of waking up every day and having to live with an empty house and in pain. It wears you down. Every holiday and birthday is a torment. It never gets better. I just got sick of it."

"What did you think would happen once you died?"

"I was hoping for nothing," admitted Dinah. "I just wanted to sleep forever and never wake up."

"Did you think about God?"

"Not really. I. . . ." Dinah hesitated. "I guess I believe that there is a God. But He's always seemed very distant to me and uninterested in what's going on down here. And frankly, I can't understand why He would allow my family to die. I thought He was supposed to be a loving God."

"You think God is responsible for the suffering and death in the world?"

Dinah shrugged. "Well, if anyone can do anything about it, it would be Him."

"Actually, God created an earth that was perfect in every way," explained Sandra. "There was no death or suffering in that world. But we ruined it by rebelling against Him. So really the fact that there is death and suffering in the world is because of us."

Dinah frowned. "I don't get it. What do you mean?"

"Let me tell you that God has two major characteristics — one is love and the other is justice. There are other characteristics, of course, but let's focus on these. He created human beings by breathing life into them, by putting something of Himself into each and every one of us. The love He has for us is the pure and unconditional love of a parent for a child. Here's the thing: He created us to have free choice. And one of the choices we can make is to reject a relationship with Him and do our own thing. When humans chose to reject God, then the earth ceased being perfect and everything started to go downhill. For one thing, everyone dies because the punishment for sin is death. That wasn't part of God's original plan. People get sick. People do awful things to one another. The world in which we live is not the one God intended for us; it's the one we chose."

"But humans are capable of good, as well," objected Dinah. "Most people live decent lives. How can you say we are all terrible?"

"Let's use the Ten Commandments as an example," suggested Sandra. "They're a guide as to how God wants us to live. Are you suggesting that people don't lie? That they always honor their parents? That they don't use God's name as a swear word? That they don't look at their neighbors' plasma TV and covet it?"

"Well, I suppose everybody has done something like that once or twice in their lives," conceded Dinah.

"Exactly. Those things are sinful, just as murder and rape are sinful. So everybody sins, and the truth is that no matter how hard we try to live up to those standards, we simply can't.

"It would have been easy for God to reject us. He could have washed His hands of us and let us continue to destroy each other. The truth is, He is too loving to do that. He still desperately seeks a relationship with each of us. So now there is a dilemma. He loves us and wants a relationship with us, but we are full of evil. How can a God who is perfect and holy have anything to do with the corrupted human race?

"Well, He's not willing to give up. We have to pay the price for our rejection of God — He requires justice, after all. So He devised a plan that enables us to come into a perfect relationship with Him and deal with sin at the same time, and the best part is, we don't have to live up to impossible standards. He sent His Son, Jesus, to earth to be both fully human and fully God."

"Okay, I know the story," said Dinah. "But why is it such a big deal?"

"God is required to deal with sin seriously because that's part of His nature. So He chose a perfect sacrifice, One who could face all the temptation to do wrong while on earth, remain perfect, and take the wrath of God. No one is strong enough to do that except God Himself — so He sent His Son Jesus to do all those things to redeem the human race. Think about it, Dinah; Jesus took the punishment for the sin you've committed in the past, but also the sin you'll commit in the future. It was a one-time solution to an ongoing problem."

Dinah nodded while Sandra took a drink of water.

"God now offers us this redemption as a free gift. There is nothing you have to do except accept it. That's the beauty of it — there are no demands on you. It's all been done for you."

A nurse bustled into the room at that moment. "Hi, guys, visiting hours are over, I'm afraid." She began checking Dinah.

Sandra stood, and Dinah suddenly realized how exhausted the other woman looked. "I'll be back tomorrow," Sandra promised. "Get some rest tonight."

\*\*\*\*

When she was left alone again, Dinah rearranged her pillows and lay back, thinking hard about what Sandra had told her. She had never been religious; had never seen any need for it. But anyone could see that her life was in the ditch. She was a broken woman and she needed relief. She had thought that suicide might provide such relief, but now she wasn't sure.

*God, if You're there, I want to know.*

She was suddenly reminded of a dream she'd had, where she'd been struggling through darkness to try and reach a light. A thought rose, unbidden, in her mind: *I have been waiting for you.*

Shocked, Dinah was silent for a few moments. *I don't want to live this way anymore. I don't want to drink myself to death. I don't want to die. I want to have some respect for myself. I need hope in my life again. I don't know how to have all these things.*

Dinah lay in the cool dark, listening to the idle chatter of the nurses, and remembered that there was always a Bible in the bedside tables of hospital rooms, and she found it. She didn't know much about the Bible, but she wanted to read about Jesus. So she opened to the New Testament randomly and began to read.

"Come to Me, all you who are heavy burdened, and I will give you rest."

Tears sprang to Dinah's eyes. *I am heavy burdened, and I need rest. Jesus, I am a wreck of a human being. What can You do with me? I haven't done a good job on my own, so I need You to help me. I have done so many wrong things and they have cost me so much. Please forgive me. I want to accept the free gift of freedom You have offered through Your death on the Cross. I need Your salvation.*

Eventually Dinah fell asleep, and for the first time in many years, slept through the night without nightmares.

\* \* \* \*

When Dinah awoke, she felt refreshed and alert, something she hadn't experienced for quite some time. Although the attempt on her life had left her weakened and sick, she realized what a pleasure it was to wake from sleep without dread of an encroaching hangover or despair at having to face another day. Finally, it seemed, she would be able to move on with her life.

The Colemans arrived after she'd eaten breakfast bearing a large bunch of flowers. "You look much better today," Andy told her. "In fact, you look the best that I've ever seen you."

Dinah laughed. "I must have looked truly hideous when you first met me!"

Andy was embarrassed. "Oh, I didn't mean that! I just . . . well, I thought . . . you know, that. . . ."

Dinah patted him on the arm. "I know what you mean. Hey, here's some good news for you. I gave my life to God last night!"

Andy and Sandra looked at Dinah in disbelief, then at each other, before both breaking into enormous grins. "Wow!" exclaimed Sandra, her eyes shining. "What a miracle. Congratulations on the start of your new life."

Andy hugged her. "That's fantastic. We've both prayed long and hard for you."

"I read some of the Bible last night," continued Dinah. "But I've realized I have no idea what I'm supposed to do now. I know nothing about being a Christian."

"We can certainly help you there," said Sandra. "Keep reading your Bible — I'd recommend you begin with the Gospel of John. And start talking to God regularly, every day if you can. Being a Christian is not about being religious; it's about a relationship with Jesus. To keep any relationship growing, you need to spend time communicating with Him."

"What are you going to do now, with regard to work?" asked Andy. "Are you going to go back to the FBI?"

Dinah sighed. "I don't think they'd have me. Despite the last 24 hours, there was a much longer history of bad behavior on my part. I think they'd be much happier if I faded into the background."

"So you've thought about what you'll do then?" asked Andy.

Dinah nodded. "Only fleetingly, but I think I could put my profiling skills to use as a consultant for the police and business, maybe."

"Have you thought any further about going to AA or rehab?" asked Sandra.

"Yes, I think I'll go to AA. I need help, I see that now." The thought of actually going to AA made Dinah's skin crawl, but she knew it was necessary.

She paused for a minute, hunting around in the little drawer of the night table next to her hospital bed. "Can I ask something of you?"

When Andy and Sandra nodded, Dinah showed them an envelope and asked, "Are you on good terms with the FBI agent based in Cleveland?"

"Special Agent O'Donnell?" Andy said. "Yeah, we talk quite regularly. Why is that?"

"I need to take some precautions. I'm not convinced that the threat to my life has ceased," explained Dinah, thinking of the hollow eyes of David Winters. "I've written down everything that has happened during this case, and included some details of some people who can support me, such as Ferguson. I have stored a copy of the statement on a number of online sensitive document storage sites."

"Sorry, you've lost me. I'm not into computers," admitted Andy.

"There are several websites that have set up virtual vaults for storing sensitive documents," said Dinah. "They are heavily encrypted and have state-of-the-art security. I've sent a copy of my document to several of these sites in the United States, Canada, and Australia. The envelope I'm about to give you contains the URL addresses and passwords to these sites. I need you both to memorize them and then destroy these envelopes. In the event of my untimely death, or that of Ferguson, then I need you to log onto one of those sites, obtain my document, and send it to Special Agent O'Donnell immediately."

"Okay. That I can do. What's in it?" Andy asked curiously.

"I'd rather you didn't know; I believe it would endanger your life, also. I don't want that. Would you feel comfortable doing this for me?"

Andy and Sandra glanced at each other. Andy shrugged. "Sure. If you are really worried about your life being in danger, it's the least we can do."

Dinah smiled. "Thank you. I feel as if I can finally relax."

Sandra stood up. "Well, if you'll excuse us we need to slip away, but we'll come back to visit you tomorrow."

Dinah watched them go, marveling that such special friends had been provided for her in her darkest hour of need.

It was a clear indication of the unseen hand of God, reaching out to save her.

Dinah picked up the phone on the night table next to her and dialed the most powerful building in the country. She was put through to the senator's office, where a chirpy office girl tried to refuse Dinah's request to speak directly to Winters.

"Tell him that I'm the woman who came back from the dead," Dinah told the secretary. "He'll want to speak with me, trust me."

It must have worked, because seconds later, she heard his voice.

"Dinah Harris, I suppose?"

"Yes, it is, Winters," Dinah said. "Are you surprised to discover I survived your attempt to have me murdered?"

Winters chuckled. "I don't know what you're talking about, though I'm sorry to hear of your misfortune, Ms. Harris. I hear that the police have apprehended two fellows responsible for your attempted murder. I'm sure that you must feel relieved."

"Funny enough, I'm not relieved," said Dinah through clenched teeth. "I know one of the killers is still roaming free."

"That's a troubling thought. I do hope the authorities find him and arrest him." Winters was infuriatingly cool, refusing to incriminate himself. "But I fear there is no evidence of a third party being involved."

"Maybe not, but there is an eyewitness account," rejoined Dinah. "That eyewitness account has been written down and stored safely."

"From what I understand, the credibility of said eye-witness is questionable at best," Winters said. There was no mistaking his mocking tone. "I believe any defense lawyer worth his salt would have a field day with such an eyewitness in court. And there really is *no* other evidence to support the testimony of the eyewitness, is there?"

"You're probably right," agreed Dinah. "So let me get to the point of this call: the written account was not written to serve as evidence in court; it was written to ensure the safety of *all* the witnesses involved."

"You're scared this so-called third party might not have finished with you?" Winters asked scornfully.

"And you're scared that the written account might be used against you in a court of law?" snapped Dinah. "It's a pretty big gamble for you to take, given your position. Even if you were cleared of charges, I wouldn't expect you to be electable again. Then how would you achieve your whacked-out agenda? What would you do then?"

There was silence for several moments and Dinah knew she'd struck a chord. She was banking on the fact that the senator was indeed worried about even being associated with the case at all. It was not the sort of exposure he could bounce back from. The American public usually didn't take kindly to their elected officials being involved in murder. And Dinah knew that Winters knew it.

"So," continued Dinah, "I think a deal might be struck — where the written account will stay locked away safely as long as Ferguson and I remain alive and well. Should either one of us meet with an untimely death, no matter if it appears to be an accident or not, the account will be made available to the FBI immediately."

"You're an imbecile if you think a shred of paper can't be destroyed," snarled Winters.

"Well, thankfully I'm not an imbecile. The account is held in a large number of virtual vaults, impervious to attempts to destroy or sabotage it."

"Do you know how easy it would be for me to get a subpoena to obtain that record?" gloated Winters. "And have it destroyed?"

Dinah laughed. "Perhaps in this country you might be able to do that, assuming you could find the companies with which I've lodged the account and the name under which it's been filed. I can assure you that I'm not imbecilic enough to lodge it under my own name. But I do think you'd have more trouble explaining to the sovereign states of Canada and Australia why you need to obtain such records. A U.S. subpoena holds vastly reduced sway on foreign soil." Dinah affected a bored tone of voice. "And again, you'd have to find the companies involved and the name under which I'd filed it. Oh, and did I tell you that every company I've opened a virtual vault with will contact me anytime someone makes a query on my account? So if you do start digging around, I'll find out about it and give the document straight to the FBI. I just love the worldwide web, don't you?"

There was more silence.

"Obviously, Hanlon and Petesky thought that they could trust you," continued Dinah. "You allowed them to take the fall for you, after all. On the other hand, I see you for the purely evil person that you are, and I don't trust you one little bit. So you'll forgive me for wanting to take out an insurance policy. Now, do we have a deal?"

Winters made a peculiar noise, as if he were choking. "Fine."

"I don't want to see anyone lurking around, following me, or watching my house. I don't want any bugs or listening devices. I know what they look like and where to find them. If I see anything remotely suspicious, the deal is off. Okay?"

"Fine."

"Great. Well, I'm glad we had this little talk, aren't you? Hopefully I'll never have to speak to you again."

"Likewise," growled Winters. He hung up on her.

Dinah hung up and exhaled. She had done all she could to protect her own life and Ferguson's life from Winters. She knew that she'd never be 100 percent safe from someone with the resources of Winters, but she'd done her best. She just had to hope that his need for power outweighed his desire for revenge.

Now it was time for a fresh beginning, with a new outlook on life. A strange sensation bubbled inside Dinah, and it took her a moment to realize that it was anticipation and excitement.

And who knew? Perhaps she might even do away with the sarcasm. Dinah contemplated it for a moment — on second thought, probably not.

\* \* \* \*

David Winters hated Thai food, but Chief Justice Maxwell Pryor loved it, so they had agreed to meet in the tiny restaurant on the edge of Georgetown. While he was worse than useless with a pair of chopsticks, he was at least glad of the relative anonymity the place gave him. It was time to lie low, as much as the senator could, until he sorted out some loose ends.

Pryor slid the sheaf of documents across the table and elegantly picked up a piece of chicken with his chopsticks. "Have a look," he invited. "I think you'll be pretty happy."

The document was headed "Proposed Vilification Bill," and Winters immediately began to read. He was quickly impressed.

The bill outlined its major new idea: that it should be illegal to publicly incite hatred against others because of race, religion, sex, gender, or sexual preference.

"So, let me be sure," Winters said, ignoring his rice and chicken satay. "If this bill is passed, it will be illegal for a pastor to teach that homosexuality is wrong?"

"Absolutely," confirmed Pryor. He chewed for several seconds. "The crucial elements of the bill, which you must not allow to be amended, are 'public' and 'hatred.' Our government cannot control what people say or think in the privacy of their own homes. However, the inclusion of the word 'public' will include churches, auditoriums, lectures, classrooms, and even a public gathering within a private home. This will broadly cover the places where fundamentalists like to stir up their religious fanaticism. It covers all forms of communication including speaking, the written word, displays, broadcasting, distributing materials, and playing of recorded material. It covers conduct also, which includes the wearing of clothes or displaying signs, flags, and emblems.

The term 'hatred' can include any negative connotations whatsoever, and any good lawyer would be able to interpret the law to include teaching that homosexuality is wrong or that abortion is wrong. It would be seen as the pastor inciting hatred amongst his congregation toward those who are gay or pro-choice."

"Excellent," said Winters. "Now, can the bill be used by the fundamentalists against *us*?"

Pryor smiled briefly. "A good point. It's important to remember that we're not saying Christianity is wrong or that their beliefs are wrong. We are simply trying to stop them from spreading their beliefs around the rest of us. It's beautiful in its simplicity."

"Wonderful." Winters sat back in his chair and grinned. He had won after all. Not only would he introduce this bill and introduce the right for the public to prosecute those he described as irritating evangelicals, he had effectively stopped the encroachment of creationism and Christian fundamentalism on the scientific establishment. Whitfield was gone, and in his place would rise someone with truly unimpeachable and mainstream credentials.

There was, of course, work still to be done. Winters would have to file progress reports on his efforts to the others. The very idea of this grated on his nerves, but ultimately it was a mutually beneficial relationship: he wanted their cash, they wanted his power.

The plan he intended to put into action would be considered unpalatable by some, but that was the difference between the average person and one who strode the halls of power. First, he would silence the opposition — no small feat in a country that prized freedom of speech. He'd already proven several times over that he was willing to take extraordinary measures to snuff out the cries of any who resisted him. Second, he would lay the groundwork for social restructuring based on the simple Darwinist premise: survival of the fittest. The perfect opportunity to achieve this had just erupted on the political scene.

The president wanted health care reform, for the good of the people. Winters wanted to progress the acceptance of euthanasia and eugenics in the legislation. While the media and politicians noisily scrapped over Medicare and private health insurance, Winters could do his work quietly in the background, so that nobody would even know until it was too late.

Winters grinned again. Darwin had been wrong, he thought. It doesn't take millions of years to change the world. It took only the actions of one man, in the right position of power, at the right time, to envision a future where the value of human life was determined by government under guidelines he himself would draft.

He stood on the precipice of a new world order, and soon there would be no one to stop him.

*All in a day's work,* he thought proudly. It was one of the upsides to being in one of the most powerful positions in the world.

And who had the power to stand up to him?

### THE WASHINGTON POST — DECEMBER 12

A large riot broke out in the maximum-security prison at Lorton, Virginia, just a few months before the prison was due to close. Inmates armed themselves with homemade weapons made from steel and plastic, took a prison guard hostage, and embarked on a spree of destruction around the facility.

It is unclear what sparked the tension. Prison officials say relations between the inmates and guards had been good in recent times and there were no incidents that had caused the rebellion.

No prison guards were injured or killed in the riot, but the bodies of two inmates were found in their cells once the mutiny was controlled. George Hanlon, 47, a former FBI agent implicated in the attempted murder of fellow FBI agent Dinah Harris; and Peter Ivanov, a Gulf War veteran accused of one count of murder, were both found with their throats slashed in their cells. Both were awaiting indictment on their respective charges.

Authorities at this time have no leads on the deaths of the two inmates.

**Enjoy a sneak preview of the second book in the compelling new Dinah Harris mystery series,**

# *The Shadowed Mind,*
**available fall 2010!**

*The victims had already been living on borrowed time, and no one really cared about them alive or dead. It would have been easy for the murders to have been overlooked in a city where crime was a daily part of life. But this killer had a mission, and a message. Will Dinah unravel the clues before the faceless danger in the shadows claims more victims?*

Surreptitiously he checked and the card in his pocket was still there. It would be an important part of the staging.

"Well, gotta go," she said with a sigh, finishing her coffee. He stood, too.

"I'll walk you back. It's not safe," he said.

Amber gave him a wry look that conveyed that she was perfectly capable of looking after herself. *Not tonight.*

The alleyway he picked was only a block away, and it was quiet and ill-frequented. The lighting there was particularly bad. He walked street side, so that she couldn't try to escape in that direction. At the mouth of the alley, he grabbed her arm with sudden force. She swung around to look at him, bewildered hurt on her face. She hadn't expected violence from him.

"I have a gun," he said very quietly. "It has a silencer. I will use it if I have to."

She quickly understood as they moved into the dark alley. "You can take the money," she said desperately. "Whatever you want. Please don't hurt me."

It was funny, he thought, how someone completely accustomed to being hurt still had keen self-preservation instincts. "I'm sorry," he said. "Truly, I am. But someone has to stop the cycle, you see."

She was momentarily confused, but was clearly concentrating on how to escape. She pulled out a small but deadly knife from the waistband of her skirt and lunged toward him. He dodged her, moved behind her, and seized her arm. Ruthlessly, he twisted it behind her until she cried out, dropping the knife to the ground. Still not giving up, she drove one high heel into his shin and he let go of her, the sharp pain shooting through his leg. Making the most of her freedom, she ran toward the street. The blinding rage erupted through his veins, and he caught up with her — high-heeled boots being completely impractical to run in. He had to end this, quickly, before someone noticed.

He roughly subdued her and dragged her back to the original spot he'd picked out. It had to be exactly right.

He was efficient. He was not a torturer.

He didn't do it for his own sick pleasure.

He did it for the good of society.

That was why he placed her body gently and respectfully sitting — well, slumping — against the wall of the tenement. He wrapped a cord around one of her upper arms. From a distance, she looked like one of many residents of the area, sleeping off a big hit of heroin.

He pulled the card from his pocket and read it again, enjoying its simplistic message. He slid the card down one of her high-heeled boots and stood back, drinking in the atmosphere.

Then he left, as smoothly and quietly as he had come, his thoughts already turning to his next hunt.

*Download your exclusive first look at chapter 1*
*of this exciting story at juliecave.com.*

## Julie Cave

Julie has loved books all her life and began writing at the age of 12. At the age of 15, she heard a creation science speaker at her church which ignited her interest in creation science and sparked an enthusiasm for defending the Bible's account of creation. It wasn't until she was in her mid-twenties, after re-dedicating her life to Jesus, that she began thinking about combining the two as a Christian ministry. In the meantime, she obtained a university degree in health science, worked in banking and finance for ten years, and is currently completing a university degree in law. Julie is married with one daughter and lives on the east coast of Australia. Her interests include reading, writing, and spending time at the beach.

*Keep track of Julie's latest writing projects through:*

- her blog at juliecave.com; be sure to sign up for updates and exclusive preview chapters of the next books in the series
- her tweets on twitter.com/julieacave

**Join** the
Conversation

**Ask** the experts

**Build** relationships

**Share** your thoughts

**Download** free resources

# Creation
# Conversations
# .com

This is your invitation to our
online community of believers.

# In God We Trust

## Steve Ham

Do you know why you believe in Christ? If challenged, it is not enough to simply recite a simple answer, but to grasp actual reasons that matter in our lives. It's not just about defending the faith, or even simply about winning the lost, but it is also about an intimately relational worship of a God we can truly call Father. Author Steve Ham goes to the heart of why faith and trust truly matter. He looks at some of the consequences of rejecting the authority of Scripture and what authority really does mean. An intriguing exploration of why man was never meant to rule himself, but instead to operate within an authoritative structure designed by God.

- Discover how to restore the authority of God's Word and enrich your Christian life

- A guided journey that will help you rediscover the truth of authority in both God's Word and in His very nature

- Identify how secular ideology and human experience have compromised the authority of God's Word and its relevance

- Experience a true understanding of biblical authority and how to apply it to your Christian walk

ISBN 13: 978-0-89051-583-9 • $12.99
5.5 x 8.5 • 224 pages • Paper

*Available at Christian bookstores nationwide or www.nlpg.com*